A Summer of War

A novel

Lynn Mason

Book Cover by Damonza

ISBN 978-1-7373422-1-2 (paperback)

ISBN 978-1-7373422-0-5 (Amazon ebook)

ISBN 978-1-7373422-2-9 (ebook)

Visit the author at lynnmason.com

A SUMMER OF WAR

1

— • —

The day Chris McKenna learned she was going to war was a day like any other. No chorus of angels announced the momentous news from on high; her colleagues in the newsroom didn't stand and applaud her courage and determination; deadlines still loomed. Rather, her editor-in-chief called her into his office one afternoon and told her to get her ass out to Vietnam by the end of the month. Deadlines were non-negotiable, but Chris thought she deserved the chorus of angels.

Now it was the end of the month. The window of time in which to reevaluate her choices had disappeared. Chris and her photographer sat before a confused major in the press liaison office of the Military Assistance Command, Vietnam, the Saigon-based headquarters of U.S. forces in country.

"Ma'am, I think there's been a misunderstanding. We have you registered with the press contingent here at MACV. I don't see a clearance for your travel to a forward operating base."

"Check again, please. I filled out the forms, in triplicate, as requested, and filed them with the Pentagon well in advance of our departure."

The major failed to stifle a sigh, but he did as she requested. Chris drummed her fingers on the desk between them and raged silently against the mean-spirited, woman-hating, pencil-necked paper-pusher lost in the bowels of the epicenter of the nation's military might who had decided to fuck her over for sport.

"Here we go. We had the forms filed under 'Lane.'"

Chris managed to refrain from rolling her eyes.

Paul Lane, her photographer, grinned and snapped a photo of her profile in all its indignant, self-righteous glory.

"All right, everything appears to be in order. This is a list of bases with robust facilities catering to the press." The major slid a typewritten sheet of paper across the desk. "I personally recommend Danang, given its ideal location on the coast and the accessibility of personnel from all branches of service."

"I'm not here for a beach vacation," Chris said.

"Ma'am, Danang is far more than—"

"I'm not interested, Major."

"I can also offer you Hue, which maintains a large and active combat division."

Chris wrinkled her nose. "I'm looking for something a little more remote."

"Remote?"

"Yes, you know, forward, as in forward operating base or forward deployed. Saigon, Danang, Hue, Pleiku, they're all so...crowded."

"I see." The major rubbed his temples. "And where would you prefer to go?"

Chris had given this question considerable thought and had yet to arrive at a suitable conclusion. She wanted action and combat, of course, but mostly she wanted to be left alone to do her job. She would go just about anywhere to escape the hordes of journalists fighting over the same tired stories. It was late April 1969; the war in Vietnam had long since become just another depressing segment on the nightly news, but it still deserved thoughtful, objective coverage. Let everyone else file breathless dispatches on the Danang beach scene.

The major rested his chin in his hand. Chris stood and walked to the large map of South Vietnam on his wall, a map that identified each and every base, firebase, airstrip, and supply depot in the country. Chris's eyes found Saigon and traveled outward in concentric circles until she reached the southern Mekong Delta. She squinted and jabbed a finger at the map.

"Tell me about this place. FOB Jane."

The major laughed. "You can't be serious."

"Why not?"

"FOB Jane isn't just remote. It's basically off the grid, and 'hostile territory' doesn't even begin to describe the operating environment."

"So you don't often send journalists there?"

"I've sent a few. They didn't last long."

"Sounds perfect."

He shook his head. "Miss McKenna, I need to be clear: MACV cannot guarantee your safety that far forward."

"I don't recall asking you to."

"May I be candid, ma'am? Off the record?"

Chris leaned a shoulder against the map and gestured for the major to continue. Off the record.

"The base is commanded by a terminal O-6 whose brigade is getting trounced by the Viet Cong. His staff is a circus act, and not the entertaining kind. There's no story at FOB Jane."

Chris smiled. "Sorry, Major, but whenever the army tells me there's no story, I know there's a good one."

He glowered silently for a beat. Then he clasped his hands together on his desk, lacing his fingers. "Allow me to be blunt. FOB Jane is no place for a woman."

Chris held his gaze. It was a common refrain, this proclamation of which places and professions suited women, a proclamation often followed by a derisive laugh or a condescending shake of the head. But the major simply watched her. Waiting for her to choose.

Chris turned back to the map. The cities beckoned, and so did the mountains and highlands where American and South Vietnamese forces engaged their northern counterparts in large-scale actions. But the Delta's call captivated her imagination, an imagination fascinated by the intensity and intimacy of small-unit combat that raged in the villages and paddies and jungles that were the heartbeat of this broken country. She wanted the stories that didn't make the evening news.

She caught Paul's eye. A smiled tugged at the corner of his mouth.

"We'd like to check out FOB Jane," she said.

The major looked at Paul, who held up his hands as if to signal defeat.

"Fine. But don't say I didn't warn you when you roll back into town after a couple of days looking for a hot shower and edible chow." He slid a sheaf of papers across the desk. "Please fill these out. In triplicate." He looked at Chris, daring her to make a wisecrack. "You will be restricted to the base for the duration of your stay, and MACV strongly advises that flak jackets and helmets be worn at all times outside of hardened structures. Vietnamese for 'journalist' is *báo chí*. When they're shooting at you, give it a go."

The major excused himself and left the two journalists alone with their thoughts and forms in triplicate. Paul looked at Chris and raised his eyebrows.

"I'm sure it will be fine," she said.

"And yet..."

"What can I say? He had me at 'FOB Jane is no place for a woman.'"

***

Two days later, after countless briefings on rules, regulations, and standard operating procedures governing the activities of journalists in Vietnam, Chris and Paul waited near a fleet of UH-1 Iroquois helicopters; one of the Hueys would be their ride to the Mekong Delta. A teenaged soldier on the flight line soon approached the reporters and asked where they were headed.

"FOB Jane," Chris replied.

His eyes widened and he glanced at Paul as if to verify that Chris was of sound mind. The photographer nodded.

Like the MACV major, the young soldier shrugged and stepped aside so she could continue her pigheaded march toward certain death. He motioned them toward an idling Huey and told them to watch their heads.

"Good luck," he shouted.

Chris and Paul leaned forward into the Huey's rotor wash and climbed aboard. They took seats on the forward-facing bench in the cabin and within minutes the helicopter lifted from the airstrip.

As the Huey gained altitude and banked southwest on a trajectory into the Mekong Delta, a thrill of excitement vanished into doubt's gaping maw. Did she expect to be welcomed into the boys' club by men who would sooner relinquish a kidney than allow a woman into their circle of trust? It seemed a silly proposition at best, more likely an ignorant wish. She knew deep down that it was foolish to believe she would be anything but a distrusted outsider. Not only was she a woman, she was also press, a bad combination in a war gone awry.

***

Saigon's urban sprawl passed below them, the shanty ghettos and makeshift refugee camps receding into the distance. Paved roads crumbled to dirt, flanked by tall swaths of elephant grass that grew into lush, dense jungle that devoured the sun's rays. The jungle melted into miles of flat rice paddies, the monotony broken only by crisscrossing rivers and canals. Farming villages dotted the landscape, some surrounded by high walls and fortifications, the South Vietnamese government's ostensible defense against the pervasive Viet Cong and their northern enablers. The government had virtually imprisoned some of its own population in their villages, but the efforts had done little to deter attacks and cooption by the guerrillas.

The Mekong River Delta was the lifeblood of Vietnam, the most productive agricultural region of the country, but years of conflict had taken their toll and the rice harvests had diminished, straining both the local and national economies and driving more villagers toward Ho Chi Minh and his cause. Chris watched the villagers bent over in knee-deep water, working their endless paddies, turning to glance at the passing Huey before resuming their backbreaking labor.

Paul moved to the opposite bench and took a photo of Chris. She knew she was grinning stupidly, but she couldn't help it. Paul was a former Marine who fought in World War II's Pacific campaign and a twenty-five-year veteran of the news industry who had covered many of the world's worst conflicts with a camera in hand. He looked the part of a bona fide war correspondent, sporting broken-in boots, stained green cargo pants, a loose khaki field shirt, and a well-worn photographer's vest. She envied his calm demeanor and wealth of war experience, and wished her boots didn't look so brand new.

Thirty minutes into the flight, the chopper dropped several hundred feet and banked sharply. Chris crushed her bags between her feet to prevent them from tumbling out the open door. The crew chief motioned to the door gunners, and then he turned to Chris and Paul, drawing close to shout into their ears.

"Sir, ma'am, Charlie ambushed an aid convoy just east of here. We've been diverted to assist with casualty collection and troop transport. I need you to stay in the helicopter and keep the cabin floor clear."

Chris nodded her understanding. The crew chief allowed Paul to take a seat on one of the side benches so he could have a clear shot of the convoy as they approached. He strapped himself in and leaned over the landing skids with his camera at the ready. Chris scooted to the edge of her bench and peered out.

The Huey descended into a surreal scene, touching down behind three flaming transport trucks and a disabled armored personnel carrier. Chris jerked when one of the door gunners engaged his machine gun against an enemy she couldn't see. Just as she rose to join Paul closer to the door, two soldiers ran to the Huey with a limp body on a stretcher. Before Chris could jump out of the way, the soldiers shoved the stretcher into the cabin and nearly took her feet out from under her.

Chris backed away from the injured aid worker and found herself at the edge of the door opposite Paul. The gunner was trying to clear his jammed M-60 and paying her no attention. She looked out and a saw a small group of aid workers and Vietnamese villagers moving blindly through the smoke toward flashing muzzles in the thick underbrush flanking the road into the village.

"No!" she shouted. "Hey! Get down! Get down!" But the roar of battle and aircraft drowned out her voice.

Glancing behind her, she saw Paul working two Nikons. The crew chief was on his knees applying pressure to the aid worker's shoulder wound. Chris yelled again and waved her arms, but the group blundered toward enemy guns. She swore, and before her brain had a chance to participate in the decision-making process, she jumped out of the helicopter and ran toward the civilians. What did they tell her to do if attacked? Stay low behind a vehicle's engine block or wheel wells? Seek concealment in the brush? Scream *báo chí*?

Chris overtook the slower villagers within seconds and shoved people off the road or behind trucks, away from the Viet Cong positions. They tumbled head-first into sharp elephant grass, packs spilling contents, sandals flying through the air. The guerrillas intensified the attack as the mass of people dispersed, but the heavy smoke afforded some concealment.

Chris ran for a nearby jeep, seeking protection from the machine gun fire. She was several yards away when a grenade explosion threw her sideways. She found herself wedged halfway under the jeep, the scream of the guerrilla who took the brunt of the grenade and the throb of a good smack to the head reverberating in her ears.

She pushed herself up holding her ringing head and tried to focus her blurry vision. Two Viet Cong soldiers ran toward her, raising rifles. Chris's head cleared instantly and she sprinted in the opposite direction as they launched a volley of

AK-47 rounds. She rounded the back of a flaming transport truck at full speed and smashed into a body coming the other way.

Her breath left in a whoosh. She bounced off the man and stumbled backwards, barely able to stay on her feet. The soldier in her path leveled his rifle at her. She stiffened in a half-crouch, poised for fight or flight, certain she would die.

But then she found clear blue eyes under the brim of a floppy bush hat, and golden hair, almost white at the sideburns. He stood a full head taller than the tallest pajama-clad combatant and wore U.S. Army insignia on his chest.

And she knew she would not die.

He lowered the rifle a few inches and stared at her in confusion. They locked eyes for what felt to Chris like a very long time, yet it was only seconds before the soldier began struggling with ropes that bound shut the canvas flaps on the back of the truck. The truck rocked and Chris realized it was filled with Vietnamese civilians. He slashed at the ropes with his bush knife and tore open the flaps. He lifted screaming women and children to safety and pushed them away from the truck.

Chris remembered her Viet Cong pursuers and sprang forward to redirect a mother and her child who had turned into danger, unseen through the billowing smoke. The soldier reacted even faster, yanking both Chris and the woman back from the barrage of gunfire and scooping the young boy off his feet. Chris ended up sprawled on the ground and the soldier dumped the child on top of her. Then he whirled, took a knee, and, oblivious to the rounds ripping through the canvas near his head, lined up his shot at the two guerrillas materializing through smoke.

He fired twice and the AK-47s fell silent. Strange how a small amount of pressure exerted on a trigger mechanism could have such tremendous effect, Chris thought. He kept the rifle in a ready position and scanned the area. She held tight to the child and tried to catch her breath. The gunfire had stopped, and the only voices she heard belonged to Americans. Cursing, expressions of disgust, even raucous laughter as men stepped over dead bodies littering the road.

Then she heard a cry of relief at her side. Chris placed the boy in his mother's arms and watched her hurry toward the other villagers and aid workers, who were extricating themselves from the brush and retrieving their possessions. Chris stumbled away from the truck and the acrid smoke of the engine fire, coughing and trying to focus her vision through the cleansing tears rolling down her cheeks.

She thought now might be an excellent time to make her way back to the Huey and apologize to the crew chief and her photographer, but within seconds she was surrounded by gawking American soldiers. Two men pushed through the semi-circle of soldiers, the taller of the pair asking why in the fuck they were standing around and not mopping up or fishing refugees out of the jungle.

One of the soldiers, a gangly man with wild hazel eyes, pointed at Chris. "LT, it's a *girl*!"

The officer wrinkled his nose as if he had just stepped in a pile of fresh water buffalo dung. He glanced at his older counterpart, who looked less appalled but just as surprised. The second man shrugged and smirked, prompting an eye roll from his superior.

The lieutenant turned again to Chris. "And you are?"

"I'm a reporter."

"Were you in that convoy?"

Chris turned to point to the Huey, but there was no longer a Huey hovering nearby. Her stomach seized. How would she get to FOB Jane? For all she knew, this lieutenant might make her walk.

"Is that your ride?" the older man asked, pointing to the Huey touching down a second time.

Chris felt her legs tremble in relief when she saw Paul waving frantically from the door. She waved back.

"Idiot journos," the lieutenant muttered. "You trying to look good for the cameras or are you just insane?"

"I'm sorry, I didn't mean to—"

The blue-eyed soldier interrupted. "It's cool, LT."

"Spare me, Rawlins. Just because she's cute doesn't mean she gets to play soldier."

Everyone laughed; everyone but Rawlins. His jaw muscles twitched. He cocked his head and glanced at her thoughtfully.

"You see that group of civilians, sweetie? That's where you need to be. The rest of you, do something useful. Medevacs and transports inbound."

Chris met Rawlins's eyes briefly, gave the rest a cursory glance, then turned and walked toward the Huey and her anxious photographer. Of course she was expecting this, she had spent weeks trying to prepare herself for the stares and the disdain and...

"Holy hell! What have we here?" An enormous soldier with an M-60 machine gun at his hip ogled her from waist-deep in the brush as she passed. The man—the boy—by his side bounced up and down, jabbering incoherently and pointing at her.

...And that. She ignored it.

And then she stopped short. Two dead Viet Cong soldiers lay sprawled in the road. Her pursuers. They each had a chest wound, a palm-sized wet patch soaking through their black tops. Lifeless eyes stared at the hazy sky.

"Chris!"

Chris walked around the bodies and tried to smile at Paul. He ran forward and crushed her in a hug. Chris held onto him, feeling herself tremble. It was adrenaline, she told herself. Paul spoke to her in a low voice, but a roar had formed between her ears.

"Excuse me."

She turned. It was the blue-eyed soldier, Rawlins. His bush hat was off, hanging by its cord around his neck. His face was streaked with dirt and soot from the vehicle fires. He stepped forward and reached a hand toward her face. Reflexively she leaned back, and his hand stopped in midair.

"You're bleeding," he said.

"What? Oh..." She touched her head and searched for pain.

He tipped her chin and examined her face. She kept her eyes on his extended arm between them, focusing on the rumpled green fabric stained with sweat and mud and paddy water.

"I think there was a grenade or something," she murmured.

His hand dropped from her chin to her left arm. He held her by the wrist and examined the bloody scratches down the outside of her forearm. "You're lucky you weren't badly injured." He stepped back and waved to a man walking toward them, another youthful soldier. "This is Doc Kearney. He'll patch you up."

"Really, I'm fine."

"Ignore her," Paul said.

"Ma'am," said Kearney as he dropped his pack on the hood of the jeep and rooted through it for some gauze. "Please, it's no problem."

Rawlins nodded to her and Paul and rejoined his platoon. Kearney pressed a piece of gauze to her forehead to stanch the bleeding and asked her to hold it in place before he secured it with a strip of tape.

"We got Hueys, LT!" the radioman shouted. "Three minutes!"

Kearney taped a bandage over her arm, smiled, and touched his temple in a casual, two-fingered salute. "Enjoy the flight."

The thump of the rotors grew louder and a grouping of helicopters appeared over the tree line, their movements mirroring the curve of the road. Chris shaded her eyes to watch the spectacle. After Paul took a few photos of the incoming helos, they made their way back to their Huey. Several soldiers were busy loading additional bodies onto the helicopter, mostly Vietnamese. The crew chief glared at Chris and tossed the reporters' luggage out of the Huey. The duffel bags and rucksacks landed at their feet. Chris and Paul stared at the baggage. The Huey lifted off.

"Excuse me, ma'am!"

Chris barely heard the shout above the roar. She turned to face a young soldier with sergeant's stripes on his collar.

"Ma'am, where are you headed? My Tho?"

"No, farther into the Delta."

"Where?"

"FOB Jane. It's south of—"

"Yes, ma'am, I'm familiar with it. Please follow me."

The sergeant brought them to the lieutenant. "LT, these two need a ride to FOB Jane."

"Conlon, if this is a joke..."

"No joke."

The lieutenant scratched the dark stubble on his chin. "I need to see your credentials and travel authorization."

Paul pulled his credentials from his breast pocket. Chris had to drop her bags and rummage through her rucksack to find her press card and the requisite paperwork. As she dug through her clothing, she watched the lieutenant tap the toe of his black leather jungle boot on the ground, a not-so-subtle hint that his time was valuable and she was wasting it. Finally, she pulled out the credentials and a folded authorization letter, signed by the major at MACV, allowing her and Paul passage to FOB Jane.

The lieutenant made a show of examining the documents, like a jack-booted thug at a Soviet border crossing. Chris kept her mouth shut; her newly heightened sense of self-preservation understood how badly she and Paul needed a ride.

"Miss McKenna, Mr. Lane, FOB Jane is situated in a very dangerous area of the Mekong Delta. I would ask that you reconsider this decision, as it may have an adverse impact on your life expectancy. The facilities at My Tho are better equipped to handle press and, more importantly, it is considerably safer."

"I appreciate your concern, but we'll continue on to FOB Jane as planned." He handed the paperwork back to her. "Follow Sergeant Conlon."

***

It didn't take long for Chris to figure out that she and the lieutenant's platoon were headed to the same place. She spent most of the helicopter ride muttering profanity under her breath and ignoring the wide-eyed stares from Sergeant Conlon's squad. She was already on the lieutenant's bad side and she didn't even know his name. This was not the start she was hoping for at FOB Jane.

Upon landing, Conlon ushered Chris and Paul out of the helicopter toward the sandbagging that ringed the helipad. Another Huey disgorged the lieutenant and the second half of his platoon. He strode toward them and with a flick of the wrist motioned her to follow.

Chris hurried to keep pace with his long strides. Movement caught her attention; her gaze settled on a group of men ambling toward tents and barracks in the distance. The tall soldier in the back stood apart from the rest, whether by design or circumstance Chris couldn't tell. The burst of laughter from the group put a grin on his face. Then he looked her way and for a second their eyes met. His smile faded.

"Staff sergeant," the lieutenant snapped at a soldier talking with two men in a jeep outside a low, heavily fortified building. "Where's Lieutenant Wheaton?"

"Danang, sir. Can I be of assistance?"

"These two are press and they need to be someone else's problem."

"Understood, sir. I'll get them settled."

"First, please escort Miss McKenna to the hospital so her injuries can be treated."

"That's not—"

13

"Roger, sir."

"Thank you." The lieutenant stalked into camp without a backwards glance.

The staff sergeant turned to address Chris. "Ma'am, FOB Jane has no dedicated accommodations for journalists, as we rarely see press this far south, but we do have a large hooch that can house you both temporarily, until we find you a more suitable arrangement."

"Thank you, Sergeant, that's fine."

"Follow me."

The staff sergeant led them through camp toward the center of the base, where a sprawling village of thatch huts lent a little local flair to the military's soulless array of tents, barracks, and bunkers, built around the remnants of an abandoned hamlet. He stopped in front of a large hooch that stood slightly askew on its mud and clay foundation and opened the door.

The temperature inside was stifling, but Chris saw two small windows that might provide a cross breeze and clear out the stale air. Two cots against the left wall stretched into the middle of the room, sheets and wool blankets folded at the foot of each. A rickety field table stood in one corner. Chris put a hand to the bandage on her head and stared at the field table, already envisioning reams of insightful, prize-worthy reporting. All she needed was a typewriter and a chair.

"Lieutenant Wheaton, our public affairs officer, will return from Danang later this week. Showers and latrines are located just down the path, sir. Ma'am, female-only facilities are near the nurses' quarters behind the hospital. Now, if you'll please accompany me, we'll get you checked out."

Chris sighed but dumped her bags at the foot of the far cot and left Paul to unpack his equipment. The young staff sergeant led her to the hospital and greeted the nurse manning the triage station.

"Is Captain Nichols available?"

The nurse, who stared at Chris the way one might gawk at a highway car wreck, finally nodded. "I think so."

She directed them toward an exam room and went in search of Captain Nichols. Chris felt a surge of irritation toward that insufferable lieutenant; she did not need medical attention, and she most certainly did not need to waste the captain's time. No doubt he had real casualties to which to attend. That was assuming he was even competent, given the MACV major's assessment of the quality of officers at FOB Jane. Chris was prepared to bolt at the first sign of ineptitude, but her injuries were so minor that if the triage nurse could have picked her jaw up off the floor, Chris thought even she could have cleaned out a few scratches and changed some Band-Aids.

She read a few of the public service announcements taped to the wall urging soldiers to wear helmets and flak jackets, to stay hydrated, to take their malaria prophylaxis, to avoid unprotected sex. Chris smirked and figured the medical staff had seen some ghastly cases of sexually transmitted diseases in Vietnam, the stuff of medical journal legend.

She turned when she heard footsteps. The staff sergeant, standing outside the room, snapped to attention and Chris found herself facing a pony-tailed woman in teal scrubs with a stethoscope draped over her neck.

"Ma'am, this is Captain Nichols, chief of FOB Jane's nursing contingent."

Chris offered a hand, which the captain accepted. "Chris McKenna."

"Maria Nichols."

Evidently warned by the triage nurse that her patient would look nothing her usual fare, the captain was discreet in her curiosity. She closed the door behind her and gestured for Chris to take a seat on the exam table. Chris complied and assured the nurse she was fine.

"I'm sure you are." Maria pulled the gauze from Chris's forehead. "That's quite a gash. What happened?"

"Turbulence. Smacked my head on that thing in the back of the chopper. You know."

"The transmission structure?"

"Sure."

The nurse appraised Chris with narrowed eyes, but didn't press the issue. She cleaned the cut with disinfectant and pulled a tray of instruments to her side.

"You're going to need a few stitches."

"It's just a scratch."

Maria again took a moment to evaluate her patient. Chris met intelligent mocha eyes that were having none of her nonsense and noticed the purple ribbon tied around the nurse's ponytail. She was tan and fit and wearing black Chuck Taylor All-Stars, and Chris could just as easily imagine her on a California beach as the exam room of a field hospital in Vietnam. She wondered what had brought Maria Nichols to FOB Jane and, perhaps more importantly, why she stayed.

"You're a journalist?"

"Yes."

"And you chose to come to FOB Jane?"

"Yes."

Maria shone a light in each eye to test pupil reaction and then held up a finger. "Follow my finger." She moved it side to side, up and down. "Any head pain, blurry vision, hearing loss, nausea, vomiting?"

"No."

"You're sure?"

"Yes.

"But you *chose* FOB Jane?"

Chris realized the nurse was having a little fun with her. She smiled. "Seemed like a good idea at the time."

Maria returned the smile. "I know the feeling."

"I keep being told that FOB Jane is no place for a woman."

Maria shrugged. "It's not, but seeing as you ran headlong into a firefight—excuse me, a Huey transmission structure—I'm confident you can hold your own."

"I've already had a run-in with one lieutenant who seems to think I belong in the kitchen, probably barefoot and pregnant, so I'm off to a good start."

Maria snapped on a fresh pair of gloves and readied a local anesthetic. "Know his name?"

"No. Tall, wiry, dark hair, hasn't shaved in at least a week. Might be good-looking were it not for all the personality."

The nurse gnawed at her bottom lip. Chris thought she was trying to hide a smile.

"That sounds like Lieutenant Gianelli."

"Is he always an asshole, or just having a bad day?"

She laughed. "I hear he has his moments. Now hold still and I'll get you out of here in time for a late lunch."

2

— . —

"How did you sleep?" Paul asked brightly.

Chris rubbed her eyes and yawned. "Are you kidding? Between the artillery blasts and those weird catcalls, which I hope were not human, I don't think I slept at all."

"The jungle does have a unique soundtrack."

"You snore, by the way."

"Sorry."

"So what do we do now?"

"What do you mean?"

She slid off the cot, clad in shorts and a tank top, and tried to tame her unruly hair. As her legs absorbed her body weight, she yelped in pain. Now that the adrenaline had worn off, she felt the full effects of the previous day's battle.

"We're in the middle of a warzone. What do we do first?"

He shrugged. "Eat breakfast?"

***

Chris thought that was as good an idea as any, at least until they arrived at the mess hall and she got her first taste of the wall spackle masquerading as oatmeal. The coffee was nothing more than caffeine-infused turpentine. Still, she choked down two cups of it, black, and hoped her stomach lining survived the assault.

"I sneaked a peek at your story last night," Paul said. "Good start."

"It kind of wrote itself," Chris said.

"They won't all be like that. Remember, five years of hard work down the drain if you come back with nothing."

"What's something?"

"You'll know it when you see it."

Chris took a sip of coffee, cringing at the bitterness. She verbalized a thought that had been troubling her for weeks.

"Willis thinks I'm reckless."

"You are."

"I am not," she replied in genuine disbelief that Paul, her cherished friend and mentor, would agree with the man dead set against her career advancement.

"No? Did you *accidentally* launch yourself into that firefight yesterday?"

"Momentary lapse of reason."

"Then I'll direct your attention toward Exhibit B, Labor Day weekend 1967, U Street and Fourteenth. A peaceful march turns ugly by the light of a Molotov cocktail. The D.C. riot police rush in, the press gaggle breaks for safety, but one reporter lowers her shoulder and busts through the line with her interviewee, the leader of the local chapter of Black Panthers. What would you call that?"

Chris shrugged. "Dedication."

"You're reckless and mentally unhinged."

"Now you're just being mean."

"Have you ever considered that Willis might care about you?"

"Oh please, Martin Willis has made perfectly clear he cares about the news, not the people who report it."

"I think his bigger concern is your impatience," Paul said.

"Patience is the most overrated virtue." Chris swallowed the last gulp of coffee and stood. "Let's get out of here. Everyone is staring at me."

They cleared their dishes and then Chris pushed through the doors of the mess hall and walked straight into a familiar soldier. He stepped back in surprise, and Chris found herself facing a wall of twelve inquisitive young men.

"It's the reporter lady!" hissed a little redhead.

Chris's shoulders tensed as she braced for an onslaught of prying and obnoxious questions. The seconds passed but they spared her from interrogation, their curiosity palpable but held in check.

"Hey, Photo Man, that's a badass camera. Got time for a few pics?"

While Paul indulged requests for snapshots, Chris slid a glance at Rawlins. He had backed away a few feet, arms crossed over his chest, uninterested in the impromptu photo shoot.

"You sure you want to pass this up? Paul collects Pulitzers like other people collect baseball cards."

"I'm not very photogenic," Rawlins said.

She offered her hand. "Chris McKenna."

***

He regarded her coolly but accepted her hand. Her skin was soft and her nails looked manicured, glossy in the sunlight. She squeezed firmly and he returned the grip, self-conscious about the roughness of his palm against hers.

"John Rawlins."

"Thanks for not shooting me yesterday."

Her playful tone set him on edge. He had been a millisecond from pulling the trigger; the only thing that had stopped him was a swish of pony-tailed hair. She seemed unbothered by the cut on her forehead, covered by a flesh-colored bandage, and the jagged scratches on her forearm, superficial but angry red in color.

"I understand you have a job to do, but next time someone tells you to stay on the chopper, stay on the chopper."

Her expression hardened. "I guess we're not so cool after all?"

"It was a moment of pity."

"Pity?"

"Lieutenant Gianelli can be...abrasive."

Her green eyes narrowed, and he watched with some amusement as she struggled to swallow the reactionary sarcasm.

"Well, thanks anyway."

"The lieutenant isn't the chauvinist pig you think he is."

One eyebrow began an upward journey into the realm of incredulity, but otherwise her face displayed little of what she must be thinking.

"If you say so."

"Who do you work for, Miss McKenna?"

"Call me Chris. I write for *American Century*. Know it?"

"I prefer *Time*."

She couldn't tell if that was a joke, so she merely nodded. "Have you been here long?"

"About a month."

"Seen much action?"

John shrugged. "A little."

"Any other heroics I should know about?"

"Heroics?"

"You saved all those civilians."

"So did you."

That wasn't the reply she expected, but after the briefest of pauses she flashed a disarming smile and said, "We should talk sometime."

She tossed back chestnut hair, pushing some strands off her face with her left hand, a hand adorned by a silver band on her ring finger. John liked how the corners of her eyes crinkled when she smiled.

"Thanks, but I'll pass."

"Okay. Let me know if you change your mind."

He nodded stiffly.

"Ready to go?" the photographer asked. The man stuck out his hand and introduced himself. "Hey, thanks for making sure she didn't get herself killed yesterday. She gets a little carried away sometimes." Paul winked and patted Chris on the back. "Catch you boys later."

The soldiers waved and the journalists began to walk away. Chris McKenna turned and shot him a mischievous grin.

"See you around, John Rawlins," she said, right before they disappeared behind some sandbagging.

The men swarmed him as he watched them go.

"Man, I can't believe you turned down that interview!"

John said nothing.

"That's cool, Cowboy, more headlines for the rest of us. She can interview me anytime she wants."

***

After breakfast, First Squad, Second Platoon, Delta Company trudged back to the barracks to retrieve their gear for guard duty, scheduled to last throughout the heat of the day, as ordered by their company commander. Lieutenant Gianelli, Master Sergeant Travis, and Sergeant Conlon were attending a company briefing, and had left instructions for the platoon to report to their posts no later than zero nine hundred hours.

The Reporter Lady, as she was unceremoniously dubbed, dominated conversation along the walk. Who was she, and why was she here?

"She's press, Steve," John said.

"So?"

John stared at him. "She's covering the war."

"Okay, but why FOB Jane? How did we get so lucky? We ain't never lucky. Right, Hector?"

"The odds are against it," Hector said.

"What's she like, Johnny?" Steve asked. "She seemed kind of feisty. I like my women feisty. Think she'd go for me?"

"No."

"Holy shit, man. You got a thing for her?"

"Absolutely not."

"Don't lie, Johnny. You're a bad liar. You got a thing for her. I can tell."

John shook his head. "She could have been killed yesterday. Insanity is not an attractive character trait."

Steve cracked his knuckles. "What are the odds on me, Hector?"

"How many men in this brigade?"

"Don't know. Few thousand?"

"Then a few thousand to one."

"Harsh, man, harsh."

A stocky, tattooed soldier with a crooked nose slapped Steve on the back. "No chance, Jersey. I call dibs."

John felt his trapezius muscles contract into knots, and he nearly ground the enamel off his teeth as he listened to the laughter and the crass comments. He focused on his feet and kept walking.

***

Chris stood at the center of FOB Jane, a grassy courtyard flanked by the brigade's headquarters building, the mess hall, and the base club. In the center of the courtyard, an American flag flapped in the breeze. A navy New York Yankees baseball cap shaded her eyes as she studied a tall wooden signpost, painted bright blue, which rose at the convergence of several trodden walking paths. Wooden arrows painted in rainbow colors pointed every which way: Hanoi to the north, Tokyo to the east, Sydney to the south, Los Angeles, Houston, Chicago, Miami, Washington, New York, and Boston to the west. Someone had even tacked on a homemade sign for Peoria. Each city had its distance from FOB Jane in miles painted in white in the corner, a startling reminder of the gap between the world and the war.

Forward Operating Base Jane was home to the Seventy-Fifth Infantry Brigade and commanded by Colonel Matthew Brooks, the purported terminal O-6. The staff sergeant had introduced her to Brooks when she stopped by Brigade HQ in search of a typewriter, and he welcomed her warmly once he recovered from the shock of having a journalist on his base.

She was still staring up at the signpost and plotting her next story when Paul appeared at her side.

"Second thoughts?" Paul asked.

"Never."

"Then let's do this. Try to behave yourself, please."

Chris sighed. They were minutes away from what was described as a "mandatory" meeting with Lieutenant George Wheaton, the brigade's public affairs officer just returned from Danang, and Captain Arthur Kittles, the commander of Delta Company, one of the infantry units. Of course, this assertion was put forth at the captain's behest by a stammering private who had approached them during lunch. Chris was not on speaking terms with anything mandatory, but Paul agreed on their behalf and, after the private departed, told her it was too early to start pissing off the officer corps.

They were met at the entrance of Brigade HQ by the same aide who had accosted them at lunch. He escorted them down a hall and stepped aside for them to enter a cramped office.

Captain Kittles, a heavyset man in his mid-thirties, greeted them and pumped Paul's hand, clapping him on the back several times and offering effusive praise for all that was *American Century*. Paul shot a sidelong glance at Chris, one eyebrow twitching. She was taken aback by the enthusiasm, a stark contrast to Lieutenant Gianelli's animosity.

A second man fumbled and dropped a mostly empty bottle of amber-colored liquid into Kittles's trash can, a clumsy attempt to hide evidence. He stood to greet the journalists and, looking a bit unsteady on his feet, swayed forward and back until his brain caught up with his body.

Kittles made the introductions. "Lieutenant George Wheaton, this is Christine McKenna and Paul Lane of *American Century*."

Wheaton reached for Chris's hand and held on a moment too long. After Wheaton released her, Kittles gestured to a small table surrounded by four chairs. Chris sat and tried to ignore the drops of sweat rolling down her sides under her shirt, wondering how Wheaton managed to look cool and coiffed in his spotless fatigues. It was a professional package if one overlooked the glazed eyes of a drunk, she thought wryly. She would not condemn a man who drank to escape the demons of combat, but she was certain Wheaton had never been outside the wire. She disliked him immediately.

Kittles broke the awkward moment of silence with a clap that jarred Wheaton from a daze in which he stared at a spot somewhere below Chris's neck.

Wheaton cleared his throat. "Miss McKenna, I can't tell you what a pleasure it is to have you here. FOB Jane has faced a dearth of reporters over the last couple of years, and we very much look forward to working with you."

"Paul and I appreciate the hospitality," Chris said.

"It's my job to provide background information, arrange interviews, and answer your questions regarding operations at FOB Jane. I know you've only just arrived, but is there anything I can assist with?"

"Well, Paul and I would like to spend some time in the field with infantry units."

Wheaton and Kittles exchanged a knowing look. Wheaton spoke. "I'm sure you're aware that the United States Army has a policy prohibiting women from combat."

"I have no intention of engaging in combat. We would be observers only."

"It's important that we adhere to both the letter and the spirit of the law. Incidents like yesterday's attack are an unfortunate aspect of this war, and must be avoided at all costs. We take our responsibility to protect journalists very seriously."

"Yet you allow male correspondents full access to combat elements."

"I know it must seem unfair, but we have your best interests at heart," Kittles said. "The last thing we want is an injured journalist. I trust you've been seen by our medical staff?"

"I'm fine."

"We're just relieved you weren't hurt badly. The leader of the platoon responding to that ambush, Lieutenant Gianelli, has been reprimanded for his negligence."

Chris frowned. "Why? He did nothing wrong. He had no idea I was even there until the firefight was over. His platoon saved dozens of aid workers and villagers."

"Unfortunately, Miss McKenna, of all the combat elements you could have encountered, you managed to find the worst. Lieutenant Gianelli and his platoon are a stain on this brigade's sterling reputation."

"I see."

"Please don't worry, you need not concern yourself with his platoon. Now, can we assume you're here to cover women's issues?"

Paul shifted in his seat. Chris stared at Kittles.

"I'm here to cover the war," she said.

"Yes, yes, of course, and there are plenty of stories for you here at FOB Jane. For example, we have a small but skilled nursing corps at our hospital, women as close to the front lines as they can be."

"Or the refugees," Wheaton offered. "Refugee stories are always popular with the female crowd."

Chris leaned forward and looked at each man. "The war," she repeated slowly, "I'm here to cover the war. That means time in the field."

"I'm sorry, Miss McKenna, but the rules are the rules," Wheaton said. "I'll check with the public affairs office in Saigon, but their stance on women in combat situations is clear."

"George, perhaps we could keep MACV out of this. As you know, MACV has, in the past, deferred that decision to the local command."

"Yes, sir. Given Miss McKenna's enthusiasm and willingness to come all the way to FOB Jane, I think it would be appropriate to leave that decision to you."

"Miss McKenna, I am happy to take your request under advisement. However, in lieu of joining patrols, at least for now, Lieutenant Wheaton will prepare a detailed briefing book for your reference on the Seventy-Fifth Brigade and its many operational responsibilities," Kittles said. "We've used similar tools in the past in theater and found them to be quite popular with journalists, almost as good as being in the field. And no danger of jungle rot," he added with a laugh. "Lieutenant, can you have the materials ready by the end of the week?"

"Of course, sir. And I will be happy to walk our guests through the more complex aspects of the brigade's operations."

"Is that acceptable, Miss McKenna?"

"Fine," she said.

Chris and Paul stood to leave. Kittles and Wheaton jumped to their feet, eager to shake hands again. Outside, Paul waited while Chris fumed.

"Women's issues? What the fuck is a woman's issue? It's a goddamn war."

"Covered predominantly by men."

"Yeah, I know," she said with a sigh. "Hey, Wheaton is a bit of a creep, right? It wasn't just my imagination?"

"Uh, no. He's definitely an interesting choice for public affairs officer, considering his obvious alcohol problem. Seemed rather taken by you."

Chris wrinkled her nose.

"He's no John Rawlins, that's for sure. At least your favorite G.I. managed to keep his eyes off your chest for extended periods of time."

Chris elbowed her photographer. "Stop it."

"Are we planning to follow both the letter and spirit of the law?"
She laughed. "Don't be silly. Of course not."

***

As the afternoon sun beat down and baked the base, Chris had an unexpected encounter with her least favorite infantry officer, the so-called stain on the Seventy-Fifth Brigade. She had tried to start another piece, but could not pull a coherent sentence from the jumble of thoughts careening through her mind. The report of the ambush, composed and filed within hours of arrival at FOB Jane, had required no serious effort, but this second installment proved more challenging. In a moment of extreme weakness, she considered pursuing the nursing angle for all the wrong reasons; a profile of the lovely Captain Nichols would certainly attract readers, perhaps even those who would otherwise disparage the notion that women could serve their country.

The thunderous launch of artillery snapped her back to reality. Sweat dripped off her face and smeared the doodles in her notebook's margins; the hooch retained more heat than a blast furnace and smelled about as fresh. In an effort to cool down and clear her head, she took her canteen and wove her way around tents, hooches, and bunkers to the water station. She opened the spigot and filled her canteen, then splashed some over her face.

"Are you lost? The Hilton is back in Saigon."

Chris stiffened as water ran off her chin onto her shirt, soaking her chest. She took a deep breath before turning around to face the newcomer.

"Lieutenant, nice to see you again."

His intense caramel-colored eyes bore into her, looking her up and down. Unlike Wheaton's lustful eyes, Gianelli's were clinical, judgmental.

"Why are you here?"

"I was thirsty."

He cocked his head to one side. The sweat on his forehead glistened in the fierce sun. "Make it quick, McKenna. FOB Jane is no place for a woman."

"I've been here for two days. What could I possibly have done to annoy you?"

"You don't get it, do you? You're a distraction, and that's the last thing these guys need."

"Don't be ridiculous."

"Are you really so naïve as to think this is a simple matter of doing your job?"

She continued to hold his gaze, wondering what had crawled up his ass. He could not be much older than thirty, but the dark circles under his eyes and hollowed shadows beneath the scruff on his cheeks gave him the haunted but determined look of weary prey pushed beyond its limits.

"I'm here for the story."

Gianelli scoffed. "You want to be responsible for what happens because they're playing hero and trying to save your ass instead of their own while under fire? That'll be a hell of a story."

"You know as well as I do that when your men are under fire, the last thing they'll be thinking about is me."

"Really? Because one soldier already risked his life to save yours."

"That was...inadvertent. But next time—"

"Absolutely not. You are not tagging along on my patrols."

"What if I promise to follow orders?"

Gianelli laughed. "I didn't fall off the Huey yesterday."

"Come on, please?"

"Sorry. No facilities for women."

Chris wanted to throw her canteen at him. "For Christ's sake, that is the dumbest—"

"Miss McKenna, when the army drew up rules prohibiting women from combat, clearly they had you in mind. If another officer chooses to allow you to risk both your own safety and the safety of the men under his command, that's on him. The best thing you can do for everyone, yourself included, is to stay out of the way."

Chris spoke through gritted teeth. "Advice noted."

***

"Stop pacing. You make me nervous."

Paul watched her with a mixture of curiosity and confusion from the doorway. Chris ignored him and continued to pace back and forth in the hooch, agitated from the conversation with Gianelli. That type of reaction from officers and grunts alike was a natural response to her assault on the army establishment, on ironclad rules and protocol, but she was still offended.

"This place might give the newsroom a run for its money in terms of virulent testosterone. Why do men hate women so much?"

Paul shrugged. "I like women."

"I wasn't really concerned about you."

"Who'd you run into?"

Chris sighed and waved away the question. "No one. Misogyny just seems to be a common thread linking all men who wage war."

"Lieutenant Gianelli?"

"I said no one. They act like I have leprosy. You'd think they'd want to talk to me. I'm their ticket to fame and glory, right?"

"You're a terrible liar."

"That's not true."

"Yes, it is. But would you like some advice?"

"That depends."

"On what?"

"Is it good advice?"

Paul smiled. "Only the best for you."

"Then by all means. Even though you're not going to tell me anything I don't already know."

"If you already know, why aren't you doing it?"

"I'm trying!"

"The story isn't going to fall into your lap. Willis won't settle for one piece, no matter how good. You've never been afraid to butt heads before. What's wrong?"

"Gee, I don't know, they've got guns and an aversion to rational behavior."

Paul rolled his eyes and busied himself with his camera gear. "Let me know when you've got something for me."

Chris made a face at his back. What would Willis say if he could see her now? He would tell her to write another goddamn story, and quickly. The thought of Martin Willis—and her mortal enemy Anne Novak and that sniveling weasel Kent Springer—gloating over her anxiety-driven pacing only made her more anxious. But this was not vicious politicking in the newsroom; this was war and the stakes were much higher.

Prior to her departure for Vietnam, Willis had summoned her to his office and held up the most recent issues of *Time*, *Newsweek*, and *Life*, fanning them out for her to see.

"Leave the conventional journalism to the conventional journalists," he said. "I don't want fluff pieces on life in the army or diatribes on the suffering of innocent civilians. It's all been done before. Tell me something I don't know about this war."

Chris had promised to do just that, but now accepted that her confidence may have been misplaced. Not every story wanted to be told, and perhaps some shouldn't be told, but she was not here to judge truth. She was here to report it.

The problem was simple: she wanted access to combat units, and the one platoon with which she felt a connection, however bizarre, was effectively off limits. Though she could surely find compelling stories elsewhere, she wanted this story. First Squad. Second Platoon.

Chris stopped pacing and snatched her pad off the field table. Maybe there was a way around Gianelli. She found the name she was looking for, snapped the pad shut, and strode out of the hooch.

***

Chris rounded the corner and entered Delta Company's section of camp, feeling about as welcome as the Viet Cong. She tried to melt into the siding of Second Platoon's barracks, resisting the silly urge to tiptoe. Her stomach had knotted itself and she felt lightheaded. If Gianelli were to walk by, she would be dumped on the next Huey to Saigon, she was sure of it.

As she approached the front of the building, she recognized the gravelly voice peppering the troops with insults about their girlfriends, their mothers, and their collective lack of manhood. The invective ended with a pronouncement of a patrol to be run tomorrow morning, followed by groans and curses. She heard footsteps and then the burly soldier pushed through the door.

She scooted past the open barracks door and followed, hanging back a few yards. When she was sure they were alone, she took up stride beside him.

He did a double take, his eyes registering surprise. Fully intending to charm him with her winning personality, Chris held out her hand and smiled.

"You're a hard man to find, Sergeant."

He ignored her outstretched hand. "I try to avoid trouble."

She shrank back. Her hand dropped to her side. "My name is Chris McKenna—"

"I know who you are," said Master Sergeant Travis.

"I thought...I just wanted to ask..." She paused to compose herself. He stared at her like she was a particularly loathsome species of small rodent. "I was hoping you'd let me come along on a patrol." She cringed as the words left her mouth, expecting a resounding no and a healthy dose of humiliation.

Travis laughed, though not harshly. "Why are you asking me?"

"What do you mean?"

"I don't run Delta Company."

"I'm not interested in company operations."

"I don't run Second Platoon, either."

Chris felt a sense of impending doom. "I know."

"Have you asked Lieutenant Gianelli?"

"Yes."

"And?"

"He was...unreceptive. No facilities for women, apparently."

"Why should my answer be any different?"

Chris swallowed hard, eyes wandering, feeling her cheeks flush in frustration. The words tumbled out before she had a chance to moderate them. "All I want is a chance."

Travis appraised her for several long seconds. "Okay," he said. "You can come."

"Really?"

"You can squat, can't you?" He grinned at his own humor. "First Squad is set to head out tomorrow morning for two days or so, recon patrol. You up for it?"

"Yeah. Yeah, sure. I really appreciate it, Sergeant."

He waved away her thanks. "Listen, kid, I've got two rules, which you follow or you walk home. You stay the hell out of the way and you don't get yourself killed. Got it?"

She nodded. "Got it."

"Be at the northwest chopper pad by zero five hundred. You have everything you need?"

"I think so."

Travis extended a hand and gave hers a friendly squeeze. "Nice to meet you, McKenna. See you tomorrow."

***

33

LYNN MASON

Chris returned to the hooch in a hurry, running over the pockmarked paths with ease. Four Chinooks passed low overhead, churning up a wall of dust and dirt that blinded and choked her. She ignored the stares from curious soldiers as she traversed the main square.

Paul had the door open to circulate the afternoon air, but the mosquito net kept out the bugs. He was engrossed in a letter, presumably to his wife. Chris waited impatiently for him to acknowledge her presence.

"You look rather pleased with yourself," he said, still writing. "Am I to assume young Mr. Rawlins turned his attention your way?"

Chris shot him a withering glare.

"No? I thought for sure…"

"Knock it off, would you? We'll be busy the next couple of days."

"We will?"

"Travis is letting us come on patrol. It really was as simple as asking."

Paul dropped his pen and sat back, running a hand over his mop of curly hair. "When I said find something to do, I meant an interview or a briefing."

"A briefing?"

"Sure. You know, the Five O'clock Follies. Perfectly ridiculous, perfectly safe."

Some of Chris's excitement diminished. "Really?"

Paul's smile reflected both amusement and concern. "No, not really. But have you thought this through? Remember what it was like to be shot at? Remember what dead people look like?"

"I know, it's dangerous. But other reporters go. What's the difference?"

Paul shrugged. "Nothing."

3

— • —

C hris and Paul arrived at the designated helipad early, owing to Chris's
concern that Travis would rethink his decision and leave without her.
They took a seat against some sandbagging and waited for the squad. Chris
rummaged through her rucksack and tried to ignore the tornado ravaging her
small intestine. She carried a reporter's notebook wrapped in a plastic bag,
several pens, a poncho, bug repellent, basic first aid paraphernalia, malaria pro-
phylactic, iodine to purify water, salt tablets for hydration, a toothbrush and
toothpaste, plenty of toilet paper, several days of C-rations, two full canteens,
and no weapons of any kind save a Swiss Army knife, mainly for the can-opener
function. Paul carried the same plus two Nikons, three lenses, and enough film
to stock a corner store. He fiddled with one of the cameras while they waited
and snapped a few shots of her.

"Stop it. I look terrible."

"Just practicing."

The men of First Squad cleared the sandbagging, deep in conversation about
the '67 Cardinals, the '68 Tigers, and the ever-hapless Red Sox. The soldier
whom everyone called Jersey loudly informed a muscular man with a crooked
nose and an Olde English B tattoo on his shoulder that the Mets were poised to
make run at glory. The Bostonian was in the throes of a vehement rebuke when
he caught sight of Chris and Paul. He left unfinished a thought on anti-Red Sox
conspiracy theories to ask a more pertinent question.

"No way, Sarge, you're letting her come? Christ, if it ain't new guys, it's chicks."

"I think it's swell," Jersey said with a goofy grin as he sidled up to her. "Maybe me and you can share a foxhole later, honey."

John Rawlins looked sternly at Jersey, who shrank like a puppy caught piddling on the carpet. Chris knitted her eyebrows, her pride bristling. The expression on John's face suggested she had ruined his morning, as if a morning in which one rose before the sun to battle insurgents in the jungle was not, by definition, already ruined. Before John boarded one of two waiting Hueys, he turned to Travis.

"Something on your mind, Rawlins?" The sergeant's tone suggested he knew exactly what weighed on John's mind, and implied he not voice his thoughts if he knew what was good for him.

John shook his head. He climbed aboard the chopper and took a seat across from Chris and Paul. She looked down at the pack between her feet, uncomfortable with the intensity of his gaze from under the brim of the bush hat. As the ride over the treetops smoothed out, she forced herself to meet the cold blue eyes. His expression never softened.

No one talked over the roar of the rotors. The door gunner occasionally fired a burst into the brightening jungle, their home for the next two days. Chris wished John would look elsewhere.

The pilots descended and held the helicopter in a hover over a small clearing outside the jungle. Travis jerked his head and John jumped into the swaying grass. One by one the men clambered out, and then Travis guided her forward with a hand to the small of her back. As she faced the doorway and stared down at the flattened vegetation, the chopper drifted sideways and bucked. Startled, she launched herself out of the open side and landed hard. She pitched forward onto hands and knees, but sprang up and scampered toward the tree line after the rest of the squad, hoping no one noticed the wipe-out. John's smirk indicated otherwise. Paul and Travis brought up the rear as the two Hueys ascended and disappeared.

They assembled their gear, the men rechecking their rifles to ensure a chambered round. Chris put on the Yankees cap and adjusted her pack. The Red Sox fan glowered at her.

"Don't you got a helmet, sweetheart?"

Chris shook her head. Nor did she have a flak jacket. The angry crew chief had forgotten to toss her armor out of the Huey when he dumped the rest of her luggage. She had promised Paul she would acquire a new set, but then had promptly forgotten to do just that.

"Goddamn journos," the man mumbled.

Chris threw a glance over her shoulder at Paul. The photographer snapped a picture of her and grinned. The squad moved out behind John Rawlins at point.

***

Oscar, the hulking black man, stood six inches taller and a hundred pounds heavier than the next biggest man, who happened to be John. He provided introductions for Chris as the squad pressed deeper into the jungle.

"I'm Jersey!" the wild-eyed man said much too loudly.

Travis socked him in the shoulder and told him not to speak. Oscar ignored the outburst and spoke to Chris in a low rumble.

"This here's the Little Man. We call him Bullseye," he said, patting the helmet of the spastic redhead who was the size of an adolescent and seemingly glued to Oscar's side. "Put an M-60 in this kid's hands and watch out."

"What's his real name?"

"Hell if I know."

Bullseye waved to Chris and grinned, exposing crooked teeth.

"That there is my boy Murphy," Oscar said, pointing to the Red Sox fan.

Murphy looked her up and down and flexed his left biceps, highlighting the Boston B on his shoulder. Chris was unsure if he was more offended by her gumption to venture outside the wire or the fact that she was a Yankees fan.

Oscar's tone turned prim and mocking. "And the crown prince of South Carolina's Turner Dynasty, established circa 1708, brave defenders of states' rights, his plantation a bastion of Confederate values."

Turner smiled in good humor.

"The dude next to him is Cook. Also a good ol' Southern boy, wishes he had a dynasty like Turner. He'll settle for king of the trailer park."

Cook, a tall soldier with a stooped walk, laughed and shook his head.

"That guy is Doc Kearney, platoon medic. Med student back in the world. Decided to be a good American and not defer when his number got called."

"Name's Ben," the young medic called. He had wavy blond hair and sunburned cheeks and looked as though he was not old enough to shave. "Hope you're changing those bandages regularly."

Chris nodded.

"The little Mexican is Hector. The best klepto this side of the seventeenth parallel. Just last week he requisitioned a stash of excess deserts from the mess hall and distributed them to needy combat elements," Oscar said, patting his stomach.

Hector flashed a peace sign in her direction.

"But he cheats at cards," another man muttered.

"And Darwin, squad asshole."

Darwin scowled and leered at Chris. She drifted closer to Oscar to escape Darwin's uncomfortable stare, and nearly tripped over Bullseye. She noticed that John had half-turned to watch Darwin's every move. Oscar then pointed to a slightly built teenager who hadn't spoken a word in Chris's presence.

"That's Billy Farrell. He don't say much. One of the fucking new guys."

Chris smiled at Billy, but got nothing in return. His brown eyes were blank, looking past her into the middle distance. Beside Billy, Steve stared at her in fascination, quiet only because he feared Travis.

"My brother spade there next to you is another one of them FNGs, too."

"Dan Peters," the man said and shook her hand. "Say hi to Steve Schaefer before he hurts himself."

"Hi, Steve," Chris said.

Jersey blew a huge sigh of relief and waved again. "Want to interview me?"

"Maybe later."

Oscar continued. "Jersey is FNG number three. At point we have FNG number four, also known as Cowboy."

"Why?"

"Because of that ridiculous headgear," Ben Kearney said.

"Hmm," Chris said. "I would have gone with Gilligan."

John Rawlins pulled the bush hat more snugly over his head and said nothing.

***

Some of them had something scrawled in black marker on the green canvas covering their helmets, like the months of their tours, bible verses, or a quote. The back of Oscar's helmet read, "Fuck this shit." Little Bullseye had written the same in his childlike handwriting. Turner had paraphrased General William Tecumseh Sherman: "War is hell." Billy Farrell had written only one word: "Help." Ben Kearney wore a medic's armband around his right biceps. Dan carried a picture of his girl in his breast pocket under his flak jacket. Cook carried a photo of his car—a Pontiac GTO—in the same pocket. Hector stuck a laminated card of the Virgin Mary under the band around his helmet. Darwin had taped a magazine cutout of a nude woman to his canteen. Murphy carried both his army-issue M-16 assault rifle and a contraband Uzi submachine gun, and wore two belts of M-60 ammunition crisscrossed over his chest. None of his shirts had sleeves. Steve's helmet, sitting askew on his head, was covered in scribbles and a half-played tic-tac-toe board.

John wore a soft bush hat instead of a helmet and moved with a self-confident ease that belied the intensity in his watchful eyes. He walked far ahead, blending into the trees and brush, often disappearing from view as he cleared their path. Chris knew her story was out here, the forgotten Delta, its paddies and jungles an afterthought in the wake of the Tet Offensive and major engagements farther north.

Just before sunset, the squad paralleled the tree line along a wide swath of a Mekong River tributary. On the other side of the water, the jungle thinned and abutted a rice paddy near a small hamlet. The squad had no intention of engaging the hamlet, not today. They saw little activity in the sleepy village, only a few farmers in the distance. Dogs barked, but there was no sign of hostile human contact. Then a whistle pierced the air.

"Get down! Get down!"

Chris and Paul dove into a thicket. The explosion rocked the ground behind them and to the left. A minute passed. Travis called orders to his men. John approached the river in a crouch, scanning the distance for any signs of movement.

"What was that?" Chris asked.

Another whistle. Explosion in the canopy, closer to them but off to the right.

"Mortars." Paul's eyes darted everywhere.

"They have crummy aim."

"They're triangulating our position."

"Oh."

"Sarge, I don't see anything," John said.

The third mortar splashed down in the river. The explosion launched a plume of water into the air.

"They see us. Let's roll."

First Squad began an orderly retreat into the jungle until the fourth mortar landed on the riverbank mere yards from where the squad had first taken cover.

"Move, move!" Travis yelled.

Chris kicked into a higher gear, spurred on by the distressing thought of being mowed down by shrapnel. Beside her, Paul struggled to run with his camera equipment, which in typical photojournalist fashion he refused to jettison. She reached out and grabbed his sleeve, urging him to run faster.

They ran until the bombardment stopped. Chris's lungs burned. The men slowed their pace. Steve Schaefer continued to tear wildly through the brush at full speed.

"Jersey!" Travis hissed. "Stop!"

The sergeant closed his eyes and listened to the jungle. Beyond the sound of panting soldiers and squawking birds, Chris heard nothing.

She pulled off the Yankees cap and hung her head between her knees for a moment. Then she chugged half a canteen of water, oblivious to the metallic taste of iodine. Several of the men lit cigarettes. Murphy held a pack toward her and she accepted gratefully. Oscar offered her a light. She took a deep drag and looked at Paul.

"That was exciting."

"I hate that whistle sound," he said. "Hate it."

She paced along the outskirts of the group, smoking and rubbing her forehead under the cap, captive to the thoughts racing through her mind, too fast to comprehend.

"Are you all right?"

"What?"

"I asked if you're all right," John said.

"I'm fine."

He regarded her skeptically. She held the cigarette toward him.

"Don't smoke."

"Good for you. I promised myself I would quit. That was before I got shot at." She laughed.

"Are you sure...?"

Chris dropped the cigarette butt and squashed it with her boot. "I'm alive. Frankly, I couldn't be better."

"Rawlins! Let's get the hell out of here, son."

***

The morning after completing her first patrol, Chris sat alone in the mess hall, her back to the entrance. She ate the pancakes without tasting them and drank the toxic coffee without so much as a grimace as she read the latest issue of *Stars and Stripes*. FOB Jane's latest issue, anyway. The newspaper was four months old. With a sense of manufactured nostalgia, she read an earnest article on Nixon's promise to achieve an honorable end to the war. Chris had always considered peace and honor to be mutually exclusive principles in wartime, at least for the loser.

She failed to notice the soldiers until they were upon her, jostling for prime seating. She watched the commotion apprehensively.

"Ow!" Steve Schaefer howled.

Oscar had just stomped on his foot in the process of settling his enormous frame on the bench next to Chris. Hector slipped between her and Turner. Ben Kearney, Billy Farrell, Murphy, Dan, and Steve lined up across from her. Bullseye sat on Oscar's other side, jabbering incoherently. Cook and Darwin sat on the end next to Turner. John Rawlins, the last to arrive, reluctantly took a seat on the opposite bench next to Steve.

"You don't mind some company, do you, honey?" Oscar boomed. He occupied more of her personal space than she did.

Murphy shoveled a forkful of pancakes into his mouth. He snatched the *Stars and Stripes* from her. "This is bull. All bull. Don't believe anything the army tells you."

Chris couldn't understand a word he said around all the food. She started to reply, but Oscar cut her off.

"You scared of us?"

"No. Are you scared of me?"

Oscar's laughter shook the table. Chris smiled.

"I been thinking," Murphy said, without food in his mouth. "I been here a few tours. In fact, a bunch of us have been here a while, and never once can I remember a woman tagging along on my patrols. Boys?"

They shook their heads.

"Fuck, what's this world coming to when a chick fights a war?"

"Murph, that's no way to talk to a lady," Turner said.

"She's a Yankees fan," Murphy grumbled.

"Have other journalists come along on your patrols?" Chris asked.

"Sure. Journos ain't nothing special in 'Nam."

"And I'm a journalist." She shrugged, aware that she was possibly the only one capable of reaching the logical conclusion.

"Don't worry," Dan said. "Nobody minds having you along for the ride."

Out of the corner of her eye, Chris saw John press his lips together and shake his head almost imperceptibly, concentrating on pushing his food around his plate with his fork.

"Thank you. I appreciate that." She leaned forward, elbows on the table, and focused most of her attention on Murphy. "Besides, maybe I'm not so bad to have around. I can make you famous."

"I guess me and you will have to talk later." Murphy's eyes roamed lower and lower.

"I guess so." A flirtatious smile at Murphy. That got John's attention. She felt his eyes.

"Hey, I want to be famous, too," Steve said.

"Me too, me too!" Bullseye bounced on the bench beside Oscar.

"Easy, Little Man, easy." Oscar patted Bullseye on the head and turned back to Chris. "Here's the deal, Reporter Lady. You want to get to know me and my boys, me and my boys want to get to know you."

***

"Sergeant Travis!" a voice shouted.

Travis paused on his way to Brigade HQ, where he intended to file his after-action report of First Squad's patrol. Based on his information, another unit—or a squadron of bombers—would return to that village sooner or later. Travis looked down at his scuffed boots, a knowing smirk on his lips.

"Good morning, sir," he said.

"What were you *thinking*?" The pitch of Gianelli's voice climbed an octave.

"Oh, come off it, Sam," Travis said. "No harm done."

"Are you nuts? It was all over this place the second that helo set down last night. Kittles just read me the riot act in the ops meeting. Claims Brooks gave him control over all her movements."

"I don't think that's true."

"That's not the point."

"Then what is the point? Your army career? The stunning rise and spectacular fall of a reservist?"

Gianelli gave his master sergeant a scathing look.

"Listen, she's different than most of the other journo hotshots we got running around these parts. Until *you* order me otherwise, I got no problem with her."

Gianelli rubbed the stubble on his chin. "She's ballsy, I'll give her that."

"Persistent, too."

The lieutenant snorted.

"What's really bothering you?" Travis asked.

"You know how things work around here."

Travis grinned. "It's gonna be one of those summers."

***

Chris finished explaining her job with *American Century* to twelve men. Eleven of them paid rapt attention to her discourse on international affairs and how she sought unique and compelling stories, wherever they could be found, as a features writer for the magazine. One man paid her scant attention; rather, he read the discarded *Stars and Stripes*.

"Hey," Steve said, "are *you* famous?"

"No. I just write."

Murphy reached into one of his cargo pockets, pulled out a silver flask, and took a swig. "So seriously, what the fuck are you doing here?"

"Murph!" said Turner.

"Yeah, yeah, sorry. Same question, minus the fuck."

"Just doing my job. Isn't it a little early for the hard stuff?"

"You last more than a week in this hell, you'll understand. You ain't gotta be here. So why?"

"It's important. The news is—"

"Gilligan, pay attention!" Oscar roared.

Everyone at the table jumped. Chris nearly toppled off the bench. John Rawlins glanced at Oscar, took another bite of his breakfast, and continued reading the newspaper.

"Cowboy marches to the beat of his own drummer," Oscar said to Chris. "He's a hopeless cause. Now, you was saying?"

"What she was saying is not nearly as revealing as what she isn't saying," John said, still pretending to be engrossed in the newspaper. "She's about to feed you a line about how she's here because it's her duty as a journalist to present the war objectively to the American people. The real reason she's here is because it's hard to get ahead in her business unless she covers a major conflict and makes a name for herself."

Everyone stared at John.

"Holy shit, Cowboy," Oscar thundered.

"What?" John looked at Chris, who watched him with forced equanimity. "Am I wrong?"

Chris knew when she was beaten. She also knew she had to regain some ground. "This war is important, and people back home deserve to know what's really going on." She looked steadily into hard blue eyes.

"Ignore him," Dan told her. "We do."

John grunted and returned to the newspaper. Chris wanted to ignore him, but it irked her to be read so quickly and accurately by a man she barely knew.

She realized everyone—even John, who had visibly tensed—awaited her answer to the next question. "Sorry. What?"

"I asked what his name is."

She looked quizzically at Dan. "What whose name is?"

Dan held up his left hand and wiggled his fingers.

Chris looked at the cheap silver band she wore on the ring finger of her left hand. She had hoped the band would discourage unwanted advances, but that would likely require an appreciation of nuance and subtlety the average grunt lacked.

It was a valid question, but she wavered. Then for a split second she met pale blue eyes and the decision was made. "His name is Edward. Edward Sinclair."

"Sounds like a rich boy name. Is he rich?" Steve said.

Chris shifted and hid her hand beneath the table. Edward had, indeed, presented her an engagement ring, one with a large and ostentatious stone. He hadn't been shy about working the cost of the ring into casual conversation. That ring had cost a year's salary—her salary, anyway.

"He does well. He's a lobbyist."

"Figures," he muttered. "The rich boys get all the pretty girls."

"How long have you been married?" Dan asked.

"We're not."

"Engaged?"

Twelve men waited, their hopes and dreams hanging on her response. Chris's sister had set Chris up with Edward, a Yale classmate of the elder McKenna's husband, six months ago. Chris, who found Edward's arrogance and overbearing nature intolerable, not to mention his lack of intellectual curiosity appalling, had decided to play along temporarily both for the sake of her sister—and by extension her parents—and for the professional opportunities that walking into a party on Edward's arm presented.

Unbeknownst to anyone, but especially to Edward, Chris had been working on an in-depth examination of the lobbying industry and its growing impact on executive branch policy decisions and Congressional oversight activities. Edward and his friends and colleagues had the tendency to forget she was a journalist when they drank, which was often, though not that they cared much in the first place. Women weren't real journalists, as Edward had proclaimed on countless occasions, both privately and publicly.

Edward wanted arm-candy, and this Chris had accepted for a time as she gathered background and made contacts, but the last three months had demonstrated the danger of leading on a man like Edward, who was used to getting his way, especially with women. He had proposed to her multiple times, each time Chris declining. She had finally accepted the ring, though not the marriage proposal itself, in an attempt to stave off a late-night confrontation that had escalated rapidly, fueled by his copious consumption of expensive scotch. The fact that she hadn't actually agreed to marry him didn't stop him from telling everyone they were engaged, however. Details were not really Edward's thing.

And then she had the nerve to seek and accept an assignment to Vietnam. If he had been generally unsupportive of her career to that point, save for the access he sought to the publisher of *American Century*, access Chris had denied, he became positively disdainful after learning his would-be future wife had the gall to defy his wishes and cover a war a world away. He had forbidden her to go; she had ignored him. This last month had been the best of their ersatz relationship, as during this month they had not spent much time in each other's presence.

"Just last month." She smiled and tried to blush as she imagined a happy bride-to-be would. "I'm planning a spring wedding. Maybe around cherry blossom time."

Dan stroked his chin. "How'd he do here?"

Images of Edward stumbling through the jungle in combat gear, swearing up a storm, flashed through her mind. She resisted the urge to laugh. "Probably not fantastic."

"Funny," Dan mused with a sly look in Chris's direction. "I thought for sure you'd have roped yourself a cowboy."

Chris threw daggers at Dan with her eyes. Ben Kearney snickered. If John had any reaction to the comment, he hid it well.

"LT made the short list?" Hector said. "Thought you didn't like him."

Chris looked to her right. He grinned and wagged her reporter's notebook, liberated from her cargo pocket, under her nose. She snatched at it, but he held it away from her, laughing.

"You little snake," she said.

"Look, Lieutenant Sam Gianelli and Master Sergeant Jack Travis, right below some dude named John Rawlins."

The squad guffawed. After exerting considerable effort, Chris succeeded in wresting the notebook away from Hector. She rose from the table with as much dignity as she could muster, crammed the notebook back into her pants pocket, and mumbled something about needing to send a telegram before striding out of the mess.

"Thanks for talking, Reporter Lady," Oscar called.

***

Back at the barracks, Hector went straight to his footlocker and retrieved a bright yellow fedora with an ace of spades card stuck in the black hatband circling the crown. He got down to business with a pen and a small black ledger.

"Pick a date," he said to Oscar.

"Tough," boomed the big man. "Don't got a good feel for this one yet. Let's say Memorial Day."

"Murph?"

"May fifteenth."

"That's only a week away. You sure?"

"I'm sure."

"No way," Ben Kearney said. "At least until August."

"August, all right, Doc's in it for the long haul."

"What's this all about?" Dan asked.

"Bullseye, name a date."

"Fourth of July. That's Independence Day."

"No shit. Darwin."

"Come on, what are you doing?"

"May twenty-first."

"The old-timers are not optimistic. Pick a date, Danny."

"Hector!"

"Come on, Danny, it ain't rocket science. Johnny?"

John looked up from the *Stars and Stripes* he had taken from the mess. "June fourteenth. Flag Day."

"That long?"

"I might have provided some extra motivation." He went back to the newspaper.

"Wait a minute," Dan said. "You're picking the date she bugs out?"

Hector grinned. "Maybe."

"Jeez, Murph, a week?"

"She only thinks she's tough."

49

"You in?"

"September," Dan said without hesitation. "No earlier than Labor Day."

Several of the men whistled. John raised his eyebrows. All twelve men picked dates, and Hector collected ten dollars from each of them and put it with his own.

"What happens if you get greased?"

"You're shit out of luck, Jersey. Don't get dead if you want to win. Betting is closed. Thanks for playing."

***

Chris sat in solitude at the western perimeter of FOB Jane, away from the airstrip and the heavily trafficked areas of the base. Notebook in hand, she began to outline her first week's experiences, the beginnings of her second story, planning a subdued follow-up to the rock 'n' roll feel of the first submission. She focused on the personalities and each unique view of what it meant to be a soldier and wage an unpopular war. Viewed with a journalist's objectivity, they were cogs in a vast machine, devoid of identity. But they were more than that.

Chris leaned against the sandbagging in her perimeter niche and stretched her legs. She knew that the story, already taking shape in her mind, would be the most challenging story she had ever told.

She heard the scuff of boots before she saw their owner. She assumed the man would pass by her position, but a broad figure towered over her.

"Sorry," he said, and turned to leave.

"Wait, don't go," she said.

"I'll come back later."

"Come on, John, I don't bite. Is this your spot? It's peaceful." As she spoke, a howitzer launched a shell into the jungle. "Relatively speaking, I guess. Please stay."

"I don't talk to reporters, Miss McKenna."

"For the last time, call me Chris."

"Fine. Chris, I already told you—"

"Yeah, yeah, that you don't want to be a story. Not to worry. We're off the record."

"Somehow I have trouble believing that."

"I promise nothing you say will be used against you."

"Ask someone else."

"I will. I'll ask plenty of people. But I want to talk to you, too."

"Why?"

"You know why. I was right there, John, right there when you risked your life to save innocents. If that isn't a story, I don't know what is. Definitely worth a cover shot and a catchy American hero headline."

He squatted and met her gaze. "If I find out I'm the newest American hero, courtesy you and your employer, you and I will have words, and they won't be the printable kind."

"Is that a threat?" she asked with raised eyebrows, feigning disbelief. She didn't believe for a second that his objections to being lauded in print were representative of his true feelings. Chris had been a journalist long enough to know that all humans craved attention. "You would threaten a woman? A defenseless woman?"

"I would hesitate to call you defenseless."

"Should I be flattered or insulted?"

"This is war, not the country club."

"Do you and Gianelli rehearse these quips?"

"Is everything a joke to you?" he asked.

"Only what's funny. You, on the other hand, don't seem to like jokes very much."

"I like jokes just fine. But this isn't funny."

"You know, you really nailed me at breakfast."

He said nothing, but watched her with renewed interest.

"Suffering—yours or anyone else's—is not something I would ever take lightly," she said.

John moved off his haunches and sat. "Good. You wouldn't be much of a journalist if you did."

"Nor much of a person. I'm going to bug you until you talk to me."

He allowed himself a grudging smile. "I know."

Chris watched him from the corner of her eye, wrestling over whether to give him a heads up about the forthcoming issue of the magazine. "Where are you from?"

"Iowa."

She laughed. "And you grew up on a farm, right?"

He looked at her, eyebrows knitted and eyes hard.

"Oh, God, you did grow up on a farm. Sorry. It's just...never mind."

John frowned and looked down at his notebook. She followed his gaze, her eyes drawn to his tanned hands, remembering the feel of the calloused tips against her chin, on her wrist.

"You don't get my type out in Iowa, do you?"

"Women who volunteer for combat duty? No, not really."

"At least you'll have something to tell the folks back home."

John rose and dusted off the seat of his pants. "My youngest brother wants to be a journalist. He reads *American Century* every week, in fact. Know who his favorite writer is?"

Chris named several well-known *American Century* writers.

"Nope. His favorite writer is Chris McKenna. But know what's funny? We both thought Chris McKenna was a man."

He began to walk away.

"John," she called. "Who's your favorite writer?"

"I told you, I read *Time*."

His eyes showed a hint of warmth as he left the niche. Chris watched a key piece of the story disappear into the dusk.

4

— • —

"Johnny!" Steve screeched. "You're famous!"

John heaved a final bench press, the last of a set of ten reps, and Dan helped him lower the bar to the rack. He sat up on the bench, breathing heavily, as Steve entered the huge open-air tent that shaded an array of benches, racks, barbells, dumbbells, and sundry workout gear. He scampered over obstacles and around his squadmates, waving a magazine above his head. He reached John and brandished his prize with a flourish. John rose and felt his heart pound a little harder when he saw the *American Century* logo emblazoned across the top of the cover.

"You're famous," Steve repeated. He opened the magazine to the feature article and thrust it forward. "See?"

John took the magazine and reclaimed the bench, perching on the edge and hunching protectively over the pages like a hungry lion over a dispatched wildebeest. Steve abandoned him to announce yet again to the rest of the platoon that John was famous, drawing sarcastic speculation that he had already managed to nail the reporter lady. John ignored him and instead admired Paul Lane's eye for drama. The opening photo was a stunning panorama of the convoy ambush: everything in the scene was on fire.

He steeled himself with a deep breath before he began reading the article, afraid of what he might find buried within the paragraphs that followed Paul's photography. The prose was sharp and pointed and honest, laced with genuine urgency and emotion.

John read the article three times in an effort to find the passages where she extolled her own actions in saving civilians from almost certain death, but the writer seemed nothing more than an observer, someone who had followed orders and remained on the Huey. He easily found his name in the first reading, but he glossed over it, unready to confront her interpretation of his character or his courage. On the last reading, he forced himself to accept that his name was in a major newsmagazine. She had an undeniably sharp eye for detail, and he reluctantly admitted that she presented an accurate and thorough recap of the battle.

But now he was a story. John rolled up the magazine and cut short his workout to seek solitude.

***

Kittles stormed into the base club in search of George Wheaton, who occupied his favorite table near the bar. The captain wielded a rolled-up magazine like a billy club. He smacked the table and Wheaton jumped.

"Have you seen this?"

"Seen what?" the public affairs officer said, well into his third drink of the afternoon.

Kittles unrolled the *American Century* and flung it into Wheaton's lap. Some of Wheaton's vodka sloshed out of the glass and onto his hand. He slurped it off the webbing between thumb and forefinger.

"Feature story," said Kittles.

Wheaton glanced over the article and shrugged. "So?"

"So? *So?*" Kittles's eyes bulged from their sockets. "It's all that son of a bitch Gianelli."

"Have a drink," Wheaton offered.

"I need a clear head."

Wheaton thought a clear head was about the worst thing to have in Vietnam. He took another swig of vodka.

Kittles plopped into a chair and dropped his head into his hands. "She's mine," he said plaintively. "Gianelli hates reporters. He's doing this to spite me. Against my explicit orders!"

"Do you think he's fucking her?" Wheaton asked.

Kittles looked startled. "What?"

Wheaton called for another vodka. "Swear to God he better not be fucking her. I want that ass."

"Jesus, George, take a cold shower. Rumor is that she's engaged."

"Kinky. Any girl who comes to Vietnam pretending to be a journalist has a wild side. Not like those uptight nurses."

"Setting aside your base carnal desires for a moment, we need a plan."

"For what?"

"Good publicity, of course."

"For FOB Jane? Who the fuck cares?"

"No, not for FOB Jane. For me. For us," Kittles corrected quickly. "What's the biggest problem with this war?"

"The fact that we're not winning?"

"Not ideal, but no. At a more granular level." Kittles waited a moment. Wheaton looked blank. "Nothing but bad news!"

"Because we're not winning," Wheaton said slowly.

"Since the start the media have run amok, subject to no oversight. They publish whatever the hell they want to publish with no regard for the men in uniform. It's time for us to start controlling the narrative."

"I'm listening," said Wheaton.

"We give her exactly what she wants. Combat."

"You really want a woman in the bush with you? If she gets hurt..."

"That would be unfortunate. But a necessary risk. The real danger comes from Gianelli. I don't trust him, but it's her choice." Kittles shrugged. "Not a great career move for him if he gets a journo killed. A female journo at that."

"Wait, I'm confused. Do we want Gianelli to get her killed?"

"No, of course not. We need her alive. I'll be the first to admit that *American Century* is not *Time* or *Life*, but it's an up-and-comer. I made a few calls back to the States. You know, doing your job." Kittles looked pointedly at Wheaton. "The publisher is new to the game but he has some major sway in both parties. Passed the oil business to his sons to indulge in a couple of hobbies and bought *American Century* when the previous publisher went bankrupt. He brought in some real talent and circulation is way up, especially with the younger crowd. Given the publisher's status, I for one wouldn't mind being on his radar. If it takes indulging Miss McKenna's desire for a bit of adventure, so be it. Not like she'll last long here anyway."

"They never do," said Wheaton. "Did I mention I want to fuck her?"

Kittles sighed. "Several times."

***

When it was time for Chris's stitches to come out, she returned to the hospital in search of Maria Nichols. A corpsman informed her that the captain was teaching a training class for her subordinates, but he asked her to wait while he searched for a medical professional.

The corpsman hadn't been gone more than two minutes when a tall man in blue scrubs swung by the nurses' station to drop off a handful of patient files.

"I'm sorry," he said to Chris. "But we don't treat Yankees fans here."

"Another Sox fan? God, you people are everywhere."

"Cubs, actually. But they break my heart every year." He crossed his arms over his chest. "You must be the infamous Chris McKenna."

"I plead the fifth."

"You don't look too worse for wear, so I assume you've recovered from your auspicious start to this assignment."

"Just need some stitches out. One of your corpsmen went looking for adult supervision."

"As luck would have it, you've found an adult. Or at least a man-sized child who supervises." He grinned. "Major Pat Jacobson. Care to join me in exam room three?"

Inside the room, Jacobson peeled off the bandage on her forehead and examined the wound.

"This healed nicely. In fact, it may not even scar." He pulled back and looked at her with twinkling eyes. "Unless you want a scar."

"Only if it comes with a killer story."

Jacobson laughed and set to work removing the stitches. He covered the wound with a fresh bandage and told her to keep it covered for a few more days.

"Otherwise, good as new."

"Thanks, Doc."

Chris hopped off the exam table and pulled the Yankees cap back on her head. She watched him as he cleaned up. He appeared to have gone days without sleep. Dark circles accentuated his deep-set, brooding midnight blue eyes. The skin on his face was pinched and drawn, emphasizing his high cheekbones.

"I hear this is a pretty busy hospital," she said.

"Unfortunately."

"What's your specialty?"

"General trauma surgery. We save and stabilize, then ship off to the major hospitals for treatment by specialists."

"How many surgeons here?"

"At the moment, just me. At least technically."

"Technically?"

"It's complicated."

"I'm sure." She waited in silence for him to continue.

He didn't bite. "We're expecting a second general surgeon later this summer. Of course, this is not the first time we've been promised personnel only to see people reassigned to more desirable locations at the last minute." He shrugged.

"I don't understand how one surgeon handles an influx of traumas."

"I have nurses and corpsmen. And Captain Nichols is more competent than most board-certified surgeons I know."

"She sews a mean set of stitches, but isn't she just a nurse?"

"That's what the army calls her, yes."

Chris cocked her head. Jacobson avoided meeting her eyes. Chris flashed back to the MACV major's dim view of FOB Jane and wondered what diverged more: his perception or her reality. While a remote base in IV Corps, a low-priority tactical zone for MACV in the aftermath of the Tet Offensive, might be an appealing dumping ground for officers like Kittles and Wheaton, Chris didn't believe that they were representative of FOB Jane's officer corps as a whole. She had just begun to penetrate the layers of military bureaucracy, but even she could see that FOB Jane was understaffed and struggling for resources.

"I get the sense that some of you have been here a bit longer than the typical tour," she said.

"A few of us have masochistic tendencies, I suppose. Over two years for me, almost three for Maria, longer for the colonel. Several of the infantry officers are also gluttons for punishment."

"Have you thought about transferring to Saigon or Danang? At least there you might get some sleep."

Suddenly conscious of his disheveled appearance, he ran a hand over his head to smooth down his dark hair. The defiant cowlick at the crown of his skull popped back up. He smiled sheepishly.

"That obvious?"

"Just a lucky guess," she said.

"You know, I've been waiting years for someone to tell me what I'm really doing here. You, I think, might be able to get the real story, whatever the real story is."

Chris laughed, taken aback. "I'll try not to disappoint. But I think defining the Vietnam experience will be easier said than done."

"Regardless, I look forward to reading your work. Be safe."

***

Chris's fingers flew over the keys of the typewriter. She occasionally glanced at her notes—a particularly pithy observation here, a colorful quote there—but otherwise the floodgates had opened and all she could do was hope to keep pace with the narrative. She had decided what, and who, her story would be.

She would be the first to admit that Martin Willis drove her nuts. He was ornery, stubborn, and impossible to please. But in that moment, Chris thanked her muse that she was blessed to have an editor who sought the unconventional. She grinned around the pen clenched lengthwise between her teeth. Willis was going to get exactly what he asked for: an unconventional story from his most unconventional journalist.

***

According to Colonel Brooks's detailed reports of enemy kills, weapons confiscated, villages searched, and sectors patrolled, the pace of combat operations had lagged throughout April. May's activity had to increase to compensate and satiate MACV's hunger for enemy casualties, a firmly entrenched sign of progress. After Vietnam, the metrics of war would never be the same.

The colonel and his staff understood that the decrease in ops tempo stood in inverse proportion to the rise in temperature. The summer months averaged temperatures in the low nineties with astronomical humidity levels, conditions that could be fatal without proper precautions. Complicating matters, South Vietnam's monsoon season ran from May through September, dumping upwards of a foot of rain per month. Without adequate rest, combat elements quickly succumbed to heat-borne ailments and exhaustion, a fact Brooks did not take lightly, not after the summer of 1967 when he neglected to monitor the pace of his rifle companies and nearly drove his entire brigade into the ground.

But the war would not stop, and so Delta Company steamed toward several large villages on the eastern coast at the mouth of the Mekong River: Cau Ngan, Ba Dong, and Tra Cu. Major Rick Gardner, the brigade's senior intelligence officer, had lost a valuable source last week; the Ba Dong village chief, a personal friend of Gardner's after years of collaboration against the Viet Cong, had been dumped in a field, tortured, throat slit. Brooks and Gardner had deemed the area too important to ignore.

Much to the shock of Brooks and Gardner and his four platoon lieutenants, Captain Kittles accepted the assignment with enthusiasm. He insisted that Chris and Paul join his company; the two journalists warily accepted the invitation, and Chris's muttered sarcasm regarding a woman's place in war went ignored or unheard. Chris suspected the latter.

As the company made its way toward Ba Dong on foot, Kittles spent the entirety of the march regaling her with his life story. Chris tried to keep an eye on Second Platoon, which occupied the point position, but both the platoon and her story disappeared from sight. Relegated to the middle of the company—the captain's invitation failed to include the caveat that her movements would be restricted for the duration of the operation—Chris paid scant attention to Kittles and instead plotted her escape. The Yankees cap kept the sun out of her eyes but baked the top of her head; beads of sweat rolled down her temples. She concentrated on the tickle as each droplet ran its course from hairline to cheekbone to jaw, plummeting off the side of her face to splash her thighs or her boots as she walked along the recently widened path.

Kittles had drifted into post-war employment scenarios. "When I retire from service, I plan to explore a run for office. Wars may be fought on the battlefield, but they are won and lost in the halls of Congress. We need a new breed of leader, a man who has served on the front lines and knows what it takes to overcome the enemy. Don't you agree, Miss McKenna?"

"I didn't think you spent much time in the field," Chris said innocently.

Kittles puffed out his chest in an effort to add dignity and gravitas to his response. "Please don't let Lieutenant Gianelli's platoon of hooligans color your thinking. I spend a great deal of time in the field, and without my leadership this company would have lost far more men and failed to achieve its current high level of operational success. As I'm sure you're aware, Delta Company has the highest kill rate in the brigade."

"Congratulations." Her tone suggested it was more of a question.

"Indeed, it is this type of operational prowess that has caught MACV's attention. I'm told I'm a shoe-in for major during the next promotion cycle."

A bead of sweat rolled down the length of her nose. As it plummeted off the precipice, she caught it with her tongue. Salty.

Paul snapped a picture of her.

"For instance, during a recent operation in Bac Lieu, we were ambushed by the insurgents, due in large part to Lieutenant Gianelli's incompetence and refusal to follow orders. The Viet Cong offered ferocious resistance, but they were no match for my tactical prowess. I led the counterattack that rescued Gianelli, although tragically he lost several men that day. And at my previous post in Hue, I led a mission that was credited with saving the lives of two downed aircrews. Goodness, there are so many operations to discuss with you. I expect you need to take notes?"

Chris made a show of whipping out a notepad and pen.

"Excellent. Please let me know if I'm going too fast."

Chris pulled the baseball cap lower and concentrated on putting one foot in front of the other during the halting journey to the South China Sea.

***

Hours later, with camp established on the beach outside Ba Dong, Chris and Paul watched Kittles disappear into his tent for a nap. Chris hopped to her feet and brushed off her sandy backside.

"Now's our chance. Let's go."

Camera equipment in hand, Paul climbed up from the sand. He snapped a few shots of the tranquil sea, glassy in the face of distant storm clouds off the coast.

"This is a nice beach."

"Hurry up."

They passed Lieutenant Jenkins's men on the perimeter and reentered the village. Clumps of women and children watched the soldiers in silence. Cooking fires smoldered in their pits and squawking chickens shuffled about the lines of hooches, pecking at bugs and feed on the ground. The men of the village had disappeared, rounded up at gunpoint for questioning. She glanced at Paul. He took photo after photo, but the faraway look in his eyes unnerved her, as though he tried not to see the truth of what his lens captured. Whether it was clairvoyance or past experience that led him to anticipate what came next, Chris never knew.

The soldiers of Second Platoon were scattered about the village. Gianelli stood with Travis and Conlon near several penned donkeys, all three focused on a map spread between them. A light breeze fluttered the paper. Paul murmured something about rain and snapped the shutter as they approached the men. Gianelli glanced at his watch but didn't look up.

"That didn't take long. Does the captain know you're here?"

Chris thought it best not to respond.

"Didn't Jenkins's boys have orders to shoot them on sight?" Travis said with a wink in her direction.

"Nobody obeys orders anymore, especially hotshot journos."

Travis turned his back to Chris and spoke to Gianelli too quietly for her to hear, but Gianelli waved away the concern.

"Miss McKenna is here to cover the war. This is war. Enjoy the show."

Chris tensed. The village fell still in the afternoon heat.

***

Though Lieutenant Jenkins was not much taller than the average man, he appeared to tower over most of his peers, perhaps elevated by his unparalleled skill as an interrogator of indigenous sources. He stood in Ba Dong's central square and cracked his neck and rolled his shoulders.

Jenkins examined the meter-long bamboo rod in his hands. With a flick of his wrist, the rod bounced, bending just enough to prevent breakage. Captain Kittles gestured to an expressionless young villager who sat shirtless and cross-legged on the dirt with his hands bound behind him.

"Start with him."

Two of Jenkins's men grabbed the Vietnamese under the arms and hauled him up. Jenkins circled slowly and deliberately. The bamboo rod whistled through the air and struck bare skin. A thin line of blood appeared on the villager's back. The man cried out. Kittles flinched, but he nodded to his lieutenant, who tapped his free hand with the rod. Kittles knew it always started this way with the Cong, but Jenkins never failed to break them. Someone always knew something. The rod would not rest until someone broke.

Neither would the fist. Jenkins threw a punch into the man's jaw. A quiet whimper escaped. His men pulled the prisoner to his feet again. Another strike on the back with the rod. A punch in the kidney. A tumble to the ground, hauled up yet again to stand on quivering legs. Taunts in English, taunts in pidgin Vietnamese. A knee to the groin. The rod drew more blood. Kittles turned away and shuffled back and forth in the dusty square, rubbing his forehead as if deep in thought.

With the prisoner on the verge of unconsciousness, Jenkins took a water break.

"Has he said anything useful?" Kittles asked.

"Hard to tell. Don't speak Vietnamese, remember?"

"I want every fighting-age man interrogated."

"Understood."

Kittles paused. "Give me the rod."

"Sir?"

"Now."

Jenkins handed Kittles the bamboo. Kittles wielded the rod clumsily, unsure of the lengths of its power or the depths of its persuasion. The first swing was ugly, across the neck, leaving behind a deep gash on the throat; Jenkins cringed. The second swing, smoother, struck the side of the villager's face, slicing him from ear to jaw. Kittles paused, pleased with his handiwork. He looked to Jenkins for approval.

"If you kill him, we lose a potential source of intel."

"A simple laceration," the captain replied. The villager's vacant eyes stared at the ground. "Hardly life-threatening."

"If you say so."

After a few minutes, Kittles tired of the exercise. He motioned Jenkins forward and held out the rod. "When you're done for the evening, report to me at camp."

"Yes, sir." Jenkins then jerked his head toward a gathering of huts on the outskirts of the square. "Were you aware that we have an audience?"

"What?"

Kittles scanned the bodies milling about, noting the men of First Platoon and a few curious onlookers. Then he saw them, one reporter and one photographer just visible in the shadows of a hooch.

***

The platoon approached Ba Dong's sister village, Cau Ngan, from the south and fanned out to cover a wide swath of ground. A light rain had fallen steadily since the early morning hours, making sleep on the beach huddled under steamy ponchos impossible. The village appeared in the mists along the edge of the flat paddy land, huts dotting the landscape, smoke rising from the breakfast fires and casting a cloud over the hamlet.

They crossed a brown field, watching for mines and other booby-traps rigged by the Viet Cong. Chris and Paul followed in John's footsteps, but Chris paused when a splash of white caught her eye. She stooped to pick up the piece of paper and unfolded the soggy mess. It was a leaflet written in Vietnamese with a picture of an American soldier at the top of the message. He was dead, shot through the face. He was missing his left cheekbone, and his lifeless eyes stared back at her. Chris dropped the leaflet and smashed it into the mud with the heel of her boot.

The scraggily grass gave way to the dirt paths of the village outskirts. Barefoot children materialized and trotted alongside the platoon. Gianelli motioned to Travis and the men snapped into action, bursting into hooches with rifles drawn, shouting, searching, dragging out villagers.

"Move it, mama-san. How about you, papa-san? You VC? Get over there."

Warning shots rang out. Withered men and women stumbled in the mud, prodded by rifle muzzles to the back. Stooped and scared, they were herded to the center of the village, penned in like farm animals.

Chris walked toward a huddled group of children. She crouched down, tilting the Yankees cap up on her head. She held out a hand and felt a lump forming in her throat.

They poked their toes in the mud, staring at her. Rain beaded on their faces, the droplets coursing over smooth skin spared the physical scars from a war that had touched everyone. One of the more adventurous toddlers reached out a hand to meet hers. Their fingertips touched. He moved his fingers over her palm. She closed her fingers over his tiny hand and sat down in the mud.

Paul clicked the shutter.

The platoon tore through the villages, looking for arms caches and tunnels and propaganda and signs of the Viet Cong, signs real or imagined.

The boy moved his tiny fingers off her palm to her face. He took his thumb out of his mouth and used both hands to trace over her jaw and her cheekbones. Then he ran off.

"You find anything?"

"Nothing, LT. It's clean, or else they got real good hiding places. Sorry. I know the captain won't be too pleased."

"No matter. We carried out orders. Let's head back."

Chris pushed herself up from the mud as the rain intensified. Paul touched her shoulder and pointed.

John sat in the mud with a little girl on his lap. She snuggled into his arms, two small hands clenching one of his wrists. He held a piece of chocolate to her mouth and she sucked on it hungrily. He bent over her to shield some of the rain.

Chris turned away before she started to cry.

***

Though it pained Anne Novak to admit it, Chris McKenna's most recent work was compelling, even impressive. Earlier in the week, Anne's editor at the *Washington Dispatch* had handed her the latest issue of *American Century* and implored her to reconsider an assignment to Vietnam.

"This could be us," he said. "This is the talk of the town."

About the last thing Anne wanted was to be pinned down in a jungle firefight with an aid convoy, but an assignment to Vietnam, perhaps just a few weeks long, would enhance an already storied career in Washington reporting. No one would ever again question her commitment or toughness; her detractors liked to note her lack of overseas war experience during an era of constant conflict. Indeed, Washington had grown rather mundane since the tumult of 1968 and Nixon's January inauguration. Perhaps a change of scenery would reinvigorate her, though the thought of a month without creature comforts made her twitch.

And then there was the small matter of the endless and unforgiving war of attrition between her and Chris McKenna, a battle for stories and prestige that had ignited during Chris's first year on the job. At an open Senate Armed Forces Committee hearing, Anne had taken a seat beside an unfamiliar face in the press section, an attractive young woman who seemed interested in what was being discussed on the floor and unappreciative of Anne's snide remarks throughout the hearing. During a break in the testimony of the deputy commander of EUCOM regarding tensions with NATO partners over the escalating American involvement in Vietnam, Anne wandered off to chat with a friendly senator and made the mistake of leaving her notebook unattended on her seat. When Anne returned ten minutes later, the woman was gone.

Two days later Anne's editor stormed into the newsroom, threw a copy of *American Century* onto her desk, and demanded to know how a reporter named Chris McKenna had stolen Anne's exclusive on President Johnson's plan to nominate an African-American to his cabinet—the first such nomination of its kind. Anne had let loose a barrage of profanity that would have shocked even the most hardened Marine, and then confronted Chris outside the *American Century* building, intending to spread the pain and make clear the journalistic pecking order in the capital of the free world. But Chris had the nerve to laugh and suggest Anne not leave her notebook out for any nosy reporter to see, especially if she was going to lack the decency to pretend to be objective. Anne was not often rendered speechless, but Chris had landed a blow strong enough to knock her ego flat on its ass.

It was this memory in particular that spurred Anne toward her editor's office, where she informed him that she would accept the assignment, but only under the condition that she pick the location and stories. Her editor readily acquiesced; Anne was the most popular writer on the *Washington Dispatch* staff and maintained the best sources. Also, he was not ashamed to admit that he was afraid of her.

Since she had no shortage of contacts at the Pentagon, most of whom owed her a favor, she phoned an army colonel in the public affairs office and told him she wanted authorization to visit FOB Jane.

***

Chris felt some of the tension leave her body when the Hueys and Chinooks touched down at FOB Jane. The days at the beach had passed with interminable slowness, allowing Chris plenty of time to ponder the Vietnam quandary, the story it was and the story it could be. She was stuck in her own head, unable to see past the moment, yet unwilling to face the moment. The next chapter in the story remained elusive, the words lost in the depth of war's emotional abyss.

As she and Paul moved off the helipad, Captain Kittles yelled for Gianelli to approach and engaged him in heated discussion. Chris grabbed Paul's arm to stop him.

"Wait a minute."

"What's wrong?"

"I'm not sure."

Gianelli turned his back on the captain and stood before his men in silence, incapacitated by anger. Travis and Conlon exchanged a knowing look and Conlon jogged to one of three Hueys with rotors still spinning and spoke with the crew.

"Back on the helos!" Travis bellowed.

No one moved.

"You're fucking kidding," Murphy said.

"Yeah, we just spent a week putting our asses on the line while everyone else screwed around on the beach," Darwin said. "What the fuck's up with that?"

"Don't give me lip. I said get back on those birds."

"LT," said Oscar, "you can't let that jackass push you around."

Gianelli sprang forward and grabbed the big man by the open flak jacket. He jerked, but Oscar didn't budge. The lieutenant's lips turned up in a snarl.

"Don't you fucking tell me what to do."

"Whoa, LT, I was just trying to help."

Gianelli released Oscar's jacket. "Then get on the Huey."

John and Dan moved to the choppers. One by one the men followed until Chris and Paul stood alone with Gianelli and Travis.

"This is probably my fault, isn't it?" she said.

"Now why would you think that, Miss McKenna? Could it possibly be your willful disobedience of the captain's orders?"

"I'm sorry if by doing so I caused you any...inconvenience."

"You certainly have a penchant for understatement."

"May we come?"

"No. Go take a shower, get a hot meal, relax, do whatever it is journalists do when they're not getting in the way. I look forward to your forthcoming exposé on your week with baby killers and torturers. I'm sure it will be riveting. After all, it's a far less arduous effort to comment on the process than participate in it. Now, scamper off and crucify us."

"I'm sorry," she repeated, because she could think of nothing else to say. Words seemed inadequate for the circumstances she would soon be forced to address on paper.

She and Paul headed toward the center of camp. Chris studied her boots to hide her face.

"His problems with Kittles aren't your fault," Paul said.

"Maybe not, but I sure didn't help."

"Take solace in the fact that the military has always hated journalists. You're not the first to aggravate a junior officer. In any case, I'm sure he appreciated the offer to suffer alongside his men."

Chris grunted. "Sorry I didn't check with you first."

"The Mekong Delta is a cakewalk compared to Guadalcanal."

A voice roared, drowning out the idling Hueys. "McKenna! Get back here!"

"You were saying?"

"Me and my big mouth."

They jogged back to the sandbagging. Travis took one last drag on a cigarette and flicked the butt away, smirking. Gianelli waited for them with his arms crossed over his chest, looking like he had just conceded defeat to his master sergeant. Chris was suspicious, but then a touch of humor reached Gianelli's eyes.

"You ready for a wild summer, McKenna?"

She grinned.

They boarded one of the Hueys and took a seat at the end of the back bench. She looked into piercing blue eyes across the cabin. The iciness melted away, replaced fleetingly by friendliness. John nodded a greeting.

As Chris settled back, her anger over events at Ba Dong began to dissipate. Anger, for the moment, solved nothing. She didn't like the story it was, but she held onto hope for the story it could be.

5

— • —

The men of Second Platoon watched the Hueys ascend and disappear over the jungle canopy. Steve heaved out a theatrical sigh, gazing forlornly into the distance.

"I sure could use some loving," he said. He turned to Chris and grinned. "How about we disappear behind that big tree over there and get to know each other?"

Chris rolled her eyes.

"Shut up, Schaefer."

"Aw, LT, I was just trying to be friendly."

Gianelli grabbed Bullseye by the collar and dragged him closer. He yanked the radio out of the cradle on the teenager's back and raised FOB Jane. The operator on the base end summoned Captain Vasquez to speak with Gianelli.

"Grid thirty. Any reports of hostile activity in the last month?"

"Negative. Grid has been clear."

"Copy." Gianelli signed off and slammed the radio down. He appraised his tired troops. "Rawlins, think you can get us to the river by sundown?"

"No problem, LT."

"Don't go too fast. McKenna's a week behind on her beauty rest."

"Roger that. She's delicate," John replied, looking at Chris with an expression of affected Midwestern politeness.

Paul laughed. Chris elbowed her photographer, her nostrils flaring in irritation. John enjoyed watching her squirm, and he noticed an unfamiliar flutter in his chest when her green eyes latched onto his, daring him to challenge her toughness again.

John took up position at the head of the loose formation and set the pace. Chris slipped in between him and Dan; he felt her closeness and tried to ignore her. He had more important things to worry about, like ambushes and booby-traps and the malarial mosquitoes buzzing around his head.

Without realizing it, John walked faster and faster to escape her, but she kept up with him step for step, never pausing as she hopped over fallen trees or skirted thickets of brush, just waiting for him to let down his guard, just waiting to pounce.

***

"You in a hurry?" Chris asked as they waited for the rest of the platoon to catch up.

John listened to the jungle pressing close around them. The afternoon sun dripped through the canopy and cast waving shadows on the copper earth, but his focus was inevitably drawn to her. Sleepless nights on the beach at Ba Dong had provided ample opportunity to ponder that which vexed him; finally, after three nights of vacillation, he concluded that her eyes were the color of an Iowa meadow after gentle spring rain. She wore a black tank top under the half-open fatigue shirt, oddly seductive despite the outfit's utility. Already her face and chest were tanned golden. Her forehead glistened with sweat, but she was not as winded as he hoped she would be.

"I'm not sure you understand what a point man does."

"I'm quite sure I do. But I don't think you were supposed to outrun your platoon by a mile."

"Do I tell you how to do your job?"

"You really don't like having me around, do you?"

72

John said nothing, despite having much to say. The platoon appeared behind them, men laden with anywhere between fifty and a hundred pounds of equipment crashing through thick underbrush, stumbling and swearing. Chris drew close.

"Next time, maybe you'll think twice before calling me delicate."

"And you think I don't take jokes well?"

Chris smiled faintly. "We both know that wasn't a joke, John."

"Maybe it was, maybe it wasn't. It doesn't change the fact that you shouldn't be running with the point man. You're not even wearing a flak jacket."

"Take it up with your superiors. Every time you turn around, I'll be here."

John kept his expression neutral. *A nerve,* he said to himself with childish glee. *I touched a nerve.*

"Gilligan," Oscar boomed, "nice of you to wait. She riding you hard?"

Even Travis and Gianelli laughed along with the men. John ignored the comment and took off through the jungle. Ever conscious of the presence on his tail, he focused on keeping a steady pace until he came to the banks of the river.

The Hau Giang River wound through the paddies and jungle until it merged with the Mekong farther south. Gianelli ordered them to set up camp on the eastern bank, where they could seek concealment behind thick brush. The men dropped their rucksacks and equipment, everything except their rifles. Travis and Conlon organized a perimeter defense and anyone not on guard duty knelt at the edge of the river and filled canteens. Bullseye promptly chugged a full canteen of river water without purifying it. Ben Kearney nearly fell off the bank while lecturing him on the proper procedure for purifying the water with iodine tablets. The redhead stared at the medic, incomprehension written across his freckled face. Kearney finally gave up.

"It's not even his first tour. You'd think he'd know better," he grumbled to John and Dan.

"Can't save 'em all, Doc," said Dan.

"No, unfortunately, stupidity is an incurable affliction."

John watched Chris mentally file away the medic's cogent quote for future use.

"Speaking of stupidity, does anyone else get the feeling we're out here for all the wrong reasons?" Dan said.

Steve, who had just dunked his head into the river to cool off, ran to them and dripped all over their gear. "Know what I heard? LT and that fat-ass captain hate each other."

"Really?" John replied dryly.

"Oh yeah," Steve continued. "Fat-ass thinks LT doesn't follow orders."

"Where did you hear that?" Turner asked.

Steve shrugged. "I got sources. We're stuck out here until he decides LT's had enough punishment."

"You're full of shit, Jersey. But for once I think you might be right." Murphy peeled off his shirt and exposed tattooed flesh: a shamrock on his right pectoral to complement the Olde English B on his left shoulder. "Wake me when it's time to go home." He stretched out and rested his head on his pack.

Steve turned to Chris. "Hey, Reporter Lady, I got a quote for you: this blows."

"That's your quote?"

"Hell yeah, that's my quote."

"Profound."

"Yeah? Well, all right. Anytime you need something, you call me or my boy Johnny here. Got it?"

Neither John nor Chris responded.

***

The following day, First Squad took guard duty until noon and then switched with Second Squad. As they settled into a loose circle for lunch, they whispered excitedly about their fantastic fortune. No patrolling. No seeking out the elusive Viet Cong. Kearney wondered aloud if Gianelli suffered from an undiagnosed malady. Heatstroke, maybe, or a brain tumor. Neither the lieutenant nor his two trusted sergeants offered an explanation for the inactivity, but everyone knew the reason. In a subtle manner, Gianelli was telling Kittles to shove it. And for that the men loved their lieutenant.

Oscar sent Bullseye over to Chris with an invitation to join the squad for lunch. Her photographer had struck up a friendship with Travis and Gianelli and had left her to her own devices. She sat against a tree with a notebook in her lap, nibbling on a cracker, lost in the story, or least pretending to be. She accepted the invitation and took a seat between Turner and Dan. Murphy instigated an argument over baseball during which he questioned her character, her intelligence, and her patriotism, but she held her own.

John helped Billy open a can of beef stew before attacking his own lunch. The boy slowly and with obvious effort brought a spoonful to his mouth. His hair, not trimmed since boot camp, was matted to his upper forehead, a scraggily mess of sweat-soaked strands. He ate a few bites of stew, then with shaking hands lit a cigarette. His eyes closed and his head lolled to the side.

John put down his tin can of spaghetti and meatballs and touched Billy's shoulder. "Billy, you need to eat."

"I ain't hungry, Johnny."

"Get some food in your belly, drink some water, and you'll feel a lot better. This afternoon we'll go for a swim and cool off. Sound good?"

"Okay. Can you help me write a letter?"

"No problem. Who's it going to?"

"My ma."

Billy's mother and older sister had sent several letters during Billy's short time in Vietnam, always to complain that they were short on money. But the words meant little to Billy, who could barely read. The first time Billy had asked John for help deciphering his mother's cramped cursive scribbling, John had been appalled by the lack of empathy for a son at war. Looking into Billy's sad eyes, he didn't have the heart to read the letter verbatim. He softened the language and was rewarded with a smile of genuine happiness.

"We'll write it after we swim."

Billy smiled shyly. "Thanks, Johnny."

John returned the smile, prompting Steve to throw a blackened sock at him. John gagged on the stench and flicked it away with his booted foot.

"You want to help me write a letter, too?"

"No. And if you throw another sock at me, I'll beat you senseless."

"Liar. You're a bad liar. Ain't he a bad liar?" Steve asked Chris.

"I'm not sure he's lying."

"Johnny wouldn't hurt no one. Hey, if you beat me, I can't write home about you no more."

Chris turned to John. "You let him write about you but not me? I'm a much better writer, you know."

John stifled his immediate reaction to snap at her. Paragraphs of neat type flashed in his mind, stark, honest writing; he had entire sections memorized and like a movie reel the words scrolled down the blank screen in the part of his brain obsessed with one particular newsmagazine, one particular reporter. Indeed, she was a much better writer than Steve.

"Steve wants him to marry his sister," Dan said. "Not his type, though."

"What's wrong with my sister? Got someone better?" Steve asked indignantly.

"Yup," Oscar said, drawing a wide grin from Dan.

"Who? Who?" Bullseye poked Oscar's arm.

"You got some nice farm girl back home? That where all those letters go?" Steve demanded. "I knew you wrote to a girl. I knew it. Why don't you ever tell us anything?"

"Fine, you caught me, I have a girl back home."

"She hot?"

"Not really, but she knows her place, so I can't complain."

"I bet she'd never be so brazen as to run around the jungle," Dan said.

"No, never." John looked at Chris. "Really no aspirations of any kind."

"Just the way you like it?" Chris said.

"Why don't you keep assuming? It's worked well for you so far."

"Uh oh," Hector murmured.

She laughed imperviously. "On behalf of intelligent, ambitious women everywhere, I take offense to your staggering lack of enlightenment. But then again, what did I expect from a farm boy?"

In fascination, John watched green eyes flash with anger.

"Dude, I think you just crashed and burned," said Murphy.

John stood. "Come on, Billy, let's write that letter now."

***

As he plunged under the surface, John enjoyed the refreshing cool of the Hau Giang. He and Dan relaxed in chest deep water with feet digging into the sandy bottom, leaning against the southerly drift of the current and ignoring a raucous game of keep-away with Oscar's football.

"This is an ambush waiting to happen," John said with a look at each sloping bank of the river and the dense brush that would conceal the approach of danger.

"Speaking of ambushes..."

John sank underwater for a few seconds. Dan waited impatiently for him to surface and continued with the question.

"Why do you antagonize her?"

"We were just talking. It's what she wants, as a matter of fact. To talk."

"Yeah, she wants to talk. Not be lied to and insulted."

John raised his eyebrows. *She started it*, he thought to himself.

"Your girl?"

"You don't know that was a lie. I might have a girl back home."

"Do you?"

John shrugged.

"You don't, but if you did, it wouldn't be that girl."

"She sounded good to me."

Dan shook his head. "You mad because of that article?"

"Which one?" Chris's second installment had arrived at FOB Jane to much fanfare just before the company departed for Ba Dong.

"Either."

"I'm not the one who should be mad. That second piece was an insult to the entire squad."

Dan smiled. "I don't know, Johnny. I think she nailed it."

John swallowed his retort. He traced a circle atop the ripples with his right hand.

"So you're not mad?"

"No."

"You sure? Because you seem awfully pissed at her."

"Nothing I can do about it. I'd prefer she write about someone else, but she's made clear that she won't let anything get in the way of doing her job."

"Why don't you just admit you like her a little bit?"

"Where'd she go, anyway?"

"Probably set up Paul's zoom lens to check out that shapely white ass of yours."

John shot him a dirty look.

"Why don't you ask her to come for a swim?" Dan said innocently.

"I doubt she brought her suit."

"Too bad for you."

"She's not my type."

"Sure, keep telling yourself that. Let's play some ball."

Dan swam into the fray, where Murphy and Darwin had teamed up to drown Steve. Along the banks of the Hau Giang, Second Squad patrolled under the direction of Sergeant Conlon. Gianelli, Travis, and Paul conversed in the shade of the jungle. Ben Kearney, stretched out on his poncho, read a tattered copy of Graham Greene's *The Quiet American*. No journalist in sight.

Yet the need to seek her out was irresistible. John sneaked away from the violent game of football and moved through the water like a crocodile, only his eyes and forehead above the surface of the water. He swam upriver, using a powerful breaststroke to propel forward, and scanned the bank.

She was deep in concentration and failed to notice his approach. Back turned to the soldiers, she had propped herself up against the base of a rubber tree with her notebook on her knees. Like the men, she had opted for comfort in the heat. The olive drab fatigue shirt and combat boots had been discarded; she wore a white tank top and flip-flops. John liked the subtle muscle definition in her arms and the way the fatigue pants hung low on her hips. He watched her for a few minutes—write a sentence, scribble out a word, rack her brain for a better one, pen another thought—and marveled at her ability to focus on her work despite the chaos around her.

He slunk closer to the riverbank where he rose to his full height, waist deep in the water. The splash caught her attention.

"Need a quote?" he asked.

"Nope. Your friends have proven quite loquacious whenever I'm around."

"Good. They've requested the string bikini, by the way."

"Very funny."

"You're not going to swim?"

"I'm working."

"Too bad. The water's nice. I bet you're hot up there."

"I'm fine."

"Okay. I won't bother you."

John turned and took a step downriver. Then he froze in place, arms out to the side for balance. He stared down at his feet.

"What was that?"

"What was what?" she said.

"Jesus...did you see that thing?"

"See what?" Chris leaned to the side, peering into the water.

"Look at it!"

"John, what are you—"

He jerked as if something had knocked into his legs. She rose, looking at him in concern.

"Are you all right?"

"Help me!"

Chris dropped her notebook and moved to the edge of the riverbank. He flailed his arms again.

"Chris, help me!"

She held out her hand. John lunged for it, grabbed her wrist, and yanked her off the bank headfirst into the river. The splash of water muffled her startled yelp. She shot to the surface, sputtering and swearing at him. Distant applause broke out.

"You are unbelievable," she said through clenched teeth.

"I told you the water was nice," he said, laughing.

She dunked her head a second time to smooth back tangled clumps of hair. "Looking for cheap thrills, John? Can't get a wet T-shirt back in farm country? At least not one that looks like this?"

John snapped his focus back to her face, feeling the guilty burn in his cheeks. Her eyes wandered down his chest to the waterline.

"Guess I'm not the only one after a cheap thrill," he said tightly.

She arched an eyebrow and smiled. "You don't have anything I haven't seen before."

John felt every muscle in his body contract, his default reaction when forced to acknowledge she was not his, and never would be.

"Thanks to you, the barbarian horde is advancing. I think I'll change into something a little less revealing."

Most of First Squad paddled toward them, hooting and whistling at Chris. John kept himself between her and the approaching men.

"No one will bother you."

"How chivalrous."

Chris retrieved her floating flip-flops, dislodged when she hit the water, and waded to the bank where she tried to climb the muddy slope. She finally took hold of an exposed tree root and hauled herself out. Towering above him, she glowered at him for several long seconds before snatching her pack off the ground and stalking into the jungle for some privacy.

John sank back under the Hau Giang to his eyeballs. Better to be the hunter than the hunted.

***

Lieutenant Colonel Simpson sent word through an aide to Kittles and Wheaton to meet him at the club that evening. Kittles, who had been staring at a blank after-action report form for the better part of two hours, rubbed his fleshy face. The operation at Ba Dong weighed on him. He could not have cared less that his company failed to meet strategic and tactical goals; that was the norm at FOB Jane. Rather, Kittles felt his efforts to manipulate and influence Chris McKenna into providing good press had been somewhat derailed.

Kittles collected Wheaton, already tipsy, and they walked to the club. Simpson was at their usual table in the back, and a bottle of scotch awaited them. Kittles glanced around the dim club, but he saw no sign of Gianelli or his two sergeants, or Chris McKenna and her photographer.

"You look like you could use a drink, Arthur," said Simpson. He poured three glasses. "Straight from Saigon on the last supply flight. Enjoy."

Kittles, seated with his back to the door, glanced furtively around the club one more time. Simpson raised his eyebrows and looked at Wheaton, who was staring at a table of nurses, and then turned his attention back to Kittles.

"Something on your mind, Arthur?"

Kittles took a fortifying slug of scotch. "I think there may be a problem."

"Oh?"

"This op at Ba Dong...things did not go exactly according to plan."

"And this is different than any other op in what way?"

"She saw me."

"Saw you what?"

"You know how Jenkins likes to get a bit...handsy...with the locals? It's possible I assisted one of his interrogations." He cringed.

Simpson swirled his scotch. "How much did she actually see?"

"I don't know."

"Did she say anything?"

"Not a word."

"Then I wouldn't worry too much. We'll categorically deny the incident took place when she asks for comment. My word carries far more weight than that of some baby girl journalist. Where is she now?"

"She went with Gianelli. I put him and his men back on the helos as soon as we touched down. I needed a couple of days to sort this out."

"What's the deal with her and Gianelli?" asked Simpson.

"I can't figure it out."

"He better not be fucking her," Wheaton said.

"Shut up, George."

"It is a bit strange," said Simpson. "Most reporters are focused on the brass. Gianelli is just a platoon lieutenant, a reservist at that. He's never shown the slightest interest in advancing. The fact that he reupped for another year shocked us all. He's got a good job back home, from what I understand."

"I really wish you'd transfer him. At least to another company."

Simpson looked thoughtful. "Perhaps Miss McKenna's affinity for Gianelli will prove useful."

"How so?"

"Look at it this way. If everything you've said about Gianelli's incompetence is true—"

"It's true," said Kittles with a bite to his voice.

"Then Miss McKenna will witness it firsthand. And you get to open a second front on Gianelli. Let her do the damage for us."

"You mean just let her do what she wants?"

Simpson shrugged. "Brooks gave strict orders that she receive whatever access she requests. Unless there's a legitimate operational reason to restrict her movements, she can go wherever she wants. If she wants to run with Gianelli, let her. And then that's the story in *American Century*. His incompetence, not whatever you may or may not have done at Ba Dong."

"I suppose..."

"You and I have both been here long enough to know that every journo in 'Nam is out to make a name for themselves. She's dying for a story, so we give her this one. We just need to help create her reality."

"It could work."

"Keep your hands clean for a bit. Give her a little space and you'll look like Patton after she spends some quality time with Gianelli."

"I'm going to fuck her," Wheaton declared.

"Is he always like this?" Simpson said to Kittles.

"Yes."

"I pity the nurses."

***

Lieutenant Gianelli visited the hospital the evening of Second Platoon's return to FOB Jane, his limp barely noticeable as he skirted the nurses' station and walked down a hall past treatment rooms and supply closets. He rounded the corner heading toward quiet offices when he heard the squeak of Chuck Taylor All-Stars on clean tiles. A lone nurse turned the opposite corner and headed toward him, wearing a set of teal scrubs and a yellow ribbon around her dark ponytail. Gianelli could tell by the way she walked that she had been on duty for at least twenty-four hours. Her shoulders sagged in relief and she quickened her pace.

"Good evening, Captain Nichols."

She beckoned him into her office and closed the door. "Delta Company got back three days ago."

"Yes, ma'am."

She waited with arms crossed over her chest.

Gianelli sighed. "Long story. Are you going to prolong the torture?"

She stepped into his arms and they held each other for a long time. He slid a hand under her scrub shirt and rubbed her taut back muscles, the main repository of a unique kind of stress that would kill mere mortals. She pressed a kiss to his neck just below his jaw.

"I'm a wreck every time you're out there," she whispered.

Gianelli hugged her tighter and nuzzled her temple. "I told you that you would have been better off falling for a so-called culinary specialist. Far fewer patrols."

She laughed into his chest and released him. "You better have a good reason for not wearing sandals."

"Until about fifteen minutes ago I was engaged in work that required toe protection."

"Sit. Let me see."

Gianelli perched on the edge of a chair and bent to unlace his boots. He gingerly removed the boots from his feet and then peeled off his nylon stretch socks. Maria sank to her knees and took one foot at a time into her hands. Her fingers prodded the hardened soles and skimmed the raw patches on the tops of his feet. Gianelli suffered from immersion foot syndrome, caused by wet feet inside wet leather combat boots. At friction points, the boots would rub away chunks of skin and the cracked soles would retain water and become infected. The condition was always painful and often debilitating, common to infantry soldiers who spent time in rivers and paddies.

"The sole swelling seems to have gone down a bit. How do they feel?"

"Better. The nylon socks have helped. They dry much faster than the wool."

"You need to stay off them as much as possible. And you must wear sandals whenever you're not in the field. Clear?"

"Clear."

She took a tube of ointment from a table and spread the cream over the raw patches. Gianelli winced.

"Sorry." She slid a set of his flip-flops toward him, one of many pairs she had stashed in her office and in their respective quarters.

He eased his feet into the sandals. "How was your week?"

She stood and sighed, shaking her head. "The usual. Alpha Company lost a few guys to mines and booby-traps. One kid fell through a pit onto poisoned punji sticks. Not a good way to go. Three of the medevac Hueys are grounded for mechanical trouble, which prompted another screaming match between Jacobson and Hawke during Thursday's staff meeting. I didn't think Pat had the energy for that kind of fight, but he tore Hawke a new one."

"Par for the course at FOB Jane."

"Pretty much." She dropped her stethoscope onto the desk and sat beside him in another chair. "Let's hear it."

Gianelli leaned forward with his elbows on his knees and rotated his aching neck. The muscles at the base of his skull screamed in protest. "McKenna got me in trouble."

"Really?"

"Total disregard for standard operating procedures and, more importantly, the wishes of one Arthur Kittles."

"What did she do?"

"Typical freewheeling journo stuff. Saw some things she shouldn't have seen."

Maria tensed. "Another Jenkins interrogation?"

"Yeah, but this time Kittles joined in. Put a journo anywhere near him and he loses his mind."

"How does that involve you?"

Gianelli sighed. "I told her where to find the show. I knew what was coming and I wanted her to see it. But I had no idea Kittles would get in on the fun, and he didn't realize she was there until after he had already fucked up a villager. She was not impressed."

"He and Jenkins should be court-martialed."

"Or taken out back and shot," Gianelli grumbled.

Maria waited several seconds before speaking. "This is the first time I've seen you pay the slightest bit of attention to a journalist."

"Jealous?" he asked teasingly.

"No. Just an observation."

He looked down at his feet and flexed his stiff toes, struggling to find the right words. "This is the first time I've felt like a journalist could tell the story."

"What if it's a story you don't like?"

"I just want someone to tell the truth."

"I hope you know what you're doing."

"Not a clue," he said with a rueful smile.

"I assume she still thinks you're an asshole?"

Gianelli laughed. "Your tone suggests that despite only one brief interaction with her, you've still managed to embrace some twisted notion of sisterhood that pits the both of you against me."

A smile tugged at her lips. "Us girls have to stick together. Besides, I enjoyed her last piece. Most accurate description of a certain lieutenant that I've ever seen."

"God help me."

Maria ran her fingers through his sweaty hair, massaging his head. "Brooks would have Kittles's ass if he knew he sent you back out there without rest."

"I can handle it."

"It's not good for you or your men to be pushed like that. Not in this heat, not in these conditions."

"It's not your fight, Maria," he said gently.

Her dark eyes hardened. "Not my fight? Who treats your men for heatstroke, exhaustion, injuries, combat wounds that might have been prevented with some rest? Who treats your destroyed feet that you refuse to take seriously?"

"Okay, okay, calm down."

She may have inherited her Mediterranean beauty from her mother, but Gianelli had learned the hard way that she had her father's Irish temper. He wrapped an arm around her and pulled her close. She smelled soft and clean. He closed his eyes and rested his cheek on the crown of her head.

"I don't want you in the field any more than you need to be," she said. "Please talk to Kittles."

"Yes, ma'am."

She cupped his face in her hands and kissed him. "Thank you. Now get out. I have rounds. I'll see you later tonight."

***

As the sun began to set, the base spewed forth a barrage of heavy artillery, shelling a nearby VC position. The ground shook with each blast and sent a shock wave up Chris's spine. She gazed into the distance, watching the burnt orange sun approach the jungle horizon.

Clean for the first time in over a week, she sought the comfortable familiarity of John's favorite sandbagged niche on the western end of FOB Jane. There was much to ponder as she sat with her notebook in her lap. She thought of the little boy at Cau Ngan and wondered when he would see peace. She thought of two tiny fists clenching a hand, a hand that had chosen to protect rather than harm, and in that moment Chris wanted to be something more than an observer. But that was her role in this war, and nothing would change it.

The wind picked up, swirling dust and smoke from the artillery positions. She tossed her hair back, inviting the breeze to dry the sweat on her neck. She felt a presence and as she turned, a man vaulted the sandbagging and dropped down beside her. She flinched, though the visit was not unexpected.

"Here to write more letters to your girl?"

"Do you plan to make incursions into the bush a habit?"

"What, no foreplay?"

"I like to get right to it." John's striking eyes roamed over her face, watching for the slightest hint of deceit.

"Which could explain why you don't actually have a girl."

"Could you please answer the question?"

"Why bother? You already know the answer. Just like I know you're here to tell me that if I do plan to make infantry duty a habit, it's a bad idea. You, John Rawlins, are rather predictable."

"It's that kind of thinking that gets you tossed in a river."

"Touché."

"You can get the story without putting your life on the line."

"Then it's only part of the story, and probably not the most compelling part."

He rested against the sandbagging and stretched out his legs. His eyes left her face and followed a plume of bomber exhaust miles above them until it dissipated. She watched him fight emotions he refused to acknowledge outwardly. A muscle at the base of his jaw twitched as he gritted his teeth. She didn't doubt that he could sit in silence and stew for hours, but she herself was not so gifted at internalizing anger.

"You're mad."

"I asked you not to write about me."

"It's my job to report the news. I wrote about you because you did a good thing. I tried to portray the situation accurately and without bias, and to be honest, I think I did a damn good job. I know you're a private person, but I really don't understand why you're so upset about this. I had nothing but praise for you."

"Do you remember I told you that my brother reads *American Century*?"

"Yes."

"Robby—that's my kid brother—will definitely see your stories. He reads every issue cover to cover."

"Your family will be proud of you, John. You saved lives."

John's laugh rang hollow. "The first thing he'll do is show it to my parents. My mother, unfortunately, thinks I'm attached to a support element in Saigon, not a rifle platoon in the Mekong Delta. We can debate the merits of that lie some other time, but trust me when I say I had her best interests at heart. No point in continuing with that charade, since it's hard to stumble into a jungle ambush when you're supposed to be a paper-pusher. Will she be proud of me? Sure, if the stress of having a child at war—I mean, really at war—doesn't kill her first."

Chris could think of nothing to say, but her eyes remained glued to the side of his face until he turned his head and met her stare.

"That's why I didn't want you to write about me."

"I didn't know. Why didn't you tell me?"

"It's really none of your business. Besides, I get the impression it wouldn't have made a difference."

Chris looked the pen in her hand, a different sort of weapon than what he, a soldier, wielded. She forced herself to consider whether she would have written the same had she known the truth behind his misgivings. What mattered more to her? Her job or sparing the feelings of a distant mother of a soldier she barely knew? Was that even a fair question to ask? John's instincts were correct; it probably would not have mattered much that he had legitimate and understandable reasons for wanting to remain anonymous. She felt a stab of resentment toward him.

"What's your position on this war?"

Chris considered the question, grateful for the change of topic. His tone held curiosity, not malice. "Personally, I'm opposed. Professionally, I don't have an opinion."

"So you're not yourself when you're holding a notebook?"

"I didn't say that. I just do my best to leave my own politics out of the job. There's no place for them in my notebook or on the printed page."

John nodded slowly. "Tough gig."

"Yours is tougher."

"Which is why you should limit your search for truth to within the confines of FOB Jane."

She shook her head in frustration. "I'll never be able to explain this so you understand, will I?"

"I'm just concerned for your safety. And I want to shower more often if you plan to be downwind of me on every patrol."

Chris allowed herself a small smile. He returned it.

"It was a rough week, wasn't it?" he said.

"About what I expected."

"Nobody expects to see that."

Chris said nothing. Her nights were sleepless since Jenkins and Kittles had invaded her dreams, where the bamboo rod split flesh, where heavy fists broke bones, where screams shattered the illusion of seaside tranquility.

"I'll leave you to your work."

She reached out to stop him from rising. "What would you do if they ordered you to hurt people?"

Her hand rested on his forearm. John looked deeply into her eyes and she felt as though he peered into her soul. The sensation was like that of falling.

"I'm a soldier. I do hurt people."

"Not like that." She pulled her hand away, shaking her head. "Not like that."

"I'm not the only one who has to make a choice. What about you? You have to decide what to report, how to report it." He paused. "And how much a part of the story you become."

"I'm just an observer."

John smiled. "No man is an island."

Chris felt hot emotion rush through her, anger, frustration, fear of failure, but tamped it down with a deep breath. "It's my job to stay objective, and I will."

"You've chosen a challenging path."

"In your footsteps."

This time she allowed him to stand.

"It's a bad idea," he said.

"The good ones usually are."

"Sleep well, Chris."

"Good night, John."

She turned her attention back to the pastel sky, armed with answers that led only to more questions. The notebook remained untouched.

6

— • —

T he river, a shallow tributary of the Mekong, carved a path through the jungle, flanked on either side by triple canopies and tall water grass. The Viet Cong traveled its winding course in canoes and flat-bottomed boats, transporting weapons and supplies along the gentle currents or launching attacks against American and ARVN forces from its muddy banks.

The river was quiet when the platoon crossed just after dawn. The rising sun reflected off the lazy ripples and silhouetted the trees of the mangrove swamp to the east. The brown filth riding the current disappeared behind nature's glory, the short time at the beginning of a bright Vietnam morning when all things were possible.

John Rawlins waded into the calm waters at the point position, walking slowly over the soft sand riverbed. He held his rifle above his head, submerged to his ribs. On the other side he climbed the bank, boots sinking into soggy grass, and turned to help his shadow. Chris ignored his outstretched hand and hauled herself out of the water. Perhaps she couldn't see him under the brim of her Yankees cap, John thought. But he knew that wasn't true. He recognized stubborn pride when he saw it, as surely as he chose to ignore his own.

John brushed past her and took his place at the head of the platoon. She waited, her thumbs hooked in the straps of her pack, taking in the sights and sounds and smells of the dawn, as wet and sweaty and dirty as any of the men. John had never heard her complain about the heat, the dirt, the bugs, the aches and pains, the tangible terror that spawned from the depths of the jungle. She was just one of the grunts.

But was she? Who was the real Chris McKenna, and what was her angle? What was the next story and was he a part of it? The first story had been received with stoic resignation in the Rawlins household, but there existed a thin line between stoicism and paralyzing fear. The letters from his family reflected their acceptance of his role in the war, but they failed to disguise their apprehension that the next article extolling his heroism would also lament his death.

John's focus drifted back to the reporter responsible for the emotional mayhem in Iowa. He tensed against the anger welling up from the part of him that could not get past the words, would not forgive and forget. He touched his flak jacket and wished he felt less exposed. The vest might stop shrapnel, but it would not protect him from her penetrating gaze, the eyes that saw too much.

"You should be wearing a helmet," he said coldly.

"So should you."

If only Gianelli would pull her back to the middle of the pack where she belonged. John suspected that even Gianelli, notoriously hot-tempered and obstinate, knew he had met his match in Chris McKenna. She and the lieutenant appeared to have come to a tacit understanding: she would have unlimited access to his platoon as long as she stayed out of the way. She stayed out of Gianelli's way, all right, John reflected, but now he had to baby-sit.

"Wake up on the wrong side of the foxhole this morning?" she asked.

"Just be alert. And drink plenty of water. It's going to be hot. Do you need me to carry anything?"

She laughed without humor. "No, I think I can manage."

"As you wish, Miss McKenna."

***

They fanned out across the field as they approached the hamlet. The sun beat down and fried the tops of steel helmets, radiating heat into over-stimulated brains. Many of the men popped salt tabs to stay hydrated. Some furtively popped other pills, uppers, downers, anything from the intrepid dealers at FOB Jane.

Jagged low ridges broke the monotony of the flat topography. Scraggily brown grass grabbed at John's trousers and an incessant insect hum reverberated in his ears. A bead of sweat trickled down his nose. He fingered the trigger of his rifle and squinted under the brim of the bush hat.

The hamlet was still, lifeless. Dilapidated huts baked in the sun. Tin cups and various utensils, haphazardly discarded and never retrieved, lay by the remains of a cooking fire. Intel said the hamlet was nominally under the control of the government, and the village chief was amenable to assisting Americans if the price was right.

Intel was often wrong. And it was too quiet. Much too quiet.

"Rawlins, hold up," Gianelli hissed. "Fall back."

John turned just as the rifle slug passed through Weinberg's forehead beneath his helmet and exploded out the back of his skull. He jerked, arms flailing, and seemed to hang in the air before he collapsed flat on his back, eyes still open, staring at the hazy sky.

***

Chris never felt the breath leave her, never felt her ribs smash the half-buried rock as she threw herself to the ground. Time slowed and she saw shimmering heat waves hovering over the pungent earth, followed the path of each tracer round that sliced through the heavy layers of subtropical steam, knew men would die.

She watched John blast the phantoms hiding in hooches, concealed behind earthen fortifications, ducking in foxholes. He turned and motioned to her and said something. Machine gun chatter and the ear-popping explosions of grenades devoured his words. She nodded, trying to understand.

Paul lay prone beside her, his finger holding down the Nikon's shutter button as if it were the trigger of an M-16, the tinny click of the shutter inexplicably carrying over the din of combat. John paused to reload; Paul paused to change film; it took mere seconds for the empty magazine to fall and the replacement to click home, for the spent roll of film to disappear into a pocket and the fresh one advanced to the ready. Chris was fascinated, and a little jealous. Paul was a real war journalist, not an imposter with his face buried in the dirt, too busy lamenting this unfortunate development to be useful.

She felt an irresistible urge to giggle. Would her readers appreciate the ironic understatement? Or would they decide they did not want to read anything written by a woman who giggled during a firefight? Would insightful commentary on this unfortunate development—oh hell, call a spade a spade, she decided—this goat rope qualify as unconventional journalism and maybe earn some long overdue praise from her asshole editor? Fuck him and every man who said she couldn't hack it in a warzone. Let's see their asses under fire, she thought.

When had she become so angry? Was it when people started shooting at her?

"What the fuck am I doing?" she asked aloud.

No one answered. They were busy fighting a war.

She thought she should do something, but she didn't know what. Then the piercing whistle of a mortar launch obliterated her internal monologue. The shell impacted the field and men screamed.

Chris McKenna moved.

***

John scrambled back to the main body of the force. Shouts and howls drowned out the clatter of the M-60s. Chris crawled on her stomach commando-style toward Cook, who was sprawled on his side, covered in blood. John reached out and grabbed her ankle. She flipped over and kicked at him, panic in her eyes.

"It's me, it's me. Get behind the ridge."

"But he's hurt."

"We'll get him. Go." John jerked his head toward a series of ridges fifteen yards to their left.

John and Dan took Cook under the shoulders and dragged him. Chris stayed low, but the enemy gunners launched a barrage in their direction, spewing dirt into their faces. She covered her head and sprinted the last few yards to where Kearney and his pack of medical supplies waited behind the ridge with other wounded men.

The medic pulled out a large compress and placed it over Cook's destroyed midsection. Cook spasmed and clawed at his tattered flak jacket with bloody hands, trying to see.

"Don't look, don't look," Kearney urged, pushing Cook's shoulders to the ground. "It's okay. You'll be okay."

Gianelli ran to his men in a crouch. "How bad?"

Kearney shook his head once.

"We have to hold them off until the choppers get here. Fucking nowhere to go. Not with this many wounded. I can't fucking believe this. Fuck!" Gianelli punched the side of the ridge. His fist, covered in someone else's blood, left an imprint in the dry, crumbling dirt. Then he took a deep breath and looked at Chris as if noticing her for the first time. "You all right?"

Chris stared at Cook, but managed to nod.

John caught Gianelli's eye and asked a question without a word. The lieutenant pulled his Colt pistol from its holster and handed it to John. John checked that a round was chambered and flipped off the safety. He took hold of Chris's shoulder, forcing her to face him. He slapped the gun into her hand.

"You see anyone who doesn't look like us, you shoot him. Got it?"

She nodded. Her chest heaved under the open fatigue shirt, and her neck and cheeks were streaked with dirt and sweat. He looked into her eyes, and behind the fear he thought he saw a flash of the true Chris McKenna.

***

Chris stuck the gun in the waistband of her pants against the small of her back and assessed the situation with professional objectivity. She had reached a firm conclusion somewhere between the first mortar launch and the sight of a gutted man: war was all fun and games until it wasn't.

She made a mental note of Paul's position—he had taken cover with Conlon and much of Second Squad behind several nearby ridges—and tried to find John, but he and most of his squad had disappeared into the tall grass near the hamlet.

The medic moved along the ridgeline in search of wounded. Chris followed a few steps behind, occasionally peering over the berm to scout approaching danger. The Colt in her waistband felt much heavier than it was, foreign and cumbersome. Kearney stopped to treat a shoulder wound, Sanders from Second Squad who was lying still and calm. Chris squeezed Sanders's forearm.

Kearney was out of bandages and nearing despair. He mumbled to himself as he rooted through his pack for anything that could double as a patch. Cook and the other wounded had depleted his stash of supplies. He turned to her, on the verge of tears.

"There are too many."

"Let me help you." A grenade explosion rocked the ridge. They ducked and covered their faces against flying debris. After the dirt shower, she grabbed him by the shoulder and shook him. "Just tell me what to do."

"No, it's too dangerous."

She shook him again. "Ben. Let me help you."

"Okay. Okay." He took a deep breath. "We need to get him over there behind the other ridge. I have to be near Cook. He needs me most."

"Then let's get him over there. Can you walk?" she asked Sanders.

"I think so."

Chris found an extra T-shirt in Sanders's pack and used it to apply pressure to the wound while Kearney helped him stand. It was a distant fifty feet to the safety of the next ridge, but they were able to move Sanders without further injury. Turner joined them, distraught over Cook's condition. Kearney reached into his pack and pulled forth a half-eaten bag of melted, deformed M&Ms. He shook out a few candies and placed a green one on Cook's tongue. Cook's chin was covered with blood and his head rested on Turner's lap while Turner laid down covering fire.

Chris looked away, swallowing hard. She pushed the Yankees cap off her head, flushed and soaked in sweat. She looked down at her hands to find them covered in blood and trembling. Bile welled up in her throat.

***

John jumped up to chuck a grenade into the hamlet and then ducked behind a ridge. Another mortar shrieked toward the platoon.

"We have to take out those mortar positions," he said.

"You nuts, Johnny?" Steve said.

"Oscar, can you and Bullseye cover us?"

"Fuck yeah," he bellowed over the machine gun fire.

"Murph?"

Murphy peered over the ridge. The platoon had destroyed two of the three forward machine gun nests, significantly improving their chances of advancing into the hamlet. If Oscar and Bullseye focused their fire on the third position while they moved from hooch to hooch, they had a chance at eliminating the mortar positions, or at least delaying their fire until helicopter gunships arrived.

"Doable," he replied.

"Hey, Cowboy," Oscar called. "LT know you about to pull some crazy shit?"

John squinted into the sun, tracing their path through the hamlet in his mind. It was risky, especially with their small numbers, but he saw no other choice. The mortars were savage, indiscriminate killers, and the platoon had sustained too many wounded for a backward retreat. "LT's got bigger problems. Ready?"

Dan tightened his helmet. "Lead on."

Oscar touched two fingers to his forehead in a casual salute. "Don't get dead, boys."

***

An hour later, as grenades destroyed mortar tubes and several Viet Cong soldiers lay dead near the mouth of a tunnel, the distant drone of helicopters reached their ears.

"Choppers incoming!" yelled Gianelli. "Move, move!"

Five Hueys flew low over the field. One circled the hamlet, mowing down structures and surviving enemy soldiers. The other four hovered to take the platoon to safety. Small arms fire rattled their hulls and pinged off landing skids. The remaining Viet Cong fighters advanced from the wreckage of the hamlet with rifles and grenades, disrupting the extraction.

Turner and Kearney picked up Cook and ran him to the medevac. The corpsmen inside slid him toward the back to make room for the other wounded. Gianelli followed, carrying his injured radioman over his shoulder. Bullets tore through the Huey's walls, opening silver dollar-sized holes. The pilots and door gunners screamed obscenities, urging the platoon to hurry.

John helped load a body into the chopper, which the medics shoved under the litter shelves. He looked out into the field to see Darwin and Murphy running with the M-60s at their hips, firing bursts, and Bullseye following, pulling Sanders toward another helicopter. Oscar lumbered out to help his small friend.

"Come on, come on, in the helo!" yelled Travis, lifting up Billy Farrell by the back of his pants.

"Where's Chris?" Paul shouted. He tried to jump out, but the sergeant blocked his exit forcefully.

Dan spoke to him as they loaded men. "John, she's still—"

"I know."

He threw up the last leg, turned on his heel and sprinted toward the ridge. The gunfire mirrored his moves. An explosion on the opposite side of the ridge knocked him off his feet and he landed at her side, face first in the dirt. The blow to the bridge of his nose brought reflexive tears to his eyes. She was with Hector and a wounded man. She was trying to calm them both.

John seized an arm and a leg and pulled the man across his shoulders. Hector ran ahead, firing at two Viet Cong soldiers about to launch a rocket-propelled grenade. Gianelli and Travis, waiting in a crouch outside the last remaining Huey, shot them dead. At the door, Oscar lifted the wounded man off John's shoulders. John turned and in one swift motion picked up Chris and tossed her inside. He pushed Hector in and pulled himself up, Travis and Gianelli on his tail, as the pilots lifted off.

***

The Huey shuddered and banked in an evasive maneuver, and Chris fell atop the dead man on the floor of the cabin. John grabbed her shirt and hauled her up, pulling her onto his lap.

The smell from the body wafted to her nostrils, the metallic scent of blood. The helicopter bottomed out and what remained of Weinberg's helmetless head bounced against the metal of the floor, a sickening thud over the thunder of the rotors. She felt the nausea rise up.

John clamped his arm tight across her waist. She gripped his wrist with hands still covered in blood, eyes fixed on the dead man at her feet. Oscar tossed a poncho over Weinberg's face, then lit a cigarette and closed his eyes.

She stiffened as John lifted the back of her shirt, clutched his wrist tighter when his fingers brushed her skin as he slipped the Colt out of her waistband. He handed it to Gianelli. She exhaled and let herself sink back against his chest.

***

Pat Jacobson and Maria Nichols faced this mass casualty event as they faced all others: calmly and with a focus on those who could be saved. Kearney's tightly taped compress held Cook's intestines in place. The arm of Gianelli's radioman hung on the shoulder by a thread of muscle. A machine gun slug had obliterated most of the ball and socket joint. He would lose the arm. He still wore the radio pack.

Maria cut the fatigues off the unconscious radioman and unbound the injured arm belted against his body. The radio crackled static. The soldier's labored breathing grew fainter. He had lost all the blood that could be spared. She clamped off the visible axillary artery that had been severed by the bullet. She jabbed a syringe of epinephrine into the rubber base of the IV tube to keep his heart beating. Then she took a scalpel and with a flick of her wrist amputated the arm. It fell with a thud at her feet. A nurse scrambled to move it out of her way.

"This one's a mess," Jacobson said as he assessed Cook. "You?"

"He's had better days. We're going to need a lot of blood to get him through tonight," said Maria.

"The call went out for donors, ma'am," said the nurse.

"Good. Please get him prepped."

"Make that two for the funhouse," said Jacobson. "I'll need help with debridement."

101

"Yes, sir."

As nurses and corpsmen circled around them, moving bodies and equipment, Maria joined Jacobson over Cook. The shrapnel had perforated multiple organs.

"I didn't see him," Maria murmured, her voice barely audible behind her mask.

Jacobson looked at her but didn't pause in his work. She had spoken evenly, but her eyes betrayed her. "If he were hurt, he'd be in here already."

"Unless he went straight to the morgue."

"Don't think that."

"Hard not to."

Two nurses flung the doors open to take Cook and the radioman into the pre-op ward, and Jacobson scanned the crowd outside for a tall, scruffy officer. A mismatched pair of men helped nurses direct traffic and attend to non-critical injuries.

"He and Travis are right there. He's not hurt."

Maria took a ragged breath. She and Jacobson tore off their gloves and ran toward the surgical ward to scrub.

***

Following the unfortunate development in the nameless hamlet, Paul hopped a Huey to Saigon in order to file a large tranche of photos with *American Century* through the local *Washington Post* bureau, where he had friends. Chris threw herself into the story, but the words on paper sounded uninspired and insignificant.

Her thoughts invariably shifted to Cook and his shy smile and stooped walk, of the conversations about her Mustang and his GTO, his black GTO with the white racing stripes and the souped-up engine and the performance clutch. How he had pushed her to sixty in under six seconds on the rural roads near his

Kentucky home. How he scrimped and saved his meager private's pay, avoiding the bars and brothels and black market, because he wanted to buy his kid brother a junker for them to fix up together when he came home from war.

Would she remember that she had barely scratched the surface of Ted Cook, or would she remember only his screams, his terror, his pain as shrapnel ripped through him? How could she have thought of him only as a story?

Chris jumped to her feet when Paul pushed through the door three days later, walking with the tired gait of a man who would sleep only when war was a distant memory. He dropped his bag of photography gear and hugged her. She bit hard on her bottom lip to fight back tears.

"It doesn't get any easier," he said in a flat voice. "It just becomes routine. You need to understand that."

Chris pulled away and swiped at the tears with the back of her hand. "I'm sorry I dragged you into this."

"I chose this assignment. I chose to be here with you. Don't forget that, okay?"

"Okay," she said unconvincingly.

He sat on the edge of his cot and rubbed his temples. "This war...it's just different. I can't explain it. I've seen a lot, but this is something else."

"I don't think a single one of these guys really knows what they're doing here," Chris said.

"At least I knew what was at stake when I fought."

She shook her head. "I have no idea how to tell this story."

"Speaking of, the staff sergeant had a telegram for us."

"Willis?"

"It's like he was right there screaming in my ear."

"That bad?"

Paul shook his head, a thoughtful frown crossing his face as he pulled the telegram from his breast pocket. "He seems more confused than angry. I thought you were set with the third piece. Lord knows you had enough material to work with."

Chris plucked the telegram from his hand. "I guess not."

"I know I'm just the photographer and shouldn't pry, but..."

She waved away the concern. "I made some last-minute edits before I filed the other night. I might have gone a little overboard. Nothing that can't be fixed."

"Glad to hear it. I brought back some Coca-Colas for you. In my duffel."

"You dear, dear man."

"Mess hall still out?"

"Yes, and it's unacceptable. I don't know how people live in these conditions."

"All yours. I'm getting some chow."

Chris waited until he departed before she opened a bottle of warm Coke and took a seat at the field table. She unfolded the telegram and stood it between the middle rows of the typewriter's keys. Paul's assessment had been correct, or at least mostly correct; Willis seemed genuinely confused, but Chris sensed an undercurrent of his famous temper rippling through his words of encouragement, urging her to dig deeper, to not pull punches. She had no one to blame but herself. The story she had so painstakingly composed was not the story she had filed. It reached *American Century* with one glaring omission, a hole that couldn't be filled with words designed to distract.

Chris took a swig of Coke and set aside the telegram. Never had a blank page so intimidated her. It had become clear that she and her muse were not on speaking terms. Had she left it behind at a makeshift interrogation area near the South China Sea, or maybe cowering behind a ridge during the unfolding of an unfortunate development in her quest for truth? She readied her hands over the keys and took a deep breath. With palpable trepidation, she began to type.

***

Ted Cook died later that week. Most of the men went about their usual business, eating, sleeping, getting high, and preparing themselves for their next patrol. Chris found Turner seated atop a bunker watching the movement of men and helicopters. His youthful face had aged overnight: pale beneath the tan, skin pinched over cheekbones, lips drawn.

It was strange how people could act like nothing had happened, Chris reflected in silence; strange how intellectual awareness of an event did not necessitate an emotional response. If she had been elsewhere during those hours of battle, perhaps safe within the confines of FOB Jane as the world insisted, would she act as if the death of just another soldier meant little? If she had been elsewhere then, would she sit by the side of a distraught young man now?

"He was my friend," Turner said. His bottom lip quivered and his wide eyes glistened. A tear rolled down his cheek.

Chris tried to smile. She reached out and brushed away the tear. "I know, sweetie, I know."

He leaned into her and she wrapped an arm around his shoulders. He sobbed quietly into his hands. The Huey hovering above the helipad blurred through her tears.

***

When the staff sergeant rapped on the door and asked Chris to accompany him to the colonel's office, Chris thought for sure she would be sent back to Saigon, an inglorious departure after an ignominious month just fucking around, as Martin Willis apparently thought. The men, ecstatic to shed dead weight, would line the path to the helipad and cheer her departure, although anyone capable of basic math would compute that the odds of getting laid dropped exponentially. Chris briefly considered preempting the colonel and leaving of her own volition before he could order her off his base.

The staff sergeant's neutral expression betrayed nothing of the nature of the visit. With slow deliberation, Chris arranged a sheaf of paper face down on the field table and placed her Swiss Army knife atop the stack, then took up stride with the young NCO. For the first time she noticed he walked with a limp. She felt her hands grow clammy as they approached Brooks's open office. The staff sergeant announced her and stepped aside for her to enter.

Brooks stood. "Chris, thanks for seeing me."

"It's no trouble, Colonel."

She took a seat opposite his desk, covered in open files. He closed two folders and smiled as he sat across from her.

"Classified," he said.

After stashing the documents away from her prying journalist's gaze, he watched her for long seconds with his fingers pressed in a steeple under his nose. Chris felt a puff of air conditioning on her neck and heard the staff sergeant's voice outside in the anteroom. If he planned to kick her out, she wished he would get on with it.

He pulled a sheet of paper from the pile on the desk. "Lieutenant Gianelli's most recent after-action report has come to my attention. He said you took it upon yourself to assist his medic while under heavy fire."

Chris saw her dream of big-name print journalism take a rifle round through the heart and sink below the surface of the foul paddy water. She resisted the urge to slump in the chair and pout. So Gianelli had won. It took him a month and she put up a hell of a fight, but in the end, he emerged from their scrap victorious. She knew going into this assignment that the cards were stacked against her, and the lieutenant, a cunning opponent, had brandished his four aces—and his army-issue .45-caliber Colt M1911 pistol for good measure—at just the right moment. Remember to congratulate him on the way to the Huey, she told herself. Then spit in his face.

She measured her words. "Yes, it's true I assisted the medic, who couldn't possibly keep up with the mounting casualties on his own. I recognize that my decision to help was in violation of the army's standard operating procedures regarding women in combat, but I'm disappointed that Lieutenant Gianelli would use this incident against me."

Brooks regarded her curiously, the three deep crevices creased into his brow now accentuated by surprise. "You think Gianelli is upset with you?"

"He usually is."

The colonel glanced down at the report in his hands. "I see."

"I understand if this was a step too far. Paul and I can be on the next flight to Saigon. Thank you for the opportunity to cover life at FOB Jane." She stood and offered her hand.

Brooks studied her. His eyes were the color of storm clouds, and emotion swirled in them as violently as the monsoons that formed over the sea. Chris saw intrigue in the storm, and the hint of a smile on his lips. She held her hand steady and thought it rude of him to look so amused.

"Lieutenant Gianelli said that without your bravery and presence of mind to move the injured to safety, more men might have lost their lives."

"Oh." Chris dropped onto the edge of the chair, her mind racing to process this turn of events.

His tanned face took on an unfamiliar expression, a faraway look of contemplation, as he rubbed his chin with the fingers of one hand.

"Sometimes I wonder what it's like to be a woman in a man's world. Then I try to imagine what it might be like to be *you* in a man's world. We barely know each other, so forgive my presumptuousness, but this assignment must be terribly frustrating for you at times."

"It has its moments."

The soldier appeared lost in a distant memory. "I can't get over how much you remind me of someone."

"Who do I remind you of?" she said softly. *Is her name Jane?*

"It's not important."

"Even when I'm not being a journalist?"

"Even then."

"You'll tell me someday."

"Perhaps."

He stood and she stood and the meeting was over. The staff sergeant appeared in the doorway to escort her back to her hooch.

"Thank you for your time, Colonel."

"Thank you, Miss McKenna."

He turned back to his paperwork and she left with the staff sergeant, pondering the intentions of a conflicted warrior and his subordinates.

***

The next morning, following an early morning photography expedition to the base perimeter to acquire the obligatory shots of sunrise over the jungle, Paul dumped his camera gear onto his cot and shook Chris.

"What?" she mumbled.

"Are you awake?"

"No."

"Wake up, then. This is important."

"It had better not be another telegram."

"It's not. Worse."

"Then just tell me."

"Brace yourself."

"Get on with it."

"Anne Novak arrived at FOB Jane this morning."

Chris blinked. "What?"

"Anne Novak is here."

"That's not funny."

"No, it's definitely not funny."

"How the hell did she pull this off?" Chris sprang off the cot and began to pace. Suddenly dizzy, she hung her head between her knees until the unsteadiness passed. Then she worked up a rhythm, walking from her cot to the door and back to her cot.

"Probably the same way we did."

"This is a combat zone. Didn't anyone think to examine her for mental illness? Didn't anyone speak to character concerns? The army should be more careful whom they credential."

"Then what are we doing here?"

"She writes for a fascist rag. Fascists should not receive press credentials."

Paul laughed. "Damn that First Amendment."

"I can't believe you're so calm." She whirled and pointed at him. "Go tell her there's a killer story in Hanoi."

"I'd really rather not."

"Just do it. Take one for the team."

He laughed again. "This is your story. Just make sure you get it printed first." He retrieved his camera gear and left the hooch.

Chris sighed.

***

"Shit, boys, you ain't gonna believe this! More women!" Steve ducked under the tent, stepped into the middle of a poker game, and waited for congratulations on his hard-earned scoop.

"Really?" John said. "Perhaps the Playboy bunnies?"

Darwin perked up. Steve made a face at John.

"Funny, Johnny. Almost as good. Another chick journo. We're definitely going to be famous."

"Go see Chris. She'll make you famous."

"I don't know. I ain't heroic or nothing. She don't seem to like my quotes."

John refrained from pointing out that his comments were unprintable without serious grammatical and editorial revision. They would never get past the obscenity censor.

"Move your dumb butt, Jersey. Stakes are high," Murphy said.

He and John and Kearney were embroiled in a tense hand of seven-card stud. Kearney had just made the third raise on the last card shown; John had called and Murphy was torn over whether his jack-high straight could compete with the medic's two visible pairs and John's three diamonds, potential flush. One card remained to be dealt, face down. Murphy called the bet, tossing in five dollars' worth of chips.

"Somebody didn't shuffle these cards," he muttered and waited for Darwin to deal the last card.

"But *another* chick! How'd we get so lucky?"

Kearney peered through Steve's legs to examine John's diamonds one last time before he began the betting. "You got two under there?"

"Maybe. You got that full house?"

Hector, in the yellow fedora, provided hushed commentary on the proceedings. He lived for these moments, to see hard-earned cash won and lost on blind chance. Another thirty dollars disappeared into the pot. John, who made the last raise, showed his cards. Ten-high flush.

"Shit," Murphy grumbled. He tossed his cards to Darwin.

Ben Kearney tried to play it smooth, but he broke into a smile as he flipped his cards, showing a full house, sevens over queens.

Bullseye whistled. "Dude, that's a sweet pot. Can I borrow a few bucks for some smokes?"

"Absolutely not," the medic replied.

"Guys, listen to me. A *woman*."

"Yes, Steve, a woman. We heard you the first seventeen times," Dan said. "Who does she work for?"

"Some magazine. All that matters is that my chances of getting laid just doubled."

"She look like Chris?" Dan asked casually.

"Word is she's older. But I ain't picky. I'd do an older lady. They's had more practice."

Murphy lay on his side, resting on his left elbow. "I had me an older woman once, a neighbor. One night I come home from my mechanic's job all greasy, just want to clean up and have some chow. She's sitting on her stoop like she's waiting for me or something. I say good night all polite and everything, and she attacks me. Drags me into her house and does me on her dirty kitchen floor. That woman could have sucked down the entire ocean through a straw, I tell you."

"Oh man, oh man, screw fame. I'll take *that*," said Steve.

"Them older women know how to talk dirty, too," Oscar boomed. "One fine thing in my 'hood had a mouth that'd make you blush, Murph. She'd—"

"Who's that?" said Turner.

The woman, of average height and build, sauntered through camp followed by an entourage of photographers who snapped pictures of anything that moved and most things that didn't. She wore freshly pressed designer fatigues and mirrored aviator sunglasses. Her press credentials hung from her neck by a black lanyard and proclaimed for all to see that her name was Anne Novak and she worked for the *Washington Dispatch*.

"Whoa, whoa, look alive, boys." Steve snapped to attention in anticipation of sexual satisfaction at the hands of a journalist.

The woman stopped at the tent and perched her sunglasses on the tip of her nose.

"Shouldn't you be out winning a war?"

The men all waited for someone else to speak. Even Oscar and Murphy seemed unsure of themselves. John and Dan glanced at each other, sharing the same thought: Anne Novak was no Chris McKenna.

"Since that appears beyond the ability of this army, I will settle for one of you pointing me in the direction of the dining facilities."

They continued to gape like mute schoolboys.

"Anyone?"

"I bet she can definitely suck down the ocean through a straw," Bullseye murmured.

Several men snickered and Anne's eyes roamed over the squad to catch the offending party. Bullseye hid behind Oscar. Before there was bloodshed, John climbed to his feet and directed Anne and her crew toward the mess hall via a nearby footpath. Anne looked him up and down and leaned in to hear his instructions.

"Thank you."

Before John had a chance to sit, she trailed a finger along his chest as she moved to join her crew. His dog tags clinked together. John fought back laughter.

"Robbing the cradle, Anne?"

The men guffawed. Chris McKenna strode forward, looking every inch the battle-tested, scrappy war correspondent that she was, and John couldn't resist a smile.

Anne heaved an affected sigh and faced her and Paul Lane. "Well, if it isn't G.I. Jane. And for Christ's sake, Paul, isn't following her across the globe like a wayward puppy a bit beneath you?"

Chris smirked. "Scared, Anne? Worried about a little competition for the story?"

Eyes widened. A catfight in the jungle? This was too good to be true. Hector hissed the odds—five to three on Chris.

"Please, McKenna, I keep *American Century* on hand in case I run out of toilet paper." Anne motioned to her crew and they followed her down the path.

Chris's bright eyes wandered to John. "Suddenly I don't seem like such a heinous bitch, do I?"

John grinned. "This jungle big enough for the both of you?"

"She's all talk."

"Looks like you might be after the same thing."

"Then one of us will have to lose, and I always get what I want." Chris winked. "Take it easy, boys."

"Hot damn! Summer in the 'Nam is heating up!"

7

—— • ——

As the temperature rose in the Delta, so did the tension at FOB Jane. Whenever they were together, the mood changed perceptibly; everyone waited for the inevitable explosion. Would it be a blinding flash of white phosphorus, or a two-thousand-degree fireball and billowing black clouds of napalm?

The men often debated which of the two more frequently provoked the other with snide remarks or outright insults, but what was clear to all onlookers, detached or invested, was that the tension was most definitely sexual in nature. Her ability to be coy far exceeded his, and so most casual observers assumed he was chasing her. Those on whom her attention did not linger wasted no time attempting to capitalize financially. If the subjects of the base-wide betting pool had knowledge of the rampant speculation regarding the intimate nature of their private lives, they concealed it well. They felt little inclination to squash Hector's scheming, because to acknowledge it would be to accept that it, whatever "it" was, existed.

At the moment Chris's career worries obscured all else, although in a moment of stress-induced clarity she saw how her two biggest challenges—improving substandard reporting and reconciling conflicting feelings about John Rawlins—were not mutually exclusive concerns. Martin Willis's most recent telegram, a terse follow-up to the critique of her rather conventional third effort, had ordered her to file a finished product by Friday, close of business Washington time. In Vietnam it was now Thursday, just past noon, twelve hours ahead of the east coast. Through the cloud of cigarette smoke swirling about her head, the situation looked dire.

Tortured writing sessions produced little of substance; rather, the words formed images of a mother collapsing to the floor in grief, a family withering under the burden of truth. She couldn't silence the chorus of voices begging to be famous, pleading to be made heroes, insisting that she tell the story of the war in Vietnam as no writer before her. Then there was her own voice, louder than all the others, reminding her how far she had gone to get this assignment, so don't screw it up.

Chris had always imagined herself as the next great voice in American journalism, pounding out compelling insights into the human condition, promoting virtue, exposing frailties, and instilling hope in the disaffected. She would be the spark of life in a profession dominated by an old guard struggling to adapt to a new American identity in an evolving world. And why not her? She had a fancy journalism degree, world-weary cynicism, a trusty Underwood typewriter with a sticky R key, expensive taste in alcohol, and a killer pair of legs that had never met a short skirt they didn't like.

Then Vietnam happened, and the universe enjoyed a good laugh at her expense. The jungle and the realities of war limited her sartorial choices; she was clad in a sweaty beige tank top and baggy fatigue pants that did nothing for her figure. Rather than a slow-burning Camel to calm her nerves, she had chain-smoked enough high-tar, unfiltered Bulgarian death-sticks to choke a water buffalo. Substitute a fine single-malt for a bottle of warm Coca-Cola and a borrowed typewriter with all keys fully functional, and one had all the makings of a journalistic train wreck. She was no Murrow or Cronkite or Didion; she was Chris McKenna, a junior writer for an upstart magazine owned by a man with an agenda that didn't always jive with her fanciful devotion to truth.

As she opened the door of the hooch to clear out the smoke before Paul returned and pitched a fit, she thought she might just as well prepare herself to cover women's issues for the rest of her undistinguished career.

***

It was another late night at the office for Martin Willis, another late night behind the scarred desk with shirtsleeves rolled to the elbows, a blue pencil in the right hand, the fingers of the left hand massaging the left temple, both palms smeared with purple carbon copy ink.

His eyes needed a rest, so he poured a glass of whiskey and let the liquid soothe frayed nerves. The blue pencil had pulled yeoman's duty this evening, tasked with tearing down and rebuilding an uninspired effort from a usually inspired writer.

Gary Crosby sauntered into Willis's office at half past eight, just as Willis finished scribbling a series of questions for the reporter in one of the margins. The publisher dropped into a chair across from his editor-in-chief.

"How's our girl doing?"

"Which girl?"

"Come now, Martin, let's not be evasive. It's been several weeks since her last story."

"She's doing her best." The words on the page blurred from the intensity of his stare, but Willis didn't look up from Chris's work.

"I did not send her to Vietnam to do her best. I sent her to produce."

"She's producing."

"*What* is Miss McKenna producing, aside from my irritation?"

"Chris is a good writer. She'll come through for us."

"Did you give her a deadline?"

"Yes."

"And?"

"She met it."

"That's hardly a ringing endorsement."

Chris's section editor had been so excited to receive her revised piece that he spent ten minutes offering enthusiastic praise for his young writer in the morning staff meeting. Willis, woozy with relief that Chris had finally gotten back on track, asked for a copy to review. His relief morphed to disappointment and confusion. Unlike her stellar initial efforts, and even her somewhat baffling third submission, this story exhibited serious flaws that the features editor had either missed or overlooked. On the surface, the piece read well; Chris was an engaging writer, witty and charming and thoughtful in all the right places. But she had used several thousand words to say very little of substance. Chris had much to learn about her craft, but she never shied away from addressing difficult issues. Until now.

Willis could not tell the story of men he had never met. For whatever reason, the writer had missed the story, too. Or, more accurately, Chris had glossed over the real story and tried to skate by with superficial coverage of what Willis suspected were compelling events at an isolated American base deep within enemy territory. Either she was being played or she was playing him. Willis would bet on the latter because Chris was far too sharp for this crap. And now he was stuck between her and Gary Crosby, a man whose quest for political relevance threatened to trump the news. Willis felt his frustration rise, the whiskey fueling the fire.

"Martin? Is that her work? Will it run in the next issue?"

"Just let me do my job."

"So it won't run?"

Willis rubbed his brow. "Damn it, Gary, I'll take care of it."

"I don't want you to take care of it. It's not your job to rewrite lackluster efforts. I expect more from my reporters."

"Give her a break. She's at war."

"That's no excuse. I want Kent out there as soon as possible."

"You can't just—"

"Send him, Martin. This was supposed to be his assignment anyway."

Willis swallowed his belligerent response. Not for the first time did he wonder how Crosby had managed to talk him out of retirement to take the reins at *American Century*. Had it been the promises of editorial autonomy and complete control over personnel matters? Promises that had been kept, until recently? What had changed, and why? Willis pressed his lips together and nodded curtly. He picked up his blue pencil and attacked the opposite margin.

"And please inform Miss McKenna that this magazine will not pay her medical bills should her ridiculous crusade to be one of the boys result in injury, or worse." Crosby stood and buttoned his suit jacket. "Good evening, Martin."

Willis said nothing, but watched the publisher's back as he left the office. As soon as Crosby disappeared across the newsroom, Willis threw down the pencil and knocked back the last of his whiskey. He swore once and began to pace.

***

The hooch was too small for her to work herself into a good pacing rhythm. The two cots and the field table were easy to avoid, but she tripped over her gear piled at the foot of her bed on every pass. Paul shot her strange looks.

"Genius at work," he muttered, shaking his head as he cleaned the innards of his cameras with a soft brush.

She ignored him. As she walked, she tapped her cheek with her pen. She stumbled on her rucksack again.

"It's over and done with. Move on," he said.

"Easy for you to say."

"Not so easy yesterday when you had my hand in a vise grip while it went over the wires."

"Writers are fragile souls. Anything but unqualified praise for our work will sink us into the depths of despair."

"Prone to melodrama, too."

"You wouldn't understand. You're just a photographer."

Paul examined a lens for scratches. "I don't know why you're so worried. You always manage to pull off a winner, even if you do have a nerve-wracking tendency to wait until the eleventh hour. Put it out of your mind and start work on the next one."

"Shit, I have to do this again?"

"Sarcasm does not become you, my dear."

"I'll be back in a while." She stuffed a small notebook and pen into her pocket.

"Tell John I'm ready to shoot his photo spread once you two work out the details. I'm sure you'll offer an appropriate compensation package in return for his cooperation."

Chris paused between the flaps of mosquito netting hanging in the doorway, unamused by the double entendre. "Could we try to maintain a modicum of professionalism?"

"I'm not the one with a silly schoolgirl crush on a soldier who refuses to succumb to your charms."

"I knew I should have brought a different photographer."

"You'd be a wreck without me."

She grumbled an unintelligible affirmative and walked out into the humid sunshine and the palpable edginess. The base was on high alert, as the ever-elusive Viet Cong had intensified their incursions into the surrounding area. Several enemy mortar rounds had cleared the base perimeter yesterday morning, wreaking havoc amongst those not accustomed to taking fire while using the latrines. Chris thought she might have slept through the incident, an impressive feat considering the level of noise that generally accompanied a mortar attack. According to Steve and his sources, FOB Jane's infantry elements would see constant action this summer on MACV's orders. Peace with honor did not happen overnight, and peace was easier to enforce if one's enemy had been vanquished.

LYNN MASON

Chris approached Second Platoon's barracks with a journalist's sense of purpose. John and Steve lounged outside on the grass, playing a heated game of War with a deck of cards. Steve mumbled obscenities at John around his cigarette whenever he lost a hand, which was often. Steve was clad only in red boxer shorts and combat boots, John in his fatigue pants and flip-flops. She stood over Steve, who was stretched out on his stomach, and stepped down lightly on his backside. He yelped and swatted her foot.

"Jesus, woman, don't be sneaking up on people like that. I could have greased you."

"Not likely. I've seen you shoot."

He climbed to his feet. "I suppose you want to talk to him now. I don't understand," he muttered to himself, "why he gets all the girls."

"He's not getting any girl, Steve," Chris replied as she dropped cross-legged to the ground across from John.

"Sure, sure. Listen, I need to find Oscar." He lowered his voice. "Me and him and Bullseye are running a racket, selling all kinds of shit to the new guys at way high prices. Uppers, downers, weed. Good booze, too, none of that watered-down piss they serve in the club. You guys need anything? We give discounts to people we like." They shook their heads. "Okay. Later." He scampered off with his rifle in hand and helmet askew on his head.

John shifted to a sitting position, forearms resting on his elevated knees. "How can I help you, Miss McKenna?"

"Do you have a few minutes?"

"If it keeps Steve occupied elsewhere, I have all the time in the world for you."

Chris half smiled. "He worships you."

"He worships those he perceives to have power. Murphy, Oscar, Darwin, any number of guys who punch first and ask questions later."

"I disagree. He respects you."

John cocked his head. "We could debate Steve's intellectual and character deficiencies for hours, but I doubt that's why you're here."

"No. I wanted to talk to you about Anne Novak."

He kept his expression neutral and began shuffling cards. "Okay."

"She'll want to interview you."

"That's quite a leap."

"It's not a leap. And you need to know something about her. She's bad news."

"No pun intended, I assume."

"Take me seriously. I speak from experience."

"Should I believe her when she says the same about you? In case you missed it, she has said the same about you, in pretty colorful language. Steve has surprisingly good sources."

"If nothing else, I hope I've proven you can trust me."

"Trust?" John paused to let two Chinooks lumber past overhead, drowning out conversation and rattling structures. "You couldn't honor a simple request not to write about me."

Chris gritted her teeth and felt her blood pressure spike. Over a month of working to earn their trust—his trust—on the battlefield, with real lives at stake, and all he cared about was whether or not he was a story. He could take great pleasure in knowing that she had sacrificed good writing for the sake of his selfish desire. This time. He might not be so lucky next time.

She got to her feet, brushing off the back of her pants. "Of course. My mistake for doing my job."

He laughed, but it was the kind of laugh that cut because she knew it was at her expense.

"Come on, don't go," he said.

"No, I should get back to work. You know, capitalizing on your pain and suffering." She began to walk away before she heeded the voice suggesting she add to that pain and suffering with a booted foot to his face.

He lunged toward her and caught hold of her right ankle. She sighed in exasperation.

"Chris, sit down. Don't be so sensitive."

"You know, John..."

"I'm sorry, I'm sorry, that's not what I meant. Please stay." He loosened his grip on her leg and gestured to the ground. "Please?"

She dropped down and looked away from him down the line of barracks, where hundreds of potential stories waited for her to pop her head in the door and start asking questions. She would never be able to write enough to cover it all. And yet all she cared about was this one story.

"Did you really think it was necessary to warn me about Anne? I have no intention of speaking with her. She won't get some big scoop at your expense."

"She'll be after you. Your reputation precedes you."

"And whose fault is that?"

She managed not to snap. "Just be careful."

"Your concern is touching."

"Have you ever read the *Washington Dispatch*?"

"No."

"Before you take a sanguine view of Anne and her motivations, you should. It's not your kind of magazine."

His eyes narrowed against the sunlight. "Your assumption being that *American Century* is my kind of magazine?"

Chris ran a hand through her hair. She knew she should walk away. She knew she should find a different story.

"Right, I forgot. You prefer *Time*."

John split the deck of cards. "My brother Robby still thinks you're a man."

"How long is that going to last?"

He shrugged. "It might shatter his world to know his favorite writer is a woman."

"Seems an appropriate reaction from the Neanderthal farm boy crowd in Iowa."

A smiled tugged at his lips. "You are a complicated woman, Christine McKenna. Driven, ambitious, in hot pursuit of the story, no matter where it takes you."

Chris swatted at a swarm of gnats and tried to decide whether his tone had been contemplative or mocking or accusing.

"This assignment is a big deal?"

"Yes, of course. Five years of hard work got me here." But her stomach churned as she spoke.

He leaned forward. "Have you thought about how you're going to get through it?"

"I'm sure I'll find a way. The alternative to survival is unappealing."

His icy eyes seemed to smolder. "Always a glib response. The truth is reserved only for the printed page, right?"

She tossed up her hands. "For Christ's sake, I chose this assignment. I'm here to do my job, then get the hell out. What do you want from me?"

"In your six weeks at FOB Jane you've far exceeded the scope of your duties as a war correspondent. You had to know you'd see things no one should ever see. Is all this really worth a few articles and a lifetime of nightmares?"

Chris blinked away a memory. "It's what I get paid to do."

"That's not much of a reason."

"I'm not as cold as you think I am," she said.

"Did I ever say that?"

"You say a lot of things without saying them, John."

They enjoyed the respite from the artillery with a brief silence of their own. Steve clomped past in his unlaced boots again, this time looking for Murphy and Hector. He was still clad only in boxer shorts. A sigh escaped without Chris's permission.

"You sure you're going to make it?" he asked.

"I'm here until I'm done. Make your peace with it."

"Until you get what you want." He locked eyes with her. "Maybe I'll figure out what that is."

As she stood, she felt lightheaded and nervous that he could see right through her. "I have what I want."

"Then you have more than most people."

"I have to go."

"Thanks for talking."

***

"Load 'em up, girls!" Lieutenant Gianelli shouted to his platoon as they ran to the waiting Hueys.

Chris yawned and rubbed her eyes. It was four in the morning. What little sleep she had managed was fitful and broken by artillery fire and wrenching images of combat. Like the men surrounding her, she had learned to function with burning eyes, lethargic muscles, and a dulled mental capacity.

The Hueys lifted off the pad and skimmed the tree canopy, slicing through the heavy mist suspended in the air. They encountered no enemy resistance.

"That's because even them VC are still asleep. This fucking blows, man," Steve grumbled.

"Shut up, fool," Oscar ordered. "You's a soldier, not some Girl Scout."

"You volunteered for this shit, not me."

"I heeded the words of a great leader of our great nation: 'Ask not what your country can do for you; ask what you can do for your country.' An inspiring call to duty." Then he tapped the crudely succinct phrase on his helmet and winked at Chris.

Chris glanced across the cabin at John. They had spoken little to each other for two days, since they had established lack of trust as the dominant theme in their intertwined story. It was only a matter of time before Anne came looking for an easy piece. Chris had driven a tank through that emotional wall of his and left a trail of untold stories in the wreckage.

Murphy leaned forward to peer out the open door. The sky was beginning to lighten. "Gonna be a hot one."

"When is it not hot?" Bullseye said.

Travis grunted. "It gets hotter."

They passed over charred jungle, the work of the United States Air Force. The bombings were indiscriminate: jungles, paddies, and villages, Viet Cong guerrillas and Vietnamese civilians. Napalm had proved to be an effective method of mass destruction, and yet the Viet Cong grew stronger, a fact that seemed to baffle MACV and the politicians.

As they traveled deeper into An Xuyen Province, the jungle grew thick and lush. The air force had spared this area from obliteration. The pilots hovered near the outskirts of the jungle, over a mangrove swamp, and the men jumped down a few feet into the muck.

Chris sank to her knees in the slimy water. The goop under the surface clung to her ankles as she tried to pull away. She breathed through her mouth to avoid the putrid stench.

"Let's go," Travis urged. "This ain't the place to get lit up."

John set out along the edge of the swamp, searching for solid land. Beyond the swamp lay dense rain forest and their sector for patrol.

"We running silent, LT?" Oscar called up the line, an M-60 a yoke across his shoulders.

"What the fuck, today is as good a day as any to die."

"Hell yeah, Little Man, load it up. Let's rock to some Hendrix."

Bullseye reached up and pulled a portable cassette recorder out of Oscar's pack.

"I can't believe he carries that," Chris said.

John shrugged. "Look at him, he's an ox. You could climb on his shoulders along with everything else and I doubt he'd even notice. And walk behind me, please. I run point for this outfit, not you."

"You're so territorial."

"Do you want to take another swim?"

"Do you want to die?"

"I wouldn't mess with her, Johnny," Dan commented, a few steps behind them.

Chris thought she detected a faint flush rising on his cheeks.

Screeching guitar chords blared from the cassette player, tinny recordings made from vinyl albums. Gianelli smacked Bullseye on the shoulder.

"Turn it down, damn it. Let's not ask to be shot."

The platoon melted into a single-file line as John led them along a narrow strip of solid land between the mangrove swamp and a small tributary. They crossed the river at a shallow point farther south and traipsed into the jungle to the guitar riffs of "Purple Haze." Chris sang softly, trying not to dwell on the heat and the gigantic flies orbiting her head. *This is what you get for running combat patrols with young soldiers who do not bathe regularly,* she told herself.

Well ahead of the main body of the platoon, she followed John to a ledge where the earth dropped toward a stream. A trodden footbath led down at an angle. John peered over the ledge, searching for signs of the enemy.

"I need a refill." Chris shook her mostly empty canteen. "Think that water is clean?"

"No."

"Well, that's what iodine is for. See you down there."

Chris had moved only two steps down the path when John grabbed her by the rucksack and yanked, hard enough to sit her on the ground.

"Hey!"

John stepped over her and knelt a yard away. He unsheathed his knife and touched the flat of the blade to the underside of a tripwire strung across the path, nearly invisible against the copper earth and jungle underbrush. He looked back at her.

"This is the reason I run point," he said in an even tone, "and you do not."

Chris stared at the wire, knowing that had she tripped it, she would have killed them both. He followed the wire to a clump of shrubbery protruding into the path and carefully parted the leaves. He reached a hand into the thicket and pulled out a rusted tin can, the remnants of a C-ration entrée.

"I always knew C-rations would be the death of me," John said.

He showed her the hand grenade wedged partly into the can. The safety pin had been removed, but the edge of the can prevented the firing spoon from dislodging. Had she caught the wire, she would have yanked the grenade from its metal cocoon, unleashing the explosion.

The platoon appeared at the top of the ledge, led by Dan and Travis. Chris pushed herself to her feet.

"Nice catch, Rawlins," Travis said.

"It was all Chris," John replied without looking at her.

He threw the entire contraption, can and all, down the ledge into the center of the stream. The impact knocked the grenade loose from the can and seconds later a plume of water shot skyward. Chris retreated to the middle of the pack. She and John didn't speak for the rest of the day.

***

Jack Travis heard the rumor from Conlon, who heard it from Lieutenant Colonel Simpson's sergeant, who heard it from Captain Kittles's corporal. Despite the long and somewhat unreliable chain of acquisition, Travis thought it best to treat the information as valid intelligence and warn his commanding officer that Kittles was escalating the hostilities.

Travis stepped out of his hooch with a Louisville Slugger propped on his right shoulder and lit a cigarette. The morning had dawned overcast, the smell of rain in the air. He walked along the footpath to the officers' quarters and stopped outside of Gianelli's hooch. After crushing his cigarette on the ground, he rapped on the wooden door. When Gianelli finally answered the knock, shirtless, pants only half-buttoned, and sporting bed-head, he opened the door about a third of the way and stood between the door and the jamb.

Travis assumed he had woken Gianelli. "Hey, LT, sorry about..." His voice trailed off when he caught a glimpse of movement in the bed behind Gianelli.

The lieutenant sighed and dropped his head. "I had no choice. She threatened to court-martial me."

Travis smirked. Maria threw a Chuck Taylor All-Star at Gianelli.

"Good morning, Jack," she called.

"Morning, ma'am."

Travis had known about Gianelli and Maria Nichols from the start, when he surmised that something beyond war was preoccupying the lieutenant and set about investigating his hunch. He discovered Gianelli had become enamored with the pretty nurse treating his ravaged feet. Their relationship was mature and discreet, and those few in the know, such as Travis, Major Jacobson, Maria's second-in-command, and Brooks's staff sergeant, respected their privacy. Travis considered Maria a godsend for Gianelli, who needed someone to keep him grounded and focused on something other than casualties and army ineptitude.

Gianelli stepped outside and closed the door behind him. "What's up?"

"Kittles just opened fire, and he's using a big gun."

"That's funny," Gianelli mused. "I'd heard his dick was rather small."

Travis dropped his voice to prevent Maria from overhearing. "He's going after you hard, LT. Not pulling any punches. He's got Simpson on his side. We're getting every patrol he can throw at us until he's sure he has McKenna in his pocket. He thinks she's going to crucify him for that interrogation stunt at Ba Dong, so his aim is to make you look even worse."

"Then I guess we'll be running a lot of patrols."

Maria pulled the door open and slipped out of the hooch, squeezing Gianelli's arm as she passed. "Behave yourselves, boys."

Travis and Gianelli watched her walk the path leading toward the nurses' quarters. Her dark hair fluttered in the breeze.

"Sorry about that. Not that it's any of my business, but I still have no idea how you scored with her," Travis said.

Gianelli grinned and rubbed a hand over his mussed hair. "Me neither."

"Breakfast?"

"I'll meet you there in ten minutes. Go get Conlon. Let's talk this through."

***

Chris agreed to have a drink with First Squad mainly because they refused to leave her alone until she capitulated. She walked away from her work, eight hundred words into her next Vietnam War story, with a silent promise to the typewriter to return after a couple of beers at most. The men escorted her en masse to the bar where Oscar bought the first round.

Murphy slid bottles of Budweiser toward Hector, who distributed the beers among the group spread around a large table.

"McKenna, normally we can't get half these losers out for a beer," Murphy said. "The army thanks you for improving alcohol sales."

"I'm here because Oscar is buying," John said with a smirk in her direction.

"Next round's on you, Cowboy. You been winning too many poker games."

"Because you guys aren't very good."

"Oscar," Chris said, "I heard an interesting rumor the other day."

"Lies," he bellowed. "Falsehoods. Innuendo. Slander."

"Obviously you're a successful entrepreneur of sorts."

"If you say so."

"How do you get the weed onto base? Must come in with food shipments, right? Is that why I always see you at the helipad helping unload supplies?"

Oscar waved his hand dismissively. "That ain't shit that gets talked about, Reporter Lady."

"And yet here I am, talking about it. Who runs the network? Did you build the FOB Jane node yourself, or did you inherit it? Where does the weed come from? What's your cut? And how have you managed to escape the brig?"

He smiled enigmatically.

"Then let's talk about Ernie Pickens. Word is you beat him to a pulp the other day because he moved a load of dope through without your permission."

The squad exchanged glances. Oscar shifted in his seat. "This is the 'Nam, honey. Ain't nothin' what it seems."

"I concede your point," she said, "because when I did a little digging, I discovered that the real reason you put him in the hospital is because Pickens and his buddies attacked those kids from Bravo Company just because they're black. Torching his Confederate flag was a nice touch."

Oscar laughed in resignation. "Just don't be ruining my rep with that sentimental shit."

"You said it, man, it's the 'Nam," said Murphy. "It gets in your head. You do shit you never thought you'd do, lose control. Guaranteed to happen to us all."

The men nodded, all except one. Dan raised his eyebrows at the lone holdout, but his dimpled cheeks betrayed his amusement.

"Everyone except Johnny, apparently. The 'Nam's not in your head?"

John shrugged.

"Give it time, Cowboy. You'll do something that shocks us all," said Murphy.

"Maybe."

A non-committal response for everything, Chris thought with disdain. For a man who acted with nothing less than solid resolve, he could carry on a vague conversation with aplomb. She would give her right arm to see John Rawlins lose control, to watch that calm demeanor shatter into a thousand bits. And then she would write about it just to make him suffer. Screw trust.

John leaned forward in his seat and rested his elbows on the table. He focused arctic blue eyes on Chris. "Are you aware that tomorrow is Flag Day?"

"No," she replied. "I wasn't." She noticed that conversation had abruptly stopped.

"June fourteenth. It's a day to honor the world's most recognizable and potent symbol of liberty, though often people forget that it's not the flag that makes us free, but rather the values shaped by nearly two centuries of triumph and tragedy."

Ben Kearney snickered.

"Okay," Chris said slowly.

"I'll make a deal with you. This is a one-time offer, so listen carefully. Are you listening carefully?"

"What is wrong with you?"

"I'll agree to a no-holds-barred interview if you leave FOB Jane within twenty-four hours."

Hector laughed so hard that tears rolled down his cheeks.

"I would sooner date Steve than interview you."

"Hey!" Steve said. "Wait...so are you saying you'll date me?"

"Nice try, Cowboy," Oscar bellowed, raising a beer in John's direction.

Chris saw she had become the butt of a joke everyone knew about—everyone but her. She knocked back the last of her beer and stood, visions of the typewriter sans the sticky R key taunting her.

"Aw, only one beer? You're no fun," Steve said.

"Duty calls."

"There are Pulitzers to be won," Paul said. "She needs killer stories to complement my photos."

"Very true," Chris replied. "Thanks for the drink, Oscar. Gentlemen, always a pleasure."

Before their heated protests could pull her back to the table, Chris pushed through the door and into the humid evening.

***

John made his way to the bar to buy the next round. He motioned Dan over to help with the load. Dan wasted no time getting to the point.

"Man, you have fallen hard for that girl."

"My feelings for her, whatever you think they might be, are irrelevant. She's taken."

"I'm not so sure about that."

"She's not going to dump the rich guy back home for a soldier. Besides, she doesn't even like me."

"You can't possibly believe that."

"I'm just a story. And I don't want to be a story, so it doesn't look like there's much potential for our nonexistent relationship to advance out of its current rut."

"Could you be more stubborn?"

"A lot of things would have to be different for this scenario to work. A lot of things," John said.

"It's no fun when it's easy."

John's jaw muscles twitched. His eyes tracked George Wheaton from the bar to the door, where he stumbled across the threshold and pitched into a group of enlisted men trying to enter. "I'm going to step out for a few minutes."

"No fear in that girl."

"Not much in the way of street smarts, either."

"Yeah, but that's why you like her."

"Back in fifteen minutes."

"Don't lose control, Johnny."

"Never." He grinned and turned to follow her out.

***

The walk from the club to her hooch should take approximately eight minutes. But the night was so still, so black, that Chris slowed her pace to soak it in. Fleetingly, the war vanished and Vietnam was a land of serene, ancient beauty. The inky sky, a primordial dream speckled by thousands of shimmering stars, imbued her with a sense of tranquility. For so long she had wandered in search of something bigger, something deeper. Had she found it in the jungles and paddies of a foreign land?

The crunch of boots on the dirt path tore her attention from the stars. She stifled a sigh and turned to face him, placing her hands on her hips. "What do you want?"

John Rawlins raised his eyes to the sky. "Beautiful night."

"Is there a reason you're following me?"

He shrugged. "I don't need a reason to take a walk, do I?"

"Go stalk someone else."

"Sorry to disappoint you, but I'm just out for a stroll. However, since I did stumble across you, I'd be happy to walk you back to your hooch."

Chris planted her feet shoulder-width apart, crossed her arms over her chest, and refused to move. "Oh, I see. You think I need a big strong man to protect me?" She opened her eyes wide and pouted her lips, radiating faux innocence.

By the light of the moon, she watched his jaw set. He glowered at her before he leaned down so their noses were practically touching. She tried not to shake or even breathe. What the hell was he doing? Would he kiss her? The thought hit her so hard she broke into a sweat.

"You have proven time and time again you need one."

What if *she* kissed him? What would *he* do? Then his words registered.

"Go to hell, John."

He straightened, his eyes still locked on her. She whirled on her heel and stalked down the path, swearing to herself. She most certainly did not need a big strong man to protect her. Last time she checked, she had survived firefights and mortar attacks and jungle insects the size of Chihuahuas the same as him. She tossed a glare over her shoulder, but he had disappeared. Leave it to John Rawlins to ruin her night.

***

Upon exiting the club, Lieutenant Wheaton lost the bead on his target as his full bladder took priority. He moved toward the closest building, a supply bunker, and relieved himself against the side. He ignored the laughter of nearby grunts. Then, as he scanned the dimly illuminated pathways, he thought he recognized a female shape in the distance. He picked up his pace, eyes straining to follow the slim figure as she wound through base.

Wheaton gained as she strolled and occasionally looked to the stars. Normally she was with her photographer or surrounded by grunts like she was in the club. Gianelli's platoon of America's finest societal dregs, he assumed. As he downed vodka shots at the bar, he had decided that tonight was his night. Now he was in a state of painful anticipation. He wondered how she would compare to the girls at his favorite brothels in Saigon and Danang. He was seized by a sudden concern that he would catch a grunt STD if she had already given it up to one of Gianelli's trailer trash. The madams at his preferred brothels made the girls get checked weekly—except the girl who had given him the clap a few months ago, apparently. He supposed it couldn't be much worse than that. Then he considered logistics; he preferred to take her back to his own quarters, but tonight he wouldn't be picky. She might be one of those women who preferred her own bed.

He lost sight of her around a corner as the path cut through an array of bunkers and tents. His brain swimming in vodka, he never saw the man lurking under the empty gym tent until the soldier sauntered into the path and blocked his progress. Wheaton tried to sidestep him, but the man mirrored his moves like an unwelcome dance partner.

"Get the fuck out of my way," he slurred.

"Sorry, sir, I can't do that."

Wheaton tried to concentrate. The man stood loosely, comfortably, his hands hanging at his sides. He was tall, taller than Wheaton, and his broad shoulders made him seem disproportionately large in the shadows. Wheaton managed to discern hair so blond it was almost white, but he couldn't read the name stenciled on the man's half-open fatigue shirt. His eyes drifted in and out of focus.

"Who the fuck do you think you are?" Wheaton tried to shove past, but the man put a warning hand to his chest.

"John Rawlins, Second Platoon, Delta Company."

Wheaton registered none of it. He tried to peer around the soldier, but Chris McKenna was nowhere in sight.

"You fucking mope. You're about to cost me a shot with a hot piece of ass. Now move."

John grabbed Wheaton's throat with his right hand and squeezed just hard enough to silence any thought of a scream. Wheaton's eyes bulged in terror and his hands clawed at John's wrist, then slapped at his face, connecting with mouth and cheek. John squeezed harder. Wheaton stopped flailing.

"I need you to listen to me, sir," he said. "Are you listening?"

Wheaton's vision turned spotty. He gasped.

"I'll take that as a yes. Here's the deal: Miss McKenna is off limits. Do you understand?"

The soldier released his grip on Wheaton's neck, and the lieutenant sucked in several huge gulps of air. He rubbed his neck and coughed. A large handprint would be visible for days.

"I'm an officer," he said in his snottiest tone, his voice raspy. "I don't take orders from grunts."

The soldier smiled pleasantly. "This time you will. Or I'll kill you."

Wheaton felt a chill. He stared into eyes that did not lie.

"Off limits," he reminded. And then he disappeared.

The vodka and lack of oxygen overcame Wheaton. His legs buckled and he crumpled to the ground.

***

She made it back to her hooch without incident, still fuming over his arrogance and ignorance. *Dumb farm boy*, she thought to herself. As she reached toward the door, a hand clamped over her wrist.

Her reaction was instantaneous. She lashed out with her foot and kicked her attacker in the shin. Hard.

John released her wrist and jumped back, hopping on one leg. "Damn," he said through gritted teeth, tentatively putting his weight back on both feet.

"What the hell are you doing? You scared the shit out of me." Chris clenched her fists to conceal her shaking hands.

"Good. You need to be scared. Do you pay any attention to what's going on around you?"

"Of course I pay attention."

"Did you see that pig of a public affairs officer follow you?"

Chris stared at him in the moonlight. Had she seen George Wheaton? Or had she been so preoccupied that she missed a potential assault? And was that blood at the corner of his mouth? She resisted the urge to reach out and wipe it away.

"That's what I thought," he said. "Unfortunately, your lack of situational awareness puts me in a difficult spot. I think there's a certain way that women should be treated, and his plans for you fell below my standards. But you were off in feminist la-la land, so tough choice for me. Do I come to your rescue, or do you get pissed that I tried to help? I'm a big strong man, after all, and you don't like my sort. Don't think of yourself as special, though. I would have done the same for Anne Novak."

Chris had to resist another urge, the urge to bloody that lip even more. Instead she turned to enter her hooch. "The white knight to my rescue once again. Forgive me if I don't swoon."

"I don't understand you," he said.

She ignored him, pulling the pad out of her cargo pocket and tossing it on the field table.

"Did you see Wheaton dead on the path?" a voice asked.

"Do you understand her?" John challenged Paul, who appeared from the darkness.

The photographer held up his hands as he slipped into the hooch past John. He chuckled. "Now here's a conversation I want no part of. But really, I think Wheaton is dead on the path back there."

John shook his head impatiently. "He's not dead." Energized, he questioned Chris with a fervor she hadn't known he possessed. "Beyond personal glory, do you have any other motivation for taking this assignment?"

Chris tore off her fatigue shirt and worked it into a ball. "Yes. And forgive me if I don't feel compelled to share my reasons with you."

"Wait a minute. Did you do that? I thought he was just drunk." Paul stepped forward to study John, saw the blood on his lip, and turned to Chris. "What happened?"

"Have you shared them with anybody? What does what's-his-name think of this, that guy you're going to marry? Edward? What does Eddie think of this? Must be thrilled, his girl off in the jungle with a bunch of killers, throwing herself into danger every chance she gets. I'd be worried if I were him. Look at you. Yeah, I'd be damn worried."

"Look at me?" she snarled, flinging the shirt toward her cot. "What am I, just some sex-crazed bimbo who can't resist young soldiers? Get over yourself, John."

"What's he like, this Edward? Paul? Decent guy? Supportive of her adventurous spirit? She doesn't talk about him much. What's the deal?"

Paul opened his mouth to respond, but thought better of it when Chris whirled and set piercing eyes upon him. Then she faced John.

"The best assumption you've made here tonight is that you don't understand me. I suggest you stick with that."

John smiled without humor, his gaze wandering to her left hand. "Everything you want, huh? You don't even know what you want."

"Good night, John."

His glittering eyes watched her for a second longer. Then he disappeared.

Chris stood with one hand on her hip. The other massaged her temple. Paul busied himself by stowing his camera gear under his cot. Then he sat and pulled off his boots. She was still in the same position, staring out the open door.

Paul's voice was quiet. "Why do you hide behind that ring?"

The hand at her temple dropped. She pulled the silver band off her finger, examined it, and dropped it in her duffel bag. After kicking off her boots, she stretched out on her cot and turned to the wall.

8

—•—

The Hueys dipped low over the Delta and strafed the paddies with machine gun fire. Hundreds of rounds disappeared into the muck, razing delicate rice plants and leaving gentle ripples along the surface of the water that masked the ferocity of their impact. Brass shell casings littered the floor of the helicopters, rolling under green canvas benches and over booted feet before sliding out the open door and raining down on the flooded earth.

One of the young door gunners whooped. "Hey boys, watch these fuckers run!" He mimicked the moves of the farmers with the machine gun, terrorizing a half dozen scrambling women and their water buffalo before the pilots ascended to clear the oncoming tree canopy.

John kept his gaze focused on the line of men across from him on the Huey. He didn't need to look out the open side to know what he would see: women screaming and running, their wide, conical hats torn off by air friction, sprawling for cover in the paddies. The gunner, who was barely old enough to vote, giggled each time one of his slugs came close to cutting down a peasant.

Their Huey, the center of five helicopters carrying the two squads of Second Platoon plus a week's worth of supplies, pulled ahead and nosedived once they cleared the jungle. Gianelli ordered the gunners to cease firing and peered out the door to survey the landscape and their approaching landing zone. The paddies collided with high grass and low shrubbery that flanked a rutted dirt road winding from one small hamlet to the next, through the jungle and deep into the Delta and the heart of Viet Cong resistance in the province. Major

Gardner's intelligence assets had reported that Charlie had begun moving more supplies and personnel into some of the more remote villages of the south, widening their reach.

Kittles had given the order to Gianelli with glee: Second Platoon would stay in the bush as long as it took to decimate the next supply convoy. The general consensus was that the mission was a wild goose chase. Charlie Cong had a sixth sense, honed over years of successful jungle warfare and resistance; he knew when the army was after him.

"Get ready!" Travis shouted.

The men strapped on their gear and tightened their helmets. John took one last swig of water from his canteen and pulled the bush hat low on his forehead. His eyes sought Chris, who watched him with a curious mix of loathing, aloofness, and well-disguised apprehension. Then on Gianelli's order, he was the first man out the chopper.

He jumped four feet to the ground, expecting as always to take a barrage of hidden rifle fire through the heart. Once the platoon disembarked and unloaded the supplies and secured the area, the lieutenant waved away the Hueys.

The platoon melted into the high grasses and shrubs, hunkering down to the moist earth until nightfall. Crickets chirped and insects buzzed, blending seamlessly with the quiet chatter of men concealed in shadows and thickets. Soon the dusty, winding road would fade to black. In the thick Vietnam air, time slowed to a crawl.

***

As the minutes of another long night in the bush slowly ticked by, Chris felt the ache of weeks of combat patrols deep within her bones. Every muscle in her body hurt; the knotted, rope-like tendrils were prone to random spasm as she lay silent and motionless under the canopy. Finally, she could stand the pain in her lower back no longer. She rose stiffly and crept to the encampment's eastern perimeter, where small teams of men kept watch, strung out along set intervals and concealed within the brush.

"McKenna!" a voice hissed.

Chris, who was moving in a half-crouch to remain hidden by the thick growth, dropped to a knee.

"Right here," the voice hissed again.

She recognized it as Murphy's voice and doubled back to his position. He and Dan and Hector sat in a loose clump, but they rearranged to make room for her. She took a seat next to Dan.

"You're lucky LT didn't see you out here," Murphy commented as he lit a cigarette. "What's up?"

"Couldn't sleep."

"I'll never take a bed for granted ever again," Dan said, wincing as he shifted and stretched his legs.

Chris reached over and plucked the snapshot out of Dan's hand, holding it in such a way as to catch the metallic glow of the moon. "She's beautiful."

"Knew I was in love with her the first time I met her."

Murphy made a gagging noise. She smacked his knee.

"Hadn't pegged you for a romantic, McKenna."

"Deep down every woman wants a man who can't live without her."

"You ever been in love, Murph?" Dan asked.

"Hell no. Love's for women and wimps."

"So tough-guy soldiers can't fall in love?" Chris asked.

Murphy grunted. "You tell me," he said, shooting her a pointed glance. "Can they?"

She remained silent, focused on the sounds of the night and the swaying leaves just out of reach. Murphy laughed at her hesitation.

"He's way down the perimeter. Just us, honey. You can trust us."

Dan sighed. "Murph..."

Chris handed the photo back to Dan. "He's just teasing."

"I ain't teasing, sweetheart. I wish you two would get it over with. The sexual tension is killing the rest of us."

Chris felt heat rise in her cheeks. "I'm here because I have a job to do and it doesn't involve sleeping with anyone. I have a hard enough time getting even the slightest bit of respect, so what makes you think I'd throw away my one chance to nail the big story by jumping in the sack with John, or anyone else for that matter. I mean," she said with a short laugh, "the guy needs to get laid, but I'm not about to jeopardize everything I've achieved for the sake of mild physical attraction. How stupid do you think I am?"

"All that nasty stuff between you two ain't for real."

"Yes, it is. He wants nothing to do with me and I've reached the point where I want nothing to do with him. He had story potential, but now he's just another sullen soldier with an attitude problem. I can't sell that. So I'm moving on."

"That don't sound like Johnny," Hector mused.

"And you." She leaned around Murphy to get a better look at Hector. "Don't think I don't know what you've been up to."

With a mischievous grin, he tossed up his hands and shrugged his shoulders. "*Lo siento, no hablo Ingles*, Reporter Lady."

"You think people around here don't respect you?" Dan asked.

"I think you guys tolerate me because I make your officers uncomfortable, and I think every single one of your officers wishes I were someone else's problem. Let's not insult everyone's intelligence by pretending otherwise."

"I respect you," he said.

Chris sighed. "I'm sorry. It's just...it's just not that simple."

"It should be," said Murphy.

"Never been a woman, have you, Murph?" she asked wryly.

"At least I got enough sense not to care about the bullshit. Don't know how much longer I got left, so I might as well go after what I want."

"Grunt wisdom. Not really applicable to the real world, but I appreciate the sentiment."

"You don't have to be so mean about it."

Chris rolled her eyes. "How about we drop it? I have enough to worry about without you on my ass."

"Just looking out for you. He ain't the only one who needs to get laid."

"Not happening. And furthermore—"

"Look, a shooting star," he said, cutting her off and pointing to a streak of light just above the horizon.

"That's not a star."

"Star, dud artillery shell, whatever. Close enough. Make a wish."

"Who are they shooting at?"

"Fuck if I know. Come on, make a wish. Ain't that what chicks do when they see a pretty light in the sky?"

"Leave me alone."

"Suit yourself." Murphy exhaled. "It's a nice night. Vietnam, Vietnam..."

As his voice trailed off, Chris heard the faint whistle of another shell ascending toward the stars. Despite herself, she made a simple wish, a wish for just a little bit of courage.

***

Chris willed herself to write under the intense Vietnam sun. She started cautiously, writing around what she really wanted to say in hopes of freeing her muse from invisible shackles, of pushing through the uncertainty and the fear. Sentences became paragraphs, paragraphs became pages, but still the story eluded her.

She worked while the men played and relaxed and staked out a deserted road. She lost herself in thought while they spread out around her, teasing her, harassing her, suggesting she strip down to rid herself of unsightly tan lines. When that failed, they settled for naps under tarps and ponchos strung between trees. Chris watched it all with a reporter's detachment, willing herself to remain nothing more than an objective observer in the most subjective of wars.

On the fifth evening, Gianelli decided it was time to find the Viet Cong.

"Rawlins."

"Yeah, LT?"

"Need you to take your squad on a scouting run tonight. Few hours, check the area for any sign of Charlie."

"Sure."

"You leave at sundown." He silenced the groans with a look and disappeared to radio base.

"Ten bucks says Charlie never comes through here. Ten bucks says a month from now our own guys come busting down the road and wipe themselves out on the mines we laid," Steve mumbled.

No one, not even Hector, took the bet.

"Hey, McKenna," Murphy called.

John whirled to catch his eye and avert the conversation, but Murphy never looked his way. Chris, who lay on her stomach in the grass, legs kicked up at the knees, saw his pained look. She wrote another sentence about him out of spite.

"What?"

"You're coming tonight, right?"

"If it's acceptable to Field Marshal Rawlins."

Ten pairs of eyes watched John. No one, not even the densest among them, missed the sarcasm.

"I'd prefer if you didn't."

"Aw, Johnny."

"Cowboy, what gives?"

Chris turned her attention back to her work, but not before shooting John a look of smug superiority. She was content to let the Greek chorus defend her, the same chorus of men who only two months ago had deemed it crazy and dangerous for a woman to run combat patrols. How ironic, she thought, that she had won over a platoon of macho soldiers but had failed to win over her editor.

"Sarge," said John.

"You're kidding, right? Shit, that girl's a better soldier than the rest of these jokers. If she wants to go, she goes." Travis lowered his voice conspiratorially. "You'll thank me later." Then he smirked and socked John in the shoulder.

Chris threw Travis a dirty look before he walked away laughing. John gave Chris a wide berth while he searched for his equipment and a dinner ration. But on the way back to his squad, he paused and squatted down beside her. She ignored him, making elaborate doodles in the margin of one of her notebooks as she vetted a sentence in her head. He touched her bare shoulder. She turned to him and offered a mirthless smile.

"Are you sure you want to come? It's probably a waste of time."

"I have a job to do."

"Right. Your job. Then of course we'll accommodate you."

"Thank you. Your selfless cooperation will be noted."

They ate an early dinner and prepared their equipment for the patrol. Oscar left his cassette deck behind and complained that he felt naked without it. Turner suggested that if Oscar really wanted something else to carry, he should shoulder Chris's gear. Horrified, Chris stood protectively over her rucksack while Oscar teasingly inquired as to why she shunned all their gentlemanly efforts.

"Because I can carry my own damn gear."

Oscar shrugged. "Okay," he said, and turned his attention to more important matters. "Yo, anybody got extra grub?"

***

The recon squad had found the Viet Cong, and they were headed straight for the platoon. As the early morning mist settled over the jungle, Gianelli, Travis, and Conlon roused the platoon. Bleary-eyed and fighting exhaustion after last night's patrol, the men of First Squad rose to hear their orders. They would be the main thrust of the attack. This they accepted without complaint.

John concealed himself in the mix of brush and high weeds along the road, accompanied by Steve and Billy. Steve lit a cigarette and kicked his legs out, tossing his rifle aside and making the most of the opportunity to relax before the fighting began. Billy sat so close to John he was practically in his lap. His hand shook as he tried to light his own cigarette. Succumbing to a bout of pity, John took the matchbook from him and touched the flame to the cigarette. Billy took a drag and closed his eyes.

Chris crept up to their position and crawled to the other side of Billy. John silently urged her to safety with a quick jerk of his head. She raised her eyebrows in mock confusion.

"Chris, get back to camp."

"I'll stay out of the way."

"You're going to get killed." He reached around Billy and grabbed her arm, harder than he meant to.

She yanked free from his grasp. Steve let out a low whistle.

"Knock it off, John," Chris said.

"This is going to be a huge bloody firefight. Use your head, will you?"

"Let's get one thing straight: I don't take orders from you."

John spoke slowly and deliberately. "You have two choices: return to camp under your own power, or return to camp under my power."

"Don't threaten me."

"You have ten seconds to decide."

Chris stared at him. He didn't blink.

"Five seconds."

Chris's eyes hardened and she set her jaw. Both of them knew he intended to forcibly remove her. She stood and retreated toward camp without a backward glance.

146

John exhaled.

"What's the matter with you, Johnny? Why you so mean to her?"

"Because she's out of control."

"Come on, you know she'd stay out of our way when shit starts going down."

"That's not the point. All it'll take is a stray bullet to send her home in a box."

Steve shrugged. "If you want to get laid..."

John's fingers tensed around his rifle, and he shot Steve a look of warning.

"I'm just saying you got it bad for her. Don't want to see you screw it up. You're my boy, Johnny."

"Then stay out of it."

"Aw..."

The wait was interminable. Billy chain-smoked; Steve fell asleep. John remained vigilant, ears straining for the sounds of a caravan or a scouting party. Last night, the squad had found the Viet Cong encampment miles north of the platoon's position. The sheer number of trucks and jeeps suggested the fighters were moving significant amounts of weaponry and materiel, as Major Gardner's intelligence sources had reported. Gianelli, always skeptical of the major's sources and their veracity, was pleasantly surprised that the platoon might secure a tactical win with the destruction of a supply convoy. However, as he sarcastically noted to John, although accurate intelligence was helpful, the problems generally occurred during the implementation of mission parameters.

As dawn approached, distant rumblings reached John's ears. He elbowed Steve and thrust Billy's rifle into his hands. Gianelli ran by each group and ordered them to advance after Murphy blew the Claymores. They would sort out the mess when it was over.

For the next several minutes, John concentrated on repressing the nausea forcing its way up through his system. He had not eaten breakfast; now he felt lightheaded and twitchy. Peering through the brush, he caught a glimpse of dim headlights bobbing up and down as the small trucks rumbled along the pockmarked road. In less than a minute, the convoy would be within the kill zone.

The first vehicle entered the mine grid. The others vehicles followed slowly, navigating the narrow curves with caution. John counted black-clad guerrillas, many wearing conical hats or military-style caps, all carrying small arms. As a truck pulled even with his position, he stared in shock at villagers crammed into the open cargo area. There had been no villagers with the Viet Cong last night.

John swore and scrambled to find Gianelli, leaving Steve and Billy alone and bewildered. He ran in a crouch to Dan and Kearney.

"Where's LT?"

"With Murph, I think," said Dan.

"There are villagers. Women and children. Murphy can't blow those mines."

"Oh God," Kearney murmured.

Just as John turned to continue his search for Gianelli, the lead vehicle reached the far end of the grid. A rocket-propelled grenade streaked out of the brush and impacted the side of the truck. The truck exploded and flipped, blocking the road. Thunderous fire from two recoilless rifles disabled several more trucks.

Vietnamese peasants and their Viet Cong escorts piled out of the vehicles and ran toward the jungle. Women screamed and tried to gather their children.

Murphy blew his first mine. The shrapnel mowed down four Vietnamese. John wanted to close his eyes, yet found himself mesmerized by the spectacle, the chaos. He watched as an old man tripped a Bouncing Betty, took the explosion in the back, and pitched forward, dead.

Murphy set off a line of Claymores, mangling vehicles. One jeep, directly above a mine, flopped onto its side.

Gianelli and Travis yelled for the surge. Dutifully, John pushed through the brush and into the battle. Through the smoke he picked his first target, an alert machine gunner on one of the trucks who sprayed his fire in a panic. John paused and aimed for the gunner's chest. He shot twice. The man fell backwards and toppled off the truck.

Steve, bent over at the waist, punched John in the thigh and yelled, "What the fuck's the matter with you? Get your ass down! Shit!" He whirled and fired haphazardly into billowing smoke from an engine fire.

"Don't shoot civilians!" John shouted back.

"Civilians? What civilians?"

His platoon shot at anything that moved. Women and elderly took bullets in the back, and young men, all of whom were presumed to be combatants, had entire rifle magazines emptied into them.

Watching the ground closely for any sign of the unexploded Bouncing Betties, John ran along the road into the fray. He covered his nose and mouth, choking on the smoke, and stumbled over a dead body, falling and skidding onto hands and knees.

Still on the ground, John watched as a young guerrilla moved toward him, shouting and trying to reload his AK-47 on the run. John brought his rifle from his hip to his shoulder and shot once. The bullet tore through the man's throat. He collapsed in a heap. For just a second, John closed his eyes.

"You hit? You hit?" Standing above him, Dan shook his shoulder.

John jumped up, startled and alert, the memory of the dying VC soldier evaporating. "What?" he yelled back over the tremendous din of explosions and gunfire.

"Thought you were dead!"

They ran along the road together, searching out any armed Viet Cong. They came across a group of three men, stunned from an explosion but seemingly uninjured. Dan trained his rifle on the little circle and John searched each man for weapons. He reached under torn shirts, into pockets of pants, and down near their ankles. He came away with one long blade. They had lost a grip on their rifles in the confusion. John kicked the Kalashnikovs toward Dan and began binding the prisoners with parachute cord.

"Can we leave them here?"

John shrugged. "Don't know what else to do with them."

The explosions tapered off. Murphy had blown all the Claymores, and many of the Vietnamese lay dead or wounded. Every Bouncing Betty and M-14 had been tripped. The soldiers of Second Platoon appeared through the dense smoke, calling for cease-fires.

"That was fucking wild," Steve said.

Murphy ran toward them, pumping his fist. "All me, boys, all me. How about them fireworks?"

Oscar slapped him on the back.

First Squad spread out to take prisoners and help care for any wounded, as ordered by Sergeant Travis. John had no interest in prisoners. He sought out Ben Kearney and offered his help. Kearney accepted with a tight nod.

Sporadic bursts of gunfire from American M-16s punctuated the calm. As the smoke cleared, they saw the full extent of the slaughter. Unidentifiable body parts littered the lumpy dirt road. Blood on the ground filled cracks and crevices, snaking long, winding paths around bumps and pebbles, pooling in potholes.

Kearney stared out over the wreckage. "I don't know where to start."

John did. He slung his rifle over his shoulder and strode to an elderly Vietnamese woman with a leg wound. She risked a glance at him with wary eyes.

The medic dropped his pack and his satchel and cut open the woman's lower pant leg, exposing the wound. As Kearney looked through his supplies for a bandage, upwards of ten successive rifle shots rang out nearby. John dropped to one knee and readied his weapon. Then they heard familiar laughter.

Kearney examined the leg, checking for an exit wound and signs of a broken bone. She winced, but maintained her stoic silence.

"Is it broken?" John asked.

"I don't think so. Looks like a flesh wound, through and through."

They helped her into a sitting position and Kearney applied a pressure dressing. All the while she stared at John. Her old, gnarled hand clasped around one of his. He was startled by her strength.

Kearney steered her to the makeshift triage area, from where she would be transported to American military medical facilities by helicopter. Holding tight to the medic, she limped off. John continued down the road, searching for the injured.

As the morning sun gained intensity, the platoon stripped to the waist and went about dragging bodies to piles for easy collection when the choppers came through. The jokes flew at rapid-fire pace, the laughs came even faster. Gianelli stood with Travis and Conlon, his hands on his helmetless head, looking dismayed by his tactical victory.

As John rounded a mangled transport truck, he found Dan yelling at Murphy, Darwin, Levens, and Huntington. Joining the group, he saw they stood over three VC soldiers, all bound at the wrists and ankles. Now they were dead, riddled with bullets.

"They're fucking Viet Cong, Danny," Murphy yelled back.

"They were bound, Murph, *bound*. They were helpless, no threat to anybody."

"Yeah, I made sure of it."

John walked away.

He approached another small group of soldiers, Steve, Billy, and Bullseye. The three were quiet and focused on their task, all in a squat. Unnoticed, John stood over them. Awed and impressed, Steve and Billy watched Bullseye slice the ear from a corpse with his knife. Bullseye explained in a low tone the proper procedure for a clean cut and proceeded to demonstrate again, slicing the second ear from the skull in one smooth motion without excess blood. He held it up triumphantly.

John grabbed Bullseye by the back of his grubby white tank top and hauled him, protesting, to his feet. Bullseye dropped the ears to the dusty road.

"What do you think you're doing?"

"Let go, Johnny, let go."

Still holding tight to his shirt, John cuffed him on the head. "Answer me."

Steve and Billy jumped up. Billy fiddled with his cigarette and wouldn't look at John.

"I was getting some souvenirs." Bullseye rubbed his head where John had smacked him.

"Ears? You think human ears are souvenirs?"

"Everyone else has them."

"Like who?"

"Oscar, Murph, Darwin...me, I got a bunch, too. I was just showing—"

"Showing them what?"

Bullseye swallowed. "I was just showing these boys how to get a good cut."

"I suppose you'll show them how to make a necklace, too?" John said.

Guilty silence was his answer.

"What is *wrong* with you?"

"Nothing, Johnny. It's what everybody does."

John stared into Bullseye's confused, pleading eyes. He dropped the teenager. "I don't."

Again, he walked away.

9

— • —

C hris McKenna had never taken orders well, and she would be damned if she started taking them from John Rawlins. Despite his threats, she had doubled back and entered the combat zone armed only with five senses and her notebook. That was the story, that rutted road in the Mekong Delta and the men who stormed it. Stray bullets missed her; trees and ditches shielded her from shrapnel; wounded Vietnamese civilians looked on in disbelief as a young journalist materialized from the smoke and tried her best to tend to their injuries.

Perhaps they wondered what could drive her to such lengths. Was it the story? Or was it something more?

She was both angry and grateful that he sent her away. She saw a man uninhibited by anyone or anything, who acted in the only way he knew how. Hers was a simple conundrum: the story was more than John Rawlins, and John Rawlins was more than a story.

But she was here for the story, and on the ride back to FOB Jane, as she stared into cold blue eyes and listened to the jubilant chatter of young soldiers ecstatic in victory, she felt the rage building, kept in check by ruthless self-control. Chris jumped out the instant the Huey's skids touched the pad and stalked through base to her hooch. She had to get to her typewriter. Voices shouted, probably to her. She didn't give a damn.

Her fatigues clung to her, saturated with days' worth of dirt and sweat. She smelled terrible, like rancid rice paddy and gunpowder and fear. Halfway to her hooch, she broke into a jog, her rucksack bouncing against her back, and scrubbed her hands with her shirttails to remove a child's blood from the crevices in her palms.

She rounded the corner to the hooch and its rings of sandbagging, the sandbagging that could never protect her from the memories of war in Vietnam. Heavy steps pounded the ground behind her; a voice called and then faded. All noise ceased except the screaming in her head. In the doorway she shrugged off the pack, left it in a heap, and moved to the field table in the corner.

Her fingers attacked the keys. She let raw emotion rule, couldn't bear to read what she wrote. Thought became a luxury. The words were in her. She had to get them out, onto paper in their brutally honest form.

Someone burst through the open door. "This is what happens in war. It's not right, but it happens," John Rawlins said.

She kept writing, refused to look his way.

He stepped over her gear and walked up behind her. "Chris, listen to me. It's not right..."

His voice trailed off. Without looking, she felt him tense as his eyes took in the words, the sentences. The truth stripped bare, in all its glory.

"What are you doing?" he asked.

"My job."

"Your *job*?"

She turned in the chair. "My job."

"You think *this* is your job? Passing judgment on men you barely know? I swear, for as smart as you are, you don't have a clue." He strode out of the hooch and headed for the path to his barracks.

Chris knocked over the chair in her haste to follow. She sprinted to his side, the wave of anger crashing over her like a storm surge.

"What happened today? What am I supposed to think?"

John stopped and faced her. "Report the news. Don't spin it."

"I have a right to tell the truth."

"Then tell the whole truth!" he hissed as his squad wandered toward them and stopped a few yards away. "We're not all like that."

"Oh, so now this is about you?"

"No, it's about you. You rolled into town armed with preconceived notions and stereotypes. You never gave us a chance to prove we're more than just mindless killing machines."

"That is flatly untrue. If I hadn't given you a chance, I wouldn't still be here. Think what I've seen, John. Torture and slaughter of innocent civilians, ambushes and bombings and death on a grand scale. I should be holed up in a hotel in Saigon recounting all the dirty little details of a dirty little war and putting your platoon in the starring role."

"That's all we are? Just more casualties for the sake of your career?"

"Don't you dare accuse me of using you." She dropped her voice for only him to hear. "How many people died needlessly today? How many? And how many of these guys are proud of what they did?"

"I told you to stay away. I *told* you. Why can't you just listen?"

"You think pretending the problem doesn't exist will make it go away?"

"I think putting the problem in the hands of an ignorant, misguided reporter will make it even worse."

"You arrogant son of a bitch."

"Tell me what you hope will be the outcome of this misadventure."

Chris was poised to snarl a response. But none came. What *was* she doing here? Did she still expect a career boost, to earn the respect of Martin Willis and her male peers, men who refused to take her seriously? Could she still achieve her dreams of winning the most prestigious reporting awards with writing that captured the confused and fractured zeitgeist of the Vietnam era? If nothing else, could she write her way to a better understanding of the world despite having failed to understand the man in front of her?

"Well? You want everyone to think you're bulletproof, the tough chick with a sharp mind and a sharper tongue, when you're nothing more than a pretty little thrill-seeker on some whirlwind tour of rebellion. Are you really so weak?"

The fury spiked, nearly blinding her, and she took a step forward, fists clenching. "Fuck you, John. Fuck you!"

"Who *are* you?"

Every muscle in her body burned with the effort to remain coiled for attack. His icy glare dared her to speak, to defend herself, to prove to every onlooker that she was not the pretender he accused her of being. But her sharp tongue failed her.

He shook his head. "Exactly."

She watched him push through the men who had gathered. Dan urged the squad to the barracks, and one by one they turned and started down the path. Tears rolled down Billy Farrell's cheeks. Dan put an arm around his shoulders as they walked.

Chris bit down hard on the first knuckle of her left hand. She so badly wanted to hit something. Or someone. Who did he think he was? What right did he have to tear her down? She let her hand drop, felt the pain.

Paul staggered past her, his head slumped. Sweat and dirt matted his curly hair. He turned his haggard face to her, unshaven for a week.

"I'm too old for this." He sighed and made straight for his cot.

Chris followed him into the hooch, her jaw set. She stalked back and forth a few times, a pace not meant to stir creative juices. Finally, she bent and yanked off her boots and threw them into the far wall with enough force to shake loose dried mud, then tossed her blackened socks into the corner and shoved her feet into her flip-flops.

"Aren't you going to say anything?"

"Such as?" said Paul.

"Oh, I don't know," she replied, "I thought maybe you'd offer up one of your trademark smart-ass comments."

He smiled thinly and extended his hands. "All out."

"Good," she muttered and tore off her fatigue shirt.

"Do you want to talk about it?"

"No."

She had to leave. She had more barbs to hurl. She pushed through the door.

"Gather ye rosebuds while ye may, Christine," Paul called.

And there it was. Chris rolled her eyes as she broke into a run down the beaten path. The thin shoes flapped against the soles of her feet. He wouldn't have gone back to the barracks. He would want to be alone. Chris knew just where he would go.

***

The run from her hooch to the supply bunker on the far side of base seemed to take forever. She slowed when she saw the broad back rising from the corrugated steel roof, facing the jungle. Without hesitation she scooped up a rock and chucked it onto the metal. John jumped and covered his head as the rock skipped past him. Breathing heavily, he glared at her. She glared back.

"Get down here."

"I have nothing to say to you."

"You're a coward."

He eased down the eight-foot drop and confronted her, standing inches away, daring her to say it again.

"You're a coward. Yeah, sure, you're a real hero when it comes to battle, but you're a coward in every other sense."

"What the hell...?" He paused at the sound of approaching men, threw open the bunker door, and pushed her inside. "What the hell is that supposed to mean?"

Chris's eyes needed to adjust to the lower light. He stood so close she could feel him trembling.

"When's the last time you went after something you wanted? When's the last time you took a chance, John?"

John's face flushed a deep red. He turned away from her, hands gripping his head as he walked a few steps. Then he whirled to face her so suddenly and with such force that Chris flinched.

"Don't talk to me about what I want. You know nothing about me."

"You're right. I don't know anything about you. I can't get through all the goddamn walls you put up. But I'm sick of this runaround, so I'll make it easy for you. You answer one question and then we're through. Agreed?"

He regarded her warily. "Agreed."

The pain left her head, her muscles eased. It would all be over soon. "Do I mean anything to you?"

John's eyes left hers. His jaw muscles twitched. She saw the tension in his body. So now she knew.

Chris struggled against the tears springing to her eyes, the one reaction she would have given anything to avoid. "Fine," she said, and turned away.

He grabbed her left wrist, firmly but gently. She made no effort to resist as he tugged her toward him. His expression was inscrutable. Without warning he dipped his head down and kissed her. She froze, her mouth responding to his without direction from her. Then he broke the kiss and rested his forehead against hers.

"Yes. You mean something to me."

She pulled her wrist free from his grasp and wrapped her arms around his neck, bringing his head down to hers. He walked her backwards a few steps, trapping her between his body and the wall. She fought to get his shirt off, and once he relented her lips skimmed over his bare chest, tasting salty sweat and the Vietnam earth. He cupped her chin and kissed her deeply. Blindly, she pawed at the front of his pants, struggling to undo the buttons, then pushed his fatigues and shorts past his hips. As soon as her hands closed around him, she felt something change in his kiss. She pulled away.

"John?"

"It's just that..." He looked away from her, a hint of pink rising on his cheeks. "I've never really..."

Chris smiled and placed her hands on his chest. The tips of two fingers reached the hollow at the base of his throat. She felt the thunder of his heartbeat.

"Do you want to stop?"

"God, no." He grinned sheepishly. "But—"

She put a finger over his lips. "It's not complicated."

He studied her. "How are you still fully clothed?"

"You were distracted."

"Not anymore." He took his time, making skilled use of both hands and mouth. Finally, after he pulled off her last and skimpiest item of clothing, he held her at arm's length and let his eyes roam. "Are you sure you want this?" He swallowed. "Me?"

She stepped into his arms and kissed him hard. "Yes. Right now."

He grabbed the backs of her legs and lifted, settling her around his waist and bracing her against the wall. She bit her lip and forced herself to relax.

"Are you okay?" he whispered.

She responded by gently kicking his backside with one of her heels. He needed no further encouragement.

***

Chris collapsed against his chest, trying to catch her breath. John, half-seated, half-sprawled on a large metal case of ammunition, leaned against the wall and held her close. She was pleased to hear his matching pant and feel the heaviness of his arms around her.

"Those Iowa farm girls have no idea what they're missing," she murmured into his neck.

John laughed and kissed her forehead. "Now you're just pandering to your audience."

"No." She pulled back to look at him. "I didn't know it could be like this."

"Hot and sweaty and dirty in a supply bunker in the Mekong Delta?"

Chris smiled and felt an unexpected surge of emotion. She curled against his chest again, hiding her face before he could see the tears in her eyes.

His arms tightened around her and they enjoyed a moment of silence. "But it was hot and sweaty and dirty, right?"

"Very." She reached between them. "How are you...?"

"Hey, I've spent months fantasizing about you. It's going to take more than a couple of times."

"I'm not complaining. How much longer do we have?"

"About an hour before the debriefing. Or until someone looking for grenades busts through the door."

She could just make out the door, which he had jammed with a pipe from the tools section of the bunker, in the dimness.

"I'm confident you'll make the most of that hour."

***

Limply, she lay beneath him. Their sweat pooled together on her belly north of where they were still joined. One hand reached up to touch his cheek, pink from exertion. He captured her hand in his and kissed her fingertips.

"I could stay like this forever," he said.

Then he heaved himself off her, with some effort. He gazed down on her as he redressed. He slipped out of the bunker, but she knew he would wait nearby.

Eventually she rose and dressed. Outside, a light rain swept through the area, but dissipated within minutes. The shower cooled her skin, still warm and flushed. She found Paul napping on his cot with a camera resting on his chest. Chris eased it from his hand. He started.

"I'm sorry. I didn't mean to wake you."

He rubbed his face. "Where have you been?"

"Thinking."

He studied her with soft brown eyes bleary from exhaustion. "I don't believe you."

"Suit yourself." Chris dropped onto her own cot, hoping for a nap to kill what remained of the afternoon.

"You gathered your rosebuds."

"Think what you will." She turned away from him, closing her eyes.

But sleep never came.

***

Later that evening, the staff sergeant delivered a telegram while Chris and Paul debated which of Paul's photos might best fit with Chris's next story. Chris took the telegram from him with a fake smile, feeling a wave of apprehension pass over her. He clicked his heels and left the *American Century* reporters in solitude.

Even before she opened the envelope, she knew the telegram was for her and her alone. Paul busied himself with his equipment in an effort to give her privacy. Chris sat on her cot and with trembling hands unfolded the paper.

Her stomach dropped and her heart beat faster. She felt a humiliated flush rise on her cheeks. Chris had worked for Martin Willis for five years, but never had the editor-in-chief given her such brutal feedback. She sat still for several minutes, her mind as blank as the fresh sheet of paper in her typewriter.

"Are you all right?"

Chris turned to Paul, who watched her with concern, and offered him a tremulous smile. "Yeah, I'm fine."

Paul sat beside her on the cot. "Has Martin Willis's soul-crushing constructive criticism claimed another victim?"

"I think I prefer being harangued to within an inch of my life." Chris handed him the telegram.

He skimmed it. "What on earth prompted this?"

Chris stood and began a slow pace. "He's not saying anything that isn't true."

"This is awfully harsh."

"Paul."

"What?"

"I said Willis is right. My latest piece was vague and two-dimensional. If I were him, I wouldn't have printed it, either."

"I don't understand. You were on such a roll. What happened?"

"I don't know. I just can't...I just can't find the right words."

"Did you get too close?"

Chris smiled ruefully. "Maybe." *Or not close enough.*

"Still, Willis has to understand that other factors sometimes preclude a sterling piece of writing."

"I asked to come here. I won't use the war as an excuse for why I can't write a decent story."

Paul eyed her cautiously. "I'm sorry to keep asking this, but will you write about John?"

Chris hung her head and felt an intense pounding in her temples. "Forget whether I will or I won't. I don't think I *can*. Every time I sit at that typewriter, I freeze up or I get so angry I want to hit someone. I haven't written a printable sentence in weeks."

"Maybe stop trying so hard? Let it come?"

"I know how to write, Paul. It hasn't worked. If I don't force myself to write something, I'll have nothing."

"Then force yourself. You must continue to produce. I've known Martin Willis for a long time and I can tell you that he won't hesitate to send someone who will get the job done."

Chris nodded and resumed her slow, deliberate pace from field table to door. Paul read the telegram once more and sighed.

"I'm finally starting to understand writers. No wonder you all despise editorial input."

"I despise criticism, constructive or otherwise, because I have an ego the size of Montana. That said, even I can admit when I submit crap. Martin Willis is a bastard, but in this case he's right. I didn't get the job done."

"Fine. I'll stipulate to forced, bland writing if that's your assessment. But this isn't a message to kick-start your literary engine. This is mean. This is cold. Why?"

Tight-lipped, Chris shrugged. "Don't know."

"I'm here to help however I can."

Chris stopped pacing and kissed him on the cheek. "Thank you. It'll be fine. Everything's under control."

"Famous last words."

Paul went back to his photos, Chris to the field table. She forced herself to read the telegram once more, this time with analytical detachment. Her eyes were drawn to one sentence, one sentence that worried her more than the rest: *The only story I want is the story you're trying to hide.*

***

First Squad took dinner in the mess after they showered and absorbed Travis's debriefing on the ambush. Best of all, Gianelli had cleared them for a week of R&R in Saigon. They would depart the following morning, released into the wild of Saigon's seedy back alleys and famed red-light district for a week of drunken debauchery, a week of living outside the war.

The mess served stew consisting of chewy chunks of beef and semi-cooked potatoes drowned in salty gravy, with peas and carrots on the side. The men ate greedily, taking little time to savor their first hot meal in days.

Murphy opened his hip flask and downed Jameson Irish whiskey by the mouthful. "What a day, boys, what a day. Gotta say, we sure know how to fuck the place up. About time we had a win."

"Old Man's been playing it safe," Oscar boomed. "Glad he and LT found their 'nads and let us do our thing."

"What was the point?" John asked.

"What do you mean, what was the point? We wasted them fuckers," Murphy said and pounded the table for emphasis.

"No, tell me, what did we gain from today? We killed for the sake of killing. We took the hill and then we abandoned it. At best it's a short-lived tactical victory."

"Good for morale," Oscar said with a straight face. "We ain't ever going to win this thing unless we hit 'em where it hurts."

"Women and children?" Ben Kearney said acerbically.

"If it ain't us, it'll be ARVN, so what's your point?" Murphy said.

"Just that it doesn't take much of a man to waste a woman."

"Fuck you, Doc. I didn't see you leading the charge."

"I was busy collecting the intestines of the toddler you blew up with a Claymore."

Murphy's face turned the mottled red of Irish anger. His light eyes bore holes into the medic. But Kearney refused to avert his gaze and the squad saw the quiet rage of a young man who had the worst job in the world. John put down his fork and swallowed the stew with difficulty. The mine had ripped through the child, nearly cutting him in half.

"Collateral damage," Darwin said with a shrug.

"If there's ever a time you're bleeding out and screaming for your mommy, you had better hope I don't remember you said that."

"We have to know where to draw the line. Like shooting bound and helpless prisoners," said Dan.

"Get over it, Danny. They were VC. You wouldn't have bound them if you didn't think they were dangerous."

"That's not the point, Murph. And besides, don't you think they were more useful alive than dead?"

Murphy laughed caustically. "Listen to yourself. What do you think would have happened to them once we got them back here? Jenkins or ARVN would have gotten their hands on them, and what do you think they would have done with them? Politely asked them to provide intel on troop locations and weapons caches? Fuck no. Jenkins would have beat the living shit out of them until he got what he wanted, then he'd keep beating them until he got bored. And have you seen what ARVN does to VC prisoners? They're doing the same to them as the NVA do to our guys in the POW camps, so don't give me shit about my supposed cruelty when all I did was shoot them. It was a waste of a bullet, but a better fate than they could have had."

"I just thought we were better than that."

"Not anymore."

***

"We killed so many people today." Gianelli shook his head and looked into his glass of warm scotch, which he had not touched since pouring it two minutes before Maria arrived at his hooch. "I should have seen the civilians. I should have stopped it."

"Sam." Maria reached for him, but he pulled away and stood facing the opposite wall.

"I lead trigger-happy kids into questionable operations, and worst of all, I can't seem to control anything they do. I hope there's a special place in hell for people like me."

"We managed to save a lot of the Vietnamese."

"Don't bullshit me, Maria. I saw their injuries. They will never be whole again."

She didn't respond. She and Jacobson had spent upwards of twelve straight hours in surgery putting people back together piece by piece.

He picked up the glass of scotch and moved to take a drink, but the whiff of alcohol turned his stomach. He had already vomited once upon returning to base, and he didn't want a repeat performance.

"I hate it," he said. "I hate everything about this war. The jungles, the paddies, the strategy, the tactics, the generals, the politicians, everything."

"She's not going after you."

Gianelli's stomach lurched again at the allusion to the reporter. Too often, he found himself forgetting Chris McKenna's *raison d'être*, and the death of Vietnamese civilians in the right hands, in her hands, could become newsworthy in an instant. He sat heavily on the edge of his bed. His head dropped into his hands and he massaged his temples, feeling his pulse beneath his fingertips.

It was not the printed word that brought him pain. The pain was John Rawlins apologizing for not seeing the civilians that hadn't been with the enemy the night before; it was his medic treating the injured regardless of color or creed; it was the woman he loved saving the lives of those he hurt.

"She might."

"She won't."

"Well, maybe she should. God knows I deserve it."

"She gets it."

"Maybe," Gianelli said. He knew Maria had been right; Chris would tell a story he didn't like. But it was a story that needed to be told.

She was quiet, looking down at her hands. Three years ago yesterday, he thought to himself.

"I wish I had been here to hold you," he said.

Maria looked at him with glassy eyes. She tried to smile. "It's supposed to get easier with time."

"It will. Someday it will."

"I know what it's like to be ashamed, Sam. Even though those people had nothing to do with my brother's death, part of me wanted to see someone else's family suffer that same loss. They took from me, so I wanted to take from them. When they brought in one of the kids I just stood there staring stupidly at the little body on the gurney, hoping someone else would save his life and spare me the choice."

"But you did choose. You made the right choice."

"It never should have come down to a choice. I can't remember the last time I made a conscious decision to save a life. I act because that's what I'm supposed to do."

"And tomorrow you'll act again."

"I know," she said with a sigh. "Tomorrow just seems like a long way off."

"Your brother would be proud of you." He touched the hand closest to him, a hand that had acted despite the mind's paralysis.

She smiled tremulously and brought his hand to her cheek. The backs of his fingers rested on soft, faintly pink skin.

"Hold me now?"

Gianelli wrapped her in his arms. "For as long as you'll let me."

10

— ◆ —

J ack Travis sloshed through the mud puddles dotting the paths. The skies
had cleared overnight, and the day had dawned hot and humid. He tapped
his Louisville Slugger against one shoulder and wiped the sweat from his brow
with a burly forearm as he rounded the corner.

Chris McKenna paced outside her hooch, cigarette in hand, oblivious to
the world around her. Travis felt an unexpected surge of protectiveness toward
her, the woman who had turned his platoon upside down. Travis so clearly
remembered the first time he laid eyes on Chris, when she was a bloodied mess
surrounded by gaping soldiers. After four years in Vietnam, the master sergeant
thought he was impervious to surprises, but the young journalist had been a
jolt. Far from resenting her or underestimating her, as was the army way, he was
intrigued by her cavalier attitude toward risk, her dedication to her craft.

She nodded toward the bat. "A new twist on corporal punishment?"

"Tempting. Bet it'd get me sent home, right?"

"Sure, straight to Leavenworth. Paul isn't here, if that's who you're looking
for. Went for a shower."

"I'm here to see you."

"Oh?"

As she spoke, she retrieved a pack of Marlboros from her pants pocket, shook
out a cigarette, and touched the end to the glowing tip of the one between her
lips. Then she dropped the stub and crushed it with her boot.

"That ain't good for you, kid."

"This from the man who's volunteered for every war since the turn of the century." She laughed incredulously and took a long drag.

He cocked his head to the side. He knew nothing about the carnivorous world of print journalism, could not identify with her private gender war, and was the last man who should ever give advice to a woman on her love affairs. Although, he reasoned as he dwelled on that last point, he would be more than happy to smack some sense into John Rawlins. Chris and John had plotted the most roundabout collision course Travis had ever seen, but he supposed some discretion was called for, given the circumstances.

The Louisville Slugger moved from his right shoulder to his left shoulder, the grip changing to match the shift.

"Switch hitter?"

The comment startled the master sergeant.

"Catcher, right?" Her eyes roamed over his powerful frame, analyzing. "Definitely a catcher. The brains behind the operation. Not about to take shit from some prima donna pitcher or a know-it-all lieutenant."

"Long time ago," he mumbled.

"Who signed you?"

"It was a long time ago," he repeated.

She took another drag, threw her head back, and expelled the stream of smoke. When she looked at him, her eyes crinkled in amusement. She held the pack of cigarettes toward him.

Travis accepted the offering and flipped open his Zippo. "You don't miss much, do you?"

She shrugged. "We are not the enigmas we pretend to be."

Travis smirked. "The platoon's headed to the rear for a week."

"Good. They need a break."

"You're going with them."

"Excuse me?"

"I don't care how you get there, but I want you in Saigon by evening."

169

"I have a thousand things to do right here. I'll use the time to finish my own work. Can't bring a typewriter into the jungle, after all."

"I'm not about to take shit from a journo, either. For the last couple of months you've lived through the same hell as the guys. You need a break. Take a week off."

"I don't need a break. I've never felt better."

"Is that why you're out here pacing and chain-smoking and looking like you haven't slept in a year? The rest will do you good."

"I'll think about it."

"By evening. Or I'll drag you to Saigon myself."

"Yeah, yeah."

"Only carrying out orders, kiddo. Take it up with Gianelli if you're pissed." He turned to walk away, then paused and looked back at her. "Hey McKenna, just be smart. Love and war are a tough mix."

Chris's unnerved expression told him all he needed to know. She and John had collided.

***

It took a while for their breathing to return to normal. Chris thought she might have killed him. He lay sprawled beside her, on his back, relaxed and drowsy, one hand lazily caressing her inner thigh.

The air conditioner kicked on, a whining hum, pumping cool air into the room, which had grown unbearably hot yet again. Finally, John retrieved the pillows from the floor, and they lay facing each other, close together. He stroked her back, running his fingers from the nape of her neck to her tailbone. She rubbed his upturned hip, following the contours of defined muscles.

"I'm sorry about yesterday," he said.

"It's all right. I often drive people to uncontrollable rage."

John rolled onto his back and stared at the ceiling. "I wasn't mad at you."

"I saw you, John. You did everything you could to protect those people."

"I should have stopped it. I should have known there would be civilians. There always are."

"Hey, look at me," she said, tilting his face to hers with a touch of a hand to his jaw. "Please don't do this to yourself."

John turned back toward her and trailed a finger down her left arm, from her shoulder to her hand. He examined the unadorned fingers, running his thumb over the delicate bones.

"It was never real, Edward and me."

"So it's not my fault?"

Chris smiled and intertwined her fingers with his. "I dumped him by telegram the morning after my first patrol."

"That's cold." But his eyes shone with laughter.

"It's more than he deserves."

"I'm a little concerned about your taste in men."

She kissed him. "Funny, me too."

He smiled in good humor and nuzzled her throat. She breathed in his scent, clean and fresh. Cleanliness was godliness, it was said, and she had made sure of it during a very long shower. As she rubbed his back and shoulders, she felt him relax. It wasn't long before his hands and mouth went exploring and she found herself at his mercy, only dimly aware of anything beyond his touch.

Then his weight shifted and his body separated from hers. He positioned himself over her, fists digging into the mattress on either side of her head.

"Do you think I could take you on a date sometime?"

"I was hoping you'd ask."

"Tomorrow?"

"Sure, but you might have to drag me out of your bed. Kicking and screaming."

John trailed a line of kisses down the center of her body until he ran out of real estate. He settled himself between her legs, his shoulders nudging her thighs apart. Chris felt his warm breath and tensed in anticipation.

"Well, as long as you're screaming."

***

Anne Novak and Arthur Kittles had come to a mutually beneficial understanding: the captain would acquire whatever information and access she desired, and the *Washington Dispatch* reporter would reciprocate by dropping his name with a few well-placed friends in the upper echelons of the United States government who might facilitate a career in politics in his post-army life. Plus, she had promised to quote a "high-ranking military officer" in her next article in honor of his willingness to share sensitive information on army plans for the Mekong Delta. For days Captain Kittles strutted about FOB Jane with his chest puffed and his nose thumbed at the mere mortals around him, giddy that he was now a "high-ranking military officer."

Anne came to his office one sweltering morning, a welcome diversion from reading Gianelli's dry after-action report on the ambushed convoy. She informed him that her first body of work had gone over the wires to Washington and suggested he special-order a bundle of next week's issue so as not to miss his newly acquired fame. The sarcasm in her voice was unapparent to Kittles, who thought it a smashing idea. He made a mental note to send one of his aides to Saigon to do just that. And to procure another humidor of *Cubanos*. He and Simpson and Wheaton hadn't had a good smoke in a while. Between the cigars and the booze and the—

"Now I need you to get me a grunt."

Kittles blinked. "Pardon?"

"I want a grunt."

"Good Lord, why?" he blurted out. "Not that it's any of my business," he continued hurriedly, feeling his collar constrict around his neck. "I'm sure we can find a discreet way to attend to your needs."

"For fuck's sake, I need an interview, not a screw."

Kittles felt his knees wobble in relief, but he soon regained a businesslike demeanor. "Not a problem," he said, rubbing his hands together. "Any particular qualities you seek?"

"Young, white, handsome, heroic. The usual."

The captain considered her request. Young and white, he could do. They were all young, and even some white kids, inexplicably, had failed to escape the draft. If he tried hard enough, he might even be able to scrounge up a handsome face, maybe one who embraced the virtues of regular grooming and hygiene. Would it kill these bums to get a haircut once in a while? This was the United States Army, not some civil rights sit-in. Christ, half his men looked like bearded Joan Baezes or Janis Joplins, those hippie freaks who—

"Well?"

"It will be a challenge, but I will find you a young, white, handsome, heroic grunt."

"As a matter of fact," Anne said, examining her fingernails, "I have one in mind."

"You do?" Kittles was skeptical not only that she actually knew a grunt, but that a young, white, handsome, heroic grunt existed.

"A John Rawlins. He's one of yours."

"He is? I don't recognize the name."

"He's assigned to your company, Second Platoon, I believe. Didn't you read McKenna's story? He saved all those refugees and aid workers."

Kittles stifled a groan, wondering how Gianelli and his men always managed to capture the limelight. The captain rejected the assertion that he would benefit from reflected glory; he wanted the glory all for himself. It galled Kittles to lose the attention of a prominent reporter like Anne to a spiteful lieutenant and an insignificant foot soldier.

Anne snapped her fingers in his face. "My interview?"

"Consider it done."

***

"All I ever wanted to be was a journalist. I wanted to journey to far-flung lands, meet people who made history, report the stories people would remember. Your dream comes true, and then all of a sudden you have to do what you dreamed you could do. I actually have to write the words people will remember. It was so much easier before I had to put pen to paper," Chris said.

"You've done that already. What's stopping you from doing it again?" John asked.

"I don't know. I have so much to say, but it's just not coming out right."

"Writer's block?"

"Everyone thinks that writing is all about finding the right words. But it's more than that. So much more than that," she said quietly.

"What's missing?"

Chris forced a smile. She knew what she was missing. She felt the emptiness every time she sat down at her typewriter. But this was not anything she could express to the man across from her, in whose calloused yet gentle hands her own rested. Perhaps on some distant intellectual plane he would understand; but to say the words aloud would bring a humiliated flush to her face, and despite her best intentions an anger borne of the deepest frustration she had ever experienced would surge to the surface of her consciousness and she would say something to ruin the moment.

So she dodged. "Good question. If I knew the answer, I doubt we'd be having this conversation."

His eyes narrowed, but he chose not to press the issue. "What does your editor say?"

"The usual chauvinistic, piggish things men say when women annoy them." The corners of John's mouth turned up. Yes, Chris thought bitterly, at least she could be amusing. "I'm sure he's poised to send in the cavalry to drag me out."

"Prove him wrong."

Perhaps at that moment Chris understood the biggest difference between herself and John Rawlins. One word popped into her mind: colors. He saw in black and white, whereas she saw every color of the spectrum, including gray. Something needed to be done, so he did it. He would not be able to wrap his mind around the reasons why things were not so simple for her.

She laughed sardonically. "Martin Willis is never wrong,"

"Are you?"

"I won't admit to fallibility on the first date."

For a time, both were silent. Cars honked along the street near the café, chickens squawked and fluttered in their stacked cages on the backs of bicycle-drawn rickshaws and donkey carts, and impatient motorcyclists wove through traffic. The smell of sizzling meats and vegetables mingled with car exhaust and rotting garbage in the heat. John stroked the tops of Chris's hands with his thumbs.

"My brother wants to be just like you," he said. "Wants to write for a major newsmagazine, travel the world, chase war."

"This scares you?"

"I want him to do what makes him happy, but of course it scares me. You think this is what I want for him? It's hard to explain to an idealistic seventeen-year-old kid that the nature of war is not glamorous or glorious. I don't know how to tell him that reality shatters the illusions we create for ourselves, and the bigger and grander the illusion, the more it hurts to face the truth." John paused, his jaws muscles working. "You're living it. What would you tell him? Is all this worth it?"

She replied without hesitation. "Yes. I wouldn't change a thing." She felt John's hands tighten around hers and she struggled to find the words to explain. "Look, maybe it's silly, but coming here and writing about this war is my contribution, however small. I know everyone thinks I'm crazy, but I love what I do. I hope your brother finds that same happiness, despite what he might see along the way."

John's gaze drifted to the hazy afternoon sky. Chris looked at their joined hands, hers small and delicate, his large and rough. An unlikely pair. A city girl and a farm boy. A journalist and a soldier.

"I suppose that isn't what you wanted to hear."

He looked back at her and smiled. "I was just thinking it's too bad no one's here to write about you. You'd make a much better story than the rest of us."

"Doubtful."

He took in a sharp gulp of air, as if he had forgotten to breathe. Chris had anticipated his next words long before he said them. At least she hadn't gotten her hopes up.

"This doesn't change anything," he said in a low voice, an honest voice. "I still don't want to be a story."

"I didn't expect it to change anything. That's not why this happened. Not at all."

"I know."

Chris doubted he was being entirely truthful. If she were sitting in his place, she too would question the sincerity of her words, considering her past disregard of his wishes. But the past did not always predict the future, she reminded herself.

The men in her past were always used for a specific purpose—usually to advance her career—and were discarded as soon as possible after the initial coupling. She consoled herself with the knowledge that all of her most recent conquests had used her just as she used them.

John was nothing like the scum she normally bedded. The one thing he could gain from her was the one thing he didn't want. He seemed to want her, nothing more. And, perhaps more importantly, nothing less. For Chris, who was accustomed to walking away before the fallout, without the slightest regard for the possibility of emotional attachment, this was disconcerting.

"A penny for your thoughts," he said.

"Cost you at least a buck."

"On a private's salary?"

John tossed a wad of Vietnamese dong on the table for their meal and pulled her up. They walked hand-in-hand through the streets of Saigon, stopping to browse the vendors' stalls for deals on black-market items. Chris bought several bottles of Coca-Cola and, under John's disapproving gaze, a few packs of Marlboros. If he ever had to churn out a Pulitzer Prize-worthy series on the Vietnam War, he would understand why she smoked. She was just thrilled to find an American brand. She had heart palpitations every time she lit up those Eastern European butts that Oscar and Steve smoked.

"Do you need to work this afternoon?"

"I should. Why?"

John shot her a sly look. She sighed in mock exasperation.

"I guess work can wait."

***

But work could not wait. The handwritten pages accumulated in the bottom of her rucksack, under dirty clothes and spare notebooks. She wrote as if her life depended on it. Each word came from deep within, honest words, passionate words that felt no trepidation over a certain soldier's reaction.

But she saw trepidation beneath his smile, felt his worried gaze as he watched her write stretched out beside him on the bed, knew he wondered how he fit into her Vietnam story. And he was there, because no Vietnam story would be complete without him.

As the week passed, they both narrowed and widened the gulf between them, the truth lost somewhere in the blackness of the fears they would not—could not—confront, because to confront those fears would make them real.

Chris took Paul up to the roof of the hotel toward the end of the week, surprising him with lunch laid out on a small wrought-iron table, a sad reminder of a civilized past. Paul chatted happily about long phone conversations with his wife, and Chris noted with relief that the time away from the front lines had done him good, although he still had dark circles under his eyes and she thought some extra gray shooting through his hair. All that mattered was that he smiled readily as he regaled her with stories of yesterday's photography expedition to the red-light district.

"It's wild, like something out of a bad movie. You know that stereotype of Vietnamese prostitutes? The miniskirts, the high heels, the excessive makeup, the pidgin English? It's all true."

"Must be in the official hooker handbook," Chris replied, stabbing stir-fried vegetables with her chopsticks.

Paul watched the violence against the vegetables with concern, wincing as she speared a peapod. "Is everything all right?"

Chris set aside the chopsticks. "I need a second opinion." Paul was the only non-writer she had ever trusted to read pre-published works. She handed him a sheaf of papers. "Please be honest."

He leaned back and began to read. Chris stared at the overcast sky, her mind empty. Ten minutes later, he spoke.

"You just saved your career. Hell, I think you catapulted it into orbit. I love it."

She offered a drained smile. "Thanks."

"Let's go send it right now."

"I'll take care of it later. I want to tweak it a bit."

"I wouldn't change a thing, but I'm just a photographer. Speaking of photos, I think I know exactly which ones to use." He reached under his chair and pulled forth a leather portfolio of newly developed prints. "How about these?"

Chris was still staring at the gathering storm clouds above the city, oblivious to his outstretched hand.

"Chris?"

"I thought they would be just names on the page."

Paul smiled. "If you don't care, how will anyone else? What did John say?"

"John hasn't seen it."

"You should show him. It's a beautiful piece. I can't imagine he'd object to it."

Chris sighed. She could imagine John objecting to it in strong language. "He still doesn't want to be a story. He's not going to change his mind. Look, John and I don't make a lot of sense right now."

"No new relationship ever makes a lot of sense."

"'Relationship' is a charitable term for what we have going. We excel at arguing and sex, not honest communication. I can't seem to convince him that I'm with him for reasons unrelated to my career. Thus we find ourselves at a bit of an impasse."

"He's in a bad spot. He's just not thinking clearly."

Chris attacked her lunch with renewed vigor, attempting and failing to scoop rice with the chopsticks. "Damn it, why can't these people use forks?" She slumped in her chair.

"Are you in love with him?"

Chris spoke to the ground. "A week ago I couldn't stand him. It's a little presumptuous to throw love into the mix."

"I'll overlook the fact that you didn't actually answer my question and toss an even harder one your way. If it comes down to John's wishes or your career, are you prepared to choose?"

This time Chris looked at her photographer. "It's not going to come to that. There's got to be some suitable compromise for everyone."

"Do you want me to talk to him?"

"Absolutely not."

"But—"

"Promise me, Paul. Promise me you will say nothing to John."

Paul held up his hands, a vain attempt at protection from her penetrating stare. "I promise, I promise."

Chris held his eyes for a few more seconds to let her point sink in. She rested her elbows on her knees and dropped her head into her hands. Her hair fell forward and obscured her face. "What a disaster. It was never supposed to be like this."

She hated to admit it, but she saw how Paul was right: she might very well have to choose between John and her career. The realization made her nauseous.

"What are you so scared of?"

Chris picked up her head and smiled wanly. It all seemed so very clear. "That everyone will see right through me."

***

John awoke to the sound of Chris's whimpers, his heart beating fast. He reached a hand toward her and felt perspiration on her forehead, tears on her cheeks. In the throes of a nightmare, Chris had curled up in a tight ball, knees to her chest, fists clenched near her head.

John scooted close and wrapped his arms around her. Her whimpers gave way to a sigh and she relaxed, stretching her body against his. John kissed the top of her head and whispered soothing words, words to drive away the war. Still sleeping, she buried her face in his chest.

John lay for a long time listening to her even breathing, hoping that the sights and sounds tormenting her in her dreams would not return. He held her until she awoke in the morning, wrapped in his arms with her head nestled in the hollow of his shoulder, her warm breath condensing on his chest, her legs intertwined with his. As her eyes adjusted to the light, he saw in them an expression he couldn't name, something deep, something heartfelt, as if the storm in her dreams had left clarity in its wake. The purity of the moment made something inside John ache. He kissed her softly. The moment lingered.

11

— • —

N othing had changed during First Squad's R&R. It was still hot; it was still humid; the base still reeked of gunpowder, sweat, and human excrement; and their overall mission was still strategically and tactically questionable. The summer dragged on.

News of the sexual liaison between Chris McKenna and some grunt they called "Cowboy" spread as rapidly as herpes through the red-light district. Anne Novak learned of it the morning of the squad's return to FOB Jane, but without hard evidence she was skeptical of its veracity. What was the point of scoring with a grunt?

Nonetheless, the information was intriguing, if only to torture George Wheaton, who lusted after Chris in a manner Anne thought worthy of a restraining order. As the news reached even the most oblivious officers and infantrymen, the resulting firestorm of hypocritical outrage and jealousy was impressive in scope and intensity. Anne decided she would be derelict in her duty as a loyal *Washington Dispatch* reporter if she didn't add to Chris's misery.

She stationed herself outside Captain Kittles's hooch and pounded on the door until he opened it, looking confused and agitated in the sunlight.

"Have you heard?" she asked, leaning against the doorjamb.

"Anne, good morning. Heard what?" Kittles rubbed the sleep from his eyes and blinked rapidly.

"Oh, nothing really, just that McKenna slept with a grunt in one of your platoons."

Kittles's mouth fell open. "A grunt? Why would she...? Do you happen to know which platoon?"

She shrugged. "Second, I think."

The captain turned the color of eggplant. Anne raised her eyebrows in mild concern, unable to conceal a smirk. Kittles would be sure to fan the flames of the inferno, and Anne could swoop in and, like an eagle dive-bombing a nest of prairie dogs, snatch the John Rawlins story while Chris was preoccupied defending her sullied reputation. Anne was surprised by Chris's lax work ethic, her reticence to dig deeper; at best, she had left the story half-told.

"Unacceptable," he sputtered. "Unacceptable. Has Gianelli no sense of propriety? Has he no sense of discipline?"

Anne rolled her eyes. "It's just sex."

A smile snaked its way across Kittles's lips. "Yes...just sex."

***

Gianelli despised Kittles's décor. The captain appeared to derive his interior design inspiration from what could be described as a *Jungle Book* massacre. Furs hung from each wall, most impressively the enormous pellet of a Bengal tiger, and two large, curved tusks of an African elephant were prominently displayed on either side of the door. To top off the barbarism, Kittles used the gray horn of a rhinoceros as a paperweight.

Gianelli tried not to twitch like a heroin addict coming off a high while Kittles huffed about the hooch and lectured him. His mind raced, unable to focus on the diatribe. He hadn't slept in quite some time for a multitude of reasons, in no particular order: the heat, painful feet, an overwrought nurse, and the inescapable nightmares. Despite a brief reprieve from operational activity, Gianelli was as tired and disgruntled as ever.

"Are we in the habit of allowing enlisted men to screw journalists?"

Gianelli's head snapped up. "What?"

"You heard me. Goddamn it, Lieutenant, you and your men are out of control."

"Wait, what?" said Gianelli, holding up a hand, still stuck on the accusation that a man in his platoon had bedded one of FOB Jane's two female correspondents. He had shut himself off from human contact with anyone not named Maria Nichols this past week, and as a result was woefully disconnected from the rumor mill. Nonetheless, it was about damn time, he thought to himself.

"I asked if you were in the habit of permitting enlisted men to engage in sexual relations with journalists. This is why women should not be allowed within a continent of a combat zone," Kittles said, opening his collar and fanning his face with a magazine.

"Do you know the soldier's name?"

"Some dumb farm boy. I want you to end it *now*." Kittles pointed a meaty finger at Gianelli. "If this happens again, you and your men will be on patrol until Christmas. Clear?"

"Yes, sir."

"By the way, Anne Novak has requested an interview with one of your men, a John Rawlins, I believe," Kittles said. "See to it that he cooperates."

"I'll do my best," Gianelli replied with a straight face.

***

Sam Gianelli burst into Chris McKenna's hooch and slammed the rickety door behind him. Chris whirled to face the intruder and flung a stream of water from her canteen across the room, splattering one side wall.

"Holy shit."

Gianelli walked to within a foot of her. "What are your intentions here?"

"Haven't you heard of knocking?"

"Answer the question."

184

Chris's tone was measured. "My intentions are what they've always been: to complete my assignment and return home. What the hell is this about?"

"Are you playing John?"

Her eyes widened. "How is my relationship with John any of your business?"

"I'm his commanding officer—how is it *not* my business? And now I have to do damage control because you two couldn't keep your clothes on. So please, enlighten me as to why I should believe you."

Chris placed the canteen on the field table beside the typewriter. She waited a beat before speaking.

"My priorities haven't changed. It's still about the story."

Gianelli sniffed. "My men would not be happy to learn they hold your attention only because you think they'll sell your magazine and advance your career. For whatever reason, they've grown rather fond of you."

"You've said it yourself, I'm just a distraction. I could leave tomorrow and in a few days they'd forget all about me."

"And John? Would John forget all about you? A wild week in Saigon with a beautiful woman?" Gianelli smirked.

Chris shook her head and fiddled with the canteen. "John's a big boy. He can take care of himself."

"Yes, he can. But let's not pretend he stands a chance against you."

"I'm not playing him."

Gianelli took in everything, her expression, her body language, and the tone of her voice. Seconds later, he stormed out.

***

The end of June went as quickly as it came and the American war machine rumbled onward. Despite the official statements from MACV proclaiming progress against the North and the Viet Cong and Nixon's June 8 speech promising a withdrawal of twenty-five thousand American troops, the men in the field knew the war was no closer to conclusion than a year ago, or four years ago, or six years ago. Nixon had not started the war, but he would not accept the North Vietnamese and National Liberation Front's terms for ending it, and so more American servicemen would die in the highlands and jungles and paddies.

Colonel Brooks entered the briefing room and faced his assembled officer corps. "I need to brief General Franklin in thirty minutes. Major?"

Gardner stepped forward. "My intel units report movements of VC cadres concentrated in the villages surrounding Bac Lieu, Phuoc Long, and Phu Loc. Charlie's rebuilt since their Tet losses. We blow their tunnels and ambush their supply lines, but they bounce back every time. They have no shortage of new recruits. Seems like everyone in the Delta is against us, no matter what crap MACV feeds to the press. We're outnumbered four to one, easy."

"And that's where our boys come in," Brooks said. "ARVN is stretched thin in the cities; they need us to pick up the slack in the rural areas. More ops, more kills. Shift the balance of power. I'm under no illusions that we'll recapture the moral imperative, but we have to help the government retake control and make them see we're a better choice than Charlie."

Lieutenant Colonel Simpson grunted. "Last thing we need is more bad press."

"Which begs the question, what do you think Miss McKenna's next story will cover? The slaughter of innocent Vietnamese civilians by undisciplined, trigger-happy American soldiers from the Seventy-Fifth Brigade?" Captain Kittles asked rancorously, flushed and sweating in the crowded room.

Gianelli met the captain's glare and spoke through clenched teeth. "My orders were to decimate any supply convoys. Unfortunately, civilians used by the Viet Cong as human shields were caught in the crossfire. Miss McKenna is aware of the trying circumstances under which the tragic deaths occurred."

"She tags along on every single patrol, which means she witnesses every single incident we would prefer the press *not* witness, and somehow she has so deeply embedded herself into your platoon that to remove her might provoke a mutiny among your men. This is going to bite us in the ass," Kittles snapped.

Gianelli directed his response toward the colonel. "Sir, based on your orders, I've accommodated Miss McKenna's requests to accompany my platoon on patrols. Captain Kittles himself has taken her into the field."

"At least I haven't ceded my authority to a woman!"

Gianelli managed to stifle his immediate reaction, which was to insult a higher-ranking officer in profane and sexually explicit terms. The rest of the officers shifted uncomfortably. Colonel Brooks feigned disinterest, but Gianelli took note of his coiled posture at the head of the table and wondered how Brooks's undying loyalty to the army would impact this fight. If forced to cast someone aside for the greater good, who would it be? Gianelli, Kittles, or Chris McKenna?

Simpson continued for Kittles, trying a more diplomatic approach. "We wonder if your body counts would be higher if you were not worried about offending the fragile sensibilities of a woman."

"Fragile? You think she's fragile?" Gianelli blurted out before he could catch himself.

"This is an untenable situation," Simpson said. "We're running a war here, and I do not appreciate being the launch pad to Miss McKenna's celebrity."

"She's risked her life to save civilians. She's treated my men on the battlefield under intense fire. My men. American soldiers. You didn't see that in *American Century*, did you?"

"This is an interesting turn of events. From what I gather, when she first arrived you were dead-set against her running with your platoon. What's changed?" Simpson asked.

Gianelli shrugged. "She's done nothing to warrant this kind of talk."

Kittles pounced. "Oh, really? As if fraternizing with enlisted men was not enough to warrant this kind of talk?"

Simpson raised his eyebrows. "Lieutenant? Should we allow our boys to sleep with press?"

The fidgeting stopped. All eyes watched Gianelli, who mentally berated himself for not seeing the ambush in time to head it off. Brooks visibly tensed, but remained silent.

"I wasn't aware there was a specific regulation prohibiting it." Gianelli stared straight at Simpson.

"This sets a dangerous precedent."

"I disagree. This is an isolated incident, and a private matter. As for her reporting, I trust Chris McKenna to—"

"You *trust* her?"

"I trust her to tell the truth," said Sam Gianelli.

A thick silence descended on the briefing room. The officers, Gianelli's peers and his superiors, stared at him as if awaiting a punch line. Then Kittles laughed airily.

"Trust? How charming. Whom else do you trust? The Viet Cong? The North? How about your men, Lieutenant? Do you trust your men? Do you trust them not to pillage and rape and murder?" Kittles dropped his voice. "Don't look now, but some of your men are animals and Miss McKenna, for all her superior talk on truth and devotion to the cause, is just another glory-seeker who will burn us all in the end."

"That's enough," Brooks said.

"Colonel, I think this bears further scrutiny," said Simpson. "The role of the press is a worrisome issue theater-wide, and Miss McKenna's role in particular has become a major distraction."

"We're losing this war and it has nothing to do with Chris McKenna or any other reporter. Absolutely nothing. As long as Sam is comfortable with her in the field, she's allowed to be there. That's final."

The men murmured affirmative understandings. Gianelli and Kittles continued to glare at each other. It was a story that needed to be told, Gianelli reminded himself, a story that needed to be told.

***

As John pulled on a clean T-shirt after a shower, he heard his name spoken and turned to see Gianelli standing near his footlocker. "What's up, LT?"

"Need you to do me a favor."

"Sure."

Gianelli shifted from one foot to the other. He put his hands on his hips. Then he scratched his beard stubble, grimacing. John raised his eyebrows.

"Shit," Gianelli muttered to himself. "Listen, Anne Novak convinced Kittles that she needs to interview you for a story. I know you don't much like talking to reporters, and under the circumstances it'll be tough..."

John shrugged. "No problem."

"You sure? I know Chris won't be too happy, but I'll smooth it over with her. You're just following orders."

"It's no big deal."

"Chris is going to be furious."

"Probably. But I'd prefer if you didn't mention it to her."

"I won't inquire as to why you're so amenable to this arrangement, but if you fuck this up..."

John stiffened. "Fuck what up, LT?"

"You know exactly what. Make nice with Novak for an hour and then you're done."

"Anything else?"

"That's it. Good luck."

***

John had volunteered to do the interview as soon as possible, mostly to get it over with. The *Washington Dispatch* crew collected him late that afternoon and escorted him to the open-air tent that the much hated, much loved villain of Washington reporting had commandeered for use as her personal newsroom. The photographers treated him like a specimen in a Petri dish, blinding him with flashbulbs as they captured his every move. One photographer urged him to look his way, but John ignored him, preferring instead to make this process as hard as possible for those tasked to make him a story. The more reticent he appeared, the better his chances to avoid being splashed across the pages of a major American newsmagazine for the third time.

John had spent much of the day pondering why he had so readily agreed to the interview. He thought Chris's fears over Anne's motives were overblown, and he had no intention of allowing their evolving relationship to dictate his choices. Perhaps there was also an element of revenge for one woman's unyielding devotion to her job, but John didn't like to think he would ever be so base as to seek payback for a couple of well-intentioned magazine articles. With any luck, Anne would abandon her interest in John after the interview and Chris would never find out he had spoken with her chief competitor.

It was an inherently flawed plan, he would realize later, as it failed to account for the unpredictability of the aforementioned women, both headstrong and striking in their tenacity to outdo each other. At the time, though, the plan was logical and John had every intention of manipulating all sides to his advantage.

Cool and confident, John entered the tent and greeted Anne Novak politely. Lounging on a spare cot like a modern-day Cleopatra, she eyed him with mild curiosity. With his hands clasped behind his back, looking every inch the wholesome young soldier, John waited for Anne to finish flipping through her magazine, a recent issue of *American Century*.

"Checking up on the competition, ma'am?"

Anne held out the magazine with two fingers as if it offended her and dropped it to the ground. "This is not my competition." She fanned her face with a second magazine, studying him. "Have we met?"

"Once. I believe you suggested to my squad that we were not working hard enough toward victory."

"Ah yes, now I remember. I've heard good things about you, John. Your superiors rave about your bravery."

John couldn't imagine Gianelli raving about anyone, especially not to Kittles, and he was certain Anne had pulled his name from *American Century* in hopes of capitalizing on an easy story. John knew what Anne and Kittles were after, and he had no intention of helping them get it.

"Just doing my job, ma'am."

Anne motioned to a chair. "Sit."

John obeyed and felt her severe gaze sweep over him. Her initial disdain for his rank vanished; before long, she eyed him like a hungry jungle cat and he kept his expression pleasantly impassive, hoping to appear naïve and uninterested. Unlike Chris, Anne held no reporter's notebook at the ready. John would have to tread with care, be boring and unmemorable, but he felt a surge of confidence.

She asked him innocuous questions about his pre-war life; he kept his answers short and vague. He saw no harm in confirming for her the information that she could easily obtain—he was twenty-four years old; born in Ames, Iowa; and was drafted for duty.

"You were drafted?" Her tone indicated disappointment.

"Yes, ma'am."

"Why not volunteer? You could have escaped a dead-end existence in farm country. At least you would have a future in the army."

John blinked. "Dead-end existence?"

"It must have been so difficult for you, that upbringing. Commercial farming is crushing the livelihoods of so many family farmers."

"Farming is hard work," John agreed cautiously. "My brothers and I helped our father whenever we could. I wish we could have done more. But my parents insisted that our education was the priority."

"You finished high school?"

John felt a stabbing pain traverse his frontal lobe. "I did."

"And then what? Working for your father?"

He paused, weighing the wisdom of engaging with her. "No. College."

"College?"

"Iowa State University, class of 1967. I have a degree in mechanical engineering."

Anne's eyes registered surprise. "Then how in God's name did you end up here?"

He thought of his brothers. Dave was twenty-one and headed into his senior year at Iowa State, where he was majoring in veterinary science and human female anatomy. Robby was seventeen and facing one more year of high school before he could break free and chase his dreams of becoming the next Chris McKenna. He intended to buck the family tradition and enter the University of Iowa's writing program. His mother, a professor of English and American literature at ISU, tortured her youngest with faux distress over his plans to become a hated Hawkeye, but raved to anyone who would listen about his facility with words.

The draft notice had been a gut punch, but John had received private assurances from the head of the local draft board—a friend of his father's and a man he had known much of his life—that his brothers would be spared if he served.

He shrugged. "My number came up. Better me than some teenager."

Anne stared at him in silence for several seconds. "Tell me, are you seeing anyone?

John considered this. "Yes."

"Have you been faithful to her?"

"Of course."

Anne moved from the cot to a second chair, which she pulled close to his. "You're a long way from home. Always faithful?" A hand rested on his thigh.

"Yes, ma'am."

"Lucky her."

Anne lit a cigarette, looking irritated with his obtuseness. John wondered if he might have misplayed the situation. This was not the story he wanted to be.

***

Chris ducked into the open tent in search of First Squad. She found half of them cleaning their rifles and the other half gawking over a skin magazine, which they clamored to hide when she appeared.

"Reading it for the articles, honey," Oscar boomed.

Chris rolled her eyes. "Where's John?"

"Don't know. Anyone seen Cowboy?"

"Been gone all afternoon," said Murphy. "Think he's got another chick on the side?"

Chris kicked him in the leg. "Not if he values his life."

"It's time for dinner, anyway. Let's go find him," Dan said. "Steve's sources say they got a shipment of ice cream. Vanilla and chocolate."

"Chocolate? Let's go," Chris said.

"Uh oh, must be that time of the month."

Chris kicked Murphy again amid peals of laughter. He jumped up and draped an arm over her shoulders as they walked.

"What's he got that I don't?"

"For one thing, no tattoos."

"Chicks dig ink."

"What chicks? I'm the only chick here."

"Cowboy! Gilligan!" Oscar bellowed.

***

Anne kept her clothes on and John continued to play dumb. He answered her questions about his role in recent operations with noncommittal statements, and credited Gianelli and Travis for the platoon's successes. She took no notes, and every so often she seemed more interested in her fingernails than she did in his answers.

At this point, John felt comfortable that he had thwarted the threat to his privacy—he had given her nothing of interest. Now he had to bore her so she ended the interview. His stomach rumbled in hunger. He wanted nothing more than to join his squad for dinner. Rumor had it the mess would be serving ice cream for dessert.

He was on the homestretch; he could feel it. She struggled to keep the conversation flowing; he was sure he had failed to meet all her expectations in terms of story material. John again wondered what drew these women to him. Was it supposed heroics on the battlefield? An innocent farm boy image amplified by silly stereotypes? Could they see past the calm exterior into the dark corners of his mind where the doubts lurked, where the rage struggled to escape its bonds? Could they see that he was more than the words on their pages?

"I have all the information I need," she said finally.

John stood, trying not to seem too eager to leave. "Yes, ma'am. Thank you for this opportunity."

Anne grunted and paid him scant attention as he moved to exit the tent. Until he stepped outside.

"Cowboy!"

Later, John would reflect on the difference a second could make. In that second, as Oscar's shout hung in the humid Vietnam air, John saw the plan disintegrate. He fully understood the folly of trying to outwit these two women.

Frankly, John hadn't thought Anne Novak capable of moving so fast. But there she was, shoving past him, scanning the crowd that had just appeared.

"Who's Cowboy?" she demanded.

John's stomach lurched, and not because Steve Schaefer answered the question honestly or even because the plan, so painstakingly conceived and executed, had gone to shit. No, John experienced a painful physiological reaction because he realized just how powerless he had become.

Anne turned to him. "It was you?"

Though the sound and fury raged around him, John was conscious of only one thing, the look on Chris McKenna's face as she shrugged out from under Murphy's arm. Her eyebrows shot skyward; her mouth dropped open.

Anne began to laugh. "I can't believe I didn't see it. It figures it'd be you." She turned to Chris. "Interesting choice, McKenna. Now, much as I would love to watch this domestic dispute play out, I have a real interview to get to."

Anne motioned to her crew and headed toward Brigade HQ. John thought about sprinting in the other direction. But he knew she would run him down.

Chris put her hands on her hips. John saw the telltale signs of her rage: glittering eyes, clenched teeth, taut and defined shoulder muscles.

"I can't believe you. You sat there and let her interview you? After everything...I can't believe it," she said in a voice barely above a whisper.

John was at a loss for words. She smiled coldly at him.

"You and I will finish this discussion later." She left them, presumably to find new dinner dates.

"Uh oh, Cowboy's in hot water."

"Really screwed the pooch this time, big guy."

"Dude, seriously, what were you thinking?"

"Hey, if she dumps you, think I got a shot?"

"No," ten men answered in unison.

"Aw, guys..."

***

Paul tried to get out of Chris's way as she stalked into their hooch. He was unsuccessful and took a shoulder in the chest as she barreled past him. When she threw her reporter's notebook against the back wall, he had to duck her windup or risk losing an eye.

"What's gotten into you?"

Chris put her hands to her head and tried to counteract the pounding in her temples. A growl escaped her lips.

"Chris? What happened?"

"He let her interview him. I can't believe it."

"What? Who?"

"John and Anne, who do you think?"

"Did he say why?"

"No. In typical John Rawlins fashion, he said nothing. I know she wants more from him. Women can tell. She bounces around in her Abercrombie & Fitch fatigues and fucks anything that moves. Well, not him."

"I don't think you have to worry about that. Men can tell," he added to reassure her.

It was at that moment she ran out of energy. She sat down on the edge of her cot and stared at her hands. Paul sat beside her and wrapped his arm around her slumped shoulders.

"I didn't sleep with him for a story. Everyone thinks I did, but I didn't."

"I don't think that."

"Yes, you do."

"No, I don't. I knew from the start that he would be more than column fodder. If he's worth all this, it won't matter if he appears under your byline or not."

"Until I leave Vietnam, he's going to expect that he *will* appear under my byline again. We have some trust issues."

"I take it you still haven't told him about the next story."

"No."

"Did Willis say when it would run?"

Chris focused on her feet. "I haven't filed it yet."

Paul pulled away and stared at her. "Why?"

"It's complicated. It's...it's just really complicated."

"Chris, what you showed me in Saigon is the best piece of writing I've ever seen from you. Writing like that skyrockets a career. Look, I can't tell you what to do about John, but you have to file that story."

"I'm working on another. One not so...I don't know. Revealing."

"Then it won't be nearly as good."

"You think I don't know that?"

Paul stood and put his hands on the top of his head, digesting her words, clearly as perplexed as she was by hers and John's inability to build the most basic foundation of a relationship.

"If you're going to let others dictate what you submit, if you write to spare feelings rather than tell the real story, why are we here?" he asked.

Chris's hands fell out of her hair and she stared at her photographer.

"You started off like gangbusters, but we've been here over two months and all we have to show for it is a pile of photos, an angry editor, and an amazing piece you refuse to file. Maybe it's time to reevaluate our intentions for this trip."

"You keep telling me we're here until we get the story."

"We've gotten the story. *You've* gotten the story. You just won't do anything with the story."

"Because if I do, I'll betray the trust of a bunch of guys who deserve a lot better. There's a lot of power in the written word. Long after this war ends, long after we've all gone our separate ways, what I wrote will remain for the world to see. These guys didn't ask for that. If someone is going to tell their story, maybe it should be someone with more talent and compassion and wisdom than me."

"That is the stupidest thing I've ever heard you say."

"For Christ's sake, Paul, what do you want from me?"

"I want you to do something with this opportunity. Otherwise..."

"What?" She regretted the belligerent tone immediately.

Paul offered a weak smile. "Otherwise, I don't know how much longer I can take this."

Chris nodded once. "I understand."

"Look, there's no one those guys would rather have tell their story than you."

"That doesn't mean I should tell it. There are some who would argue that truth and exploitation are one and the same."

"I know you said you wouldn't have to make a choice between John and this assignment, but it sounds like you might have to do just that. If you can't have them both, I think it's time you seriously consider which of the two means more to you."

Chris looked at the typewriter atop the field table, reflecting on the words that had come so naturally, once she stopped thinking about them. A squad of men had inspired her, but that inspiration only ran one way. She stood to gain everything, and they would be left with nothing but a memory.

"I know," she said. "I know."

***

It didn't take long for Chris and John to discuss his transgression, though longer than he would have liked. As it was, he had to spend a sleepless night pondering his sins and their possible consequences.

After Gianelli's briefing on an upcoming patrol, on which John struggled to focus, the squad moved to a shady area near a munitions bunker to inventory and clean their equipment, restock on ammunition, and kill time until lunch. John stretched out in a hammock strung up between two sturdy wood posts, hoping for a short nap. As his eyes closed, he heard Hector whisper excitedly and the crinkle of varying denominations of U.S. currency being collected.

"Get up."

So much for a nap. He reluctantly complied amid the smattering of laughter and noted that her anger had not abated. Possibly, it had intensified. Chris paced among them, eyes spitting fire. The men hung on her every move. There was serious cash riding on this fight.

"How could you, John?"

John opened his mouth to reply, but quickly realized it was a rhetorical question.

"How *could* you? Anne Novak! My sworn enemy!" She tossed up her hands. "I don't understand you. Outward appearances suggest you're a bright guy, but then you go stick your head up your ass and I'm forced to rethink my positive assessment of your intelligence."

Polite applause. Point for Chris.

"I can explain."

"Really? Please do."

"Gianelli asked me to speak with her." He cringed as the words left his mouth, feeling weak and pathetic under her black glare.

"Why would your misogynistic, anti-press, anti-establishment lieutenant ask you to do such a thing?"

"She got my name from...somewhere. She just had a few questions. I don't really know."

"Oh stop, the humble hero bit is getting old."

Everyone nodded. John resented the comment. It was her fault Anne knew about his alleged heroics in the first place.

"Now answer me honestly: Did Gianelli order you?"

As John considered her question, he admired her lithe, athletic build, the way the sweaty tank top clung to her body, the way her sun-streaked hair fell about her shoulders, how she occasionally had to flip an errant strand off her perspiring forehead. Some of the resentment slipped away.

"No."

"But you agreed to the interview? 'Sure, no problem, LT. I'm a hero and all, so Chris will just have to understand.' Is that how it went?" She jabbed a finger into his chest. "Guess what? I'm *not* understanding, not at all."

She continued to highlight his insensitivity, his immaturity, his outright stupidity. He looked down at her, at the crown of her head that fit so perfectly under his chin, at the body that formed so perfectly to his own. He felt the corners of his mouth turn up.

"Is something funny?"

"No, ma'am."

She shot him a scathing look. Then, inches away from him, she smiled. "If you ever pull a stunt like that again, the story will be the least of your concerns. Understand?"

With a flick of her wrist she rapped his groin with her knuckles. John's breath caught. Guffaws from the peanut gallery, but she silenced them with a look. Turning back to John, she steered the conversation to more serious issues.

"She's going to destroy you in print. You won't recognize yourself."

"I was careful. I didn't give her anything."

"John," she said with a sigh as rubbed her forehead. "I hope you're right."

And with that, Chris McKenna departed. The men swarmed John, laughing and offering congratulations on his survival. He sank back into the hammock, relieved it was over.

"What was the bet? Who would win?" John asked.

Murphy laughed. "Hell no, boy. That was a foregone conclusion. We bet on whether she'd deck you."

***

From April to October Gary Crosby, oil tycoon and media mogul, made the most of his membership at the Congressional Country Club in Bethesda, Maryland, home to a sprawling expanse of exquisitely manicured golf heaven plied by an exclusive cadre of Washington power brokers. Every Saturday morning during that six-month span, weather permitting, he shot eighteen holes in the company of senators, congressmen, CEOs, and ambassadors from countries in which he had done, or intended to do, business.

On this particular Saturday, however, Crosby would play with a commoner. He had instructed the editor-in-chief of *American Century* to meet him at the club by half past eight for a tee time of nine o'clock. Willis had reluctantly accepted the invitation—he was more of a contact sports kind of guy—but made clear that he would much prefer to spend Saturday morning in his home office to read in peace, as was his customary routine.

Willis entered the clubhouse promptly at half past eight, feeling uncomfortable in a white polo shirt and khaki pants. He could not remember his last visit to a country club, but suspected that it too had been under duress.

"Good morning, Martin."

Willis grunted and eyed the publisher with thinly veiled irritation. While Crosby rambled on about his prowess on the course—he shot an eighty last time out—Willis figured he would be lucky to break a hundred. He had not golfed in years. His wife thought the game failed to appeal to him because he lacked both patience and a soft touch. Willis saw merit in her argument. Before he left the house, she made him promise not to clobber Gary with a driver, no matter what the extenuating circumstances.

Willis hefted his own bag as Crosby's young caddie did the same, and they walked into the bright sunlight of a humid July morning. The expanse of green before them sparkled, dappled and dewy and pungent with the aroma of life in full bloom. At the tee, Willis stepped aside to allow Crosby to take the first shot. The publisher set his ball, took a few practice swings, and lined up his drive. With a satisfying *thwack*, the ball leapt from the club and shot down the fairway.

Willis stepped forward to drive. The club felt foreign in his hands, but he concentrated on keeping good form. His powerful swing launched the ball nearly two hundred yards, but considerably right of the fairway.

"Not bad, Martin. Heavy on the power, though. Try a bit of finesse."

"Power has its uses if you want to get where you need to go."

Crosby smiled. "True. Shall we?"

Conversation for the first sixteen holes remained pleasant, as Crosby reminisced about the many business deals he had closed on this very course and Willis spoke fondly of his father teaching him the game on the public course on the outskirts of Baltimore when he was a boy. Just when Willis noted with surprise that he was enjoying himself, despite multiple triple bogies on the back nine, he felt a subtle shift in the mood.

"I talked to Kent before he left."

Willis gripped his 9-iron a little tighter and watched Crosby out of the corner of his eye.

"I think he'll do a fine job, a fine job," Crosby continued. "His work has been outstanding as of late. We need results. The product has been...bland."

Willis pivoted and swung mightily. He sliced the shot and swore under his breath.

"I'd like you to fire her."

"I'm sorry?"

"I said I want you to fire Miss McKenna. Immediately."

Willis calmly replaced the club into his bag. "You ordered me, without explanation and against my wishes, to send a twenty-six-year-old kid to the front lines of the most unpopular war in this nation's history, before she was ready for it, I might add, and now you want me to fire her?"

"This is not up for debate, Martin. I giveth, I can taketh away."

"Spare me the God crap. You sent her to fail."

"She did that on her own."

"Damn it, Gary, she needs more time."

"She's had over two months. I pay her to write features, not gallivant around Southeast Asia on my dime."

"Chris has so much potential. She just needs to find her way."

"I'm surprised at you, Martin. It's not as if Miss McKenna has played by all your rules. She has a reputation in the newsroom as something of a rebel. How many good reporters have we lost because they disobeyed one of your directives?"

"That's irrelevant."

"Throughout all those firings, I stayed silent despite my misgivings. You are a talented editor and manager, and as a businessman I can appreciate that many of your decisions are based on gut instinct. So are mine. My gut tells me she doesn't have the edge. She's too emotional. There is a reason that women should never be war correspondents. Miss McKenna put herself before this magazine, and that is unacceptable."

"That's not a fair assessment of the situation. If I know Chris, she's in the middle of the story trying to see it from every possible angle. We'll get exactly what we need from her."

"It's not a request, Martin. Take care of it."

Willis spoke through clenched teeth. "This is a bad decision."

"But not one I'll regret."

Willis and Crosby played the final holes in silence. Back at the clubhouse, two men went their separate ways.

12

— • —

J ohn stood outside Chris's hooch for several minutes before he worked up
the courage to knock. They had not spoken since the aftermath of his
interview with Anne Novak. In fact, she had hardly looked at him. Revenge had
been sweet at first, but then the guilt had started to gnaw at him. He hadn't liked
the flash of betrayal he'd seen in her eyes before it was consumed by rage.

She answered on the first knock, looking surprised to see him. He stepped
into a cloud of cigarette smoke and stifled a cough. A pack's worth of Marlboros lay smashed in an ashtray beside her typewriter. The light breeze followed
John into the hooch and ruffled the blank sheet of paper wrapped around the
typewriter's carriage. She sat at the field table and he perched on the edge of her
cot. The silence was uncomfortable.

"Rough night?" he asked, gesturing to the typewriter and trying to sound
sympathetic.

"Please don't patronize me."

John stared hard at her. If he apologized, would she drop the attitude? Or
would Chris McKenna simply take it as confirmation that she bore no responsibility for the vast no-man's land between them?

"I'm sorry," he began to say. Then he paused, lost momentarily in the depths
of unyielding green eyes. "I'm sorry you're having difficulty writing."

"Here's an idea—you worry about the corn and the soybeans, I'll worry
about the magazine business."

"Guess I'll be the only one putting food on the table."

"Will that make you feel like more of a man?"

"If it's about me, don't you think it'd be to your advantage to actually talk to me?"

"What makes you think this is about you? You're one among many, and rather dull at that."

John smirked. "Who else would it be about?"

"Your arrogance is astounding, considering."

"Considering what?" John challenged. "The unfortunate circumstances of my upbringing? Just some dumb farm boy, right?"

Chris rolled her eyes. "Considering I haven't published a single word about you in weeks."

"You haven't published a single word about anything in weeks. Believe me, I've checked."

Chris fumbled for her cigarettes, finally knocking one free from the pack. With a shaking hand she managed to strike the lighter and touch the tip to the flame.

"What do you want from me, John?"

"How about a little honesty? You've evaded everything—your job, your past, your life outside Vietnam—and I'm tired of it. You know everything about me, but I know nothing about you. Except that I'm the latest in probably a long line of screws and you'd do anything for the sake of your career. Does that about sum it up?"

Chris laughed incredulously. "You think I know everything about you? The stoic, war-weary, intensely blue-eyed soldier who internalizes all his emotions? Give me a break. I know your name, your rank, your serial number, and that you like it best when I'm on top. That's about it. And it's not as if I haven't asked, so don't give me that crap. I'm with you because I want to be with you, not because I think *American Century* readers will give a damn about your hopes and dreams."

"You can be a real..."

"Bitch?" She shrugged and blew a stream of smoke in his direction. "Guilty as charged."

"When you look at people, do you see anything more than a word count and a paycheck?"

"Yeah, I see a lot of people who aren't worth either."

"Like all of us, right?"

"This is between you and me. Don't drag everyone else into it."

"Well, at least we're finally being honest. What am I worth?"

"Don't be a smartass. You started this." Chris took another drag on the cigarette and glared at him.

"Then I'll be the one to end it. Good luck writing." John stood and moved toward the door.

"Are you ever going to trust me?" she asked.

John walked out of the hooch without responding.

***

Two days later, Travis accosted Chris and Paul outside Brigade HQ and motioned for them to follow. They dutifully fell in behind the master sergeant as he led them to the eastern perimeter, where his squad had just completed an afternoon rotation of guard duty. He held the Louisville Slugger in his left hand and a rolled magazine in his right hand. He slapped the magazine into John's chest.

"Might want to take a look at that. Page twenty-seven. Picture and everything."

"Hey, is Johnny famous again?"

"Come on, dude, let's see this thing."

Chris stepped away from the scrum to avoid being trampled, but her heartbeat quickened as he opened the *Washington Dispatch*.

"This won't be good," Paul whispered to her.

John opened the magazine to page twenty-seven. The men crowded behind him to read over his shoulder.

"'Well-meaning but slow'? Since when has she seen you run?"

"'Simple-minded farm boy'?"

"Hey, don't you got college and stuff?"

John started to crumple the magazine, but Dan snatched it out of his hands.

"Not so fast. Can't you get a retraction or something? Isn't this libel? Isn't it?" he asked Chris.

"No."

"But he's not a simple-minded farm boy."

Chris shrugged. "Right or wrong, it's incredibly difficult to prove libel, and she's entitled to her opinion."

"Thanks for the vote of confidence," John said to her just before he turned to walk away.

Chris shared a frustrated glance with Paul before jogging to catch up with John. She grabbed his arm and tried to slow his angry stride. He stopped and faced her.

"Didn't I tell you to be careful around Anne Novak?" she asked.

"It's done."

"Look, I know it wasn't flattering, but how many people will see it? I can't imagine there's much of a market for the *Washington Dispatch* in small-town Iowa."

"That's not really the point."

"Well, I don't want to say I told you so, but..."

"When should I expect your next contribution to my wildly inaccurate biography?" John asked.

"Don't lump me in with Anne. She's not a journalist—she's a hack. She takes potshots and destroys reputations because it's easier than putting some hard work into getting the real story. People don't respect her, they fear her."

"You didn't answer my question," he said frostily.

"Why would I bother? Anne pretty much summed it up," Chris shot back.

John set his jaw and stared her down, but Chris refused to avert her gaze. Unlike Anne Novak, Chris loved her work, loved searching for truth and loved manipulating the written word to express that truth. She still held onto the fading hope that John would someday understand that her work was much bigger than either of them.

John's eyes darted over her right shoulder and she heard a familiar voice call her name, the voice of a very unwelcome colleague. The blood drained from her face and she felt lightheaded.

"You look happy to see me, babe," Kent Springer said as he sauntered up to her and John with Lieutenant George Wheaton in tow.

"What the hell are you doing here?" She looked frantically for Paul, but he and Travis had disappeared.

"Just taking back what's rightfully mine. I deserved this assignment."

"Get over yourself, Kent," Chris snapped. "You did nothing to deserve it, other than leave the womb with a Y chromosome."

"Babe, I remember a time when that Y chromosome made you scream, so don't give me that attitude."

"Scream?" Chris laughed. "I can't imagine that was the first time that *you've* heard a woman fake it."

Springer's face turned an ugly shade of puce. "You're such a bitch."

Chris's insult hit home, but it couldn't repair the damage already done. She felt a chill at her back and knew the death knell had sounded for whatever relationship she and John might have had. She was torn between turning to John and confessing everything, or knocking the affronted look off Kent's face with a well-placed right hook. She opted for neither. Instead, she asked him again why he was here. In Vietnam. On her base. Her turf.

"Gary and Martin asked me to pick up the slack. Apparently, they're not happy with the output from the current Vietnam War correspondent. You know how it is," he said, looking between John and Wheaton. "Can't send a woman to do a man's job."

Chris wanted to leave, but stood rooted to the spot. She had forgotten how to walk.

"Oh, Chrissy, by the way, I'm supposed to pass you a message. Willis wants to chat. Pronto." Confidence regained, he flashed an unctuous grin. "Better hurry. You know how he hates to wait. Later on, stop by my hooch. It'll be just like old times, if you know what I mean."

Springer and Wheaton departed, Springer laughing and Wheaton throwing nervous looks over his shoulder at John. Chris swore under her breath. John stepped in front of her, blocking her path. Cold blue eyes roamed over her face.

"Anyone else I should know about?"

Chris ignored him and ran toward her hooch to gather a bag for another trip to Saigon.

"Hey, Reporter Lady, where you going?" Oscar bellowed. He and the men were still engrossed in the *Washington Dispatch* article.

"Saigon," she yelled. "Tell Paul."

"That ain't fair, we just got back. How come you get to go again?" Steve whined.

Murphy punched Steve in the arm. "She ain't one of us, dumbass."

"Come back soon," Dan called. The squad waved.

Within thirty minutes, she was on a Huey bound for Saigon.

***

Chris gnawed on a thumbnail, pacing in her hotel room while the international operator put her call through to the *American Century* offices in downtown Washington, D.C. Evening in Vietnam was morning in the District, and that meant Martin Willis would be at his desk or within shouting distance of a phone.

Several cigarette butts lay mangled in the ashtray; one still smoldered, its tip glowing orange in the dim room. The sun had set and she hadn't turned on the light, preferring the anonymity and safety of the dark. Beside the ashtray stood a fifth of Stolichnaya vodka, a bargain purchase from an elderly street vendor a block from the Hotel Continental. Chris had not yet taken a drink.

The call finally connected. Martin Willis's secretary sounded surprised to be speaking to Chris, but transferred her immediately. Chris steeled herself. He picked up on the first ring.

"You better have a goddamn good excuse why I haven't received anything of substance from you in months," he said.

"I'm sorry," she replied, as a voice in her head urged her to transition into survival mode.

"How long did you expect me to wait? How long did you expect me to cover your ass? What the hell am I supposed to tell people around here when they ask why we have nothing from Vietnam but a correspondent in country? What the hell am I supposed to tell other writers who slack? That you get judged by different standards?"

"Martin, I'm sorry, it's just that—"

"Quiet." Through the phone, Chris heard him slam the door of his office. "I told you I had concerns about sending you to Vietnam, but you went behind my back and agreed to whatever demeaning, degrading terms Crosby demanded to get what you wanted. I'm going to take a wild guess that he enjoyed the sex a hell of a lot more than you did. You did provide sex in return for this assignment, right, McKenna?"

The rhetorical nature of the question did nothing to blunt its force. Willis's words provoked a rush of blood to her cheeks, the hot flush of shame that raced over the wires and confirmed her guilt.

"You have no patience, none at all. You know why I was going to send Kent ahead of you? So I could let you prove that you do it better. If you had just *listened* to me!" Willis shouted. Chris had never heard him so angry.

"You think Crosby gives a damn about you? He got what he wanted, and he gave you what you wanted because he knew you would fail. Now he's done with you. And he wants me to be done with you, too."

Chris broke into a cold sweat. She gripped the phone so hard she lost feeling in her hand. "He wants you to fire me?"

"What did you think would happen? You're a nobody. You're expendable. You're the woman who sleeps with the boss to get ahead."

"Martin, I can fix it, I swear I can."

"You can fix it?" Willis laughed in disbelief. "Why would I trust you after you lied to me? You've made fools of us both."

"I know, and I wrong to betray your trust. Please let me fix it."

"How, Chris? How are you going to fix this? I know you're hiding something, something that could be great. If you think you have a prayer of surviving this, you tell me what that something is right now."

Chris gritted her teeth and massaged her forehead with her fingertips. She glanced at her rucksack, in which rested a folded sheaf of papers. It would be so easy to start reading and beg for Willis's forgiveness. Honest words could save her. But Chris saw their faces, every single one of them, and the familiar distrust in a pair of piercing blue eyes.

"I'm not hiding anything. I can have something for you by tomorrow."

"I can't believe you. I'm done with your bullshit. You're fired."

Martin Willis slammed down the phone, leaving Chris staring motionless out the window, the receiver still pressed to her ear. Then the receiver slid from her grasp and tumbled downward, landing on the carpet with a dull thud.

Chris sank to the edge of the bed and let her head drop into her hands. The tears began to fall, followed by silent, wracking sobs.

***

Paul pounded on the door and called Chris's name until she stumbled to open it, then pitched forward into him.

"Whoa, careful! Are you all right?"

Paul guided her back into the dark room and sat her on the bed. Then he reached for the table and switched on a lamp. The light, the first she'd seen in hours, blinded her. She clamped her hand over her eyes to shield them from the assault.

Paul surveyed the room. The phone was still on the floor in the middle of the room, the dial tone buzzing insistently. She'd gone through most of a package of cigarettes, and beside the loaded ashtray the bottle of vodka stood two-thirds empty.

He dropped to his knees in front of Chris and pulled her hand away from her face. She looked at him with glassy, red-rimmed eyes, struggling to sit up straight. Paul held her steady, one hand on each of her bare arms.

"Talk to me, sweetie."

"He fired me," she said dully.

Paul sighed. "I'm sorry, Chris."

"It's not your fault I'm a fuck-up."

"Don't say that. Willis is just angry. I know him, he'll change his mind."

Chris broke into helpless laughter. "No, probably not." She tipped to the left, still laughing, and Paul righted her. "Want to know why? Want to know why he fired me?"

Paul said nothing.

Chris managed to focus her bloodshot eyes on his. "Because I let Crosby fuck me. All for this shit." She swung her arm to indicate the mess her world had become, and Paul ducked just before her elbow knocked him in the head. "Our little quid pro quo." She giggled again. "God, I am totally sloshed."

She lunged for the bottle, but Paul pushed it out of her reach.

"I think you've had enough. At this rate you'll be drunk for days."

"Who cares? It's over. Might as well be shit-faced. Then I won't have to contemplate my meteoric rise to ineptitude."

"Ever the writer, even when bombed out of your skull," Paul murmured to himself.

"What?" she said listlessly, her eyelids fluttering. "Can you make the room stop spinning?"

"Chris, honey, look at me. Keep talking."

"I just want to...sleep."

She tried to lie down on the bed, but Paul kept her upright. "No sleep. You need to get some of the booze out of your system."

The mere suggestion was enough to compel her body to action. A look of pain passed over her face, and with a quickness surprising for someone so inebriated, she shot up and sprang toward the bathroom, bowling him over in the process. She misjudged the size and placement of the doorway and slammed into the doorjamb, but ended up where she needed to be, on her knees in front of the toilet. With a tremendous heave, she vomited hours' worth of vodka consumption into the bowl.

Paul held her hair and rubbed her back. Wearied from the exertion, Chris lowered her forehead to rest on the chipped toilet seat, an act that under more sober circumstances would have disgusted her. Paul passed her a square of toilet paper and she wiped her mouth.

"You knew, didn't you?"

"Knew what?"

"About me and Crosby."

"No."

"Don't lie to me, Paul. Even when I'm wasted, I know when you're lying to me," she said, not unkindly.

"I didn't know," he said, settling himself on the floor beside her.

"But you suspected."

"It occurred to me that something must have happened between you, yes. Willis was adamant about waiting to send you until you had a little bit more experience. Crosby was the only one who could overrule him."

"He said he would give me what I wanted, and I wanted this more than anything," she said. "Why didn't you say something?"

"It's not my place. Besides, what would it have changed?"

"I'm sorry I let you down."

Paul laughed gently. "Chris, I know you won't believe this, and tomorrow you might not even remember it, but you've never let me down. Your means might have been dubious, but your end was pure. That counts for something."

"I guess it was a nice dream while it lasted, you and me fighting for truth and justice and the American way."

"The dream doesn't have to be over."

Chris opened her mouth to respond, but then turned her face to the toilet again. Several minutes later, she was able to talk.

"It's over, Paul. It was over the second I met John Rawlins. And the bastard doesn't even know I'm in love with him."

The words sounded strange to her ears, ringing with the beginnings of a hangover. Chris had always questioned whether she was capable of love, rather preferring the image of herself as a hawk soaring high above the earth, observant but detached, solitary and self-reliant. It was a foreign idea, this idea of love.

"Maybe you should tell him."

"That's over, too. That was over before it even started. Wrong time, wrong place, wrong pasts, wrong futures, wrong everything."

"You shouldn't let something as insignificant as job descriptions keep you apart."

"It's a lot more complicated than that. And it doesn't matter. John doesn't feel the same way."

"I wouldn't be so sure about that. I've seen the way he looks at you."

"How's that?"

Paul smiled. "Like a man consumed."

He got no response. The writer had lost the battle against exhaustion and had fallen asleep with her head resting on her arms, resting on the toilet seat. It was as poignant a picture as he had ever seen, of loss, despair, hopelessness. Had it been anyone else with her arms wrapped around the toilet, the award-winning photojournalist might have run for his camera to capture the raw emotion of the scene in black and white and shades of gray.

With a sigh that made him sound a hundred years old, Paul squatted and scooped Chris into his arms. He carried her into the bedroom and laid her on the bed. She stunk of booze and vomit; against his better judgment, he stripped her to her bra and panties and covered her with the sheet. Then he lay down beside her and stared at the ceiling for a long time.

***

After rousing the platoon for patrol, Gianelli and Travis departed the barracks and took a detour on the way to the helipad. On the destination signpost, standing proudly in the center of camp, a bored G.I. had hammered up a sign reading "Hell," but instead of pointing in a specific direction, the sign denoted with a large white X that the visitor was already there.

Gianelli rapped on the door of the hooch, expecting one of the two journalists to stumble to the door, appalled at the early hour but game for a day in the bush. He rapped again and wiggled the locked doorknob.

"You think they're in the mess?"

"Maybe."

But they were not in the mess hall, not at Brigade HQ or Administration or the hospital, not at any of the showers or latrines. The lieutenant and his master sergeant tried to appear nonchalant in their search efforts, but they grew more concerned with each empty venue.

"They could have told us they were otherwise occupied," muttered Gianelli, strangely affronted.

"They got jobs, Sam. Maybe those jobs are done."

Gianelli pondered this. "No, it's something else. I think Rawlins fucked it up."

"We should bust him down to private."

"War used to be so much simpler," Gianelli said with a sigh.

They reached the north helipad with five minutes to spare, though they figured the platoon would be at least ten minutes late. Conlon nodded a greeting. Last night Gianelli had subjected his two trusted sergeants to a diatribe on the finer points of his irritation with this particular assignment, patrolling a swath of farmland supposed to be clear of Viet Cong activity. According to Major Gardner and his often vague and contradictory intelligence reports, the sector had seen increased guerrilla incursions from the surrounding jungle, but no one was entirely sure to whom the villagers had pledged loyalty. Captain Kittles had volunteered Lieutenant Gianelli and his platoon to find out.

"Kittles on approach with a bogey," Travis murmured.

Gianelli made a face at Travis and Conlon and then turned to his commanding officer and the newcomer, wearing an expression of polite disinterest.

"Lieutenant, this is Kent Springer, a correspondent with *American Century*."

Gianelli was instantly suspicious and appraised Springer with a judgmental eye. Travis and Conlon crowded around Gianelli like neighborhood busybodies.

"Mr. Springer will accompany you today. I expect him to be given the same high-level treatment as past correspondents," Kittles said pointedly.

"Have you ever been in a combat situation?" Gianelli asked.

"I'm looking to find one," Springer said with a wide grin, as if all men desired to prove themselves in war. He might have been correct in that assumption, but he was about to learn not to advertise that desire to men who had already lived through combat, men who, if given the choice, would never see, smell, hear, taste, or feel it again. Springer extended a hand for Gianelli to shake.

"So the answer is no, you have never been in a combat situation." Gianelli ignored the outstretched hand. Springer let it drop back to his side.

Kittles forced a laugh. "Just make sure he comes back whole. Knowing this guy, he'll be in the thick of it when the shooting starts."

Gianelli rubbed his beard stubble. "Let Sergeant Travis inspect your gear. We lift off in fifteen minutes."

"Oh?" said Kittles. "Then where are your men?"

"Right there." Gianelli nodded down the path. "Right on time." Ten minutes late.

"Kent, good luck." Kittles patted the reporter on the back. "Lieutenant."

"Captain."

"Hey, LT! We stuck with the FNG?" Oscar rumbled.

"What's 'FNG'?" Springer asked Travis.

"Beats me."

As Gianelli shot Oscar a warning look, he saw several of the men glance apprehensively at John, who looked as though he would happily gut Springer with Travis's machete if given an opportunity.

Gianelli knew it would be a long day.

***

Midmorning, Chris sat up in bed, confused. Her tousled hair fell over her face. As she flipped it back with her hand, the sheet slipped down, revealing tanned shoulders and a black bra.

"Good morning, sleepyhead," Paul greeted.

"Jesus Christ, stop shouting. I have a marching band in my skull. A bad one."

"That's no surprise."

She blinked away the fog of the night and took in her surroundings: the faded wine-colored carpet, the taupe walls, the Eastern décor with a hint of Buddhist influence, the photographer seated by the sliver of light streaming through the curtains with a book in his hands.

"Why am I naked?"

"You're not naked."

"Mostly naked."

"You threw up on yourself and I didn't want to smell it all night."

Chris considered that. "Good enough."

"Do you...do you remember last night?"

"Unfortunately. I think I'll be reliving it for most of today." The slightest movement sent blinding pain through her head. "I'm still fired, right?"

Paul grimaced.

"Yeah, that's what I thought." She dropped her head and muttered quietly, "Shit."

"I'll do whatever you need me to do."

She tried to smile. "I guess there's not much point in sticking around."

"Okay," he replied cautiously.

"I need to move on, make a fresh start. You want to go home, right?"

"I miss my wife."

"We should go home."

"If you're sure," he said.

"I'm sure. There's nothing for us here."

"Okay. Then let's go home."

"I thought you'd look a lot happier," she said.

"I'm thrilled. I only wish we were returning under better circumstances."

"Not like he's going to throw away stunning photography just because you happened to be on assignment with me."

"One never knows with Willis."

"He might be a dick, but he's not stupid."

218

"So, do you plan to lounge in bed all day like a hung-over princess?"

Chris gasped in mock offense. She tossed off the bedcovers and hopped to her feet, the sudden movement inciting a crash from the cymbals in her brain.

"I guess I should look away," Paul said, trying to look away.

"Doesn't bother me if it doesn't bother you."

"Have you always been this thin?"

Chris looked down at herself. "We've been eating C-rations and running for our lives for three months. I guess I've dropped a few pounds. So have you."

"But I had a few pounds to lose."

"I promise I'll gain it all back. I live on chocolate when I'm depressed."

"Go take a shower. I can smell the vodka oozing from your pores."

Chris paused at the door of the bathroom and looked back at the man who had just seen her through the most difficult night of her life. "Paul."

He looked up from his book. "Hmm?"

"Thank you."

***

Sam Gianelli sat with his C-ration—cold beef and potatoes—and watched his men. They had found a suitable clearing in which to take lunch; once the sentries were posted, Gianelli settled against a thatch of brush, strong enough to hold his weight if he leaned back, and popped open his tin of food. He ate slowly, savoring the salty stew. The salt would help him retain water and maintain proper hydration, which would help him stay alert on patrols. Or so the medical staff facetiously justified the excess sodium and preservatives, which in reality would probably just exacerbate his stress-induced high blood pressure and contribute to premature kidney failure.

First Squad had gathered together in a clump, but Gianelli noticed their conversation was uncharacteristically muted, perhaps because Kent Springer sat three feet away. Gianelli decided he didn't care for the way Springer looked at his men. Was it disdain? Pity? In fact, Springer showed little interest in the men, preferring to fire questions at Gianelli during the morning's slog through the paddies. The lieutenant had not deigned to put much thought into his answers to the reporter's rather simplistic queries into Gianelli's personal views on the war, military strategy, and life in the trenches with the grunts.

"Come on, man, you've got a correspondent from one of America's premier newsmagazines at your disposal. Now's your chance to tell the world what the hell goes on out here," Springer had said. "You. Your views. Sam Gianelli."

"I work for the army. I don't have views."

Springer had then tapped Travis on the shoulder and jerked a thumb in Gianelli's direction. "Is this guy serious?"

"Yes."

If there was one thing Gianelli could count on with Travis, beyond his leadership, his stamina, and his courage, it was his willingness to make life difficult for journalists. Most of them, anyway.

Gianelli believed his men deserved far more attention than he did, and he didn't appreciate Springer showing so little respect for the burdens they carried. They patrolled the paddies and the jungles knowing they might make the ultimate sacrifice in pursuit of often questionable and ambiguous objectives. Too often that sacrifice was ignored or belittled by people who would never understand what it meant to be a soldier fighting America's most unpopular war.

"Hey FNG, you're with *American Century*?" said Murphy.

"Sure am."

"So you know Chris, right?"

"I know her well."

"Where is she?" asked Bullseye.

"She's gone."

The entire squad looked to Springer in surprise, even John Rawlins. Gianelli watched John set his jaw and stare into the middle distance.

"What do you mean?" Dan asked.

Springer laughed. "How do you guys know her? She hang around the club a lot?"

Murphy and Oscar exchanged a confused look. "She's been running patrols with us for months," said Murphy.

"We talking about the same Chris McKenna here? The Chrissy I know far prefers a bar stool to jungle rot. Anyway, she's a goner."

"Dude, what the hell are you talking about?"

"Sorry, guys. Her time in 'Nam is up."

"No, there's no way she'd leave without saying goodbye," Murphy insisted.

The journalist laughed again. "I guess you really don't know her that well."

As he licked the last of the stew off his spoon, Gianelli felt an unexpected sense of loss. Examined rationally, the lieutenant thought the feeling might have been precipitated by the sudden departure of a woman who both understood the stakes of war and appreciated the sacrifice of his men.

13

— • —

I f anyone could see under the brim of the Yankees cap pulled low over Chris's face, they would have thought she looked about the same as she always did, if a bit tired. But who in Vietnam was not tired? Today's confident expression and bearing, however, were mere façades, practiced to perfection over her years as a journalist. Chris had always thought, possibly somewhat incongruously, that if anyone should appear to know what the hell was going on, it should be a journalist.

Despite outward airs, Chris wanted only to beeline for the safety of her hooch and pack her bags in solitude. Paul had stayed in Saigon to make travel arrangements. She needed to pack up the last of his things as well. She had not yet decided how—or if—she would say goodbye. Gianelli's men would wish her well; for a time they might even miss her. She dreaded the moment with John. Goodbyes had never been her thing.

It could be nothing more than a simple parting. What would he say? Thanks for the good times? That he would write? What would Chris say? Sorry for all the lies? That she would wait for him to come back from war? That they could build a life together?

She did not intend to share with anyone her forced separation from *American Century*. About the last thing she needed was pity; awkward, embarrassing pity. Just walk away, move on, she told herself; every adventure must end. Perhaps someday she would be a fond memory when they reflected on their summer in 'Nam.

Chris was hurrying past the hospital on the way to her hooch when she heard shouts. The hospital doors flung open and purged Major Jacobson and his entire staff. Chris paused and watched the doctors and nurses approach the medevac helipad in a full sprint, their teal and maroon and navy scrubs fluttering in the light breeze. Then she looked to the sky, eyes squinting into the early afternoon sun. An armada of Hueys appeared over the horizon, skimming the treetops like giant dragonflies.

The colonel's staff sergeant raced past, calling over his shoulder instructions to a corporal to alert Brooks. Chris took up stride and tugged his sleeve.

"What happened?"

"Air Cav accidentally took out a company patrolling a market near Vi Thanh. Medevacs are bringing in some of the wounded."

"Do we have that kind of space? Or doctors?"

"No. Hey!" he yelled to two corpsmen driving a jeep loaded with stretchers toward the helicopters. The driver slammed on the brakes. "We cleared out the club. Bring the overflow there for treatment."

The corpsmen waved their understanding and sped off.

Before Chris was conscious of making a decision, she had broken into a run toward the medevacs touching down at FOB Jane.

***

Paul stared at the phone for ten minutes before he picked it up and dialed an international operator. It took another fifteen minutes for the call to go through. When Martin Willis answered, he was less than pleased to be talking to his award-winning photographer. It was very early in the morning in Washington, D.C., but Paul was angry enough to be deliberately inconsiderate.

"If you were anyone else, I'd fire your ass," Willis said groggily.

"You're on a roll this week."

Willis was silent. Paul thought he lost the connection and was about to curse when he heard a voice.

"Did she tell you why I fired her?"

"Because of Crosby? Hell, Martin, if you fired reporters for every boneheaded decision they made, you wouldn't have a staff."

"She slept with the publisher to get an assignment. That goes way beyond boneheaded into the realm of colossally stupid."

"Please tell me why you're so hard on her."

"I did it for her own good. If she can impress me, she can impress anyone," Willis said.

"Did she impress you?"

"Yes," he grumbled after a pause.

"Then that's something you probably should have told her, just once," Paul said. "Because I don't think she knew. She respects you more than anyone."

"She has a funny way of showing it. And I don't appreciate you pinning this on me. She pissed off Crosby. He wants her gone."

"You don't give a damn what Crosby wants. This is about you."

"So what if it is? I have a right to be angry. If I can't trust her, and clearly I can't, then I don't want her around."

"She just wanted a chance," Paul said.

"You know what? You know why I didn't want to send her?"

"I know, lack of experience. Look, you don't get experience by—"

Willis cut him off. "No. It's more than lack of experience. She hasn't learned to harness her power. She has no idea what kind of impact she could have. She could be among the best. But she needs to learn the rules before she breaks them."

"You're going to regret this."

Willis waited a beat before speaking. "When can I expect you home? We could use you back here."

"You sure you don't want me to babysit Kent?"

"Your photos will fit his work."

Paul seriously doubted that. "You're not changing your mind?"

"No."

Paul shook his head in defeat. Next to Chris, Willis was the most stubborn person he knew. "I'll be in touch with our schedule."

"Fine."

"Sorry I woke you."

Paul placed the receiver in the cradle. *American Century* would not be the same without Chris.

***

"Jesus Christ. Jesus fucking Christ."

"Don't just stand there!" Jacobson shouted at a group of corpsmen who stared in horror at the soldiers and civilians being offloaded from the medevacs. "Get them to the hospital!" He turned to Maria Nichols. "I'm heading back to scrub. We'll work both ORs, keep them cycling through. Where's Lowery?"

"Prepping."

"Good. Send a few of the nurses and corpsmen to the club with the stable cases. I'll see you back there."

Jacobson returned to the hospital while Maria took charge of the chaos unfolding at the landing site. Helicopter crews unloaded the wounded at an alarming rate, depositing ruined bodies on stretchers that the corpsmen whisked away to waiting ambulances and trucks, then replaced with clean litters for the next batch.

Chris tilted the Yankees cap higher on her head, squinted into the swirling dust, and stepped forward to Maria's side. The nurse bent to examine a young corporal covered in blood and burns.

"Get him to the hospital," she ordered a corpsman.

"How can I help?" Chris asked.

Maria glanced at her, but didn't miss a beat in her cursory examination of the next soldier. "Do you have any medical training?"

"No."

"We can still use an extra pair of hands."

As the wounded piled up, awaiting treatment, Chris forced herself to look without seeing. She forced herself to concentrate on the movements of her own body, feeling time slow to a crawl. Hard as she tried, no amount of willpower could block the sight of charred flesh, of bloodied faces, of limbs torn from torsos and obliterated in the blast. No amount of willpower could block the acrid stench of rocket burns, pink and mottled like raw meat, mingling with the heavy exhaust of diesel fumes and Vietnam's oppressive heat.

In the hospital, wounded occupied every bed. In the first operating room, Jacobson treated the worst cases with Maria at his side, working as one. On her knees, Chris turned back to a teenaged soldier who kept clawing at the bandage covering a severe eye injury. She tried to calm him with words until his thrashing forced her to put an arm's length between them.

Two corpsmen picked up Jacobson's next patient, a soldier missing his left leg midway up the thigh. A makeshift tourniquet had initially stopped the blood loss, but in transit the torn shirtsleeve had loosened and a small pool of blood had formed under him on the stretcher, dripping to the floor. Jacobson and Maria set to work on him, but a nurse from the second operating room assisting Captain Lowery, the newly arrived surgeon, yelled for Maria in a panicked voice. Jacobson flicked his head toward the door. She ran out.

Chris watched the doctor through the open door. Jacobson cranked the tourniquet's makeshift windlass—a small stake of wood—and stopped the blood loss, but he needed another set of hands and his entire surgical unit was occupied elsewhere. Chris grabbed the corpsman nearest her and ordered him to subdue the young soldier with the eye injury. Then she went to the doctor's side.

"Put on a mask. Hand me that clamp."

Chris held the mask to her face and looked on his instrument tray for anything resembling a clamp. She guessed right. He took the clamp from her, in a gloved hand slick with bright red arterial blood, and dug his other hand into the leg stump until he found the receding femoral artery. He clamped the artery and removed the tourniquet.

"Torch."

Chris handed him a small blowtorch. Ignited, the flame burned blue and white. Jacobson drew the flame to the edge of the leg stub and the room filled with the stench of burning flesh. Fighting nausea and lightheadedness, Chris whirled away from the table just as Maria Nichols burst back into the room.

"Chris, don't lose it. Breathe through your mouth," Jacobson urged her as he cauterized tissue and veins. "Maria, get her out of here. She's going to pass out."

"I'm okay," Chris said, and then gagged silently behind the mask. Tears blurred her vision. "I'm okay."

"Are you under control?" Maria asked Jacobson. "Lowery's having a rough time in there."

"Go. It's your OR."

Chris slowly approached the table. The soldier's breathing was shallow and irregular under an oxygen mask.

"Come on, let's wrap this guy up. See that roll of gauze?"

Chris handed him the dressing and watched him wrap the stub tightly in the clean white gauze.

"Will he make it?"

"Hard to say. He lost a lot of blood. We'll get him started on a transfusion right away and then into surgery."

As he finished speaking, a scream pierced the air, the most tortured howl Chris had ever heard. She jerked like she had been jolted with a massive amount of electricity. Her heart pounded in her ears, momentarily deafening her. Without realizing it, she had grabbed Jacobson's forearm and dug her fingernails into his skin.

"It's a burn victim," he said. "He's going through debridement. It's exceptionally painful. It'll be a miracle if he survives the night."

He taped the dressing on the man's leg and motioned to a corpsman to take the patient out. Once the man was gone, he pulled his mask down and breathed deeply.

"I hate this war."

***

The medical staff worked through the night. Chris helped in any way she could, assisting the nurses and corpsmen attend to the non-critically injured soldiers and Vietnamese, mopping pools of blood from the hospital floor, delivering food for the surgical teams. The staff sergeant oversaw the movement of wounded and personnel between the hospital and the club. Colonel Brooks put in several hours with the nurses, he himself well versed in basic combat medicine. He could insert IVs and bandage wounds, and he did so with a certain gentleness that tempered the storm in his eyes.

Every hospital bed was filled; the overflow occupied tents and unused bunkers. Jacobson ordered the serious but stable cases flown to Can Tho and Saigon for specialized treatment. The armada of medevacs returned to FOB Jane, albeit in a more orderly fashion. Throughout the night, under spotlights rigged at the airstrip and with cover from every artillery piece at the base, the helicopters picked up their loads and lifted off one by one.

Lowery crashed after twelve hours; it was his first major trauma event and Chris, a casual observer, wasn't sure he was cut out for life at an evacuation hospital in the Delta. At five in the morning, after the worst of the traumas were stabilized, Maria sent Jacobson away to grab a few hours of sleep. Jacobson attempted to counter the order with one of his own, but Maria, who had lost track of how many straight hours she had worked, ignored him and disappeared into another surgery. He knew better than to fight with her, and promised to spell her in time for a late breakfast. Her nursing staff, with help from the corpsmen, would monitor the patients. She in turn promised to get him if the situation deteriorated further.

Chris pushed through the hospital doors into the early morning air, pausing to breathe its freshness. The night sky was just beginning to lighten. She walked toward the main square. Her Yankees cap and green fatigue shirt were right where she left them, balled up on a dusty patch of grass right below the colorful signpost. Her lower back ached as she bent down to retrieve them. She felt much older than she was.

"It's a beautiful morning," Major Jacobson remarked.

Chris turned to him. "Go to bed."

"I don't sleep. But you should."

"I'm afraid to close my eyes."

"Come with me."

Together they walked through FOB Jane to a bunker on the far eastern side of camp and used a pile of pallets to climb atop the structure. They sat close together, arms draped over their knees, gazing on the distant jungle, a shadow in the emerging twilight.

"It should be a spectacular sunrise this morning. Not a cloud in the sky." Jacobson focused on his hands, clasped between his open knees. "Thank you for your help."

"How do you do it? Every day, the horrible things you see, the cruelty, this whole tragedy. How do you do it?" Chris wanted an answer that made sense—she needed an answer that made sense.

"I do the best I can. I save those who can be saved and I try to make comfortable those who can't."

"And that's why you sleep so well?" she said wryly.

"I didn't say it was easy. It's my job."

"This isn't your job. This is a calling. No one suffers through this shit for the sake of a job."

"I suppose not. Look at yourself."

"I'm just here for the story, Doc."

"You put yourself in the same danger as the men, and you saw the worst kind of mistake today. It must be one hell of a story."

"Must be."

The doctor smiled. "I think it's about far more than a story."

The urge to tell someone overpowered her. "I got fired."

Jacobson looked at her. "I'm sorry to hear that. May I ask why?"

"Lack of production, creative differences with my editor, whatever you want to call it. The truth? I fucked up."

"I know it isn't what you want to hear, but if Vietnam has taught you anything, it should be that there are worse things in life than being fired."

"Can't argue with that." She reached into her cargo pocket for her cigarettes, and then offered the pack and a light to Jacobson.

"Thanks." He leaned back and blew a smoke ring into the mist. "I'd feed you some line about things happening for a reason, but you're too smart to fall for that crap. It is what it is, whatever you make of it. So make the most of it."

She smiled ruefully. "Journalism is all about reputation. I flushed mine down the toilet, then flushed again for good measure."

"Don't you think you're more than the job?"

She sighed. "This job is all I ever wanted. I don't think I ever intended to put my career before everything else in my life, but somehow it happened. My family doesn't know what to think, I really have no friends besides Paul, and the one person I want most to understand me just can't."

"John?"

Chris nodded.

"Doesn't he, though? I think he sees more clearly than you do that who you are has shaped every decision you've made out here."

Chris's thought of all the times John had made her laugh, and the times he made her cry, and the glimmer in his eyes when he looked at her, as if he could read her mind. Unconvinced, she said what was true: that it was over between them.

"Yet here you are."

Chris remained silent for a moment. "I'm not staying. There's nothing for me."

"Nothing? Look around. Who here wouldn't do anything for you?"

Chris bit her bottom lip to hold back a wave of emotion. The sun had begun its ascent, rising above the tree line to bathe the world in soft golden light.

"You're right," she said. "It's a beautiful sunrise."

She could feel his sad midnight blue eyes watching her. She turned to him. His cheeks reddened.

"I would do anything for you."

Chris smiled. "I know," she said, and kissed him, her lips lingering against his. The sadness in his eyes was replaced by fleeting joy.

Together, they watched the sunrise.

***

Chris watched the Huey on its approach to FOB Jane, admiring the slow, wide arc of its graceful turn as the pilots circled no man's land between the base and the jungle, waiting for clearance to land. She stood behind a line of sandbagging with her duffel and rucksack at her feet.

It was early evening now, and Chris had been awake for well over twenty-four hours. She was overstimulated and exhausted beyond measure. The air was heavy with the promise of rain, and behind her the storm clouds gathered.

She thought of Paul waiting for her in Saigon, anxious for her return. Paul had sacrificed so much, and he had done it for her. This was a summer he should have spent on the streets of Washington, camera in hand, documenting the impact of the war on the home front. This was a summer during which he should have spent long evenings with his wife and weekends tending his beloved gardens. He should not have spent this summer at war, in the paddies and jungles and villages, under constant threat of death, or worse.

And all for what? Chris knew she would ask herself that question until she made amends for her mistakes this summer.

She had not seen John; she had not seen any of the men. She should have waited until their patrol ended and they returned to base, but courage was a mysterious thing, ebbing and flowing like the tide, and her tide was far out to sea.

Chris reached into her rucksack for a sheaf of folded papers. With the pages in one hand and her Zippo in the other, she struck metal to flint. She touched the sheaf to the flame and lay the burning mass on the ground at her feet. As fire engulfed the finest piece of writing she had ever produced, Chris lit a cigarette, perched on the edge of the sandbagging, and watched the ashes scatter in the breeze. Where did one belong when one had nothing left?

The Huey landed and took off within ten minutes, having exchanged one set of cargo for another. Soon all flights would be grounded, but these pilots would beat the storm into Saigon and be safely on the ground when the rains battered the Delta.

Chris McKenna picked up her bags and walked back to her hooch.

14

― ⋄ ―

T he platoon arrived back at FOB Jane early in the morning two days after
the friendly-fire incident at the market. They stopped by the barracks to
dump their gear and Murphy marshaled the exhausted squad for a march across
the base.

"No way she's gone," Hector said as he pulled on his poncho. "Won't even
call the odds. There's no way."

John lingered at the back of the pack, a dull pain assailing his stomach.
Murphy led them through camp to Chris's hooch and knocked on the door.
They waited for her to stumble out, hair disheveled and eyes sleepy, or mumble
obscenities through the thatch. Murphy knocked again, harder. The only answer was the splash of raindrops into mud puddles.

In a semi-circle outside the door, the men shared a moment of silent disbelief.
John felt used, empty. Numb, like a cancer patient full of dreams just told he has
a month to live. Shoulders sagged; faces dropped. Men who had once wanted
nothing to do with Chris McKenna now missed her as they would a best friend,
a confidante. They had told her things they would never tell anyone else.

"Let's get some chow," Oscar said.

As they trudged to the mess hall, the rain intensified. One by one they filed
inside the dimly lit building in search of a hot meal. The heavy smell of sausage
and pancakes hung in the air.

"Mmm, sausage," Oscar said, patting his belly.

John Rawlins saw only the solitary woman at a far table who watched the rain pour down with a wistful look on her face.

"Well, son of a bitch," Murphy remarked, following John's gaze.

"Hey, Reporter Lady!" Oscar bellowed.

He lumbered toward her table, sending reverberations through the floor with each thud of his boots. The rest of the squad followed close behind. Chris managed to put down her coffee mug before Oscar lifted her to her feet and crushed her in a hug.

"Don't suffocate her," Ben Kearney said.

Chris accepted hugs and kisses on the cheek from many of the men. John met her eyes, and she quickly looked away.

"Chris, what the hell, we thought you'd left," Murphy complained.

"Who told you that?"

"The shit-eater."

"Who?"

"Kent Springer," John said.

Chris tensed, but he said nothing more.

"Yeah, that guy. Hey, you wouldn't leave without saying goodbye, right?"

"No."

"Promise?" Turner said.

Chris smiled. "I promise."

"So how come he said you left?" Steve asked.

She shrugged. "I don't know. But I'm still here."

"See, I told you," Hector said triumphantly. "We didn't even put odds on it."

"I'm touched," she said dryly, but something in her eyes gave her away.

"Why'd you run off?" Dan asked.

Chris wrapped her hands around her coffee mug and let her gaze wander to the ashtray where the rest of her breakfast still smoldered. "Had some business to take care of."

"What kind of business?"

"Magazine business."

"Everything okay?"

"Everything's fine."

"The bush ain't the same without you, Reporter Lady," Oscar said.

"Yeah, we got stuck with the shit-eater. Fucker nearly lost his mind when Charlie got a bead on us," Murphy said. "When I told him a chick half his size had a bigger pair, he got pretty pissed."

"Even LT laughed," Steve said. "LT never laughs."

"Poor Kent," Chris said. She smirked.

"You're going to eat something, right?" asked Kearney. "I can't condone a breakfast of coffee and cigarettes."

"Yeah, come on, let's get some grub," Dan said.

"Mmm, sausage," Oscar said again.

Chris's face, pale under her tan, acquired a green tinge.

"Hey, you look like crap," Murphy told Chris, eyeing her critically. "I mean, you're still hot and all, but you look like hell."

"Thanks."

"Just saying. You sure everything's all right?"

Chris downed the last mouthful of coffee and stood. "Let's eat."

"Better enjoy it. Our next one's a big one."

"Jersey, how the hell...?"

"Dude, I told you, I got sources."

***

Within minutes of landing that morning the staff sergeant had accosted Gianelli and Travis as they walked to their quarters, heads ducked against the rain. The staff sergeant informed them of the friendly-fire incident at the market.

"Sir," he said to Gianelli. "Major Jacobson asked to see you as soon as possible."

The staff sergeant hadn't even finished his sentence before Gianelli took off running for the hospital, still weighed down by his gear and rifle. He burst through the doors and scanned the crowds near triage, but he didn't see the familiar ponytail. He was about to stop a nurse and dispense with all subtlety when Jacobson appeared and waved to him. Gianelli pushed through the crowds of nurses, corpsmen, and walking wounded to reach the doctor.

"Where is she?" Gianelli said.

"She's resting. I finally got her to crash a couple hours ago."

Gianelli rubbed his haggard face with both hands, willing his racing heart to slow. He looked around again, taking in the scene with new eyes. "This looks like a bad one."

"The OR ran for thirty-six straight hours. But only one of us made it that long."

"Thirty-six hours in surgery?"

"I've never seen anything like it. She singlehandedly..." Jacobson paused and shook his head, his midnight blue eyes suddenly bright.

"What do you need from me?"

"I don't want to see her anywhere near this place for at least twenty-four hours. Forty-eight if you can manage it. Make sure she rests."

Gianelli shook the doctor's hand and headed straight for the nurses' quarters. He let himself into Maria's hooch and found her sprawled diagonally on her bed. She had managed to let down her hair and strip to her underwear before collapsing in exhaustion. Gianelli fought the urge to hold her, opting instead to shed his gear and boots.

He took a seat in a chair and, with elbows resting on his knees, watched her sleep. He couldn't help reflecting on their opposing missions. How many lives had he taken? How many lives had she saved? How much of themselves had they left on their respective battlefields, he in the paddies and jungles, she in the hospital?

Gianelli reached down and picked up her scrub shirt. The faded teal garment was threadbare. It had her scent. He was nearly overcome with emotion.

As he blinked away the blurriness, a small plastic wash basin under the bedside field table caught his attention. He pulled the basin onto his lap and dumped water from his canteen into it. In his pack he found his straight-edged razor and on her other field table he saw her shower accoutrements, including a bar of soap and a small mirror. He lathered his face with the soap and, using the mirror for guidance, shaved a week of beard growth.

She woke just as he was drying his face with his shirt. He threw the shirt aside and knelt by the bed.

"What time is it?" she asked in a voice thick with sleep.

"Doesn't matter."

"I need to get back."

She tried to sit up, but Gianelli pushed her down. "No, you don't. I was just there. Everything is under control."

"Are you sure?"

"Yes, baby, I'm sure. Please relax."

One hand drifted up to stroke his smooth cheek. "You shaved."

"All the women seem to prefer it that way."

She smiled just as her eyes closed and she slipped back into sleep.

***

Chris and Paul faced each other across the expanse of hooch. Though they stood no more than ten feet apart, the space between them felt wider. Slowly, Chris pushed the door shut behind her as rainwater ran down her poncho and pooled at her feet. They needed a welcome mat, she thought suddenly, inexplicably; a welcome mat on which to wipe their boots so as not to track Vietnam's mud into their dwelling. *Welcome to my hooch. Welcome to my home. Welcome to*

LYNN MASON

my hell. Then she focused. Paul did not appear angry; weary, certainly, and thoughtful, but not angry.

He cocked his head to the side and said, "Are you sure you know what you're doing?"

"No."

"But this is where you want to be?"

She sighed. "Want? Maybe. Need? Yes. But I don't expect you to stay."

"Do you want me to stay?"

"Don't ask me that."

"I just did. Do you want me to stay?"

"Paul, you are the best friend I've ever had. You've done more for me than you can possibly imagine. I will miss you, but please go home."

Paul looked down at his feet, lips pursed in concentration.

"I don't need you to protect me. I can take care of myself."

"I know that. I've always known that," he said.

"Then go. It's what you want."

"Please don't tell me what I want. I just need some time to think."

"I understand. I didn't mean to—"

Paul held up his hand. "Don't apologize." He began unloading his camera gear, laying camera bodies and lenses on a blanket and stowing the protective hard case under his cot. "I guess I'm not surprised to be back here."

"I have some unfinished business."

"You don't need to explain."

"It's not about John."

Paul raised his eyebrows.

"Well, not entirely about John."

"Speaking of business, are we going about this as business as usual?"

"Yes. I just...I just don't know how these things happen."

Paul smiled crookedly. "Story of our lives."

238

***

Chris found Major Jacobson and Ben Kearney leaving the intensive care unit of the hospital engaged in a technical and graphic discussion regarding the onset of sepsis around gunshot and fragmentation wounds, a major problem for doctors in Vietnam. Jacobson was uncharacteristically animated as he regaled Kearney with tales of clinical nightmares. She took a deep breath and approached the two men, who welcomed her with smiles. Chris knew that Kearney, upon learning of the tragedy at the market, had spent nearly every waking moment with Jacobson and Maria, helping them care for the wounded that remained at FOB Jane.

"I want you to teach me to do what he does," she said, gesturing to Kearney.

The doctor and the medic looked at each other, and then back at her.

"I don't understand," Kearney said.

"Bullet wounds, shrapnel wounds, sucking chest wounds, broken bones, dehydration, anything. Just teach me to do something useful. Please."

Jacobson knitted his eyebrows together but remained quiet.

"Chris, you're a journalist. No one expects you to—"

Chris held up a hand and silenced Kearney. "Journalism and first aid are not mutually exclusive occupations."

"No, but..."

"But what? I'm not asking you to make me into a surgeon. Just the basics. Enough to be useful. I need to be useful." The last sentence came out more forcefully than she intended.

Kearney looked at Jacobson. The doctor ran a hand over his disheveled hair.

"It puts you in harm's way."

"I've been in harm's way for months."

"Gianelli won't like it," he mused. "Or the colonel."

"Or Kittles," Kearney offered.

"God no, Kittles will be furious."

"Good thing you outrank him, Major," Kearney said.

"Young Mr. Kearney and I will accede to your request under one condition."

"Which is?"

A hint of a smile crossed Jacobson's face. "You tell the story. No matter what."

***

At the end of her shift, Maria Nichols shed blood-stained scrubs, showered, and pulled on fresh fatigue pants, a maroon University of Southern California T-shirt, and her black Chuck Taylor All-Stars. Her stomach growled—it had been ten hours since she had last eaten anything of substance—but she had a stop to make before chow. She strolled along the main drag en route to Brigade HQ, enjoying the sunshine after so many hours inside. A sergeant and his squad of tired men approached from the opposite direction, just returned from a patrol. She hugged the right side of the path to allow them to pass. Abruptly the entire squad stopped, spun ninety degrees, and saluted her. She nodded once, uncomfortably.

"Sergeant."

"Ma'am."

Brigade HQ was a building she normally avoided, save for the weekly senior staff meeting that she and Jacobson were required to attend, patient care permitting. Inside the building was cool and calm, nothing like the controlled chaos of the hospital. She walked past offices and conference rooms where men plotted attacks and fortified defenses, where men played war and pretended that they didn't see the doctors and nurses cleaning up their messes. Rick Gardner, holding court in a conference room with his intelligence officers, tossed a smile and a wave in her direction. George Wheaton, who had been staring into space, likely drunk, jumped up and leered. Seconds later she heard his footsteps as he fell in behind her. Gene Simpson and Arthur Kittles, deep in discussion just inside Simpson's office, stopped speaking and watched her as she walked past. She fixed Kittles with a baleful look. He drew back as if she might attack him.

The staff sergeant snapped to attention on her approach but then he moved toward her with urgency, his eyes focused on something behind her. Maria entered the colonel's office suite and waited a beat. Then she reached for her pocket, flicked open a switchblade, and spun around to face Wheaton, whose eyes had been glued to her ass.

"If you don't get out my sight this instant, I'll slice off that tiny syphilitic dick of yours and run it up the flagpole for everyone to see." She held the blade millimeters from Wheaton's groin.

Wheaton was paralyzed. Only his eyes moved, from her face to the blade and back.

"I think it's time for you to leave, Lieutenant," said the staff sergeant. His right hand rested on his holstered pistol.

Wheaton backed out of the anteroom and sprinted for his office. They heard the door slam. Maria retracted the blade and clipped the knife back inside her pocket.

"I'm sorry for that, ma'am. Lieutenant Wheaton is a pig." The staff sergeant paused, a smile tugging at one corner of his mouth. "But if you'll permit me to say, that was quite impressive."

"Turns out if you can wield a scalpel, you can wield a switchblade."

The staff sergeant closed the anteroom door. "Did you need to see the colonel, ma'am? He's in Saigon for the day, but I can get you on his schedule for tomorrow."

"I'm here to see you." She took a seat on the couch against the wall and appraised the young NCO. "You still having trouble sleeping?"

"Not as often, ma'am. The pain is better now that I've been doing those exercises you gave me."

"Good. Keep doing them. The looser you keep those muscles, the less stress on the bone and joints."

"Yes, ma'am. Now if you could only do something about the weather."

Almost three years ago, the staff sergeant, a former squad leader with Charlie Company, was a passenger in a Huey that crashed. The impact threw him clear of the helicopter, which likely saved his life; but he sustained broken ribs, a lacerated spleen, a punctured lung, and a shattered femur. The casualties from that crash had overwhelmed the former base surgeon, and Maria had no choice but to insert a chest tube and open him up to stop the bleeding or watch the staff sergeant drown in his own blood.

That former surgeon had screamed at his new chief of nursing for the breach of protocol and alleged usurpation of his authority at the next day's staff meeting in front of Colonel Brooks and the assembled officer corps. He found himself banished from FOB Jane later that morning on Colonel Brooks's orders. He didn't even have a chance to pack his bags before the MPs escorted him to Saigon and dumped him in the brig, run by a friend of the colonel's, until he was liberated by his male physician compatriots after a couple of hours. Brooks reconvened his senior staff that afternoon and promoted Maria to captain. Maria then ran the hospital, including the surgical unit, until the replacement surgeon, a Major Jacobson, arrived.

The staff sergeant had fully recovered from the internal injuries, but he required multiple orthopedic surgeries over the following year. His femur was held together by a rod, plates, and screws. He was a human barometer, able to predict the onset of Vietnam's ubiquitous storms with perfect accuracy.

"I think you're stuck with that particular talent, unfortunately. But on the bright side, there's always meteorology for your next career."

He smiled. He would be a lifelong soldier, and they both knew it. Though he would never again be cleared for combat, Brooks and Jacobson, at Maria's urging, had lobbied on his behalf to stay on active duty. It hadn't hurt that Brooks was an expert at operating beneath the army establishment's radar, and he didn't hesitate to create a certain reality to benefit those under his command.

The staff sergeant had been Brooks's aide since his surreptitious return to FOB Jane a year ago.

Maria leaned forward and rested her hands on her knees. "I was wondering if I could ask you for a favor."

Surprised, the staff sergeant pulled a chair close to the couch and sat on the edge, watching her intently. "Anything, ma'am."

"Can you pull some AARs for me? Say the last six months for Delta Company?"

"That's a lot of after-action reports. Are you looking for anything in particular?"

"I'll know it when I see it. But I need them all."

"Consider it done."

"Most importantly, can you do it without anyone knowing?"

"As you wish, ma'am. Shall I bring them to your office tomorrow?"

"That would be perfect. But Sergeant, I need to be clear: I don't want *anyone* knowing about this." She fixed him with her best officer's stare and raised her eyebrows pointedly.

"I understand, ma'am. Now, am I sworn to secrecy on just the AARs, or the knife skills, too?" He grinned mischievously.

"How hellish do you want your next physical therapy session to be?"

He laughed and followed her to the door. "I'll see you out."

"I'm sure I'll be fine." She patted her pocket and winked.

"I insist, ma'am." He patted his gun and winked back.

***

The only time Chris could reasonably expect privacy at the showers was in the middle of the night, which suited her just fine because she was still incapable of anything better than fitful sleep. She left Paul snoring on his cot and, with shampoo, soap, and a towel in hand, walked through base toward the secluded nurses' latrines and showers, anticipating the feel of cool water on her skin to ward off the mugginess of the night.

As she expected, the line of six stalls was empty. Just as Chris pulled open the door of the stall on the far right, she heard the scuff of flip-flops as someone entered the building. Not in the mood to deal with the wide-eyed, doe-like stares of Maria's young, naïve nurses who still had trouble processing the fact that a female journalist, the most predatory of predators, lurked in their midst, she let the door bang shut and turned to face the newcomer.

Involuntarily, she groaned.

"Nice to see you, too," said Anne Novak.

Chris rolled her eyes and stepped into her chosen stall. Much to her irritation, Anne entered the stall next to her. The side panels between stalls reached the women's shoulders. Chris stripped and hung her towel and garments on a rusty hook on the inside of the door, just out of the water's range. She turned on the spigot and tensed as the stream of lukewarm water hit her chest.

"Jesus, McKenna, eat something, would you? You look like a refugee."

Chris ignored the remark and stuck her head under the water. At home Chris had always viewed the shower as a time of leisure, but months at war had broken her of such fanciful notions of luxury. Water, time, and privacy were scarce commodities, and in this instance, so was Chris's patience. Her record for a full wash, including hair, was three minutes. She intended to shatter that record tonight.

Anne turned on her water and lathered her hair with shampoo as Chris did the same. "I heard a rumor you bailed."

"Sorry to disappoint."

"Springer seems to think your departure from *American Century* is imminent."

"He's full of shit."

"Likely. He's got quite an inferiority complex when it comes to you. Bit of a disappointment in the sack, too."

Chris glanced at Anne, arching an eyebrow.

"Talks a big game, but then it was just so…small," Anne mused. "If you know what I mean."

Chris did know what she meant, and she coughed to muffle a laugh. She rubbed the bar of soap over her skin and scrubbed every reachable inch with her hands, washing away sweat and dust and Vietnam's pervasive stench.

"Wheaton is worthless and Kent wouldn't stop whining about how he'd been shot at. I figured what the hell, a decent fuck can't hurt, right? Waste of a perfectly good rubber."

Anne turned to her as Chris rinsed the soap from her body. She moved closer to the wall separating them and rested her hands on the top edge. Chris was mildly traumatized by the amount of information Anne had just shared.

"Is he any good?" Anne asked.

"Is who any good?"

"The grunt. Come on, girl talk."

Chris shook her head as if to clear it. "Seriously? Girl talk? You hate me."

Anne shrugged. "So? Doesn't mean we can't dish about these pricks. The grunt. How is he?"

"None of your business."

"What do you think his farm girl back home would say if she found out you got your claws into him?"

Chris was momentarily confounded but then remembered the interview. She gave John credit for his creativity, but not his common sense. Not for the first time she wondered what other nonsense he had shared with Anne that hadn't made it into the *Washington Dispatch* piece.

"Claimed to be faithful to her. Funny…didn't mention you once."

Chris turned off the water, snatched her towel off the hook, and began to dry herself with rough, jerky movements. Her brain screamed for silence, but her mouth saw fit to ignore the order.

"That story was crap."

"That story was money. He's a hero now."

"He was a hero before it, and furthermore—"

Anne cut Chris off with a scoff. "We both know you're nothing unless the media proclaim it. Don't go soft out here, McKenna. Lucky you for landing a good screw, but you and I know that's all he is, so spare me the war journo-grunt solidarity shtick."

Chris spoke through clenched teeth. "He's not some dumb farm boy."

"Oh please. So what if he's just another dumb farm boy? It's okay because that's exactly what people want. They want to believe there are nuggets of goodness in this disaster, that people just as simple and average as they are can be larger than life, heroic. Your farm boy might be all of that, some of that, or none of that, but he'll be whatever I say he is because I wield the goddamn pen."

As she yanked on her clothes, Chris felt angry shame wash over her, anger because she had failed to protect John and shame because on some level she agreed with Anne. No one wanted to think or be challenged. No one wanted to face the truth.

Anne watched Chris with amusement. "You really have gone soft. Did I mention you look like death?"

Chris shoved through the door of the stall and stalked out of the building. Anne's laughter followed her down the path.

***

True to his word, the staff sergeant delivered six months of after-action reports for Delta Company to Maria's office the next day. He handed her the documents, concealed in a green rucksack, with a grim look. Then he clicked his heels and pulled the door closed behind him.

Maria set the pile on her desk. She already knew what she would find, but she took a fortifying breath and began to skim the reports, looking for the dry, staccato recap of each operation written in tiny, immaculate block letters by the hand of a lawyer uninterested in pandering to his superiors.

Hours later, she faced four stacks of documents, one noticeably taller than the others. Calmly, she set the stacks into her bottom desk drawer. She locked the unit, grabbed her stethoscope, and began her rounds.

15

— • —

The fleet of Huey gunships and Chinook troop transports lifted off from FOB Jane as the sun rose over the Mekong Delta. The first helicopter to take to the sky was filled to capacity with officers and journalists, and it flew in the middle of the pack surrounded on all sides by Hueys and Chinooks teeming with the four platoons of Delta Company.

Chris, seated between Paul and Gianelli on the back bench, stifled a yawn. She and Paul had stayed up most of the night talking by the light of a hurricane lamp, and finally Chris was able to convince him to go home. Teary-eyed, he made her promise to stay only as long as absolutely necessary.

This operation to several western villages near the Cambodian border would be his last; his flight departed at the end of the week. Chris suspected that more than anything, Paul wanted to see with his own eyes Kent Springer at war. Travis had confirmed First Squad's collective assessment that Springer was not cut out for combat, and that his habit of freezing in place and screaming obscenities at the enemy was less than helpful under fire.

In the beaten green rucksack at her feet, in addition to her normal load, Chris now carried an augmented trauma kit to supplement Ben Kearney's more robust pack of supplies. Jacobson and Kearney had begun her lessons in earnest, spending hours at a time teaching her the medic's trade. Jacobson often excused himself to make rounds or attend to incoming wounded, but Kearney was a reassuring presence at her side as she learned to tourniquet and bandage properly, read the signs of dehydration, and insert IV or morphine needles.

She practiced the tourniquet procedures on Kearney, doing her best to cut off circulation in one of his limbs, and the needle procedures on spoiled fruit from the mess. Though her technique was still far from perfect, she grasped the basic concepts.

Chris had told no one, not even Paul, of her time with the medical staff. She worried he would think it was silly or foolish, not to mention dangerous. When she disappeared for the better part of a week, she told him she was still interviewing and writing, despite lacking employment. Paul understood her plausible desire to regain her job and encouraged her to keep at it and prove to Willis that he had made a mistake.

Now she was simply living a lie, something different to everyone around her. To some it might not matter what she called herself; to others it was everything. If she were to admit what she had become, would she cease to be?

Chris leaned her head against the Huey's rear wall, her body vibrating in tune to the shakes and the tremors in the metal all around her. She felt Paul's leg bump hers, Gianelli's elbow brush her forearm. She was aware of silent soldiers and journalists, the smell of metal and grease and sweat, the *whap whap* of the rotors. She could not suppress her thoughts, silent but insistent bearers of truth. *I am nothing*, they said, repeating the same line like a broken phonograph to the beat of the helicopter. *I am nothing.*

***

"*Dios mio, es muy caliente!*" Hector said cheerfully.

"Fuck that *caliente* shit, it's hot, man," Steve complained as he piled his gear in a heap and stripped to his tank top.

John and Dan glanced quizzically at each other.

"Jersey, pick up your gear and get ready to move out. I don't want LT taking heat because you have the I.Q. of monkey shit," Travis said.

LYNN MASON

"Remember last time the captain got mad at us? We spent a lot of extra time in the bush," Turner pointed out.

"Smart boy, Turner. Let's do it right today. We're on point for this op."

"Of course we are," Murphy muttered.

Travis threw him a warning look. "Cool it."

"Hey, Sarge, can Chris and the photo man run with us?" Steve asked.

Travis looked annoyed by the question, but tossed a glance over his shoulder at Captain Kittles and the menagerie of journalists who surrounded him, some more reluctantly than others. The Yankees cap shaded her face from view, but Travis watched her fidget like a bored child in church on the outskirts of the circle, a sure sign that Kittles was in the middle of a long-winded monologue on standard operating procedures for journalists in the field.

"They'll be safer with the captain."

"But Sarge, she won't like that."

"Schaefer, just shut up."

"But Sarge, we can keep her safe. We been doing it for months. Girl don't got a scratch on her."

"Schaefer!" he roared.

Steve cringed. "Sorry, Sarge."

***

John walked point under the August sun, his clothing already drenched with sweat. Their landing zone was less than three miles from the hamlets, but Kittles called frequent halts to confer with his lieutenants in full view of his entourage of correspondents. John dropped down to one knee at the edge of the elephant grass and watched the group from a distance, waiting impatiently from his exposed position at the front of the column. Kittles whipped out his map and checked their position both by compass and against the sun. John, who knew exactly where they were, also knew that the hamlets were approximately half a

250

mile away to the west, through steadily thinning jungle. The *Washington Dispatch* photographers, weighed down by multiple cameras and lenses, dutifully took Kittles's picture, snapping away as the captain examined the map like a taller, fatter Napoleon.

At one point during the third halt, Gianelli made his way up to First Squad's position to kneel beside Travis, a few yards behind John.

"This is ridiculous."

"We're sitting ducks," Travis said.

"Balcolm and I tried to tell him that. But Commandant Kittles knows best."

"Then let's hope Charlie is on vacation today."

John saw that neither Chris nor Paul had touched the tools of their trade, and both appeared to be searching for an escape. One presented itself when Kittles, trailed by Anne and Springer, approached Gianelli and Travis. Chris and Paul scooted up to join Hector, Oscar, and Bullseye on the left flank.

"Lieutenant, we'll be with the point from here on out."

Gianelli and Travis shared a look. "Sir?" said Gianelli. "I don't understand. These hamlets are known to be hostile."

"All the more reason for strong leadership. I'd like to speak to the point man."

Travis waved John over and patted him on the back as he passed to join Gianelli, Kittles, and the reporters. Anne's mouth curved into a predatory smile.

"Your name?" Kittles asked.

"John Rawlins."

Kittles narrowed his eyes. Gianelli and Travis tried to pretend nothing was amiss, and did an admirable job wearing identically blank expressions. When Kittles finally realized he was staring at FOB Jane's most famous—or infamous—soldier, he tried to look at everyone at once. First Anne, then Gianelli, then over his shoulder at Chris, then back to John.

"Yes, well," he continued, "Mr. Rawlins, we will be on point. Should we receive hostile fire, I would like you to take responsibility for Mr. Springer. I will cover Ms. Novak."

"Yes, sir."

Springer snorted. "Great. My life in the hands of McKenna's boy-toy."

"I assure you that Rawlins is beyond reproach in both competency and courage," Gianelli said, his tone cutting. "And if you are still concerned about your safety, Master Sergeant Travis and I would be happy to be a close, constant presence at your side."

Springer looked between Gianelli and Travis. Both men glowered at him, and Travis made a show of fingering his rifle trigger, the muzzle rising to the level of Springer's crotch.

"Whatever," said Springer. "G.I. Joe here is fine."

"G.I. Joe is a hero now," Anne said. She casually nibbled at a thumbnail as she looked him over.

"Ah yes, Ms. Novak's article. You should be very proud, son," said Kittles.

John said nothing.

"Aren't you?"

John knew truth had no place in this discussion. The sooner they moved out, the sooner it would all be over. "Yes, sir."

"It's quite an honor." Kittles leaned forward conspiratorially. "One we share."

"Yes, sir."

Kittles clearly expected him to say something more. John waited for orders. "Well then, let's move out. Take us to the village."

As John turned to lead the company, Gianelli turned to Travis and spoke in a voice dripping with disdain.

"God bless the Fourth Estate."

***

Gianelli and Travis stayed close to the point, trailing a few yards behind Anne and Springer, who followed John and Kittles. The beaten trail led into the village; they could see a maze of huts and farmers in the distant rice paddies.

As the trail opened into the hamlet and John stepped across an invisible threshold, the shots rang out, a dozen by Travis's count.

Kittles collapsed. John whirled and tackled Anne and Springer, clotheslining each of them with an arm to the chest.

Gianelli and Travis dropped to the ground and yelled for cover. As Travis turned to shout to First Squad, he saw Chris McKenna jerk and stumble and fall to her backside, the impact knocking the Yankees cap off her head. She put her right hand to her left arm. When she pulled it away, she looked in confusion at the blood on her palm.

"Kearney!" Travis yelled. He sprinted to her side and was on her in an instant, positioning himself between her and the rifle fire.

"Those bastards just shot me," she said in disbelief.

***

As Delta Company swarmed into the village to seek out the shooters, First Squad tended en masse to the one wounded reporter. Kearney repeatedly told them to back off and give him space, but as they leaned over each other to ask Chris for the hundredth time if she would be all right, they crowded the medic and his patient yet again.

"Sarge, could you?"

"Let's go, step back. Let Doc help her." Travis allowed only Paul to remain at her side, and Paul had turned so pale under his tan that Chris thought he might faint.

The experience was surreal. Someone else had been shot, someone who looked just like her, Chris told herself. She could not possibly have been shot. She was just a journalist. She wasn't really part of the war.

She watched Kearney root through his gear for a dressing; she felt Paul ease off her pack and remove her fatigue shirt. She winced when fabric brushed the wound. Free from the torn shirt, she examined her arm. The bullet had grazed her midway between elbow and shoulder, leaving a bloody gash.

Several of the men sharply sucked in a breath, as if in all their years of war they had never before seen a minor gunshot wound.

"You ain't gonna die, right?" Steve said.

"Hadn't planned on it."

Jacobson and Kearney had taught her to properly deal with a flesh wound, and she mentally walked through the steps. The blood was dark red—a venous bleed, far preferable to an arterial bleed. A cursory cleaning of the wound and a simple but tight wrap dressing would suffice until they returned to FOB Jane.

"Don't you worry, honey, we's gonna grease the asshole that shot you," Oscar assured her.

"Yeah, grease the asshole," Bullseye echoed.

Kearney doused a square of gauze in alcohol. "This is going to sting."

As he dabbed at the wound, Chris crushed Paul's hand in her own. A yelp escaped. Her arm exploded in pain, like it had been seared with a branding iron.

"Hey, Sarge, will she get a Purple Heart?" Hector asked.

"Nope."

"She should."

Kearney wrapped a white dressing around her arm. She was now a statistic, a part of the war.

"All done. Major Jacobson will take a look at it when we return."

Chris forced a smile. "Thanks, Ben."

"You sure you're all right?"

"I'm sure." She hopped to her feet and gingerly moved her arm. It hurt, but the pain was bearable.

When she turned, she found herself facing Gianelli and Travis, both of whom stood with arms across their chests and regarded her with evident relief.

Murphy picked up Chris's Yankees cap and set it back on her head. Paul snapped a few photos of Chris, who made a face at him. Some of the missing color had returned to his cheeks, but he still looked as though he'd lost years from his life.

"Rawlins, quick thinking with Novak and Springer. We could have been up to our asses in wounded journos," Travis said.

"The captain took one," John said.

"How bad?"

"Just a scratch."

"We're going to hear about it," Travis said to Gianelli.

"You think?" he replied sarcastically. "Now then, if Miss McKenna is done getting shot, we need to make an appearance in the village."

Chris suddenly had a dozen armed bodyguards who formed a tight circle around her. "This is not necessary."

Dan spoke for the group. "Please let us protect you. Just this once."

"Do I get a choice?"

"No," Gianelli said. "So just relax."

She touched two fingers to her head in a mock salute.

"Mr. Rawlins, if you please?"

There was a long pause as everyone waited for John to acknowledge the order to move out. John's eyes, hard and vacant, were on Chris. Travis and Gianelli exchanged a glance.

"Rawlins?"

Wordlessly, John turned and led them into the village.

***

The three other medics traveling with Delta Company had spent the last fifteen minutes tending to Captain Kittles. The medics, to their credit, stopped the bleeding immediately despite Kittles's theatrics.

After taking the hit, Kittles had collapsed to the dusty earth and flopped about like a beached whale. His skin had turned pasty gray, the color of the mess hall's oatmeal, and he sweated so profusely that the medics considered starting an IV to replenish his fluids despite the minimal blood loss.

Kittles had been shot in the lower torso; a bullet had nicked the right side of his belly, now exposed as the medics taped on a bandage. He couldn't bring himself to watch the procedure, so distraught was he by the thought that he might bleed out on a dirt road in the middle of a goddamn swamp.

Through his pain, he was pleased to see Anne Novak and Kent Springer watching him with concern, though once the medics peeled away his shirt to expose the wound Anne looked merely bored. Springer, on the other hand, started to swoon and had to turn away. Kittles, playing off Springer's mortification, thrashed a bit, causing the one of the medics to bump the wound. This provoked a howl of real pain from the captain and a chorus of mumbled apologies from the medics.

Finally, Kittles struggled to his feet, assisted by a medic and one of his aides. He put a hand to his side and struggled with his words.

"Anne, Kent, are you injured?"

"G.I. Joe did his job," Anne said.

Except he let me get shot, Kittles thought. Then he was hit by a sweet revelation: he would receive a Purple Heart for his wound. He was a true warrior, christened by the droplets of blood on the path at his feet. He felt vibrant, powerful, alive...

Until Chris McKenna strolled down the road. She was surrounded by one of Gianelli's squads and on her left arm was a white bandage with a spot of dark blood seeping through the center. She walked confidently, with the top half of her fatigues tied around her waist and a maddening charisma radiating from her person.

Arthur Kittles felt himself deflate, the bravado evaporating in the humid air. He wanted nothing less than to share the spotlight with a journalist, particularly this journalist. When she paused by the captain's side, so did Gianelli's squad, arrayed about her like a presidential protection detail with rifles at the ready.

"You all right?" she asked him from under the brim of the Yankees cap. A sparkle in her green eyes danced in mocking amusement.

He drew himself to his full height and sucked in his tender gut. "Of course. But my main concern is you. I see you are injured."

"I'll live."

How could she be so nonchalant? Charlie had nearly cut them down. "Lieutenant, get your men into that village. Do you really need a squad of soldiers to take care of one wounded reporter?"

"My men were tending to the injured and securing the area," Gianelli said calmly.

"Fine, injured tended to and area secured. Now get in the fight."

A flick of Gianelli's head sent the squad into the village. Chris and Paul took up stride with the phalanx.

"Miss McKenna, please, it isn't safe!" Kittles called to her, a note of panic creeping into his voice.

Chris turned and tipped up the cap. "Kent can play it safe enough for the both of us," she said with an infuriating smirk.

Springer swore under his breath. Much to Kittles's surprise, Anne Novak followed the group and waved her photographers forward.

"Anne!"

"For God's sake, you've got over a hundred grunts in there with enough firepower to invade China. No feature story if you act like a baby."

Kittles saw it all so clearly—she wanted decisiveness, a man of action, an officer who would not shy away from the tough choices. He could be that man. He would get the job done, and he would do it in spectacular fashion.

***

Lieutenant Graves had been gunned down in a firefight and Lieutenant Jenkins had been fragged during a visit to the FOB Jane latrines, which made Lieutenants Gianelli and Balcolm Delta Company's fonts of knowledge and experience and authority. With the two new platoon lieutenants unable to maintain order, the push into the village degenerated into a free-for-all. Gianelli and Travis ordered First Squad to round up women, children, and elderly and shepherd them to safety while Conlon and Second Squad assisted the search for arms and tunnels. Ben Kearney set up his makeshift trauma center in the abandoned village meeting hall while his squad-mates, led by John and Dan, carried out Gianelli's orders. Chris, in a curious break with her own standard operating procedures, chose to remain behind with Kearney.

Kearney and Chris tried to check each villager for injury as they entered the meeting hall under First Squad's armed escort, but they were quickly overwhelmed by the numbers. Dan's half of the squad had returned first with throngs of villagers, followed ten minutes later by John and his men, who had another group in tow.

"What's going on out there?" Chris asked.

John and Dan glanced at each other, as if coming to an agreement on who would speak. Then John focused his eyes on Chris's hands as she taped gauze over a child's skinned knee.

"Just be glad you're in here," Dan said.

Gianelli and Travis joined the group. Both men looked irate, and Gianelli cursed the FNG lieutenants.

"LT, why hasn't the captain shut this down? People are getting slaughtered out there."

Gianelli considered Dan's question and carefully measured his words. "The captain possibly misinterpreted his orders."

"Bullshit," Chris murmured.

"I would argue, Miss McKenna, that some of the impetus for this behavior is the deleterious influence you and your colleagues exert over anyone in a position of authority."

Her eyes flashed. "I would never glorify this."

"Doesn't matter. He thinks you will."

"Where's Darwin?" Travis asked.

John stiffened. He retraced their steps from the last hooch to the hall. He had run point with Steve and Murphy on the flanks. Billy had been swallowed up by the mass of women, but he had escaped and now smoked a cigarette in the corner. Darwin had brought up the rear, face contorted by a familiar leer as they crossed a deserted swath of village ravaged by American bloodlust.

Without a word of explanation, John ran from the hall.

***

"Where the hell is he going?" Gianelli asked.

"Don't know," Travis replied.

Dan shrugged.

Chris looked with concern at the open door, but then turned back to help Kearney with a woman and her baby. The men watched the pretty young woman bring her hand to her mouth and mime a feeding motion, pointing to the baby. Chris nodded understanding and went about mashing some canned pears from a C-ration for the child. The young villager bowed repeatedly, gratefully.

Understanding struck all three men at once.

"Oh fuck," Gianelli said.

Like John, they hit the open doorway in a sprint.

***

LYNN MASON

The grove of banana trees on the west end of the village was quiet. Screams struggled to escape the grove, and the distant rifle shots were only muffled pops as they traveled the humid air currents.

The leaves of the thick banana trees, planted decades ago by intrepid rice farmers seeking to diversify their crops, swayed in a gentle breeze. Shadows danced along the fertile earth, mimicking the movements of the leaves. Beneath the biggest tree in the grove, Darwin raped a young Vietnamese woman.

John Rawlins grabbed Darwin by the back of the shirt and yanked him away from the woman. Darwin turned in surprise and John punched him in the face with enough force to shatter his cheekbone.

Darwin fell to the ground, moaning. John dropped down, one knee on Darwin's chest, and threw punch after punch into the man's face until it was nearly unrecognizable. He wanted Darwin to feel every broken bone, every chipped tooth, wanted him to feel the exquisite fear as his victim had, knowing that he was at another's mercy.

Just as Darwin's eyes rolled back and he drifted into unconsciousness, two hands wrapped around John's raised fist and a voice urged him to hold the last blow.

"He's not worth it," Dan Peters said.

Instinct told him to struggle against the hands that restrained him, but Dan held his fist suspended in midair.

"He's not worth it," Dan repeated.

John's muscles uncoiled; he lowered his bloodied fist and raised himself off Darwin's chest. He pushed the bush hat off his head and let it hang from his neck. Beads of sweat caught his eyelashes and burned his eyes. He heard the swish of the leaves in the breeze and Darwin's ragged breathing. The world came into focus—Gianelli and Travis standing silent to his left, Dan at his side, Darwin at his feet, and a young woman at the base of the banana tree.

Travis was the first to speak. "Go get Kearney," he told Dan.

"And Chris," Gianelli said. "We need Chris."

The Vietnamese woman cowered against the tree trunk like a beaten animal, knees drawn to her chest, eyes darting between the men who watched her. Darwin had bound her hands with his belt and gagged her with a dirty rag. Her black pajamas were in tatters; what remained of the pants was down about her ankles.

John took a step toward her, intending to at least remove the gag and unbind her, but her panicked cry, muffled by the rag, froze him. She curled into a tight ball and clenched her eyes shut. The men looked helplessly at each other.

Dan returned in minutes with Chris, Kearney, and Paul. Kearney looked from Darwin to the woman and back. Then he stepped over Darwin and cautiously approached the woman. She cried out again. Kearney looked back at Gianelli uncertainly.

Gianelli turned to Chris, who stared unblinking at the woman. "She might respond better to you."

Chris dropped her pack and removed the Yankees cap from her head. The spot of red in the center of the bandage on her left arm had expanded in diameter. She composed herself with a deep breath, brushed past the men, and knelt beside the woman.

Her cries in Chris's presence were softer and less insistent. She allowed Chris to remove the rag, covered in gun grease, and release her arms. Chris offered her the bloodstained fatigue shirt from around her waist, which she accepted and hugged to her chest. On one side of her tear-streaked face was a palm print, a match to Darwin's hand.

"Show her your armband," Chris told Kearney.

He pointed to his medic's armband and showed her his pack of bandages and equipment. Chris held one of the woman's hands and told John, Dan, Paul, Gianelli, and Travis to turn away.

Darwin began to moan, awake and in pain. Travis kicked him in the gut.

"Shut up, you piece of shit."

"I'm sorry, LT," John said.

Gianelli shook his head. "This isn't your fault."

"I would have killed him," Travis said, and John believed him.

"I'm sorry," John said again.

"What's the story, Doc?" Travis asked.

"She's a mess. Bruised, beaten, plus bleeding."

"Can you bandage her up?"

Ben Kearney's gaze drifted to the prone Darwin. "It's not that kind of bleeding," he said in a hard voice.

Not that kind of bleeding. Above him the palm fronds swished and John's eyes were drawn to the languid sway of the shadows at his feet, mesmerized by the rhythm, the harmony. The war disappeared and he was in her arms, deep within her, part of her, as close as they could be. Bright green eyes searching for his, her rapid breathing and restless hands, the unmistakable spasms of pleasure rippling through the body she pressed against him. How soft she was, soft and vulnerable and trusting. Her trust, her gift to him.

"Will she be all right?" Gianelli asked.

The medic sighed. "I would feel a lot better if Captain Nichols had a look."

"We could have a medevac here in a couple of hours," Travis said. "But Kittles will never approve it."

Gianelli rubbed his beard stubble. "We'll bring her back to the hall and figure it out."

"Only one stretcher. Darwin can't walk, and I doubt she's going to let any of us carry her," Kearney said.

"Take her first. I'll stay here with Darwin," Travis said.

"That might not be necessary," Chris said.

The men turned to see the village woman walking unsteadily into the grove. She wore Chris's shirt and the remnants of her pants, billowing in the wind, tatters fluttering in every direction. Black pajama pants. A torn black shirt at the base of the tree. A pair of sandals fashioned from old tires, one on the left foot, the other held in her right hand. The typical dress of a Viet Cong operative.

"Someone should stop her," Ben Kearney said, a hint of despair in his voice. "She needs medical attention."

But no one moved to stop her, perhaps because no one knew what to say or how to say it. It was more than a language barrier holding them back, for each felt a paralyzing sense of shame in knowing that although they did not perpetrate the act, they were all a part of it just the same.

"Let her go," Chris said softly.

***

"Burn it," Captain Kittles said.

Four lieutenants, three writers, and several photographers looked at the captain in surprise.

"Sir," Lieutenant Balcolm said, "did you say...?"

"Burn it! Burn this place to the ground! How many goddamn times do I have to tell you?" He grew more agitated with each word, sweating and gesticulating until he remembered he had been shot. Then a look of pain passed across his face as he put a hand to his side.

"Sir, the colonel—"

"The colonel is not here," Kittles roared. "This is my operation. Now do it!"

"They were just potshots," Chris said, cutting to the crux of the issue.

"Miss McKenna, those snipers opened fire on an officer of the United States Army."

"You think you were the target?"

"Of course. To strike down an officer would be a tremendous victory for the insurgents."

"I think they shot at the first soldier they saw and hit you by dumb luck."

"No, they hit you by dumb luck. Now watch yourself. I have orders from the colonel."

"I doubt he meant burning down an entire village because you got nicked."

"I am this unit's commanding officer. Show a little respect."

"Respect? When you use the actions of a few to punish hundreds? You don't deserve respect. You deserve a firing squad."

Gianelli stepped between her and Kittles. Facing her, he gave an almost imperceptible shake of his head.

"That's right, Lieutenant, get her out of my sight. That's the smartest thing you've done yet."

"You aren't worth the bullet that hit you."

Gianelli took her by her uninjured arm and led her away from the captain, who swore and kicked at the dirt, then yelled again for the flamethrowers. She shrugged out of Gianelli's grip and glared at him.

"What the hell is wrong with you?" he hissed. "Don't make it easier for him to come after you."

Chris rolled her eyes. "What's the worst he could do? Send me home?"

"And ruin your reputation faster than you thought possible. Even incompetent officers have powerful benefactors."

"Is that why you're so scared to stand up to him?"

"McKenna, stick to being a journalist."

"I *am* being a journalist. I've been watching this conflict simmer for months, and it's always your platoon that suffers. What's the deal, you afraid he might give you a spanking if you stand up for your guys?"

His voice was low, dangerous, and he didn't hesitate to meet her eyes. "Don't ever question my loyalty to the men under my command. I don't know if he makes life miserable for them because he hates only me or hates you and me equally, but I don't care. I have done my best both to facilitate your access to my platoon and shield my guys from his ineptitude, but I won't hesitate to sacrifice whatever story you intend to tell to protect them."

"Then tell the colonel he's out of control."

"For Christ's sake, McKenna, open your eyes. Brooks's responsibility is to the mission. He doesn't give a damn who Kittles sacrifices in order to get it done, because if Kittles doesn't sacrifice someone, someone above Brooks will sacrifice *him*. Haven't you learned a fucking thing?"

She smiled without humor. "Oh, I've learned plenty about sacrifice."

As she spoke, plumes of dark smoke rose into the cloudless blue sky. Half a dozen men with flamethrowers strapped on their backs coated huts, the Buddhist temple, empty livestock pens, and banana trees with flames. Within minutes, the entire village was ablaze. Its occupants watched silently from a makeshift holding area just outside the village proper, guarded by Balcolm's platoon.

"You can't save the world," Gianelli told her. "Maybe think about saving yourself instead."

She said nothing. He walked away.

The reporters stood in a small group near Balcolm and the two new lieutenants. Chris distanced herself a few feet away, dropping down to a squat to watch the destruction. Paul took two rolls of film as the village disintegrated under orange fire, whipped into frenzy by the breeze. Flames licked skyward from the canopy of the banana grove, a fitting end to a day of horror.

When she could no longer stand the sight of the blaze, Chris's gaze wandered to her fellow journalists, two people who could not be more different from her if they tried. Anne Novak watched with equanimity; Kent Springer watched with boredom. Chris watched them with an overwhelming sense of helplessness and couldn't help wondering when she had become so powerless or why that knowledge didn't bother her more. She rubbed her eyes and as her nose filled with the acrid odor of smoke, of lives destroyed, she thought only of how tired she was.

***

John had been waiting for over an hour seated under the blue destination signpost, his eyes watchful under the bush hat. To pass the time he had munched on a chocolate bar, unsuccessfully attempted to calculate the distance in miles from FOB Jane to Iowa, and gamed his approach to Chris when she finally emerged from the hospital. He would be forthright, but he did not expect the same courtesy from her. He expected her usual dance routine around vexing issues, perhaps some verbal sparring, and certainly an indignant, angry defense.

She pushed through the doors and he hopped to his feet, slung his rifle over his shoulder, and strode toward her, blocking her path. She sidestepped him and continued on her way. He fell in beside her.

"I don't need an escort."

"You almost got yourself killed today."

"Hardly."

"Chris, you got shot. All for what, some stupid job?"

"It's barely a scratch. But thanks for your concern, underwhelming as it is."

"Hey, I saved lover boy's worthless skin. What more do you want from me?"

"You are unbelievable," she said.

They walked in silence, their boots crunching on the dry earth. John watched her from the corner of his eye. She kept her gaze focused straight ahead.

"You were going to leave, weren't you? You were going to leave and you weren't going to tell me."

"No."

"I don't believe you. I was going to have to find out like every other nobody, from Steve's sources or the rumor mill. I was going to be the guy thinking I meant more to you than everyone else." He smirked. "Yup, I was going to be that guy."

"John..."

"Stop. We both know you were going to leave. What made you decide to stay? Springer? Old flame back in town, pick up where you left off?" He laughed unexpectedly, oddly amused by the thought of Chris and Springer together, though beneath the laughter black fury bubbled, thick as tar, approaching a boil.

"It meant nothing."

"That seems to be news to him. He's telling anyone who will listen how you jumped him every chance you got."

"Do you believe that?"

John laughed again. "Does it matter whether I believe it? And what the hell did you see in him, anyway? He's a jerk."

"And you're an asshole. So I guess I have a type."

"*I'm* an asshole?"

"What happened between Kent and me is years old. It has nothing to do with today."

"It has everything to do with today," he said. "Everything. How many times have I asked you about the simplest things? How many times did you dodge or lie outright? Then that creep shows up and..." His voice began to shake and he trailed off.

"I didn't stay because of him. I'm sorry you had to find out about it this way, I really am, but I never expected to see him here."

"Never the twain shall meet," he said softly.

Once at her hooch, she reached for the door, but his voice stopped her.

"Why did you stay, Chris?"

"For my work," she said evenly. "I still need the story."

"Oh, you got the story, all right. You got him good."

John saw her tense, her hand still outstretched, resting on the door. Against his will, he reached out and touched her injured arm, just above the bandage, for only a second. Then his hand dropped to his side and she disappeared into the hooch without a word.

***

"Have I ever hurt you?" Gianelli asked.

Maria Nichols picked up her head from where it rested in the hollow of his shoulder to look at him. "What?"

"Have I ever hurt you?"

"You mean...?"

"Yes."

"No, you have never hurt me."

Gianelli stared at the ceiling of her hooch, where shadows cast by the hurricane lamp flickered. He could feel her watching him, but he couldn't bring himself to meet her dark eyes.

"Talk to me," she whispered, punctuated by a kiss on the cheek.

Gianelli searched for a way to lessen the impact of his words, but found no way out. He stated the facts as he once had in a New York City courtroom, plainly, for the jury to absorb and judge on their merit. "One of my guys raped a villager today." He felt her tense against him. "Kearney treated her as best he could, but she didn't want much to do with us."

"Who did it?"

"He's in the hospital."

"The one whose face...?" She trailed off. "Did you do that?"

"No. But I wish I had. John Rawlins beat me to it."

She stayed silent. Her fingers traced over his abdominal muscles, the lightest of caresses.

"She was VC," he continued.

"That would matter to some. To most."

"If she took up arms against us, I would engage her in combat. If I had to kill her, I would kill her. But not that." Gianelli shook his head. "Not that."

"What will you do?"

"It's a long shot, but I'll submit the paperwork and hope that charges are brought. I had Paul take a few discreet photos of the scene for evidence."

"I guess having journalists around isn't the worst thing in the world."

Gianelli grunted. "How is Chris, anyway?"

"She was lucky. Another inch and that bullet would have shattered her arm. She'll be sore for a while, but she'll heal up just fine."

"I almost had a heart attack when I saw her go down."

"I knew she'd grow on you."

"She drives me nuts. She's been here for months, and nothing. She could literally shut this place down and put half these assholes in the brig. I can't figure it out. I've served it up to her on a silver platter. At this rate I'll have to write the goddamn exposé myself. They can mail my Pulitzer to federal prison."

She patted his stomach. "It's a good thing you're cute, because you're a bit dense sometimes."

"What's that supposed to mean?"

"Someday you'll figure it all out. Did you know that Pat and Kearney have been giving her lessons in emergency field medicine?"

Gianelli looked at her in surprise. "No. I had no idea."

"Something's going on."

He sighed. "I'm convinced Rawlins fucked it up."

"Well, he is a man."

Gianelli could think of no witty rejoinder to that fact and all it implied, so he opted to speak a different language. He extricated his arm, now numb, and settled himself over her, resting his forehead against hers.

"I love you," he whispered.

She smiled, a movement he felt more than he saw. "I love you more."

"Darling, are we going to be *those* people?"

"You started it."

"And I plan to finish it, too," he said, and pressed his lips to hers.

***

Chris and Paul returned to the hooch after a late dinner that ran long on conversation over rubbery chicken, tasteless rice, and mushy vegetables. Chris was exhausted, her arm throbbed, and John Rawlins had yet again come to the right conclusion based on the wrong information. She tried to push that inconvenient truth out of her mind because Paul was scheduled to leave for Saigon tomorrow morning, and she wanted to enjoy her last hours with her friend.

He ran a hand through his mop of curly hair, wild in the humidity. "What a day. How's the arm?"

"It's fine. Same as it was ten minutes ago."

"Susan won't believe me when I tell her."

"Oh, I think she will."

"Actually, she's commented a number of times that trouble seems to find you wherever you go."

Chris smiled, but it quickly faded. "Can I ask you a question? Was it the same when you were a Marine?"

Paul sighed. "Men have brutalized women since the dawn of time. It doesn't take a war to bring out the worst in us."

Seated on the rickety chair, Chris leaned forward, elbows on her knees, chin in her hands. She wiggled her bare toes, thought of the woman's makeshift tire sandals and the small feet resting among droplets of blood. Blood from her most intimate place.

"What did you say to her?" Paul asked. "She seemed to respond."

"She didn't understand a word of it, but I told her it would be okay." Chris shook her head. "But that's a lie. We all know it's not going to be okay."

Paul picked up his favorite Nikon, fiddled with the aperture setting, and snapped a photo of Chris still pensively mulling the impact of her words. She raised her eyes half a second before the click of the shutter, looking straight into the lens. He then began to rewind the film.

"What was that for?"

"To show Susan that you've taken a few hits, but you'll pull through. She likes when I include pictures with my letters."

"Except you'll be home in a couple of days."

"I'm not going home."

She looked at him in surprise. "Why not?"

He shrugged. "Not ready."

"Paul, you promised me you would go home."

He looked at her, eyes gentle. "Let's not start harping on broken promises."

"You don't have to stay."

"I know. But I'll regret it if I leave. I can't go home when you need me."

"I don't..." She trailed off, unable to finish the sentence. "What if something happens to you?"

Paul reached for Chris's hand. "I've already taken shrapnel in the back in one war. Lightning won't strike twice in the same spot. He pulled her up and hugged her. "This is where I want to be."

"Thank you, Paul," she whispered.

16

—·—

Through a cloud of cigarette smoke from her table in a corner of the mess hall, Chris watched Colonel Matthew Brooks take his breakfast alone, without a retinue of aides like Captain Kittles, without the most up-to-date Viet Cong casualty figures like Lieutenant Colonel Simpson, without a sampling of the current VC propaganda efforts like Major Gardner. Colonel Brooks simply ate his breakfast—eggs and fried potatoes—quietly and efficiently like a good soldier.

Chris sat down across from him with a mug of coffee. He looked up, surprised by the intrusion, a forkful of eggs poised halfway between his plate and mouth.

"You're up early," he said.

"Couldn't sleep. Mind some company?"

"Not at all. How's your arm?"

"Healing well, thank you. How's your sanity?"

"Dead and buried since the day I was commissioned."

"When's the last time you took some R&R?"

"Probably about 1952." Brooks cocked his head and regarded her thoughtfully. "There's a question you want to ask me."

"Yes."

"I don't know why you waited so long."

"Who is Jane, Colonel?"

"Jane is my wife. Was my wife."

"What happened?"

"She passed away in 1965. Cancer."

"I'm sorry."

"Me too."

"You were here?"

He nodded. "Saigon, waiting to take command of a forward base in the Delta. I was scheduled for home leave at the end of April. But she deteriorated quickly, too quickly. I didn't make it back in time."

Chris remained silent, watching him drift into the past, remembering what war had taken from him. When he spoke again, his voice was hollow.

"I just…I just never thought I would lose her, you know? She had gone into remission and we thought she beat it. So I followed orders like I always did and shipped off, not knowing I would never see her again. She didn't tell me how bad it was until it was too late. I went back to bury her, but I haven't been back since."

"What will you do when this is over?"

"Good question. Volunteer for the next war, probably." He shook his head ruefully, but then smiled. "For what it's worth, she would have liked you."

Chris felt the wave of emptiness pass over her, and she said without warning, "I'm sorry, Colonel."

"For what?"

"For everything." She stared into her coffee mug. It was time to start making amends.

Brooks laughed. "You know, Chris, I thought you'd be just another journo, in and out and forgotten just as fast. Instead, half my officers are more concerned with what you're doing than prosecuting a war."

"I'm glad you find that amusing."

Brooks laughed again. "Only the lunacy of it all. It's my brigade you've thrown into disarray."

"I'm sorry."

"Stop apologizing. Make your choices and stand by them. Never let the enemy see you waver."

She was tempted to inform him that not every conundrum could be solved with the simplicity of military logic, but refrained. He had a point.

He finished his eggs and leaned forward on his elbows. "When this is all over, do you think we might be friends?"

"Are you sure you'll want to be friends? It *is* your brigade, after all." She smiled because he smiled, but then turned serious because she knew it was a serious question. "Yes. When this is all over, I expect we'll be friends."

"Good. I'll look forward to that instead of the next war."

"Sir."

They both looked up at the staff sergeant standing at Brooks's left shoulder, posture impeccable.

"My apologies for interrupting, but you have a call from Saigon."

Brooks downed the last of his coffee and stood. "Chris, always a pleasure."

The staff sergeant clicked his heels and nodded to her. "Ma'am." Then he turned and followed Brooks out of the mess hall.

Alone again, Chris lit another cigarette.

***

Bullseye, the platoon's tunnel rat, had sustained a mild concussion, a perforated eardrum, and multiple contusions to the face, head, and torso after opening a booby-trapped door deep in the bowels of one of the Viet Cong's labyrinthine tunnel complexes. The steel door had blocked the force of the blast and saved his life, but Bullseye had not escaped injury. With Oscar in a state of panic, John had entered the tunnel and dragged the semi-conscious teenager to safety. The men returned to FOB Jane having little to show for their days in the field and Gianelli yet again faced the wrath of Captain Kittles.

The next morning after breakfast Bullseye, with an escort from Oscar, returned to the hospital for a bandage change. Kearney's field dressing, wrapped around headband style, had prompted ninja comparisons and offensive imitations of Japanese people. When he and Oscar rejoined the squad midmorning, the men had set themselves up under a large open tent with their rifles, beer, snacks, several decks of cards, a football, and the latest edition of *Playboy*, procured in Danang during Alpha Company's recent R&R and traded for a dime bag of Oscar's finest weed. On Gianelli's orders, they all wore sandals. The weather had cleared overnight, and it was a scorching hot day.

"Hot damn, Miss August is a babe!" Murphy said. "Check out the rack on this chick." He held up the centerfold.

"Murph! She's not a piece of meat."

Murphy looked at Turner. "Dude, she's posing in a skin mag. She is most definitely a piece of meat."

"I'd do her," Steve said.

"You'd do anything wearing a skirt, and that includes Hector."

"I slit your throat if you try it," Hector said.

"Mexicans ain't my type."

Bullseye poked Hector. "Guess what? The hot nurse patched me up."

Hector's eyes widened under the brim of the yellow fedora. He dropped the deck of cards he had been shuffling, spilling them over his lap. "Maria? My Maria?"

Bullseye grinned and pointed to his head. "She got real close to examine me, made me take off my shirt to change my bandages and everything."

Hector toppled over onto his side, an affected swoon. "Oh Maria, Maria, *mi amor*."

"Get a grip, man. That woman is light years out of your league and a fucking officer," Murphy said, still engrossed in the magazine.

"Jersey, shoot me," Hector said.

"What?" Steve's bewildered hazel eyes shot from Hector to the rest of the group, who stared at Hector in surprise. Even Murphy looked up from Miss August.

"Shoot me. I need a reason to see Maria."

"Honestly," Dan said, "you really are *loco*."

"Just shoot me in the leg and rush me to the hospital. I will be fine."

Steve shrugged and reached for his rifle. "Okay."

"Steve, don't even think about it," John said as he pulled apart his M-16 for a long overdue clean.

"Aw, Johnny, he's just trying to get a date."

"Boy, you crazy," Oscar bellowed.

Murphy flipped over onto his back, holding the magazine above his face. "Hey, listen to this. Miss August thinks it's sexier if women leave a little something to the imagination. Could have fooled me, but I'd take black lace. The sluttier, the better."

"*Rojo*. My Maria in red."

"White. On our wedding night," said Turner, staring dreamily into the distance.

"White's nice," Dan said with the same dreamy look. "Pink too."

"Come on, Cowboy, we see you trying to disappear. You ain't getting out of this one," Oscar boomed. "Pick a color."

John concentrated on wiping the gun grease off his hands with an old rag, envisioning her in something other than jungle fatigues. But they had come full circle. She was now what she had once been, only a dream.

"Cowboy!"

"Lavender," John said softly. A dream.

* * *

Travis went to check on his squad with Chris and Paul in tow, chatting about Bullseye's near miss in the tunnel. Travis had his Louisville Slugger at his shoulder—right-handed grip—and emphasized just how lucky Bullseye had been.

"That kid is a like a cat, nine lives. I have no idea how he survived that explosion. Charlie doesn't mess around with those booby-traps. Grenades, mines, poisons, pit vipers, nasty stuff."

"If John hadn't rushed in, who would you have sent?"

Travis glanced sidelong at her. "It's easiest for the small guys to maneuver in those tight shafts."

"Hector?"

"Or you." He laughed, but trailed off when he saw she was not amused. "I don't know, Chris. Hector wouldn't have been able to drag a dead weight back through the tunnel. What if there's a Viet Cong squad down there? How do you pick the next guy to die?"

"Is a weapons cache worth a man's life?"

"It's not that simple. Over the years we've found more than weapons. Lots of solid intel, from battle plans to names of village infiltrators to hit lists of politicians and ARVN officers. No one forced Bullseye to take the gig. He volunteered. He may not be the brightest grunt out there, but don't knock his bravery."

"I'm not. Just the wisdom of how this army fights."

Travis shrugged and shifted his grip on the bat. "We're making it up as we go along. We're still learning the most effective way to fight an insurgency."

"We had to make adjustments in World War II," Paul reminded her. "The Marines in the Pacific had to adapt to battling an enemy who would fight to the very last man even when they had no hope of holding the hill."

Travis nodded in agreement. "It's hard to get guys motivated to fight a ghost. Tet was a disaster, but we had a purpose again—fight an enemy that made a concerted charge against the cities. Not the invisible guerrillas in the bush."

"Doesn't it concern you that we're not winning?"

"I'm a soldier. I fight the best I can, and I leave the bullshit to the officers and the politicians."

Chris shook her head. "It drives me crazy."

Travis smirked. "That's what a magazine column is for, kid."

Chris and Paul glanced at each other, sharing unspoken thoughts. Paul surreptitiously snapped a photo of the master sergeant and his Louisville Slugger.

"Hey, Sarge! What's happening?" Oscar called. "Reporter Lady! Photo Man! Join us!"

"That cloud above your head better not be weed," Travis said.

"Good old-fashioned American cigarette smoke."

Chris ducked under the tent and couldn't suppress a grin at the sight of Bullseye, who still looked ridiculous. Cleaner and happier, but ridiculous with his shock of red hair spiked in every direction, pushed up by the wrap-around bandage. She suspected that Maria Nichols or whichever nurse tended to his wounds had mimicked Kearney's haphazard field dressing for comic effect.

"I came to see the tunnel rat," she said, standing over him.

"Me?" He looked up at her with wide eyes.

"Yes, you. How's your head?"

He glanced at Oscar, unsure of what to say. Oscar reached over to smack him, but thought better of it, settling instead for a light pat on the shoulder. "Boy, the lady's talking to you."

"I'm good."

On impulse, Chris bent down and kissed Bullseye's cheek. His freckles disappeared under his blush.

"Can I have a kiss, too?" Steve asked.

"No."

"Aw, why not?"

"Because you didn't take a grenade in the face."

"But you kissed lots of other guys."

"Like who?" she said in surprise, an edge to her voice.

"Johnny, the shit-eater—"

"Shut up, Schaefer," Travis said.

"That was a long time ago," she said.

Her eyes darted to John, who avoided looking at her. He rammed a magazine into his reassembled rifle and racked the slide to chamber a round.

"And Doc Jacobson. Up on a bunker watching the sunrise. Gave him a big wet one."

The atmosphere under the tent darkened and the men fell into an uncomfortable silence, furtively glancing between her and John. Chris wanted to break it as quickly as possible, to talk around it or through it or past it.

"It wasn't like that. It was nothing."

"But my sources—"

"It was nothing," she repeated, eyes on John.

"Then how come I can't have a kiss?"

John's rifle clattered to the ground as he jumped to his feet and took a few steps in her direction until he stood an arm's length away. He smirked at her, and she instinctively turned her back on him to avoid his piercing eyes.

"How do the other guys pay? Wad of cash on the field table? Do you prefer dollars or dong?"

Her anger exploded in an instant, like a phosphorus bomb, an uncontrollable white-hot flash of fury. Chris whirled to face him and swung wildly, punching him full in the mouth. Her fist connected with lips and teeth. John stumbled backwards and tripped over Murphy's outstretched legs. He fell to his backside, clamping a hand over his mouth as blood oozed from his split lip.

"Goddamn, Reporter Lady!" Oscar bellowed.

The pain in her hand took a second to reach her brain. She bent at the waist holding her right wrist in her left hand, staring at her bloodied knuckles.

Paul and Ben Kearney rushed to her side. "Let me see," said the medic.

Chris gritted her teeth against the agony and hoped her hand wasn't broken.

"Got some fight bite," he said, examining where John's teeth had cut her skin. "Can you move your hand?"

She flexed her fingers, feeling the pain shoot through her hand all the way to her forearm. "I'll be all right."

"We need to clean you up."

Paul left Chris's side and squatted down beside John, who was still sprawled on the ground. John refused to look at him.

"Young man," he said, "if she hadn't slugged you, I would have."

Then he took a photo of John, the perfect picture of ignominious defeat, before he and Kearney led Chris away from the tent.

***

John spat out a mouthful of blood and sat up. The eyes of every man in his squad were on him, confused, disappointed, accusing. John hung his head and ran his tongue over his teeth to ensure they were all there. The strength of the blow had surprised him, although, he now reasoned, perhaps he should have seen it coming. Had Chris McKenna been any other woman, she might have slapped him, a stinging rebuke both literally and figuratively. But she was not like any other woman, an important distinction he had neglected to note before he ran his mouth.

Travis touched the tip of the Louisville Slugger to the underside of John's chin and inched it up until John was forced to look at him. "Son, that was just about the stupidest thing I've ever heard a man say to a woman." Then the master sergeant ducked under the tent and departed, shaking his head.

John's bottom lip had already swollen to twice its normal size. He touched it with his finger and discovered it was split down the middle. He took a clean bandanna from his pocket, wiped blood from his chin, and pressed it to his mouth.

Steve sat down beside him. His hazel eyes were wild with concern. "Sorry, Johnny, I didn't mean to start nothing nasty between you two."

"Don't worry about it," John mumbled.

"It's just that my boys saw her and the doc and—"

John took the bandanna away from his mouth. "I said, don't worry about it."

"Okay. Sorry."

Murphy tossed the *Playboy* to John. "You might need this, because you sure ain't getting any from her."

John grunted and put the bandanna back to his lip. Then he laid back and closed his eyes against the pain.

***

Deep within the belly of An Xuyen Province, Second Platoon moved toward its objective, a Viet Cong encampment on the Ca Mau Peninsula at the southern tip of Vietnam. The camp was an interprovincial weapons depot, according to Major Gardner's Vietnamese intelligence agents, settled far within Viet Cong-controlled territory on the western half of the peninsula, so deep, so well hidden in the dense jungle that the VC had become complacent. It had not come under attack since the start of the war and was thought to be guarded by no more than thirty guerrillas.

Colonel Brooks had ordered a strike on the camp, and Lieutenant Colonel Simpson had taken the lead on operational planning. He and Captain Kittles had assigned Lieutenant Gianelli's platoon to the operation, with support from Lieutenant Balcolm's platoon. However, just as Gianelli's men boarded Hueys in the twilight at FOB Jane, Balcolm and his men were recalled from the tarmac. The platoon had lifted off alone, and Gianelli had stared, stunned, down at Kittles and Simpson, who stood at the edge of the helipad and watched the Hueys ascend. Kittles had the nerve to wave before he and Simpson turned their backs and retreated to the safety of their offices.

Gianelli and Travis had conferred away from their platoon at the drop-off point, both men at a loss to explain the behavior of Simpson and Kittles. With the choppers en route back to FOB Jane and having spent a week listening to Gardner rage about the importance of the target, they saw little choice but to advance toward the camp. Gianelli reserved the right to wave off if it appeared the platoon was grossly outnumbered.

A mile out from the camp it began to rain, a sudden downpour that tapered off into a steady fall. Second Squad split and took the flanks while First Squad, the platoon's battering ram, pushed up the center of the line. The camp was small, consisting of closely grouped huts in multiple clearings. Travis and Murphy silently dispatched two sentries with their jungle knives. The bodies crumpled in a heap at their feet, quick bleed-outs. The platoon entered the camp, shadows in the rain, until Levens triggered a booby trap.

The rigged Claymore mine shattered the jungle calm and killed Levens and Sutherland instantly. The Viet Cong mounted a counterattack with a ferocity that belied their platoon-sized numbers. Black pajama-clad fighters opened fire from rickety platforms in the tree canopy, from within tunnel openings, and from hooch doorways.

Gianelli shoved Chris to the ground, behind a close grouping of massive trees that would absorb rifle rounds. Paul dropped down at her side, extending one hand around the trunk and snapping photos of the action raging in the heart of the camp. Chris peered around the trees in time to see Gianelli, in a sprint, lower his shoulder and smash through a hooch. She saw the flash of gun muzzles through the doorway as shots were fired inside the small dwelling. Her chest seized, but then Gianelli reappeared, in the process of reloading his rifle and looking for his next target.

"Fuck," she muttered in relief.

Chris disentangled herself from the thorny brush near the trees. She heard shouts in English and Vietnamese, heard screams of the wounded. She ignored Paul's pleas and ran to the nearest clearing in a half-crouch, just in time to see

Sergeant Conlon take a rifle round in the thigh. He fell to the muddy ground with a cry, still firing at his attacker.

Chris dropped to her knees and slid the last few feet to his side, rolling him over and pressing hard on the wound with her hands. Conlon jerked with such force that it knocked her backwards. As her hands came off the wound, a geyser of blood spurted through the tear in his pants.

"Kearney!" she yelled.

In the distance she heard him respond. Ignoring Conlon's roar of pain, Chris jammed her knee into the inside of his thigh near his crotch, pinching off his femoral artery. Still with her knee over the artery, she fumbled for a tourniquet she kept in her cargo pocket. Willing her hands to stop shaking, she slipped the tourniquet over his leg above the wound and ratcheted tight. Conlon cried out again but managed to swap magazines and continue firing. Kearney reached her side and ratcheted the tourniquet one more click. As the shock of his injury set in, Conlon's rifle muzzle sank into the mud and his eyes closed.

"Get some gauze," Kearney said.

Chris covered the gaping exit wound in the front of his thigh with a handful of gauze, pushing down with all her strength. Blood, diluted by rain, spilled over her hands. A burst of bullets riddled the ground a few feet behind her.

"Pack it in! In the wound!" he yelled over the gunfire. He turned away from her to return fire.

Without thinking, Chris stuffed the gauze into the wound. Kearney stood and stomped on the gauze with his boot, ramming it as far as it would go. Yelling something unintelligible as he ran past, Murphy brought down a VC position thirty feet off the ground in a tree with an RPG. Chris and Kearney threw themselves over Conlon to shield him from fiery debris.

As she squinted through the smoke, a fragmentation grenade landed with a splash a yard away. Chris stared at the small lemon-shaped cylinder, black in color. Russian-made, she was quite sure. Between the raindrops she took in every vivid detail of her surroundings, of her plight. She saw every choice that had brought her to this moment, and all the future choices she would never get to make.

John Rawlins hit her like a blitzing safety, driving her down flat into the mud and covering her with his body. Searing pain shot through her injured arm, pinned beneath her. He held her tight and she heard his ragged breathing in her ear. Now they would both die, she thought to herself, and that was a shame. Long seconds passed.

John pushed himself off her and in one swift movement, picked up the dud grenade and threw it into the jungle, away from his platoon. Kearney grabbed John and spun him around.

"See that anthill over there?" Kearney pointed to a man-made mound of dirt and straw with a slit opening in the side. A rifle muzzle poked through and flashed, illuminating the driving rain. "You need to kill that man."

John pulled Chris to her knees. Chris tried to control her breathing and concentrate on Conlon.

***

John shouldered his rifle and walked toward the mound. He squeezed a round off every other step. The first two impacted only dirt. Then he found his rhythm. Every shot entered the narrow slit. Standing over the hill, John pulled the pin on a grenade and dropped it through the opening. He dove to his right and covered his head. The explosion spewed dirt in every direction and showered him with heavy clumps of mud.

He reloaded his rifle and looked for his next target, but the shooting had stopped. Flames licked the canopies of several towering trees and all the huts had been destroyed. His platoon was mopping up. There would be no enemy survivors.

"Hurry up," Gianelli yelled. "We've got serious wounded." He and Travis were in the frantic process of a head count.

"Conlon needs an evac now, LT," Kearney said.

John looked around for his squad, felt a stab of panic. He was one man short. His eyes connected with Dan's.

"Billy's missing," Dan said.

"Find him," Gianelli said to Travis.

John held up his hand, silencing the group. "Do you hear that?"

A voice, faint but insistent, calling out the same word over and over. "Help!"

They found him in a soft thicket of grass and moss, on his back, eyes wide and staring at the tree canopy, filled with a primal fear, more alive than they had ever been. He clutched his stomach.

"Can't...breathe." He sobbed, wheezing.

Ben Kearney sank to his knees and pulled away Billy's hands. The bullet had entered the lower right quadrant of Billy's abdomen and perforated his liver, then traveled upward at an angle to puncture his left lung. The squad gathered around them and watched Kearney reach into his pack to pull forth not a compress, but a handful of M&Ms and a syringe of morphine. Billy coughed blood.

Kearney injected the morphine through a vein in Billy's inner arm at the elbow, near a line of fresh track marks. Then he placed a yellow M&M on Billy's tongue.

John forced himself to watch Billy Farrell die. Kearney ran a hand over Billy's face to close his eyes for the last time.

The platoon loaded four stretchers with their dead and wounded. The rain continued to fall.

***

Sam Gianelli's knees buckled and he nearly collapsed in pain on the floor of the hospital triage station. Maria Nichols caught him around the waist and helped him through the doors to a bed, where she forced him to sit. As his arm slipped off her shoulders, her stethoscope clattered to the floor. She ignored it and began to untie his waterlogged boots.

"I need to see Conlon."

"He's going into surgery."

"Why aren't operating?"

"Because right now you need me."

Gianelli jerked away from her, sending a blinding eruption of pain through his still-booted feet. "The hell I do. Get in there and help my guy."

Maria's dark eyes flashed. "Don't be an ass, Sam."

"They are fucking feet, *Captain*. Don't you think your time would be better served in surgery saving my sergeant?"

She grabbed his left foot, untied the boot, and pulled it off. When she yanked off his wet sock and let his foot hang, Gianelli gasped.

"Look at that. You think that's not worth my time?"

Gianelli stared at his swollen foot with its soggy white sole and peeling top layers, rubbed raw at friction points within his boot. Watery blood dripped to the floor. Full blown immersion foot syndrome, enough to drive any hardened soldier to a hospital bed. She took hold of his leg by the ankle and lifted to relieve the intense pressure brought on by gravity.

"Listen to me. If you don't let me treat this right now, you're done in the field for at least a month. Understand?"

Gianelli met her glare, but she refused to back down. She removed his other boot and looked at his two feet, barely recognizable.

"Jesus, Sam," she muttered. "Why do you let Kittles get away with this?"

"Stay out of it," he said quietly.

She set her mouth in a thin line and rolled up his soaked pant legs to mid-calf. Just as she pulled a wheeled cart toward her, her deputy poked her head into the room.

"Captain Nichols, the patient is prepped."

"On my way." She snatched her stethoscope off the floor. "Jenny, please clean and treat Lieutenant Gianelli's feet."

"Yes, ma'am."

"Do not move," she said to him. "I'll check on you later."

Jenny advanced toward the cart Maria had vacated and pulled on a pair of rubber gloves. Gianelli rolled down his pant legs and retrieved his socks and boots. The nurse watched him apprehensively.

"Lieutenant, she said..."

Gianelli pulled on his socks and boots and stood, fighting the urge to roar in agony. "I heard her," he said through gritted teeth.

Without a backwards glance, he limped down the hall to the doors leading to the operating rooms. There he and Travis stood for hours waiting to learn whether Conlon would live or die.

***

Chris slumped down against the sandbagging of John's favorite niche, the effort of moving her muscles an overwhelming task. She thought she should have been crying, but she was out of tears, out of energy, out of compassion. *Nothing*, the voice in her head repeated over and over. *You are nothing.*

"McKenna!" Anne Novak stood over her, hands on her hips, looking irritated. "Didn't you hear me screaming at you?"

"What?"

"I need a favor. I want to interview the chief medical officer, Jacobson. Heard you two are tight. He keeps brushing me off with some lame excuse that he's got patients to treat. He's got a fucking army of nurses; I think he can spare thirty minutes. How about you swing your pretty little ass into the hospital and do something useful for a change?"

Chris heard none of it. She was back in the jungle, back in the rain, back under fire. It was on her, the blood, a life, on her clothes, on her hands, spurting into her face.

"McKenna?" Anne reached down and shook Chris's shoulder. "What the hell is wrong with you? You're as dirty as the grunts."

Chris looked up. "May I ask you something?"

Anne wrinkled her nose and shifted impatiently. "In the interest of obtaining this interview, I suppose."

"Why are you so angry?"

Taken aback, Anne narrowed her eyes and reappraised Chris. *What does she see? A beaten ex-journalist? A nobody? A nothing?*

"I'm not angry."

"Then what do you call it?"

Anne shrugged and dropped down against the sandbagging. "Educated. Evolved. And fine, maybe a little pissed."

"Why? You make up the story as you go along and people love it."

"I suppose you think you're some fountain of truth?"

Chris said nothing.

Anne laughed caustically. "Your idealism is quaint and self-serving. Name a single piece of objective journalism that's left this swamp. It's always a fuck you to the administration, a fuck you to the grunts, a fuck you to the Commies, a fuck you to anyone who doesn't believe what you think they should believe. I'm no different, and neither are you. Strip my writing down to the bones, what am I saying?"

"That you're too lazy to do your research?"

"Cute. I'm saying fuck you to anyone who ever made me drop to my knees for a story. Now they need me. Power is intoxicating, McKenna, the best high I've ever had. Learn how to play the game and you'll see what I mean."

"I know how to play the game."

"Intellectually you may comprehend it, but you're lost on the nuance. Not for a second does anyone believe you *want* to play it. You have to sell the performance before you make them pay for it."

"I want to be better than that."

"We all do. But you're still a woman in a man's business, and certain indignities must be endured."

Chris said nothing, only stared at the ground in a state of catatonic indifference.

Anne climbed to her feet and looked at Chris with pity. "Now, how about that interview with the doc?"

"I'll see what I can do," she said, but that was a lie and they both knew it.

"You look like shit."

"Rough day."

"Guess so."

Anne's departure precipitated Chris's unwilling return to the jungle. She looked to the sky, desperate to see something other than slippery blood gushing over her fingers, swallowing her, drowning her. She felt John's arms around her, strong and reassuring; she felt the twitch of a shattered leg, heard the screams. Terror constricted her chest, she couldn't breathe.

Help...help...

Chris clamped her hands over her ears and bowed her head. She didn't move for hours.

***

Dan found John seated atop a familiar bunker, the site of a collision with a journalist, a collision with lingering shockwaves. He climbed up to join him and set between them a fifth of Jameson. John glanced at it but made no comment.

"Murph was kind enough to spot us a bottle."

John turned his eyes back to the horizon. The sky, the color of a day-old bruise, was bloated with storm clouds. He faced south toward the jungle that had taken lives and brutalized the survivors.

Dan continued. "Maybe it was for the best. He was barely hanging on."

"Maybe. If it hadn't been a bullet, it would have been the drugs."

"There was nothing we could do." But his tone asked the question.

"No," John said. "There was nothing we could do."

"I don't feel any better."

"Me neither."

They sat in silence, each man lost in his own thoughts, each trying to convince himself that there had been nothing they could do to save a young soldier. Billy Farrell had lived a short and unhappy life, and now he was just another body with a toe tag, another Vietnam statistic.

"Got my Dear John letter," Dan said.

"I'm sorry."

"She said the war has changed me. She said she doesn't know who I am anymore."

"I thought you didn't write home about the war."

"I don't. I did—only once. The ambush. The mines. The kids we killed. The bound prisoners shot in cold blood. I'm not proud of what I've become. But she doesn't understand."

John clasped a hand over Dan's shoulder and squeezed.

"It hurts, John. It's more than Billy, more than my girl. I didn't know I could hurt this bad."

John nodded. It was Billy; it was Chris; it was the feeling of emptiness inside him. It was the knowledge he had made mistakes and done irreparable harm, and the guilt he would live with for the rest of his life. He couldn't protect the people who mattered most to him. He couldn't protect himself.

"Feel like getting drunk?" Dan asked.

John reached for the bottle and twisted off the cap. He raised it to the jungle, to the brewing storm. "Vietnam, Vietnam…"

17

— • —

The staff sergeant found Master Sergeant Travis bench pressing two hundred and twenty-five pounds under the gym tent. Travis was shirtless and sweat poured off his face and chest. He finished his set with a low roar and sat up, panting, to swig water from his canteen and mop his brow with a towel.

The staff sergeant approached the bench. Travis gulped water and nodded a greeting.

"Do me a solid, add five to each side. I could use a spot for this next set."

"Sergeant, I need you to come with me. Captain Nichols asked to see you right away."

"Captain Nichols?" Travis had just finished lunch with Gianelli. The lieutenant had been his usual irascible self, if somewhat moody and introspective, and with a more pronounced limp as a result of his immersion foot syndrome, but otherwise all had been fine. At least what passed for fine at FOB Jane. "Did she say why?"

"I need you to come with me. Right now, please."

Travis sighed and pulled on a gray T-shirt. Threatening the younger, more junior NCO with physical mayhem was pointless; the staff sergeant would be loyal to Maria Nichols to his dying day. He escorted Travis to Maria's office and left without a word, only pulling the door closed. The click was ominously loud in the silence.

Maria scribbled notes on a patient chart and hadn't yet looked at him. Travis waited with his hands clasped behind his back. He was still drenched in sweat and wished he had brought a towel. Finally, she set aside the chart and focused dark eyes on his disheveled appearance.

"I see I interrupted you."

"Just a workout."

"Lifting without a spotter, no doubt."

Travis smiled patiently. "What can I do for you, Captain?"

Maria opened her bottom desk drawer and pulled out a sizable stack of paperwork. She separated the stack into four piles. One pile stood taller than the others.

"Do you know what these are, Jack?"

"No, ma'am."

"These are every single after-action report for Delta Company going back six months. Squad recons, platoon patrols, company operations, and everything in between." She laid a hand on the tallest pile. "I'd like you to guess which platoon this stack represents."

Travis said nothing. He felt his body vibrate. He tried to convince himself it was because of the lifting.

"Sergeant?"

"Ma'am, this—"

"Your platoon, Sergeant. This stack belongs to Second Platoon. But what I find most fascinating is how many reports in this pile bear the names of Balcolm, Jenkins, Graves, and others, despite obviously being written by you or Sam or Conlon."

Travis ran a hand over his hair and stared at the four piles. "Shit," he muttered.

"Didn't you find it strange that you spent considerably more time outside the wire than any other platoon at FOB Jane?"

"Captain, this is the army. We may not like the orders, but we follow them."

"Fuck orders, Jack. Your platoon has been decimated. You've suffered far higher contact and casualty rates than anyone else, almost assuredly due to the extra patrols and Kittles's penchant for sending you into the most dangerous territory without adequate numbers, like this last disaster of an operation. That in itself is appalling, but the cover-up is downright criminal. Did you or Sam know about the forged paperwork?"

"No. Of course not."

"But you suspected?"

Travis set his jaw and met Maria's angry eyes. Finally, he sighed. "We knew something wasn't kosher. Sam was religious about completing the paperwork in hopes that someone at HQ would make some noise."

Maria laughed incredulously. "You two bozos pinned your hopes on some twenty-year-old admin clerk noticing bad forgeries? Jesus Christ. No wonder we're not winning this war."

Travis moved toward her desk and dropped into a chair. She pushed the stack toward him. He examined each report, recognizing Gianelli's impeccable block handwriting, Conlon's chicken scratch, and his own cramped print. At least half bore typewritten headers with names of platoon or squad leaders who had never been a part of those particular operations. He looked closely and saw how Kittles had done it: a thin layer of correction fluid over their names and the overlay of Balcolm, Jenkins, or Graves.

"Son of a bitch," he muttered.

"It stops now."

"Captain, you need to stay out of this."

"I'm sorry?"

"Please stay out of it. Sam and I will handle it."

"You both had your shot to handle it, and you did nothing. Now I will."

She swept the reports into a rucksack and stepped toward the door. Travis blocked her path and held her by the upper arms.

"Maria, please. Listen to me. This won't end the way you want it to." He squeezed her arms, feeling the tension coursing through her. "You're untouchable. Everybody knows that, even Simpson and Kittles. But Sam isn't. All it will take is a call from Simpson to one of daddy's pals in Saigon to get him reassigned to some firebase on the DMZ where the artillery rains down and Charlie is in the wire and there's a contact on every patrol. Not even Brooks can stop that. And Sam...he's not leaving Vietnam without you. He stays for you."

Maria slumped. She bit down hard on her bottom lip. He released her arms and guided her to the chair he had vacated. He pulled the second chair close and waited for her to compose herself.

"It needs to stop, Jack."

"I know."

"I can't..." She rubbed the bridge of her nose. "What do we do?"

"I need you to trust me."

She studied him. "Fine."

"Thank you."

He rose and moved toward the door, hand reaching for the knob. But he paused and looked back at her. She stared into space, motionless. He pulled her up and wrapped her in his arms. She held him tight.

"I will never let anything happen to him," he whispered.

***

Major Jacobson tied off a stitch, snipped the excess inch of thread, dropped his scissors onto a metal tray with a clang, and pulled off his rubber gloves with a satisfying snap. "And that is how you save a life."

The recipient of the stitches, a soldier who had gotten drunk, started a fight with a platoon mate, and been slashed in the forearm by a broken beer bottle, looked at the doctor in surprise. "Was I going to die, sir?"

"No, of course not. Next time, don't pick a fight with a guy twice your size."

"But continued transfusions can lead to an unsafe drop in body temperature," Kearney pointed out.

295

"Captain Nichols came up with the bright idea to warm the blood units in the microwave oven immediately before the transfusion. Several other evacuation hospitals have taken up the practice."

"What did I do?" Maria asked as she joined Jacobson, Kearney, and Chris.

"Nuked our plasma units."

"Well, better than fighting hypothermia in addition to the wound." She turned to Jacobson. "Conlon just arrived in Japan. The vascular and arterial repairs are holding stable."

"Good. I wouldn't be surprised if he makes a relatively full recovery."

"Lieutenant Gianelli will be happy to hear that. He took Conlon's injury hard," Kearney said.

Chris caught Maria's pained expression, but it passed quickly.

"I'm still amazed he didn't lose more blood. He took five units that first night, but it could have been much worse. That man owes you his life," Maria said.

"He owes Florence Nightingale here. She got that tourniquet on fast."

Chris shook her head, only days removed from the trauma and plagued by constant flashbacks to the rainy day in the jungle. "Just followed orders."

Maria smiled. "If you ever decide to change careers, let me know. There will never be enough combat nurses."

Chris wrinkled her nose. "I'm actually pretty squeamish. For real," she continued, seeing their disbelieving expressions. "I don't know how you do it."

Maria shrugged and tossed up her hands, as if to concede the inherent peril of peering too deeply into the recesses of one's own soul. "If we didn't, who would?"

The nurse retreated to the post-op ward. Chris was alone with Jacobson and Kearney.

"Okay, boys, spill it. What's Maria's deal?"

"What do you mean?" Jacobson asked. He looked like an antelope about to be flattened by an eighteen-wheeler.

"She's not really a nurse, is she?"

There was a pregnant pause. Jacobson and Kearney exchanged a glance. "Off the record?" said Jacobson.

"If you insist."

"In 1966, Maria Nichols graduated from medical school at the top of her class. A few months into her residency, her brother, a Marine, was killed in action near Hue. She dropped everything and joined up, but the army would only commission her in the nursing corps. Now she's three years into the world's worst residency and has become probably the finest vascular surgeon in theater."

"She's the one who saved Sergeant Conlon's leg," Kearney added.

"Steadiest hands I've ever seen. Yet she remains invisible to the army and her male peers, all of whom she puts to shame," said Jacobson.

"Well," said Chris after a moment of reflection. "That's some bullshit."

"Have you ever noticed that guys jump to salute her when she walks past? No matter who they are, where they are, or what they're doing?" asked Kearney. "There isn't a man at FOB Jane who doesn't know someone that Captain Nichols saved."

"Off the record," Jacobson reminded Chris as he and Kearney moved toward post-op.

Chris nodded. She gazed into space for a minute, then pulled a pad from her pocket and jotted down a few notes.

***

John took a swig from his canteen, taking care not to bump his tender lip. Shirtless, he leaned against some waist-high sandbagging near the airstrip and waited for the next helicopter to land so he and several men from an artillery company could unload the various supplies, foodstuffs, and weaponry. The sun beat down on his back and shoulders, long since overcooked brown. His muscles felt tight and stiff, victims of the palpable tension of the last several months. It was a day off for the platoon, but he needed to stay busy lest his mind wander to dark places.

John pushed the bush hat off his head and let it hang by its string around his neck. He watched Anne Novak approach with her luggage, looking snappy in a set of designer fatigues. Much to John's relief she was alone, no photographers in sight. She stopped in front of him and pulled off her sunglasses.

"Good afternoon, ma'am."

She reached out and cupped his dog tags, running her thumb over the silver toe tag. The back of her hand rested against his sweaty chest. "You know, I never had the opportunity to thank you for saving my life."

"Not necessary."

"Are you sure?" She moved a step closer.

"Yes, ma'am."

"What if I promised not to tell McKenna?" Anne paused and looked him over. "Oh, screw that, she'd be the first person I'd tell."

John smiled in spite of himself. He wondered again why he had thought stepping into the crossfire was a good idea. "Who's winning this prizefight, anyway?"

"I am, of course. That said, I think I'll concede this round and retreat to my corner. She got what I wanted."

"But you got the story." A warped version of it, he corrected himself silently. But whose fault was that?

"What do you mean?"

"Your article. You beat her to it."

Anne cocked her head to the side. "Did I? She's been here for months. I'm sure she has her reasons for sitting on the story."

"Like what?"

Anne's laugh startled him. "And I thought for sure she was the one using you. You fuck her but don't bother to talk to her." She shook her head in amusement. "Maybe she was right. Maybe you're not a dumb farm boy after all."

A Huey touched down and kicked up a cloud of dust. Squinting, Anne picked up a bag and tossed it over her shoulder. She had to shout above the roar of the rotors.

"I'll be in Saigon for a couple of days. Lotus Hotel if you can escape."

John watched her board the helicopter and followed it until it was out of sight over the jungle on a northeasterly course toward Saigon. He thought about the months, the countless opportunities. A realization hit him hard.

***

Chris glanced sidelong at Jack Travis as they strolled through FOB Jane. The Louisville Slugger rested on his left shoulder, left-handed grip. Outside the club, he handed her the bat, told her to wait, and disappeared inside. Chris wrapped her hands around the ash handle, worn smooth by years of the sergeant's weathered palms gripping and grinding. He reappeared carrying two open Budweiser bottles and motioned for her to follow. They stopped on the edge of the makeshift volleyball court, deserted in the fading evening light, and took a seat on the scraggily grass. Travis handed her a beer.

"Thanks."

"How's your arm?"

"Fine."

"Your hand?"

Chris glanced down at the butterfly bandages over the two middle knuckles of her right hand. "Bruised."

"I'll bet. You've got a hell of a swing. For a chick." He winked at her and took a gulp of beer.

"Next time I'll aim for something other than the mouth."

"I thought the mouth was an appropriate target."

"I've never hit anyone before."

Travis shrugged. "It's the war. Just like it was the war speaking for him."

"I don't think I like who I've become."

"It's not so much that you've changed, just that you haven't stayed the same. Make sense?"

Chris pondered the paradox. War had brought out the best and the worst in her, forced her to accept that life was more than a story, more than a career. Life would never be the same. She would never be the same.

"I deserved the comment."

"He deserved the punch. Doesn't change the fact that you two are good for each other."

Chris smiled wanly. "Thought you said love and war don't mix."

"They don't, but every rule has an exception."

"That's why we're here, to talk about my wreck of a love life?"

Travis looked down at his hands for a moment before answering. "Not entirely. I need a favor."

Chris waited, curious about what favor she could do him. He seemed unable to speak. "Have to tell me what it is, you know. I can't read minds."

He took a deep breath. "I need you to ask Kittles to ease up on the platoon. The guys are half dead and Gianelli is a mess. He needs to take medical leave for his feet, but he'll keep going until he's crippled."

"What makes you think Kittles will do anything I ask?"

"I thought a feature on the prevalence of questionable interrogation techniques or uncontrolled slaughter would be effective. Paul has the art and you have the pen. It would end Kittles and he knows it."

Chris agreed with Travis that the threat of seeing the incidents in question described in excruciating detail, an eyewitness account from her, the writer, on the pages of a major newsmagazine would be more than enough to compel Kittles to back down. The fact that she was no longer employed by a major newsmagazine was immaterial, for now.

"Who put you up to this?"

"What makes you think anyone else is involved?"

"Because I know you."

Travis looked at her, eyebrows knitted together in consternation. "Does it matter?"

"Only if Gianelli finds out. Believe me, I'm passing the buck."

"The individual in question would prefer to remain nameless. This individual enlightened me as to the extent of the problem—it was my idea to come to you."

Chris repressed a smile. She had a distinct idea who might compel the sergeant to seek such a favor. "Okay. But I want answers to two questions. First, tell me why there's such bad blood between Gianelli and Kittles."

"That's fair. Kittles ever tell you the story of the battle outside Bac Lieu?"

"The one in which he single-handedly saved Gianelli's ass?"

"That's the one. The real story is that Delta Company was augmenting a 9th Division operation run out of My Tho, and an ABC camera crew had come along with the infantry elements sent south to Bac Lieu. Kittles alerted the enemy to the platoon's position by ignoring Gianelli's recommendation to stay put so we could link back up with the company. He blundered into a major VC counterattack, our platoon got cut off from the main force, and when the shooting stopped we'd lost five guys. Never took responsibility for it. Even tried to blame the fatalities on Gianelli. Bottom line is that he gave us away because he was trying to look good for the cameras. And wouldn't you know it, but that ABC crew had absolutely no interest in a company commander from a backwater post."

"Does the colonel know?"

"Brooks is fully aware that Kittles is a walking catastrophe, but it's a little more complicated than just shit-canning his dumb butt and calling it a day. Kittles might be stuck at FOB Jane, but he's made the most of his time here."

"Simpson?"

"Are you asking me, or telling me?" Travis's eyes twinkled.

"I did a little digging. I know Simpson's father is a retired three-star and World War II hero."

"Unfortunately, that apple missed Simpson's branch of the family tree entirely. His last unit went to hell up near Khe Sanh, so they promoted him and moved him out. He's in the penalty box down here, and we're all paying the price. Simpson provides the top cover that Kittles needs. As long as he keeps it off Brooks's radar, Kittles has free rein to heap abuse on Gianelli."

"And Gianelli?"

"Trying to hold back the tide of ineptitude and protect the platoon. I've never seen anyone take it on the chin so many times and keep coming back for more." He shook his head, a small smile tugging at his lips. "You won't tell him I told you this, right?"

"It's off the record," she said, thinking again that many of the soldiers at FOB Jane needed a tutorial on working with the press.

"What's the second question?"

"Who signed you?"

Travis emitted a defeated sigh but smiled. "St. Louis, 1948, right out of high school. Played in the minors for a season and change."

"What happened?"

He shrugged. "Korea. Enlisted the day after the north crossed the thirty-eighth parallel."

"Regrets?"

"None."

"You're a good man, Charlie Brown."

"I owe you, kid."

"Consider us even."

Travis appeared perplexed. "Even? For what?"

Chris took a moment to allow the surge of unexpected emotion to recede. "For giving me a chance."

***

John found Lieutenant Gianelli, Sergeant Travis, Paul Lane, and Colonel Brooks's staff sergeant seated around a field table under a tent engaged in a game of poker. A fifth chair sat empty, Sergeant Conlon's spot. The staff sergeant folded on the fourth card of seven-card stud, Paul on the fifth. Every time Travis raised, Gianelli swore but continued to call each bet. John sat down on the extra chair to watch.

"You're full of shit, Jack. No way you have a flush. No way."

Travis shrugged and squeezed the grip of the Louisville Slugger. "Gotta pay to see 'em."

Travis did in fact have a flush of clubs, queen high, which he brandished after Gianelli called the last raise on the final card. Gianelli dropped his head into his hands. Travis laughed and slapped him on the back.

"Beers on me tonight."

"Rawlins, you want in?" Gianelli asked.

"No thanks. Stakes are a little high for private's pay."

"You don't want him to play," Paul said. "He'll clean us out."

"I just lost a month's salary, what's another month?"

"What's up, Rawlins?" Travis began to deal the cards.

"Nothing."

All four men glanced at him, but John offered no further explanation, preferring to watch the game. On the third card, Paul chewed absently on his lip and raised the bet. John was certain he had at least a pair. The staff sergeant rubbed his chin and called, probably holding nothing higher than the king already showing but doubting the veracity of Paul's raise. Gianelli touched his pile of chips, withdrew his hand, but still called. Holding nothing of value but looking to make back his money. Travis called without hesitation.

Everything was so clear, each tell. Why couldn't they see it? Every movement, every twitch, every dart of the eyes, they all said something important. So why hadn't he seen the signs when it really mattered? He had seen only the cards and hadn't liked what he'd been dealt. The cards had consumed him and he'd missed all her tells, every single one of them.

"I screwed up," he said.

The players paused, the staff sergeant in mid-bet. His chips clattered onto the ante pile, breaking the startled silence.

Travis grunted. "I'll say."

"So fix it," Gianelli said with a shrug.

John's eyes flickered to Paul, who watched him carefully. "I don't know how."

"Take your lumps like a man. What are the odds she hits you again?" Travis smirked.

According to Hector, four to one that Chris would throw another punch in his direction, John thought with some chagrin. Several men were only too willing to put their money on Chris.

"Grovel." Gianelli's weary tone suggested that John was not the only man present who had recently run afoul of a strong-willed woman.

Paul busied himself by stacking his chips into three neat towers. The staff sergeant listened to the conversation with interest but chose not to participate. John wanted someone to plot the course he needed to take to win her back. From his vantage point, at the bottom of an unfamiliar emotional canyon, the ascent did not look smooth. And judging from the looks on their faces, sympathetic but unhelpful, he would have to brave the loose, rocky terrain alone.

They finished the hand, Travis winning yet again with three of a kind. John scooted his chair closer to the table and motioned to the staff sergeant.

"Deal me in. I'll show you how to play poker."

***

Early afternoon, following a morning spent searching a series of small canals for weapons caches, Gianelli called for a lunch break. The platoon melted into a swath of jungle lining the banks of a Mekong River tributary, seeking cover from patrolling insurgents and shade from the intense midday sun.

The men dropped to the ground and discarded packs, flak jackets, and shirts. Gianelli pulled off his boots and socks to air out his feet. Steve peered at the lieutenant's feet in horror.

"LT, that's some nasty shit."

"Shut up, Schaefer."

"Does it hurt?"

"No."

"Looks like it hurts."

"Jersey, eat your lunch and leave LT alone," Travis said.

"Okay. Hey, I got some spicy beef today. Sweet!"

"LT, music?" Oscar held up the cassette deck.

"Just keep it low."

The soothing strains of Bob Dylan's guitar filled the jungle. First Squad sat in a loose circle and pulled out their C-rations and canteens, trading entrees and exchanging cigarettes for extra dessert or another can of fruit. Steve attempted unsuccessfully to trade his squares of toilet paper for Turner's tin of pound cake. Ben Kearney pointed out that the last time Steve traded toilet paper for food, he was stricken with a debilitating case of diarrhea and had to beg back the toilet paper, and then some. But Steve was not deterred and Turner had to guard his dessert with his rifle at the ready.

John ate his tin of pork and beans ravenously and then moved onto his energy bar. He watched Chris, seated alone on the trunk of a fallen tree, struggle with a can of fruit, unable to pierce the lid with her tiny army-issue can opener. She gritted her teeth and again tried to force the blade through the lid.

Before she could protest, John closed his hands over hers and took the can. He sat down beside her, punched a series of cuts through the tin, popped off the lid, and handed her the can. She narrowed her eyes but accepted the proffered food, then ate slowly and ignored him.

But John went nowhere, content to be close to her. He took a melted chocolate bar out of his cargo pocket and offered her a mushy section. She barely glanced at it.

"No thanks."

John shrugged. "Probably a good choice. You look like you've put on a few pounds."

Chris looked at him, and he saw the dark circles under her eyes, the pale under her tan, the exhaustion lining every feature of her face. In an excited whisper, Hector reminded everyone of the odds for another punch.

"That was a joke. Not funny?"

"When is it ever funny to joke about a woman's weight?"

He leaned closer so their shoulders touched and dropped his voice. "You need to eat more than just a can of fruit."

"Thanks for the advice, Doc. Got it covered." Her green eyes still on him, she lit a cigarette and took a drag.

"I was thinking more along the lines of Spam."

Chris looked away and blew a stream of smoke straight up. "Did you need something?"

"How's your arm?"

She laughed without humor. "I wish people would stop asking about my arm."

"I tackled you awfully hard the other day. I'm sorry if I hurt you."

"Don't worry about it."

John popped a square of chocolate into his mouth and chewed, still watching her. Something had nagged at him for days, since the instant before he flattened her to the muddy jungle ground in anticipation of an explosion of shrapnel. The sensible voice in his head told him to let it go, but he was resolved not to be sensible anymore. His acute notion of sensibility had gotten him into this mess in the first place.

"You just knelt there staring at that grenade."

"What?" she said in surprise.

"It was like you didn't care anymore."

She looked at the cigarette in her right hand, as if it might hold the answers to life's philosophical quandaries. The orange glow approached the filter. She dropped it to the ground and crushed it with her heel. After a deep breath, she spoke. "No matter how fast I moved, I never would have escaped the blast."

"But you didn't even try."

"John..." She paused, swallowing her exasperation. "What was I supposed to do? Leave Conlon?"

"I don't know," he said. But the truth was that he could handle Conlon's death. He would not be able to handle hers.

They sat in silence. Chris lit another cigarette. John found himself momentarily absorbed in Dylan's mellow ode to a changing world.

"Yanks are having a rough go of it," he said. "Looks like Baltimore might take the east."

She smiled tightly. "I'm learning to live with disappointment." Then she stubbed out her cigarette on the log and walked away.

Nice try, Dan mouthed to him.

John finished his chocolate bar and watched her from under the brim of his bush hat. As she moved toward the edge of the jungle, he stood and drifted in her direction. She paid him no attention. Her eyes were elsewhere, riveted on Lieutenant Gianelli plucking a small yellow wildflower from the bank of the river.

18

— · —

C hris finished typing her favor to Sergeant Travis within an hour of the
platoon's return to FOB Jane late the following day. Now that it no
longer mattered, the piece had been remarkably easy to write, split between a
simple recounting of a week by the South China Sea and a lyrical description
of a village that became a funeral pyre with a few passes of the flamethrowers.
The story was about two thousand words total; two thousand words Captain
Arthur Kittles would never want to see in print. Martin Willis, on the other
hand, would have run it in an instant because on those pages were two thousand
honest words, a story that meant something. She hid the handwritten rough
draft under her mattress and folded the typewritten pages in half.

She found him in the club engaged in animated conversation with George
Wheaton. Kittles did a double take when she walked up to their table.

"Scram," she said to Wheaton.

Wheaton leered at her over his glass. "I don't take orders from you, babe," he
said, slurring.

"If you don't leave right now, I guarantee you'll be dead by lunch tomorrow.
How do you want to go? Sitting on the can like Jenkins? Maybe jerking off in
your hooch?"

Wheaton's eyes widened and he almost dropped his vodka onto his lap.
Kittles stood and straightened his uniform. He smiled disingenuously at her,
then looked at Wheaton and jerked his head.

"George! Get out of here," he hissed.

Glaring at her, Wheaton stood and stumbled to the bar, the glass of vodka clenched in his fist. Kittles gestured to the vacated chair.

"Miss McKenna, a pleasure to see you. How can I be of assistance?"

Chris dropped into the chair and slid the article across the table. He regarded it warily, picking up the pages with his thumb and forefinger and holding them at arm's length as if they might bite him.

"Read it." She leaned back and waited.

***

John cleaned himself up with vigor; after showering and shaving, he changed into fresh pants and a tank top, and exchanged his boots for flip-flops. The plan was taking shape, its genesis in a burst of clarity after his conversation with Anne Novak, of all unlikely inspirations. He had examined his fear rationally and come to the conclusion that the printed word was not the bogeyman. His life hadn't fallen apart after his star turn in *American Century*; his mother had forgiven him his lies, his father had choked up with pride when John had called home from Saigon, and his brothers were desperate for more of the story that Chris McKenna had told, finding it infinitely more interesting and entertaining than John's letters home. The printed word had been a stand-in for what really scared him—the truth. The truth of his role in Vietnam, the truth of the John Rawlins he had lost, the truth of the John Rawlins he had become.

He left the barracks without a word to anyone, although he was certain everyone knew where he was headed. He hadn't traveled more than a dozen steps down the path when Paul Lane appeared from under a vacant tent.

"Thought you might be coming this way."

"I want to make it right. I've been a fool."

"Without a doubt."

"I want her to know that she can write whatever she needs to write. I just want to be with her."

"It's interesting how completely you've missed the point."

"What do you mean?"

"This was never about the story, not really, anyway. That's what you made it into. Nonetheless, she might have appreciated that sacrifice a month ago. But not now. Doesn't matter anymore."

John felt a sense of dread settle over him, pounding in his temples. "What happened?"

Paul shrugged. "She didn't make you a story."

"Please don't tell me..."

"What, that she got fired? She got fired. She had it, she had the most incredible, honest piece of writing I've ever seen, and she gave it up for you. So don't go in there and offer a quote. You'll need more than that."

John's shoulders sagged and he put a hand to the back of his aching neck. Paul's eyes burned with a fierceness that unnerved him, challenging him to do as he had said he would: make it right. John squared his shoulders and met the older man's gaze.

"I've got more than that."

***

Captain Kittles adjusted his collar and swallowed. The papers shook in his hands. When he spoke, his voice was hoarse. "This is slander."

Chris raised her eyebrows. "Oh?"

"A distortion of the truth."

"The truth is bad enough without distortion."

Kittles composed himself and forced an arrogant smile. "No one will believe a word of it. You're nothing more than a disgruntled journalist on a smear campaign."

"No one will believe a word of it?"

"Not a word."

"Funny. The photos seem quite believable."

Kittles's face froze in a mask of terror. "Photos?" he whispered.

"Of course. Paul doesn't miss a moment. He's among the world's best photojournalists, if you hadn't heard."

"This will ruin me."

"Yes."

"But...but why? I've done nothing but assist you, given you unprecedented access, protected you in the field—"

Chris cut him off with incredulous laughter. "Assisted me? Protected me? Gianelli and his men assisted and protected me. You tried to manipulate me at every turn and cut me off from everyone under your command."

"Miss McKenna, I strenuously disagree. It is my responsibility to maintain control over my unit, and that means regulating who speaks to reporters."

"Yet it contradicts orders from Colonel Brooks to maintain an open dialogue with the press."

"As company commander, I feel it is my right to disseminate the appropriate message to the media."

"What else is your right as company commander? To ride a platoon into the ground? Does the colonel know how you punish those who challenge your ineptitude? With extra combat patrols? Violations of the division's mandated drying out period between operations? Forged paperwork?" She watched him blanch. "That's right, I know all about the little scam you and Simpson are running. I have to hand it to you, Captain, you sure go above and beyond. Torture *and* deliberate endangerment of your own troops? That'll make for an impressive indictment."

Kittles, panting and sweating, ran a hand over his forehead and reached for the article. He tried to read it again, but his eyes glazed over and Chris knew he was envisioning his arrest by MPs and his subsequent court-martial, the courtroom filled with journalists, anti-war demonstrators, and other malcontents. How many of his ex-troops would volunteer to testify? How many of Paul's photos, snapped the exact millisecond the bamboo rod split bare Vietnamese skin, would the prosecutor use? How many forged after-action reports would be presented into evidence? The article had the potential to unleash hell and, at the very least, disgrace him.

"What is it you want?"

"I want you to ease up on Gianelli and his men. I want you to put them on equal footing with every other rifle platoon on this base. Treat them no better and no worse."

"Now Gianelli? I see you've taken a step up the food chain," he said crassly. "You two deserve each other."

Chris smiled pleasantly, unperturbed by his vitriol. She tried—but failed—to suppress a patronizing tone. "I won't dignify that with a response. Gianelli will never know we had this conversation. Ever. Is that clear?"

"This is blackmail."

"Technically, yes. Do we have an agreement?"

Kittles nodded grudgingly.

"Excellent." Chris stood and reached for the article. Then she paused and, with a bright smile, withdrew her hand. "On second thought, you keep that. Give it a read when you feel the urge to do something foolish."

The captain scowled, but folded the article and tucked it in his pants pocket. Chris turned and walked out of the club.

***

"Sorry, I'm booked. Try again some other time. But just so you know, I don't come cheap and I require cash up front. Dollars will be fine."

"Chris." John put his hand on the door of her hooch to prevent her from slamming it in his face. "Can we talk?"

"That costs extra."

"Please?"

"Haven't we said all we needed to say to each other? There's really no place to go after you call a girl a whore."

"I'm sorry."

"I bet you are," Chris said with a short laugh. "If it's a choice between me and Anne Novak...well, I mean, come on."

"Chris, please?"

Against her better judgment, she walked away from the door to allow him to enter. What purpose would it serve to talk? They were just going to fight again, because that was what they did best. She intended to recapture her dignity and if that required another punch, she would throw another punch. Perhaps with her left hand this time, because the right one still hurt like hell. She crossed her arms over her chest and waited for him to speak.

"Why didn't you tell me about your job?"

Chris silently cursed Paul. "I don't need your pity."

"I wish you had told me."

"Why, so you could swoop in and save the day?"

"So I could have done what you needed me to do."

"I didn't need you to save my career."

"That's not what I'm saying."

"Then what are you saying, John?"

"I'm saying I messed up. I messed up badly." He took a deep breath. "And I'm sorry."

Chris shrugged. "Glad to hear it. You apologize to anyone else yet, or only the people you've slept with?"

John opened his mouth to respond, but nothing came out. Chris barreled on, energized by her anger and his confusion.

"I ask because I'm sure all your buddies would appreciate some thoughtfulness for once. Doesn't have to be much, maybe something like, 'Hey, sorry for being an insensitive, uncaring dick.' Of course, it's much more complicated with women. We expect you to actually mean it."

313

"I care," he said quietly.

"Really? Because if Hector were here, he'd lay the odds at about a million to one that you give a fuck."

"I would do anything for those guys."

"Would you? That squad is a family, however dysfunctional, everyone except you, the solitary hero devoid of human emotion. I've spent months watching you, John, and you've only pushed them away."

"That's not true."

"No? Then let's play a little game we'll call 'Did You Know?' Did you know that Ben Kearney is married and has a baby girl he's never seen except by photo? Did you know that Bullseye pulled a fast one on the army and joined up at age sixteen, or that Oscar uses the money he makes from selling weed to support his sick mother back in Detroit? How about that Hector and his family sneaked across the border from Mexico one night and now he's serving in the army of a country that considers him illegal? What about Turner, who can't go home until it's over because the men in his family fight to the bitter end? Or Murphy, who won't go home because he thinks that fighting a war is the only thing he's good at? And Steve, who would do anything, anything, to win your approval?"

John looked at the floor. She saw his jaw muscles twitch and felt cruel satisfaction knowing she had punctured his armor.

"Did you know any of that? All I had to do was ask. These guys worship you, and you don't have the decency to give a damn."

"I care. It's just..."

"Just what? Easier to save a life in the heat of battle than to be their friend when they need it most?" Chris shook her head. "And then there's me. All I know is that you took extra special care not to open up to me. Best not to shit where you sleep, I guess."

"I can't believe you think that."

"You've told Anne Novak more about yourself than you've told me."

John sighed. "That was a stupid stunt. I didn't tell her anything she wouldn't have known if she'd just read my personnel file. Some of it wasn't even true."

"What, no girl waiting for you back home? Shocking."

"Chris, I—"

"You just couldn't trust me."

"I should have. I should have trusted you, and I do trust you. I would give anything to change how I treated you." John stepped closer to her. "Can we start over? Please?"

"No, I don't think so."

"I'll do it right this time."

"No."

He waited a long time to speak. "Why?"

She fought hard to keep the emotion in check, but as the tears sprang to her eyes, she knew she had lost the battle. "Because I can't go through this again." Her voice cracked and she turned away from him, wracked by a silent sob.

"Did you think I would let you get away?"

She turned back to face him, eyes red and glassy. "Let me get away? John, you are the only man who's ever had me, and you threw me away."

"I never meant to hurt you."

"This isn't about an interview or a career or an insult. I made mistakes too, I know that, but I was always honest about one thing: it was never about my job."

"I know. I was just...ashamed. Of everything. I hate that you've seen the worst of me. I've never been so scared to feel what I feel. Of how you make me feel. But losing you hurts worse than anything." He put a hand to his chest and tried to smile, his eyes bright. "God, it hurts. I just want to make you happy. How can I make it right?"

"Let me go."

"I can't do that."

"You have to."

"But I love you."

A fresh tear rolled down Chris's cheek. He reached for her, but she pulled away. One touch and it would be over. She pushed past him and left the hooch. In the humid air, she took a deep breath and tried to halt the stubborn tears, walking for a few minutes before her stride slowed and she came to a stop. She wanted desperately to keep moving, to run away from the past and toward a fresh start, but it was not so easy because no matter how hard she tried to convince herself otherwise, there was something she wanted even more desperately, and he was back in that hooch.

***

Sam Gianelli placed the delicate yellow wildflower, preserved and protected for the ride back to base in a clean beef stew tin, on Maria's pillow. Her bed was made with corners pulled snug, the pillows fluffed, fastidious even amidst the chaos of war. The little flower brightened the dim interior, a splash of color in a drab army world.

Back in his own quarters, he lay down on his bed and stared up at the thatch ceiling. He wiggled his bare toes, still stiff and sore, but the swelling around the soles of his feet had once again receded. He folded his hands over his stomach and, against his will, dozed off, dreaming of the jungle, dreaming of her.

When he awoke an hour later, she was seated by his side watching him sleep. She had the flower in her hand.

"I was thinking of you," he said drowsily. "I'm always thinking of you."

"Don't ever get mad at me for caring about you."

"I'm sorry. It just wasn't supposed to go down like that. To be betrayed by your own commanding officer..." He shook his head. "I lost three men, one of them a kid who never should have been here in the first place. And Conlon...Conlon is a good guy, as dependable and capable as they come. It's hard to watch your friend bleeding out in the mud."

She touched his scruffy cheek with the back of her hand. "Conlon is going to be all right."

Gianelli nodded. "Kearney told me." He took her hand in his, reacquainting his fingers with the slender bones, the softness of her skin, her strength. "I love you."

"I know. And I still love you more."

"I'm glad we're those people."

She smiled.

***

John, seated on the edge of Chris's cot and staring vacantly at the floor, stood when she entered. Chris stopped inches from him and placed her hand on his chest. He covered her hand with his.

"You really love me?" she said.

"I really love you."

He pressed down on her hand. She couldn't feel his heart, but she knew it beat slow and steady. She met his eyes and saw vulnerability. No more walls. No more distrust.

"Good. Because I love you, too."

He smiled and squeezed her hand. She pulled away and took a seat at the field table, then motioned for him to sit on the cot.

"I need to tell you everything."

"Chris, it's all right, you don't need to—"

She held up a hand. "I need to tell you everything. I want to."

She started from the beginning, from the truth about her relationship with Edward Sinclair to the complicated dynamic with her family, from a long-ago fling with Kent Springer to a quid pro quo with Gary Crosby and all the reasons she lost her job. She explained the depth of her friendship with Paul Lane and how much she still admired and respected Martin Willis. She couldn't hold back

317

a smile when she recounted the start of her feud with Anne Novak, but grew serious when she told him why she had kissed Pat Jacobson. She spelled out that her love for him, John, had nothing to do with her career.

He listened without comment, wearing his best poker face. When she finished, she waited for his response, afraid that with the truth on the table, he would fold his cards and walk away. Instead, he leaned forward and cracked his knuckles.

"For the record, I intend to kill both Crosby and Eddie first chance I get."

"Not Kent?"

"Kent was already on the list."

"That's sweet. I've never had anyone commit a felony for me." She rose from the chair and joined him on the cot.

"May I kiss you?"

Chris nodded. John kissed her so tenderly that it brought tears to her eyes again. After he pulled away, he cupped her face and brushed away the tears with his thumbs.

"I'm such a mess," she said, sniffling.

"But a beautiful mess."

"I really did a number on your lip." She touched it gently with her finger. The split was healing, but still noticeable.

"I suspect you got the worst of it." He looked at the butterfly bandages on her knuckles. "Aim for the cheek next time," he said, patting his own. "More padding."

Chris kissed the cheek. "Next time?"

He grinned lopsidedly. "According to Hector, odds are pretty good you'll throttle me again."

"What were the odds I'd take you back?"

"Didn't ask. Didn't want to know. Not in my favor, I'm sure."

She leaned into him and he wrapped his arms around her. "Lucky for you I can't resist a simple-minded farm boy."

In the distance helicopters lifted off from the airstrip, hovering over the base before banking for the jungle and soaring to a cruising altitude. Chris took a deep breath of the still air. How had a place so far from home become home?

"It won't be over for a while," John said.

"I know."

"There's no way I can convince you leave, is there?"

"No. Besides, you'd miss me if I were gone."

"I don't know...you're kind of a pain sometimes."

Chris smiled as she laced the fingers of her right hand with the fingers of his left hand. "All the more reason to stay."

"Then please promise me one thing." He tipped her chin so he could look into her eyes. "Tell the story. All of it."

"Are you sure?"

"I'm sure. Tell our story. No matter what. Promise?"

Chris searched the blue eyes for doubt. Finally, she nodded. "I promise."

***

John knocked on the door of the hooch until Chris flung it open and glared at him through sleep-puffed eyes. In the cot closest to the door, Paul jerked awake with a start, cutting himself off in mid-snore.

"What in God's name do you want?"

"Breakfast."

"Does this look like the mess hall?"

"Are you always so hostile in the morning?"

"Yes," Paul muttered, pulling the pillow over his head.

"I'm trying to catch up on four months of lost sleep. And you"—she stuck her head out the door and peered into the twilight—"decide to wake me before the sun is up. You're lucky I'm only hostile and not homicidal."

"Fair enough. But still, come eat breakfast with us. Platoon's got guard duty most of the day. You can sleep while Steve rambles on about his sister and I contemplate eating my rifle."

As there was undeniable merit to his argument, Chris obliged by dressing and harassing her photographer until he too vacated his cot, unaware that he had expected John's early wake-up call. Five minutes later Chris and John walked down the path together, trailed by Paul and his cameras. John opened the door for the reporters. The mess hall was empty save First Squad and they stood at attention in two lines, one on either side of the center aisle between the tables. Chris glanced in confusion at John, but he offered no explanation, only guiding her forward between the lines with a hand to the small of her back until she stood before Gianelli and Travis.

Gianelli glowered at her. *Goddamn it, what have I done this time?* she thought to herself in a panic, racking her memory for recent transgressions and possible defenses.

Then Gianelli spoke. "Christine McKenna, you are hereby awarded a Purple Heart for wounds sustained in battle on 12 August 1969."

The lieutenant turned to Travis and took from him one of the master sergeant's many Purple Heart medals, resting cupped in Travis's hand on a scrap of ivory parachute silk. Then he pinned the medal on Chris's fatigue blouse, just above her left breast pocket.

"Mr. Rawlins, would you do the honors?"

John bent down and gave her a wet, noisy kiss on the cheek while the men whistled and clapped and Paul captured every moment on film. She felt her face flush in happy embarrassment. When she turned back to Gianelli and Travis, they were watching her with something akin to fondness. She smiled and inclined her head toward the two men, a silent thank you.

"Friggin' army won't give medals to journos, so we had to improvise," Murphy said.

"I'm honored."

"So now can I have a kiss?" Steve asked.

John put Steve into a headlock before Chris could respond.

"Chow time!" Oscar bellowed, at exactly five o'clock when the mess hall officially opened for business.

The squad, including Chris and Paul, congregated around Gianelli and Travis at a table in the back of hall. The men attacked heaping plates of bacon, eggs, and hash browns. Paul snapped a few photos of the spectacle before diving into his own plate.

"Shit's actually good today," Murphy said around a mouthful of scrambled eggs, spraying the people across from him.

"You're disgusting," Chris said.

"Only a woman could spend months in the bush with a bunch of lunatic soldiers and still be appalled by bad table manners," Gianelli muttered between sips of coffee.

"You don't think social niceties matter?" she asked, shooting Murphy a disapproving look as he belched.

Steve and Bullseye snickered. Oscar lightly smacked Bullseye on the back of his still tender head.

"No," said Gianelli. "Consider our era of unparalleled suffering: war, famine, genocide—"

"Nuclear holocaust, religious persecution, racial and gender discrimination, and abject poverty. The list goes on and on. Fascinating conversation. Mind if we join you?" asked Major Jacobson.

"Not at all," Gianelli said to Jacobson and Maria Nichols. "Major, in your capacity as chief medical officer at a field hospital in a hostile Vietnamese province, would you please inform our resident journalist and self-designated platoon conscience that there are far greater travesties in this life than a grunt's lack of couth?"

"Your existential angst, delightful to some, perhaps, is pretty goddamn annoying this early in the morning," Chris said to Gianelli. Out of the corner of her eye, Chris saw the hint of a smile cross Maria's face.

Jacobson held up his hands and grinned. "Sorry, Sam, you're on your own. I don't stand a chance."

"Is your life truly nothing more than an exercise in suffering?" Chris pressed.

"Since about the time you graced us with your wit and charm, yes."

"LT, you trying to get yourself killed?" Oscar boomed.

"McKenna knows when she's outclassed."

Chris washed down a bite of potatoes—yes, they were tasty this morning—with a sip of coffee, black, of course. She rested her chin in her hand, allowing her gaze to focus first on Gianelli, then Maria, and then back to Gianelli. The lieutenant seemed to be enjoying himself.

"Truly, I have no idea what Captain Nichols sees in you. All the eligible bachelors on this base, and she chooses you? Did she lose a bet?"

Jack Travis choked on his coffee and failed to suppress a spasm of laughter. The great burden of secrecy visibly lifted off Pat Jacobson's shoulders. Maria blushed as red as the ribbon tied around her ponytail. Gianelli slumped and squeezed the bridge of his nose. Paul took a photo of them both.

"My Maria?" Hector said in a plaintive whisper, looking crestfallen.

"Damn, LT, nice," Murphy said, shooting Gianelli a thumbs-up.

"I'm sorry," Chris said to Maria. "I know that was supposed to be some big secret."

"How did you know?"

"I just...I just knew. You *are* discreet, if it makes you feel any better."

Maria shook her head in resignation, cheeks still red.

Chris grinned at Gianelli. "I win."

"Rawlins, I pity you," Gianelli said.

John wisely offered no response.

"So, back to existentialism," Jacobson said.

"Hold that thought, Major," said Gianelli, his piercing hazel eyes watching the stream of officers and grunts entering the mess.

***

The lieutenant took a fortifying gulp of coffee and stepped into the path of Simpson, Kittles, and Wheaton, all carrying trays and making a beeline for a secluded table in the back corner. Without a word Gianelli slugged Wheaton in the jaw. The public affairs officer went down in a cacophony of yowls and shattering dishes. For a second the mess hall fell silent. Then grunts and officers alike broke into applause, the loudest coming from a table of nurses. Simpson and Kittles stared in open-mouthed shock at a prone Wheaton.

"Mr. Gianelli," said a voice from behind.

Gianelli turned to face Colonel Brooks, Major Gardner, and the staff sergeant. Gardner laughed silently and the corners of the staff sergeant's eyes crinkled with the smile he tried to hide. The lieutenant made an effort to stand at attention.

"Sir."

"Can I assume you have a good reason for assaulting a fellow officer?"

Gianelli looked at his table. His squad cheered; Chris raised a coffee mug in his direction; Paul documented it all with his camera. His eyes lingered on the pony-tailed woman in navy blue scrubs and brand-new white Chuck Taylor All-Stars. She was blushing even redder now, but her eyes shone. Gianelli smiled at her and faced the colonel.

"Yes, sir."

The colonel had followed Gianelli's gaze. "Ah. Well then, carry on."

Brooks, Gardner, and the staff sergeant stepped over a moaning Wheaton and the splattered food on the floor. Gardner slapped Gianelli on the back, and then the two officers and NCO took a seat with Gianelli's men, the reporters, and the doctors.

"This looks like the fun table," Brooks said.

Gianelli stood at Maria's shoulder and spoke loudly. "My apologies, Dr. Nichols. I know a sucker-punch doesn't compare to removing his, and I quote, 'tiny syphilitic dick' with a switchblade and running it up the flagpole, but I hope it's the thought that counts."

Those assembled at the table howled in laughter. The nearby table of nurses erupted again. Maria covered her face, her shoulders shaking. Gianelli tugged her ponytail until she looked up at him. He leaned down and kissed her.

"Now that's a quote I can work with," said Chris McKenna.

***

The typewriter beckoned. It stood alone on the field table, for months a silent witness to her musings, her pacing, and her sleepless nights. Now it called to her like a siren from the deep, a song subtle and suggestive.

One afternoon, having awoken from a nap to the gentle beating of rain on the thatch roof, Chris faced the machine, the channel through which she desired to speak. She sat at the table and allowed her hands to touch the keys. The metal casing, cool in the heat, imbued her with a sense of vitality and purpose. *Just write.*

Chris had come to admire and respect the plain language of soldiers. They disdained the clever tactics of verbal obfuscation, so essential to the self-preservation of politicians, diplomats, and, sometimes, journalists. While the complexities of international relations and national security seemed to warrant such diversionary wordplay, often the most enlightening observations came from the grunts, men who stood to gain nothing from simply telling it like it was.

It had been a journey of discovery, her time in Vietnam, and if there was one thing she had learned, it was that most soldiers just wanted their story told truthfully and with compassion.

She knew she would never be an entirely honest broker, in as deep as she was. But that was not her intent. She wanted only to tell their story to the best of her ability, to show their sacrifice to the world. She had done it once before; she could do it again.

Soon, the *clickety-clack* of the typewriter drowned out the rain.

19

— • —

C hris McKenna waited patiently for Steve Schaefer to make a word. Every few seconds he contorted his face in agony, wild hazel eyes darting from the board to his tray of letters and back again. She sneaked a peek at her watch. This was the longest game of Scrabble she had ever played.

Steve finally reached for his tiles. Chris, Dan, and Murphy held their breaths. He laid down the letters triumphantly.

Dan groaned and slumped. Chris scratched her head and scrunched her nose. Murphy regarded Steve with utter contempt.

"Jersey, you fucking dolt, *wajer* ain't a word."

"Is too!"

"No, it isn't. I'm no rocket scientist, but even I know it ain't spelled like that."

"But it gets me forty-eight points!"

"All the more reason to get it off the board," said Dan.

Steve turned to Chris. "Come on, it's spelled like that, right?"

"G, not J."

"Aw…"

"Sorry. I didn't make the laws of English. I just follow them."

"Do you need help?" Dan asked Steve. "I'd really like to play another word sometime today."

"Shut your trap, I'm thinking."

Bullseye peered over Steve's shoulder. The two men conferred and then Steve placed two letters on either side of an A in the center of the board.

Dan groaned again and smacked a palm to his forehead. "Cat? That's the best you could do? After all that?"

"It's a word," Steve shot back. "Five points."

While Murphy knocked back another Budweiser, Chris examined the board. She played all seven of her tiles around an O.

"Quixotic?"

"Triple word and double letter under the X, plus fifty bonus points for using all my tiles. One hundred and fifty-two points. It's a word," she assured them.

"Isn't it a proper word?"

Chris twisted to glare at her photographer. "Perhaps you should stick to taking pretty pictures and not commenting on intellectual matters outside your realm of comprehension."

Paul clicked the shutter of his camera and blinded her with the flash.

"Is it really a proper word? Because in the rules, it says we can't use proper words," said Steve.

"It's not a proper word. It means idealistic or unrealistic. As an adjective, it alludes to the hero from Miguel Cervantes's novel *Don*—"

Murphy belched and reached for another beer. "Yeah, yeah, whatever. Let her have it. Even without it, she'd still destroy us."

"You quote a lot of high school. I didn't learn nothing like that in high school," Steve said.

"How often did you go to class?" asked Turner.

"I don't know, couple times a week."

"There you have it."

"Like you's some kind of literary genius."

"At least I've heard of *Don Quixote*."

"Who?"

Oscar's rumbling baritone cut through the marijuana smoke billowing above his head. "Philistine."

"Just so you're all aware, I have three hundred and sixty-seven points. Your scores combined don't equal half that."

Dan, Murphy, and Steve exchanged a three-way glance. Chris returned her attention to the board to plot her next move. She failed to notice Murphy squash his cigarette on the barracks' cement floor, then reach up onto the nearest cot. He snatched a pillow and chucked it at her head, scoring a direct hit. Chris yelped and toppled onto her side.

"Hey! What was that for?"

Murphy shrugged. Then he whipped a second pillow at her, hitting her flush in the face.

"It's just a game." Chris threw it back at him, but he swatted it away. "And speaking of games, the Sox are toast."

Laughing, Chris curled up in a ball to protect herself from the onslaught of pillows. Turner, in an effort to persuade Murphy to cease and desist, enumerated all the reasons why beating women with lumpy army-issue pillows was morally reprehensible. Paul snapped several photos while Murphy subjected the barracks to a tirade on Yankee crimes against humanity since 1918. Chris countered by listing the years in which New York won the World Series.

"Is the game over?" Steve asked, looking down at the scrambled board. "I had a good word."

"Hey," Dan said. "Guess what today is?"

The squad, still in the process of disengaging from the pig pile on the floor, offered a collective shrug.

"Monday?"

"No. I mean, yes, it's Monday. But it's also Labor Day. I win!"

"Win what?" Chris asked, flipping hair out of her face.

No one responded as Hector counted out one hundred and twenty dollars and handed it to Dan. He accepted the wad of cash with a grin, folded it, and stuck it in his pocket.

"Win what?" she asked again.

Dan looked at John, who reluctantly nodded his assent. "I'm collecting on a bet we all made back in May. A bet on how long you'd last at FOB Jane. Everyone else said you'd bug out months ago, but I said you'd be here until at least Labor Day."

Chris had a flashback to an evening in the club when one man had shared his inane thoughts on a minor holiday in June. She turned to John. "Flag Day?"

He shrugged. "You're tougher than you look."

She punched him in the shoulder.

"Ow!"

Four more men—Murphy, Oscar, Bullseye, and Turner—held out their hands toward Hector. He consulted his black ledger and counted out their winnings.

"McKenna, if you injure the point man, you run point," Gianelli said as he and Travis entered the barracks.

"Goddamn it, Oscar, put that shit out!" Travis snapped. "It's ten o'clock in the morning, for Christ's sake."

"Sorry, Sarge. You know how these jokers can wreck a chill." Oscar pinched the end of his half-smoked joint with two fingers and extinguished the smoldering tip. Then he placed the joint in a small bamboo box for safekeeping.

"Here's the deal," Gianelli said. "Alpha and Delta Companies are going into Bac Lieu on Wednesday."

The tension in the barracks was palpable. Murphy, Oscar, Bullseye, Turner, Hector, and Kearney exchanged glances.

"What in the fuck for?" Murphy asked.

"MACV has ordered that forward elements in the Mekong Delta begin flushing out VC cadres in the major cities and villages."

"Back into the jungle where we won't find them again," Dan murmured.

"Until they find us," Kearney replied.

"Captain Kittles is holding his briefing at fourteen hundred hours this afternoon. Do not be late."

"Or what?" Bullseye whispered to Oscar.

"There are any number of ways in which you can be left behind in the jungle," Gianelli said, glowering at his youngest soldier. "Don't be late."

***

Captains Kittles and Lewis were not enthused that their companies had been chosen to storm Bac Lieu with 9th Division units out of My Tho, as Delta Company in particular had a dismal history in the small city. However, Kittles viewed this operation as an opportunity to make amends for prior actions, which he firmly believed had been misinterpreted by Colonel Brooks, Major Gardner, and at least one journalist. As the shock of Chris McKenna's threat to expose his alleged crimes diminished, Kittles had spent the majority of his time engaged in damage control, seeking to justify some of his more controversial actions of late to the colonel, who was not interested in speaking with him; to Lieutenant Colonel Simpson, who had offered only lukewarm support and a suggestion that perhaps it was time to lay off Gianelli; and to Anne Novak and Kent Springer, both of whom seemed indifferent to—but unimpressed by—his decision to burn down a village or his inability to control the men under his command.

Kittles took some solace in the blasé attitude of the two journalists who, he noticed, were disappearing to Saigon more frequently and for longer periods of time. Nonetheless, fear skulked about his subconscious. Anne had rebuffed his pleas for good press, demurring with an excuse that her editor wanted more varied reporting from his correspondent at FOB Jane. It was enough to drive

Kittles to sleepless nights, knowing that Chris McKenna's voice might speak the loudest.

But he had to keep up appearances, so he monopolized the briefing and spoke in an imperious tone more appropriate for four-star generals outlining plans for the invasion of Nazi Germany, not company commanders providing infantry support in a backwater Vietnamese city. Ever conscious of the scorn and sanctimony twisting the features of Sam Gianelli and Chris McKenna as they watched him from the back corner of the room, he strutted like a peacock as he briefed Delta Company's assignment in Bac Lieu.

"Second Platoon will run point on this operation," he said, glancing at Chris, who shifted in her seat, her green eyes boring into him. He swallowed hard. Unfortunately, Gianelli was the most competent platoon leader in either company; he had little choice but to assign him the point position, else risk losing even more troops to Viet Cong attacks. "Followed by Lieutenant Balcolm and Third Platoon. First and Fourth Platoons will provide cover on the flanks as both companies move toward the city center, linking up with 9th Division and ARVN elements out of My Tho. Air Calvary will provide air support. With any luck, the armored battalion will have cleared most of the danger areas of the city before we move through, but be prepared for stiff resistance from Charlie. We depart at zero five hundred on Wednesday. Dismissed."

***

At sunset, Chris and John hoisted themselves atop a bunker on the western edge of camp. They sat shoulder to shoulder, gazing at the cloudless pastel sky, lavender layered on pink layered on orange over a black jungle, the menacing shadow on the edge of reason. Five F-4 Phantom jets in an inverted V formation streaked north through the pink, miniscule flecks at twenty thousand feet.

"Wouldn't see that over a cornfield," John said.

"Wouldn't see much of anything over a cornfield."

"Just every star in the sky."

"Do you think about the future?" Chris asked.

"These days, a lot more than I should."

"What does it look like?"

"Well, there's a cute farm girl..."

Chris reached for his hand and squeezed. "Very funny."

"I see you. And we're wherever you want to be."

"Really?"

"Really. And if you get bored with stability, I'll tag along while you chase another war."

"After this, my war days are through."

"That's probably what Hemingway said, too."

"I think maybe I'd like to try stargazing in that big empty field."

John turned in surprise, his eyes searching for hers. "Really?"

"Really. I can write anywhere. All I need is you and a typewriter."

"Finally, the truth: I'm your muse."

"I'm pretty sure that's not what I said."

"It's what I heard."

"Then you are my muse."

The sky deepened to cerulean, the pastel swaths fading into night. FOB Jane was tranquil, devoid of the thunder of artillery and helicopters and the movement of men. Chris was content to live in the moment, feeling John's warmth against her side and the reassuring strength of his fingers interlocked with hers.

When she glanced at him, she saw the pensive expression on his face—the slightly knitted eyebrows, the tightness around his mouth—as he moved his focus from the last vestiges of daylight to her hand.

"You worried about tomorrow?" she asked.

John shrugged. "No. Not really. It just...I don't know, it just feels different somehow. Instead of disappearing into the jungle, they'll disappear into concrete and alleys."

He chose not to finish his thought for her benefit, but she knew what it was. Instead of dying under the shade of the triple canopy or in foul-smelling paddies, they would die on shell-pocked streets or in bombed-out buildings.

"All I ask is that you don't get shot again," he continued.

"No problem. This time when the shooting starts, how about you let Kent take one?"

John smirked. "Consider it done."

"Brooks and Gardner will be taking an active role in this op," she said. "I confirmed it with Brooks this morning."

"Probably to keep a tight leash on Kittles."

"Is this a push to win or a push to take the hill?"

"Good question. Let's see how quickly we give back the hill."

"Your optimism is less than inspiring. I thought I was supposed to be the pessimist in this relationship."

"It's the 'Nam, man," John said in his best impression of Oscar.

The 'Nam, the bullet buried deep within living tissue, a constant ache, a faithful reminder of the price of duty and the pain of sacrifice. If they were lucky, the pain would dull over time and become a bittersweet memory of all that was, all that wasn't, and all that could have been.

"Please don't worry," he said. "We're hitting the city with a lot of firepower. The odds are in our favor."

Chris forced a smile. "I've seen you bluff your way to a win holding nothing higher than a single jack. You wouldn't be trying to do that now, would you?"

"No point. I'm pretty sure you can read my mind."

"And yet I'm still not comforted."

"Sweetie, I thought we had overcome our trust issues," he said lightly.

"If I'm not allowed to get shot, you're not allowed to get shot."

"That seems fair."

"I mean it, John. I will never forgive you if..." She trailed off, feeling her chest constrict.

"Hey, hey, you can't dwell on that. Besides, you think I want to deal with your rage for all eternity?" His hand tightened around hers. "One day at a time, okay?"

"One day at a time."

***

Gianelli and Travis went over the battle plans for tomorrow's incursion of Bac Lieu one more time—both agreed it would serve little purpose, but if asked, they would say that about every infantry operation—then turned their attention to Gianelli's case of Heineken. Travis raised a green bottle to the night sky, the stars blinking *cheers* in return.

"Here's to another summer come and gone."

"Think it's the beginning of the end?" asked Gianelli.

"Maybe. But this won't be the last summer, no matter what the politicians say."

Gianelli took a swig of beer. "None will ever top this one in terms of sheer lunacy."

Travis laughed, tapping his Louisville Slugger against his boot. "Tough to know who's more responsible for all the lunacy, McKenna or Kittles."

"The chick is always a safe bet." Gianelli glanced at Travis, wiggling his bare toes and thinking how much better his feet felt after a couple weeks of surprisingly light operational activity. "Kittles seems to have backed off. Wonder why that is?"

Travis shrugged. "Beats me. But I'm not complaining. We needed the rest."

"I should kick all your asses."

"Sorry?"

"I'm not stupid. You, Maria, and Chris. Except I don't hit women and I'm pretty sure you'd wreck me in a fair fight."

"No idea what you're talking about, LT."

"Every time Kittles sees Chris, he looks like he might dive into the nearest foxhole, and Maria is uncharacteristically relaxed, considering her extreme stress level. Never thought I'd see the day you became one of the girls. I bet Maria had to ask only once."

Travis looked as though he was trying not to laugh. "Have you ever tried to say no to that woman?"

"Yes."

"And?"

Gianelli sighed.

They drank silently, each man lost in his own thoughts and reflections on a summer of change. The peace of the night was broken only by the rustle of the breeze and the liftoff of a distant Huey.

"Jack?"

"Yeah?"

"Thanks."

Travis smiled. They clinked beer bottles and listened to the night.

***

Bac Lieu smelled like a cross between raw sewage and dead bodies, which may have been explained by the dead bodies littering the narrow streets lined by open sewers. They had cleared two sectors of the city in the early morning hours and were working on clearing a third in the wake of the armored battalion, meeting only sporadic resistance as they moved between ramshackle storefronts, small gated villas, and ragged shantytowns.

"I'm gonna puke," Steve said, pinching his nose and gagging.

335

Chris took several steps away from Steve on the off chance he was unable to keep down breakfast. Out of the corner of her eye, she saw Paul ready his camera to capture the spectacle on film. Someday, Paul's images would fill anthologies and histories of the war, each second in time a microcosm of the experience, sometimes funny, often heartbreaking, and usually poignant. This one, potentially, would be merely disgusting.

"Shut up, Jersey," Travis said. "You bitch like a chick. No offense, kid," he said to Chris.

"None taken."

"LT, the captain is calling for you," Turner said.

He handed the radio receiver to Gianelli, who pressed it to his ear and spoke briefly with Kittles. The captain was about a mile behind Second Platoon, moving through the city with Balcolm and his men, Anne Novak and Kent Springer at his side. Kittles was subdued over the radio, lacking his usual pomposity because Colonel Brooks and Major Gardner circled the city in a Huey monitoring all movements and radio communications.

Earlier that morning Kittles had watched with relief as Chris and Paul boarded a Huey with part of Gianelli's unit. He probably hoped she would be struck down in a Viet Cong attack, ensuring that she would not publish an exposé on his exploits in a magazine by which she was no longer employed. If only Martin Willis could see his two writers; both were held hostage by unique and different captors, both concealing the true story for reasons that would drive the editor to violence.

"Jack, Lewis is reporting resistance in the eastern sector. We need to close off the back door. As usual, Charlie's about to give us the slip. Balcolm and his guys are right behind us, they'll continue clearing," Gianelli said.

"Got it. Rawlins, get us to the southern end of the canal zone. Double time it, son."

John pulled the bush hat more snugly over his head and widened the distance between himself and the platoon. Second Squad split and ran parallel to First

Squad several streets in either direction. Chris's eyes never left the lone soldier now crossing a deserted intersection of a potholed street, moving with the power and prowess of a tiger, sweeping each blind corner with his rifle, clearing the way for the men behind him, a willing sacrifice in the quest for the hill.

***

From their circling Huey, Brooks and Gardner watched isolated skirmishes rage between army and insurgent elements. Bac Lieu was a divided city, nominally under government control yet ruled by the ruthless jungle law of the Viet Cong.

"Gianelli is moving his guys toward Lewis," Gardner told Brooks over the headset. "If he can close off the canal zone, I think we we'll have them surrounded."

"What about ARVN?"

Gardner rolled his eyes. "Two companies are pinned down near the floating market. The armored battalion is on the way to rescue them."

Brooks peered out the open side as the Huey banked north in a wide circle. The young door gunner kept his finger poised over the trigger of his machine gun, alert to ground fire from small arms and rockets. Had the colonel been in full control of the operation, rather than the My Tho-based brigadier general angling for major general, he would have sent an American company to babysit the two ARVN companies in trouble. The armored battalion still had three sectors to clear; this delay could facilitate Charlie's escape to the jungle.

Brooks pressed a hand to his headset as the radio crackled and Major Hawke's voice came over the air. He snapped his fingers at Gardner to get his attention and held up three fingers to indicate that he should tune to channel three. The logistics officer informed them that several of FOB Jane's medevac helicopters had been diverted to assist with casualty collection near Can Tho and were presently unavailable in the event of casualties at Bac Lieu. Three of the four remaining medevacs were grounded for mechanical trouble, but Hawke had teams working to get them airborne.

"For the love of Christ," Brooks muttered, looking again out the door. So far, the reported injuries were minor, treatable by medics on the battlefield, but as the day wore on, serious casualties were inevitable.

Gardner threw up his hands and shook his head helplessly.

Brooks directed Hawke to coordinate the medevacs with nearby bases and turned his attention back to the action on the ground just as several large explosions rang out near Lieutenant Gianelli's platoon.

***

The force of the simultaneous explosions nearly knocked John off his feet. He stumbled toward the first cover he saw, an overturned Opel that had once been parallel-parked at the southeast corner of an intersection. He ducked down near the passenger-side front wheel well and scanned the streets, his eyes tracking movement and color and shadow, seeking signs of attack. He saw nothing.

John was half a mile from his platoon, isolated and exposed and lacking solid cover in the event of sustained fire. He could use the shanties and huts as concealment as he moved, but a rifle round would easily penetrate the thatch and corrugated steel sidings. He could not afford to duck into one and trap himself. Not for the first time he had too quickly outpaced his platoon, a bad habit fueled by adrenaline and impatience.

He tried to see through the smoke lingering over the intersection, but the platoon was too far back. Still in a crouch, he shuffled to the side of a store shack and peered around the corner. A donkey clomped across the empty street, emboldened by a taste of freedom. John mentally mapped out his route back to the platoon, intending to circle around and approach from the right flank. After one last look in the direction of the explosions, John hugged the side of the building and set off in search of his unit.

***

The explosions forced the platoon to halt and take cover. Chris didn't miss the look exchanged between Gianelli and Travis as they moved fire teams to protect their position.

"He knows what to do," Travis said to her.

She tried to nod confidently. She had her back to a concrete building, in a crouch, with First Squad spread around her.

"What was it?" Dan asked. "A mine?"

"Possible," Murphy replied. "Maybe an unexploded cluster bomb? Could be anything in these parts. It was big, though, whatever it was."

Turner gave Murphy a disapproving look and jerked his head toward Chris. "Hush. It doesn't matter what it was. Let's just find John."

"You're not worried about him, are you, Chris?" Murphy asked. "He probably greased them all already. I give him five minutes before he waltzes back here all calm, cool, and collected, Cowboy-style."

"He's an idiot. Why does he insist on running so far ahead?"

"That's the Cowboy way," Oscar boomed.

"LT, I got him," Hector called. "Fifty yards away, coming toward the flank."

Murphy glanced at his watch. "Four minutes. Not bad."

Chris knocked Paul over onto his side as she scrambled toward Hector. Paul folded himself over his expensive equipment.

"Hey, watch the camera!"

"Sorry."

"Any sign of Charlie?" Gianelli asked.

"Looks like he's alone."

Oscar and Bullseye set up their M-60s on parallel corners to cover John's approach. Chris felt her heart rate slow as she watched him move closer and closer, soon to be enveloped by the platoon.

Her heart rate spiked when machine gun fire bisected the street, kicking up clouds of dirt and sending John scurrying behind the nearest building. Most of the rounds impacted near the entryway of a building on the far side of the street, opposite John's position.

"Bullseye!" Travis yelled.

Bullseye let loose streams of M-60 rounds at the unseen enemy as the platoon advanced toward John.

***

John ducked behind a building and trained his rifle in the general direction of his attackers. Except that he did not seem to be the target. He saw movement near the building across the street, the outlines of helmets and weapons, heard the bark of orders in Vietnamese, and realized it was an ARVN squad cut off from the main pack. One by one, the ARVN soldiers climbed out of a side window and ran though winding back alleys to escape the Viet Cong.

John watched and waited, but the machine gun fire continued in bursts, despite the retreat of the ARVN squad. He crept forward and peered down the street. A block away, crouched at the corner, Dan and Murphy waved to catch his attention. John pointed at his eyes and cut a hand across his throat, indicating he would be running blind. Even with the distance between them, John could see the grin on Murphy's face as he readied his Uzi to spray the cross street. Dan motioned John forward and John made a break for the intersection.

Then he stopped.

***

"What the hell is he doing?" Chris said. She tore the Yankees cap off her head in search of unobstructed vision.

Paul snapped a photo the instant John stopped, capturing conflicting emotions on the soldier's face—anger, determination, resignation—and pointed to what had caught John's attention. "Near the building. It's a kid."

"Fuck!" Gianelli snapped.

"No, Rawlins, no," Travis murmured. "Don't stop, don't stop..."

But the boy was in the line of Viet Cong fire and John was already moving toward him, a blur of green fatigues in the dust. The machine gun intensified and rounds followed in his wake. John snatched the child off the ground and hugged him to his chest, pivoting and sprinting back toward the other side of the street. He deposited the boy behind a car and turned to fight.

"Oscar!" Travis yelled.

Oscar swung his M-60 around and fired at the Viet Cong squad moving toward John. Murphy and Dan advanced, shouting. Chris watched a VC fighter bring a grenade launcher to his shoulder and pull the trigger. He launched two grenades before Dan shot him dead. The grenades landed near the opposite side of the street and exploded in quick succession.

The blasts lifted John off his feet and dropped him in a crumpled heap near a ditch. The world seemed to pause. Two journalists and a platoon of soldiers watched and waited, expecting him to climb to his feet as he always did. He was their lucky charm, their rabbit's foot, endowed with immunity from harm by the patron saint of grunts. But he lay still in the pocked street.

And then they all moved at once. Chris shot up, but Gianelli and Travis dove forward and dragged her down before she got more than a foot away. Travis shoved her into Paul's arms and then he and Gianelli and Kearney rushed toward John. Chris managed to kick and elbow her way to her feet, but Paul quickly recovered. He grabbed her from behind and wrapped his arms around her waist before she could advance.

"Do not let her move until I say," Gianelli called to Paul.

"Swear to God, Paul, I will kill you," Chris said through gritted teeth.

Paul said nothing, only squeezed her tighter. She heard his ragged breathing in her ear, felt him lower his center of gravity to prepare for her next bout of thrashing. She was vaguely conscious of the men attacking the Viet Cong with an anger and intensity that would have otherwise sickened her; all she saw was a motionless body on the ground. She grabbed one of Paul's wrists, not to fight, but because she needed to hold onto a friend.

***

John stared at the hazy sky through half-open eyes and thought he saw a smiling Buddha in the clouds. The white puffs soon morphed into other strange creatures that danced in his spinning head. The sensation reminded him of secondhand highs off Oscar's weed, and he wanted to laugh at the memories.

He heard far off voices and tried to focus. Where was the boy? And why couldn't he move? He should be fighting with his friends. The fingers of his right hand brushed the stock of his rifle down near his hip. He tried to grasp it, but his body would not obey his mind's commands. He felt a crushing weight on his chest, and his breath came in wheezing gasps that rattled his lungs and drowned out the roar of the ongoing battle.

And then he saw three blurry faces, familiar faces. One of them, Travis, he thought, grabbed him under the arms and dragged him behind the car. John's head lolled to the side, the bush hat hanging around his neck. Travis set him down and John looked at Ben Kearney's boyish face, flushed with tension. The medic opened his flak jacket and cut away his fatigues to see the damage. He tried to read Kearney's lips as he spoke, but Kearney's face swam before him and all he heard was a low buzz in his ears.

Kearney taped a plastic dressing over a tiny hole on the right side of John's ribcage, then he readied a thick compress and placed it over the lower left side of John's torso, just to the inside of his hip. He pressed down and John jerked, blinded by a flash of white light and agony. Then nothing.

***

"How bad?" Gianelli asked. He had already put out a call for a medevac helicopter.

"Bad. Looks like a piece of shrapnel went through the flak jacket and is collapsing one of his lungs. He's also bleeding from the hip wound. I think it nicked a major vein."

"How long?"

"If the lung fully collapses, he might not make it. The air is building up in his chest. He won't be able to breathe much longer. He needs a hospital now."

Captain Kittles came on the radio and informed Gianelli that medevacs were at least an hour out.

"I don't have an hour. My man is critical. There must be something close. Raise My Tho or Can Tho—"

"Not an option. Your man will have to be treated on the battlefield. When base medevacs become available, you will be notified. Now get your platoon down to the canal zone. Delta six out."

"Fucking Kittles," Gianelli snarled. "Fuck!"

Kearney had Travis counting John's pulse, growing weaker by the minute. They both looked at Gianelli, who was staring at John. He put a hand to the back of his neck and tried not to shake. He wanted to scream.

First Squad swarmed the little group, having finished off the squad of Viet Cong. Second Squad fanned out and continued the search-and-destroy exercise.

"LT?" Dan said.

"Get Chris."

***

"I will kill that piece of shit myself," Brooks said to Gardner. "Get us down there."

Gardner raised Gianelli on the radio and explained the plan. Gianelli provided his exact location, and Gardner then ordered the pilots of the Huey to set down near the lieutenant and his men.

As the pilots angled the helicopter for a tight landing in a four-way intersection, Brooks and Gardner readied themselves for combat, strapping on helmets, fastening flak jackets, and slinging rifles over their shoulders. They were about to become foot soldiers again.

***

Chris dropped to her knees and looked from John's ashen face to Kearney to Travis to Gianelli. No one spoke. Turner and the Vietnamese boy, who was maybe ten years old, stood together, Turner's hands on his shoulders. She looked again to John. His blond eyelashes rested against the dark circles under his eyes. He looked at peace. She touched his hand.

"We need to move him carefully," Kearney yelled above the roar of the Huey. "Onto the stretcher, count of three."

Chris stepped aside for Kearney, Travis, Murphy, and Dan to slide John onto the stretcher. Then Murphy and Dan lifted the stretcher and followed Kearney to the Huey. Brooks and Gardner met them halfway.

"Wherever you need to go," Brooks told Kearney.

"FOB Jane."

"Good luck, son."

Chris stood rooted to the spot, feeling like a swimmer who had strayed too far from shore, limbs leaden, lungs screaming for air, slowly sinking to the bottom of the ocean. Paul pulled Chris aboard the helicopter. Seconds later Kearney clambered aboard the Huey and Dan and Murphy ran back to the squad. The helicopter lifted off the ground and banked southwest toward FOB Jane.

***

Chris sat atop her favorite bunker blanketed by a Vietnam night. The stars were invisible under roiling clouds. Far in the distance lightning flashed, portending atmospheric violence. Eventually Paul climbed atop the bunker and sat beside her. For a long time neither spoke. Rumblings of thunder grew closer; the rains would soon drench them. Chris leaned sideways into Paul, shoulder to shoulder. There was comfort in his closeness.

"Did you have a chance to...?"

She nodded, unable to speak. To make a promise. To say goodbye. The tears would no longer be denied. Paul held her as the storms ravaged the Delta.

20

— · —

The day Chris McKenna left Vietnam was a day like any other. It dawned hazy, hot, and humid with a chance of rain. She rose with the sun and meandered through FOB Jane to the mess, where she downed one last mug of toxic black coffee and bowl of wall spackle. Then, after pausing at the destination signpost, she returned to her hooch where her duffel bag and rucksack sat beside the field table, stuffed with clothes and gear and invisible memories from a year at war. Her eyes drifted to her neatly made cot, the scratchy gray wool army blanket folded over the foot of the bed, and then to the neighboring cot that had been unoccupied for months.

It was May 1970. The previous day, Dan Peters and Steve Schaefer had completed their thirteen-month tour of duty in South Vietnam and departed the country on a military transport plane bound for California and the real world. The goodbye was long and heartfelt; Dan apologized for weeping. Chris, whose own eyes had clouded with tears, hugged them and pushed them to the waiting helicopter for the ride to Saigon. She watched their faces peer out of the open side of the Huey, their eyes fixed on her, until the helicopter disappeared from view.

Dan and Steve were the last two men remaining from John's original squad. Murphy, Oscar, Bullseye, Turner, Hector, and Ben Kearney had finished their tours one by one and returned home in various states of disarray. In some cases, Murphy's and Turner's in particular, it had taken all of Chris's considerable powers of persuasion to convince them to leave Vietnam.

Now only Chris remained, and she was finally going home after a year of her own tour of duty. She had seen them through a dark time; her promise to a wounded soldier, his sacrifice for his friends.

Chris focused her gaze on the rickety field table in the corner of the hooch, the site of her greatest professional triumph and her most devastating professional loss. The typewriter sans the sticky R key sat in the center of the table, a yearlong requisition from the colonel's staff sergeant, who never once came looking for his missing office equipment. Her fingers took their last dance over the keys two nights ago, laying down her final thoughts on a long year. Had the typewriter been a sentient being, perhaps it would have lauded the writer for her honesty and her vision and her guts. Perhaps it would have saluted her tenacity, her will, her survival. But the typewriter stayed still and silent, speaking only when ordered.

Then her eyes moved back to the empty cot nearest the door, Paul Lane's old bunk. Paul left in October 1969, a month after the battle in Bac Lieu. He had held her tight and told her the truth: he had nothing left to give.

But she did, so she stayed. And now it was her time.

She slung the rucksack over her shoulders and hefted the duffel in her right hand. With one last look around her hooch, her home, she pushed aside the mosquito netting and closed the door behind her. Her booted feet propelled her along the center path of FOB Jane, past the destination signpost, past the hospital, past Brigade HQ, toward the eastern helipad.

She dropped her bags and waited behind the sandbagging, her eyes narrowing against the blinding sunlight as she searched the sky for incoming Hueys. Major Hawke had promised a ride to Saigon by mid-morning, either on an FOB Jane bird or a transiting helicopter. Her flight left Saigon that evening.

How had the world changed in her absence? How had she changed? What had a year of war done to her?

The sky was still and quiet. No Hueys on the horizon. She sat on the duffel, leaning against the sandbagging, facing inward toward the center of FOB Jane. Six individuals walked her way.

She stood.

"Miss McKenna," Colonel Brooks said. "I know you wouldn't think of leaving without saying goodbye."

Gianelli, Travis, Jacobson, Maria, and Brooks's staff sergeant fanned out around them in a semi-circle. Chris tried to smile.

"I'm not very good at goodbyes."

"Try as you might, you're not getting out of this one."

Chris took a deep breath and struggled to focus through suddenly teary eyes. She looked at each of them. "I guess it's time."

"McKenna, I for one couldn't be happier that you're leaving," Gianelli said. "I don't think I'd survive another summer with you."

Travis grunted. "Don't let him fool you. He won't know what to do without you."

Gianelli sent Travis a dirty look. "Don't encourage her."

Chris laughed, wiping her eyes. "No chance of that. You finally get your platoon back."

"I've had easier campaigns against Charlie," Gianelli muttered. Maria elbowed him in the ribs.

Jacobson stepped forward and handed her a white armband with a red medic's cross. "Thank you for listening to our story, Chris."

Chris cupped his face in her hands and kissed him on the lips. His midnight blue eyes gleamed.

Then she and Maria Nichols shared a hug. The doctor had become a close friend, a confidante. "You are a saint," Chris told her.

"I know," she said with a smile.

After Maria came the gruff master sergeant. Travis wrapped his arms around her and lifted her off the ground. "It won't be the same without you, kid. Take care of yourself."

Chris faced the colonel. He rubbed his beard and appraised her with stormy eyes.

"It's over," she said. "Are we friends?"

"My brigade is still in disarray."

"Then I've done my job."

"With aplomb."

Chris stood on tiptoes to kiss him on the cheek. "Just be thankful I lasted longer than Anne Novak. Don't let the bastards get you down. Promise?"

"Promise."

The men and Maria retreated a few paces to allow Gianelli a moment. How they had managed to coexist for a year baffled her. He stood with his arms crossed over his chest, his caramel eyes looking her up and down, critically, analytically, this time with twelve months of shared experience with which to judge.

"Hell of a year, McKenna, hell of a year."

"Sorry for all the trouble I caused."

"Liar."

"Thank you," she whispered. "For everything." She held out her hand.

He looked at her hand, stepped forward, and hugged her.

As Gianelli released her, a Huey appeared low and tight over the jungle, her ride out of town. They turned away from the dust whipped up by the blades as the helicopter touched down on the landing pad. A young corporal waved Chris forward.

Brooks's staff sergeant picked up Chris's bags and handed them to her. Then he stepped back, clicked his heels, and bowed his head. "Ma'am."

Chris took one last look at the group of people who had long since resolved to stay and fight, their stories forever intertwined. She would miss them all.

"Goodbye," she said.

"Goodbye, Chris."

Chris boarded the Huey and seated herself at the end of the front bench nearest the open door. As the helicopter lifted and banked northeast, six arms raised in unison, a final farewell. It was time.

***

Chris sat for an hour on a bench at the center of Dupont Circle, staring at the *American Century* building on the corner of New Hampshire Avenue. She would have killed for a cigarette, but she had quit months ago. Finally, she stood. Her mouth was dry but the hand that held a large document envelope stuffed with a novella-length series of reporting was damp with sweat.

She jaywalked through the gridlocked lunchtime traffic and entered the building. As she had for five years, she took the stairs to the newsroom, seized by a burst of nervous energy that propelled her up the four flights two stairs at a time.

The Congressional beat reporter did a double take and the international affairs editor knocked over a stack of copy, splashing crisp white sheets and inky black carbons to the floor, as she breezed past their desks. Chris kept her eyes straight ahead. She continued to turn heads on her long march through the newsroom, a walk down the plank toward the ocean abyss, the half-open door beyond the flotsam of desks.

"Miss McKenna!" said Martin Willis's secretary, staring at Chris wide-eyed and with measurable uncertainty. "You can't go in there! Wait!"

Chris ignored her and pushed through the door of Martin Willis's office. He sat in his high-back leather chair with his burly forearms on the desk as he pored over copy with a blue pencil in hand. Just as he moved to scribble commentary in the margin, he caught sight of the reporter he had fired many months ago. The pencil halted in midair.

"Chris?"

She stopped inches from his desk and regarded her former boss with equanimity. Just as there were things more important than a career, some things needed—and deserved—closure.

She held the envelope toward him. He accepted it, his eyes never leaving hers.

"This is the story I was trying to hide. It's a story that deserves to be told."

Willis stood and walked around to the front of his desk. They faced each other for long seconds, each offering and accepting silent apologies. Willis clasped one of her hands in both of his.

They had closure.

***

Later that night, when the newsroom was dark and quiet, Martin Willis opened the envelope and withdrew Chris McKenna's reporting from her year in Vietnam. With the pages in one hand and a whiskey in the other, he leaned back in his chair and began to read.

I fell in love with a soldier.

Hours later, after Willis had read every word, sometimes laughing, sometimes biting back emotion, captivated by the cast of characters and the pathos of the writer who found herself in the midst of their most human of dramas, he placed the tome on his desk and took a sip of whiskey. Tomorrow he would order it broken into sections and run, untouched, over however many issues it took to tell the story. It was a story that deserved to be told.

Chris McKenna had gone out on her own terms. Willis smiled.

***

Chris drove for two days in the Mustang, the top down, her hair a swirling mess in the chilly wind as she navigated north and west through the heartland. The Mustang carried her up and over the foothills of distant mountains, sliced through plains that stretched forever, traversed the endless roads with a purpose.

She pulled up outside a white farmhouse on the evening of the second day. A dog, a shepherd mix, climbed to its feet and watched her from the front porch. Assessing she posed no threat, the dog scrambled down the steps and ran to greet her. Chris bent to pet the animal.

She felt him before she saw him, the figure that materialized in the doorway of the house, illuminated in the soft glow of the porch light. As she straightened and flipped windblown hair off her face, her pulse quickened. He covered the distance between them in seconds, crushing her in a hug. Chris's tears seeped into his shirt as she pressed her face into his chest. One hand drifted to his pelvis, the side where shrapnel had torn through him so many months ago.

"I can't believe you're here," John Rawlins whispered. "I was worried I'd get dumped by telegram."

"It was a tough choice between you and Steve."

John laughed and kissed her. "Does this mean I'm forgiven?"

"Not a chance."

"I promise I'll make it up to you. Where's our next adventure?"

"Ever heard of a place called Cambodia?"

"I guess I better pack my flak jacket." He held her tighter.

"No more wars," Chris said.

"No more wars."

She tilted her head to smile at him. The stars had begun to appear in the sky, barely discernable pinpricks of light twinkling over the fields. Chris saw only his blue eyes, bright with happiness, and felt safe his tight embrace. She was finally home.

The Sandstorm Series

A spy, a mercenary, and a motley crew of friends. Can they save the world, or will they die trying?

—

CIA operative Kate Devlin and security consultant Nick Cavanaugh get off on the wrong foot. After all, her accidental terrorist had orders to kill him. And if there's one thing Nick can't abide, it's creating terrorists.

But it turns out that Kate's good intentions count for something. She saves his life, in more ways than one. While creating terrorists may not be a good career move, it does lead to a most unexpected outcome: love. Kate's never been in love before, but she thinks this might go the distance.

They were made for each other, this pixie spy and caveman mercenary. Lovers, best friends, and...business partners? Is Sandstorm International big enough for the both of them?

And will they ever be able to escape the CIA? Kate may have quit the Agency, but the Agency just can't quit her. Whenever an impossible problem arises in a foreign land, the CIA calls in Kate, Nick, and their Sandstorm family.

Shenanigans ensue.

Maybe they can't save the world, but they sure can have fun trying.

The Sandstorm Series features Kate, Nick, and their motley crew of friends on rollicking adventures in foreign lands. If you enjoy action, intrigue, humor, and a love that conquers all, you'll love *The Sandstorm Series*.

—

LYNN MASON

Book 1: *The Stars Refuse to Shine*
Book 1.5: *Sandstorm Rising*, a free novella
(download at www.lynnmason.com)
Book 2: *The Edge of the Night*
Book 3: *A Gathering Storm*

ALSO BY

The Sandstorm Series
The Stars Refuse to Shine
Sandstorm Rising, a free novella
(download at www.lynnmason.com)
The Edge of the Night
A Gathering Storm

—

Historical Fiction
A Summer of War

About the Author

Lynn Mason likes strong female protagonists with a penchant for getting themselves into trouble all over the world. The only thing more fun than watching a character get into trouble is watching her get out of it.

Lynn believes that the journey of creation will take an author to wild and wonderful places. The artistic wilderness can be daunting, but the creator has a duty to leave footprints in the sand.

When she's not globetrotting in search of her next story, she and her menagerie of furry friends live near Washington, D.C.

Find Lynn at www.lynnmason.com